BLACK GOLD

'Romance, suspense and a rich historical background not only ensure an enthralling read but also reminds us that times have not changed that much since the last depression'
Publishing News

'Strikes, shortages and unemployment made life harsh. *Black Gold* shows us a glimpse of men who are driven to desperation. The women who love them must also fight, although some find it easier than others'
Books, London

'Swansea in 1926 is a divided town. Iris Gower's novel of the miners' strike, *Black Gold*, finds heroes and sympathies on both sides'
Northern Echo

'The sixth and final story in the excellent sequence by Mrs Gower . . . Iris Gower has created a host of memorable characters to tell a story packed with violence and pathos and running high with passion'
Gloucester Citizen

'A page-turning drama of love, hate and ambition, portraying a vivid picture of south Wales and its mining industry during the dark days of the 1926 General Strike'
South Wales Evening Post

BLACK GOLD

Iris Gower

CORGI BOOKS

BLACK GOLD

A CORGI BOOK   0 552 13316 7

Originally published in Great Britain by
Century Hutchinson Ltd.

PRINTING HISTORY

Century Hutchinson edition published 1988
Corgi edition published 1989

This book is set in 10 on 11 Times

Corgi Books are published by Transworld Publishers Ltd., 61–63 Uxbridge Road, Ealing, London W5 5SA, in Australia by Transworld Publishers (Australia) Pty. Ltd., 15–23 Helles Avenue, Moorebank, NSW 2170, and in New Zealand by Transworld Publishers (N.Z.) Ltd., Cnr. Moselle and Waipareira Avenues, Henderson, Auckland.

Reproduced, printed and bound in Great Britain by
Hazell Watson & Viney Limited
Member of BPCC plc
Aylesbury, Bucks, England

1

The town of Sweyn's Eye was in darkness, the sharp darkness of a January night. The blast furnaces had been tapped the brightness of the molten metal illuminating the sky before dying away into respectful silence. Even the barking of the hungry mongrel in the backyard of the Mexico Fountain had ceased.

But Charlotte Davies was wide awake, staring through the crack between the curtains into the night. The long, dark plaits of her hair hung over her shoulders giving her an appearance of innocence and her large dark eyes were blurred with tears.

There was the sound of footsteps on the stairs and she stiffened, her shoulders tense.

'*Duw*, don't you think it's time you came up to bed, girl?' Her husband was a big handsome man, his face scarred with the blue lines of the miner. He ran his hand through his hair as though puzzled by her behaviour.

'Go on, you, I'll be up in a minute,' she said with a cheerfulness she did not feel. He came to her side, resting his hand on her shoulder. 'Look, *cariad*, I'm sorry if I upset you tonight; I didn't mean to quarrel in front of Denny and Frederick.'

'I should think our sons are used to it by now.' Charlotte couldn't keep the note of bitterness from her voice. She turned to face her husband. 'Why do you have to go on about my brother all the time? You used to be such good friends.'

'Aye, well, Luke Proud is forgetting himself, now, a boss man, isn't he? Not one of the workers any more, thinks he's God Almighty, he does.'

'That's not true!' Charlotte said at once. 'It's you have changed, Gronow, not my brother. Grateful to him you

5

were for a job, mind, and still glad to pick up your pay packet in spite of what you say about our Luke.'

'Well the revolution is coming and soon,' Gronow said, his eyes alight, 'and then the likes of your brother will know their place.'

He left the room and, with a sigh, Charlotte rose to her feet, staring around her and feeling the warmth of the kitchen before switching off the gas lamp and following him upstairs. She lay awake, staring up at the ceiling – sleep would not come, however hard she tried to relax.

At her side, Gronow stirred as though feeling through his sleep the direction of her thoughts. He turned and his hand reached towards her, grasping her breast and she forced herself not to stiffen and recoil at his touch. What had happened to the young carefree girl who had fallen in love with her handsome suitor? Had Gronow really changed or was the change in herself?

He moved closer and she felt his weight press against her. He was always ready to make love to her; he was a virile man and she wished she could respond to him in the way he deserved. She knew she should be flattered that after ten years of marriage, his desire for her was as strong as ever but all she longed for these days was to be left in peace.

'*Cariad*.' His voice was hoarse, thick with sleep but his arms were around her, drawing her closer. 'There's a lovely girl, you are, my Charlotte.'

She wanted to push at him, get up from his bed and run away, anywhere so long as she did not have to endure his passion. Perhaps she was sick, or perhaps she was simply growing too old for this sort of thing.

She endured his lovemaking, even going so far as to put her arms around him and pretend for his sake an enjoyment she did not feel. She sighed with relief when he fell away and lay beside her breathing raggedly.

'*Duw*, there's a woman in a million I've got!' he whispered. 'Ready and willing for a lark even before the sun is awake.'

If only he knew, she thought as she slipped out of bed, that the 'lark' as he called it brought her no pleasure only worry that she might fall for a baby.

'No need to get up, girl,' he said, 'it's early yet.'

Charlotte washed herself from the water in the bowl on the table and dressed quickly in the darkness, afraid that if he saw her nakedness he would be aroused once more and beg her to come back to bed.

'It won't do me any harm to be about an hour or so before daylight,' she said firmly. 'There's the boys' breakfast to prepare, mind, as well as your snap box. Sleep you for a little while longer, I'll call you when the fire's lit and breakfast ready.'

Downstairs, she lit the gas lamps and watched the dark crouching shadows of the furniture spring into life. She shivered in the coldness of the dawn and hurriedly knelt before the grate setting light to the papers beneath the coals.

It was good to sit alone in the kitchen warming now with the ruddy glow from the fire. Charlotte held a cup of tea in her hands and sighed softly. Her life would be fine if only she loved her husband as she had done on their wedding day.

It wasn't as though Gronow was a womanizer or spent his wages down at the bar of the Mexico Fountain. He was a good man and a wonderful provider – perhaps it would be easier if she could find some fault in him because then she might understand her own feelings better.

She heard the sound of the boys' footsteps on the stairs and put down her cup with a sigh. There was no more time for introspection that got her nowhere, the real world was here in this house in the shape of her sons and her solid, reliable husband, and she should be ashamed of herself for being so ungrateful for what life offered her.

'*Duw*, mam, there's early you're up.' Denny came into the room like a hurricane, his shirt tails flapping like a tail between his braces. Behind him at a more leisurely pace came Fredrick, her first-born, his hair slicked down with water, his eyes bright as they looked at her.

7

'Aye, couldn't sleep, boy,' she said softly, 'which is all the better for you because you'll have time for a cooked breakfast before you go to school this morning, instead of running out with a piece of toast in your hand as you usually do!'

She deftly placed the strips of bacon in the pan and pushed it onto the hob where the bacon began to sizzle at once with a mouth-watering smell.

'That doesn't mean you get out of doing your jobs, mind,' she said evenly. 'You fetch the sticks in from the shed, Denny and, Fred, cut some bread for me, there's a good boy.'

'Why can't I cut the bread for a change?' Denny said standing near the door with the basket in his hands.

Fredrick pushed at his arm. 'You ask the same question every day and every day mam tells you that you can't cut bread until you're older.' Fredrick smiled wickedly. 'We don't want finger and thumb sandwiches do we, mam?'

'Ugh! that's enough of that.' Charlotte frowned at her sons. 'Get on and do what you're told or you won't get any breakfast at all.'

While she was frying a pan full of eggs, Charlotte heard the sound of Gronow's footsteps on the stairs. She looked up and smiled as he entered the room in his singlet and long underpants, and kissed her dutifully on the cheek. She could be at ease with him now in the presence of her sons and in the safety of the kitchen, it was only in the marriage bed that she shied away from him.

He winked at her from his chair at the head of the table. 'Hurry up with that food, missis, a man needs to keep up his strength, mind.'

She placed the plate of food before him and then served the boys, taking for herself only one egg and a slice of bacon.

'*Duw*, you eat like a bird, girl,' Gronow said reprovingly, 'and me earning a good enough wage to feed a family of ten.'

Charlotte refused to meet his eye. This was another source of contention between them – her reluctance to have another child. She poured the tea and sat down at the other end of the table facing him and changed the subject adroitly.

'Do you think I could buy some curtains for the parlour windows, Gronow?' She picked up her cup and looked at him over the rim. He chewed his piece of toast thoughtfully and after a time nodded his head.

'Aye, I don't see why not, girl, but what's wrong with the old ones?'

Charlotte put down her cup. 'Men! Can't you see that I've washed them so many times the pattern looks like tea stains? And the hems are going threadbare, another wash and they'll fall to pieces anyway.'

Gronow held up his hand. 'All right, buy the curtains, I'll say no more on the subject.'

He rose and took his working clothes – caked with slurry and dust – from the cupboard. Charlotte always hated to see him put on his dirty clothes day after day, she could almost feel the irritation of the dust against her own skin. In the early days of her marriage, she had tried to wash her husband's clothes every day but she quickly learned it simply wasn't practical, Gronow would need trousers and a flannel shirt for every day of the week and even then there was no guarantee she would be able to dry the washing. And so, she followed the practice of older more experienced housewives and did the really dirty wash just once a week, choosing a day when the rain clouds were at bay and the winds blew in strong from the sea.

She handed Gronow his snap box and watched as he patted first Denny and then Fredrick on the head in a gesture of farewell. He was not a man who could express himself easily in words and yet the gleam in his dark eyes clearly revealed his pride in his sons.

Charlotte chastely offered her cheek, as she did every morning. 'God go with you, Gronow,' she said and watched from the door as he made his way uphill towards the Slant Moira. Then she returned indoors where there was still a lot of work to be done: the boys to get off to school, the breakfast dishes to be washed and the brasses to be cleaned just for a start. Later she would dust the bedrooms, and change the sheets on her bed.

And yet, long after her sons had left for school, Charlotte sat staring at the cluttered table overcome by a feeling of inertia. She was becoming a shrew, she told herself, a discontented woman who deserved a good hiding for not thanking the good Lord for what she was given.

She was just about to rise to her feet and open the window to the early spring air when she heard the eerie, spine-tingling sound of the hooter rising above the hills surrounding the Slant Moira. She knew full well what it meant and suddenly, she began to tremble.

The Slant Moira was a small drift mine lying beneath the craggy mountains on the outskirts of Sweyn's Eye. It was a mine rich with good coal, the anthracite of Red Vein, second only, some said, to Peacock that came from the very bowels of the earth. And it was owned by Luke Proud, once carpenter turned boss, and watched with interest by the gossips who said such a venture could not succeed.

But to Katie Murphy as she made her way slowly up the hill towards the mine, Mr Proud, though she had never met him, was a hero, for he had given her little brother a job. She adjusted the bag on her arm. It was awkward to carry; bulky with the snap box of food and the canteen containing tea leaves and tin milk her young brother had forgotten to take with him that morning.

She paused, the mountain was raw and ragged in the cold air and she was breathless from the climb. The early sun was beginning to shine and an outcrop of coal gleamed like diamonds in the shaft of light.

Katie sighed. She loved Sean, he was special to her: she had been sixteen when her brother was born and even then had fancied she was a woman of the world for she had taken unto herself a lover who had taught her early the delights of the flesh.

Her reminiscences were shattered by a sudden noise as though thunder was rumbling around the skies above her head. She froze, feeling as if she was sinking in honey. She stumbled and almost fell, fear running like wine in her veins as on the heels of the blast the raucous siren from the Slant Moira sent the birds screaming into the air.

'Oh, Mary mother of God, let Sean be all right,' she whispered, forcing herself to move forward, slipping now in her haste. Her breathing was laboured; it seemed to her that she would never reach the mine. She tried to run but the rutted slope of the hill seemed to be dragging her back. At last, lungs bursting, she reached the rise above the Slant Moira and stood staring at the scene before her.

Already, coal-blackened figures were running towards the mine, some of them like monsters from a nightmare beneath the masks of their breathing apparatus. The rescue work was in progress as men struggled to lift huge stones, seeking leverage with poles beneath large coal masses that gleamed dully in the early light. Within the mouth of the mine was a solid barrier formed by a massive roof fall.

Katie bit her lip and tasted blood. Sean, baby of the Murphy family, might be imprisoned within the darkness, frightened – even injured.

As she hurried down the slope she saw a horse standing, blinkered and submissive, coat dulled with coal dust and dampness. The animal shivered as she passed and made soft noises of distress, lifting a hoof and scraping the iron rail. Katie stroked the soft muzzle. 'Sure an' everything is going to be all right then.'

She moved closer to the mouth of the mine where men from the neighbouring drift now toiled side by side with the miners from the Slant Moira, for competition was put aside when it came to disasters in the small mines too insignificant to trouble the rest of the world.

A fall at the Kilvey Deep or Craig Fawr aroused public curiosity for they were big deep pits with boilers to make steam for the winding gear and the pumping out of water, but the owner of the Slant Moira employed only five fully-grown men and a boy, so there was little for anyone outside the town of Sweyn's Eye to be concerned about.

The miners at the Slant Moira worked longer hours than most, piercing the mountainside with blasts of black

11

powder to open new faces, but they brought out of the darkness a good living, for at the beginning of the new year of 1926 there was prosperity after the troubles that had long dogged the coalfields of Wales.

Katie drew nearer to the hub of activity at the entrance to the drift and her pulse quickened as she saw at close quarters the solid mass of rock and coal that blocked off the rescuers from the trapped miners.

'Any sign of Sean Murphy?' she asked quietly and one of the men turned a blackened face to her, rivulets of sweat marking lines along his cheeks. He shook his head. She recognized him and felt a measure of relief.

Big Eddie Llewelyn was a strong man and sensible, more used to bagging the coal and selling it from the back of a cart than digging it, but he had courage and muscle and would work until he dropped.

'No, Katie love, but Rory the fireman's in there and so is Luke Proud's brother-in-law. They will have looked out for your Sean don't you worry.'

'He's so young,' Katie said wistfully, 'he shouldn't have been inside the mine at blasting time and him not yet sixteen.' She moved back quickly as another of the rescue party staggered towards her with a huge slab of shining coal.

'Get out of it, girl, let the dog see the rabbit, right?' Tanny was a short, stocky man, one of the hauliers at the mine and he spoke kindly enough, but Katie felt tears blur her vision as she moved obediently away.

She seated herself on a rock and hunched her shoulders, drawing her woollen jacket around her, shivering, in spite of the fact that the sun was warming the land now and a light wind was sending clouds scudding across the sky. Her arms ached with tension as she hugged her knees and she remembered how they had once ached from nursing Sean.

He was the youngest of her brothers, born late to Mrs Murphy. He had cried often in the nights, keeping Katie awake when he was teething, coming into her arms for comfort for mammy had slept soundly through his tears, thanks to her being fond of the gin. Still was, come to that, although she had been bedridden these past two years.

Mammy had been upset this morning and looking drawn and sickly. 'Sure and that foolish boy has gone and forgotten his food again,' she said worriedly. 'I'll give him a good pasting when he gets home.'

Mammy's eyes had been anxious, her face pale, the skin dried by the excess of alcohol that was her only relief from the pain of bone ache. 'I don't know what it is, Katie girl,' she'd said, 'but I feel real uneasy about my boy, you take his food to him and see he's all right.'

Katie had been reassuring, believing mammy's sickness was making her downhearted. She had always been strong-willed and in spite of all her drinking, Mrs Murphy had outlived her more robust husband.

She drew her woollen coat more firmly around her shoulders and told herself that thinking about her dead father was morbid, so she turned her attention instead to the rescuers who were working like demons from hell, blackened faces throwing the whites of their eyes into relief. And yet they seemed to make little inroads through the mass of stone and coal that had filled the entrance to the slant. What if there was gas within the levels, methane that would kill a strong man let alone a young boy like Sean?

She must not allow herself to become silly and tearful; as her mammy often said, looking for trouble would surely bring it to you. And yet she felt a pain within her as she remembered how much Sean had longed for a job in the mines. He had gone first to the big pit of Kilvey Deep and begged for work, and she had met him on Market Street with tears coursing down his cheeks. His thin wrists had stuck out of the sleeves of his too-small jacket, his face was streaked with dust and the cap, set at a jaunty angle that morning, was twisted between his fingers.

'They said I was too small, mind.' He spoke with Welsh intonations in his voice for he had not the Irish that mammy had passed on to Katie.

13

'Well then, prove them wrong!' She had smiled and touched his thin shoulder. 'You mustn't give up hope so easily, if you really want to be a miner then you must try again somewhere else, perhaps one of the small mines up in the hills.' And he had taken her at her word.

She heard the throb of an engine and rose to her feet as a battered Austin car drew up on the rough roadway leading to the mine. The man who swung himself from the driving seat was not unknown to her. He glanced for a moment in her direction and then he moved purposefully towards the mine entrance, discarding his jacket. He was a tall man with crisp, dark hair and clear blue eyes, a forceful man.

Katie watched as he rolled back the sleeves of his white shirt and, taking up a large shovel, began to help with the digging into the fall at the black gaping wound in the hillside.

She felt anger burn within her head, the beat of her pulse was accentuated. This then was the boss, the man who had allowed a fifteen-year-old boy to be in the mine when the dangerous task of blasting was taking place.

She clenched her hands to her sides, fighting the urge to rush forward and confront the mine owner who stood so tall in his fine clean clothes while his workers grovelled in the dark like animals trying to make a living.

She almost moved forward but then there was a cry from one of the men at the entrance. 'We've broken through! *Duw*, there's a gap in the rock and I can see someone inside.'

Katie felt as though she was walking up a long, steep hill, her footsteps dragging. Her jacket fell from her shoulders but she took no heed. She closed her eyes for a moment and willed herself to be calm. Everything would be all right, it had to be, for wasn't mammy waiting at home expecting her youngest son to return safely from his work?

The figure brought out into the sunlight was caked in dirt and slurry, his hat had gone and his hair was thick with dust. It was not her brother.

'It's Rory!' a voice said above the whirling noise in her head. 'He's alive, thank God!'

But she had wanted it to be Sean, with his long thin limbs, his bright eyes and the red hair that characterized the members of the Murphy family. Sean, her brother, the only boy left at home and mammy's two eyes. God, let him be alive and then she, Katie Murphy, would ask for nothing; she would look after mammy with infinite patience and never look for any love in her life other than that of her kin.

She'd had her share of men. After she had lost Will Owen, her first lover, she had thought she would never fall in love again but then Mark had come to her and married her and for a time she had been the happiest woman in the world.

She sighed – she was doom to all the men in her life, she was a jinx and she was better off living the life of a maiden as she'd done these past few years. And yet the memories of Mark were sweet, the way he had held her and kissed her, rousing in her a ready response. But Mark she had lost to the sea, he had been dragged beneath the rushing, booming waves off Mumbles Head and she had watched him drown in an agony of anguish, and since his death had not loved any man.

Oh, there had been lovers and for a brief interlude she had believed she would make a good marriage with Ceri Llewelyn whose brother Eddie toiled now with the other miners at the mouth of the mine. But she had deceived herself for she had known in her heart that all she felt for him was affection; passion had been missing and in the end he had found himself some one else who could really give him the love he deserved.

She had run away to Yorkshire where she had enjoyed, for a time, the hospitality of Rhian Gray who had married Mansel Jack.

Perhaps she was destined to live out her life alone, Katie thought bitterly. She was past thirty now, an old woman by some standards and yet she did not feel old. Within her beat a heart that wanted love and her body was a traitor calling out for the ecstasy of passion that she had once known.

15

She lifted her head as she heard her name called and moved forward instinctively. 'Come here, girl,' Eddie said urgently, 'see if you can help poor Rory, see how he bleeds and you standing there like a frozen statue.'

The sharpness of Eddie's tone brought her fully aware, back to the present. She knelt beside the wounded fireman and saw the blackness of blood below his knee.

'Here, let me try to bind it,' she said softly, reassuringly, in the same tone she had used to quieten the nervous horse. She quickly pulled down her clean linen petticoat and making a pad of it pressed it against the wound.

'It should be cleaned,' she said, 'he needs to get to the hospital.' She looked up into the direct, blue eyes of Luke Proud. She noticed almost absently that his clean, crisp white shirt was streaked with coal dust and that his hands were cut and bleeding.

'One of the young boys from the next mine has gone to bring the ambulance,' he said evenly. He stared down at her with a mixture of impatience and pity. 'Do you think it's any good you being here, wouldn't you be better off at home?'

'No, I wouldn't,' she said tersely, 'and if you'll give me a pick and shovel I can work as well as you.' Her tone was curt, her heart thumping again with anger. She stood up and wrested the shovel out of the man's hands, unaware of the rush of colour to her pale cheeks and the sparks of light that shone from her eyes.

'Eddie, here's the ambulance coming up the hill. Help me get Rory to his feet.' Luke had turned away, seeming to ignore her existence, and for a moment Katie watched him carry the hefty figure of the fireman over the rough ground with a strange feeling replacing the anger within her. Luke Proud was a self-made man – he'd once been a carpenter and now he was a successful mine owner, and as such he commanded respect.

Katie turned impatiently and thrust at the hole with the shovel, trying to rake the small coal and rocks away from the entrance. It was more difficult than she'd imagined. She managed to dislodge a large stone

and she fell to her knees, peering into the darkness.

'Sean!' she called, hammering at a piece of rock with
the shovel. 'Sean, can you hear me?'

'There's no sign of the boy.' Eddie was at her side. He
paused and took in a great breath. 'There's another fall
further back, see, and it looks as if Sean is deep inside
the mine.' He pointed to the crushed timbers that had
once held back the pressure of the mountain. Frail enough
protection, Katie thought, with a feeling of dread. She
moved back to the hill and sank down to her knees and,
taking up her rosary, began to pray.

Charlotte felt sick to her stomach as she left the house
and made her way up the hill towards the slant. She had
tempted fate, she told herself fiercely, she had held lightly
the love of a good man and now she was to be punished
for it.

She tried to hurry but her feet kept slipping on the hard
stones that gleamed diamond-bright in the early sunlight.
The coal was a cruel master, turning in spite on those who
sought to wrest it from the land. It could crush and maim
and it could send forth gases that burned a man's lungs
until they were useless.

Charlotte heard the whine of the ambulance engine
as it left the mine and careered past her down the rough
track. She paused, wondering if her husband was inside,
but after a moment she made her way towards the Slant
Moira, feeling sure in her bones that Gronow was still up
there.

Men were working at the mouth of the slant and as
always when there was an accident the women came to
wait, shawled and booted, grim-faced, expecting only the
worst.

She saw Katie Murphy kneeling a short distance from
the mine and made her way unsteadily forward. The young
Irish woman turned and seeing her rose to her feet.

'The other men have been fetched out,' she said,
her voice hoarse, ''tis our Sean and your man they're

17

trying to rescue but the fall is a bad one sure enough.'

Charlotte bit her lip and stared at the gaping mouth of the mine that was set like a wound in the softness of the hillside. She had never been this close to the Slant Moira before. She turned questioningly to Katie, 'Luke, my brother, is he safe?'

Katie nodded. 'Sure he's fine and working like a hero alongside his men, I give him that.'

'We've found them, the both of them!' Charlotte heard Big Eddie Llewelyn's voice as though in a dream and her hands were trembling, her legs almost failing to support her as she watched the blackened figures being carried from the mine.

'There, gentle now, boys. Lay the lads down soft, like, and we can have a look at them.' Luke was on his knees beside the still figures of the man and the slender boy as they lay face-up as though looking to the sun.

As if in a dream, Charlotte watched Katie draw closer to her brother. Katie seemed determined to force herself forward, though her legs moved stiffly, her hands hanging uselessly at her sides.

She stared long and hard at the arched back of her young brother, at the open mouth, black with dust, and at the eyes staring upward as though searching for the light.

Luke was standing beside her, trying to draw her away. 'Go on home,' he said gently, 'we'll see to things here.'

Luke turned towards Charlotte and there was a world of anguish in his eyes. 'Charlotte, there's sorry I am.'

Charlotte knelt in the roadway and gently touched the coal-blackened face of the husband who only this morning had taken her in his arms and made love to her. And, ungratefully, she had resented his attentions. How different she would have been had she known what was to happen before another night had come.

She slipped her arm beneath her husband's broad shoulders and held him to her, careless of the dust that transferred itself to her shawl and blouse.

'It's all right, my lovely,' she whispered softly, 'I'm going to take you home.'

2

Cold winds lifted the heads of the early snowdrops that sprinkled the garden of the ferry house and sent eddies of water racing down the River Swan towards the sea. On the line at the back of the house the washing danced clean and fresh, small garments that befitted a new baby, for Nerys Llewelyn had given birth to a girl.

She sat up in her bed and stared in wonder at the small, perfect features of her daughter lying in the crib beside her and tears blurred her eyes – she had given Siona the girl-child he'd always wanted.

Her husband entered the room silently, his clear green eyes seeking her face, his big frame tense as he stared at her anxiously. Siona was a man used to working outdoors, running the ferryboat from the Hafod Bank to Foxhole, and he seemed to dominate his surroundings with the force of his character.

'The midwife said to come up,' he said softly. 'Are you all right, *cariad*?' He stood uncertainly in the doorway but when Nerys smiled and beckoned him forward, his frown vanished.

'Come and see her,' she said softly, 'she's got the Llewelyn looks, a real charmer she's going to be.'

'*Duw*,' he touched the tiny hand in wonder, 'isn't she a beauty then?' He bent and kissed his wife's lips. 'She's just like her mammy as far as I can see.'

Nerys held him close, loving him more than she ever believed it possible to love any man. He was so much older than she was, but he had the strength and energy of a man half his age.

'When are you going to bring our son back from Big Eddie's house?' she asked imploringly. 'I can't wait to see Emlyn's face when he knows he has a baby sister.'

'Well the baby is only a few hours old,' Siona said doubtfully, 'I don't think you could manage that boy of ours yet, he's such a rip. Give it a few days, righto? In any case, our Eddie's glad of the company, the accident at the Slant Moira shook him up a bit.'

Nerys sighed. 'You're right, as usual. Big Eddie's a hero, marvellous he was that day at the mine, everybody says so. Come on, sit by here and give me a kiss.'

He held her close but so gently, as though she was a flower that might be crushed. She kissed his cheek and clung tightly to him. She was so thankful that she had given him a child, and a daughter at that.

She closed her eyes, her mind drifting to the days when she had worked in the ferry house, cleaning, cooking, doing all the many chores that caring for a motherless family involved. She had believed herself in love with Howel, eldest of the Llewelyn boys, and she had conceived his child; but it had been Siona, father of the family, who had married her and given her child his rightful name.

She had come to love and respect Siona more and more as the days passed and when, in the boating accident on the freezing waters of the River Swan that had taken Howel's life, she had feared Siona dead too, she had known that her husband was dearer to her than life itself.

She held him close now, loving him with every pore of her being; he was in her pulse, part of her. 'You're a wonderful man, Siona Llewelyn,' she said softly, 'you make me feel precious, cherished. Have I ever told you how much you mean to me?'

He kissed her gently. 'Hush now, you'll make my head so big I won't be able to climb aboard the ferryboat let alone take it across the water.' He smiled at her proudly, 'You're a good girl, *cariad*, you've brought me such happiness today.'

He held her hand and it was lost in his large fingers. 'You know better than most the pain I suffered when I lost my only daughter and her mother to the river.' He looked directly into her eyes. 'I'm not a man of words as you well know, Nerys, but I thank God for you every day.'

He coughed in embarrassment. 'Enough of such nonsense, I'm beginning to sound like an old woman.'

He rose from the bed and walked to the window, staring out into the slant of winter sunlight. He was not a man given to a show of emotion and Nerys knew how much it must have cost him to put his innermost thoughts into words.

Beside her the baby cried out and at once Siona moved to the crib and stared down anxiously at the baby.

'It's all right,' Nerys said, 'she's perfectly healthy, a strong child and no doubt a hungry one.' She opened the buttons of her cotton nightgown. 'Lift her up then and give her to me.'

Siona obeyed, cradling the child for a moment in his big arms, the tenderness he felt reflected in his green eyes. Almost reluctantly, he gave the baby to Nerys and she smiled up at him proudly.

'Come on, my lovely.' She turned her attention to her daughter. 'It will take you a little time to get the milk flowing but you must learn, there, that's the way, close your little mouth now.'

She smiled in triumph. 'See, she knows already that she can have milk from me, she's going to be a bright one, this little girl.'

Siona thrust his hands into his pockets. 'What name shall we give her?' He stared down at the small child, enchanted by his daughter. 'It must be something special.'

Nerys's lips curved into a smile. 'Well, Sian is the nearest to Siona and what could be more special than that?'

'Well, there's an idea for you!' Siona's green eyes glowed and Nerys held her hand towards him.

'Come and sit by here and let me tell you how much I love you.'

Siona kissed her mouth gently and then moved towards the door. 'I'd better get back to the boat, I still have to work for a living, mind.' He frowned. 'It's all right for some, lying in bed all day doing nothing.'

'Get out of here before I throw something at you!' Nerys smiled as the door closed. Siona was not a man of words but she knew how deep his feelings went, he didn't have to tell her he loved her, he showed it in every action, every look; she was so lucky to have him.

She put the baby carefully in the crib and sank back against the pillows. This giving birth was hard work. Her lids were becoming heavy and everything seemed to be misty. She must have fallen asleep for when she opened her eyes again, it was growing dark outside.

There was a tapping on the door and Nerys struggled to sit up, she still felt a little weak but she was no longer so weary.

'Mona, there's a good girl, coming over here to help me. Come and have a look at the baby.'

Siona's daughter-in-law was a quiet, kindly girl and a hard working one. 'I've been here for hours,' she said, 'but when I peeped in earlier, you were having a little sleep.'

'How's Ceri?' Nerys asked. 'Apart from being a very successful business man, of course!' Ceri was a silver-smith. He had started in a small way a few years before and now employed other men to do the work.

'He's very well, thank you.' Mona came into the room and went at once to look into the crib.

'*Duw*, there's beautiful she is, oh, Nerys, can I hold her, I'll be very careful, mind.'

Nerys smiled. 'Of course you can hold her but she's going to be ruined, spoilt rotten I can see it now!'

Mona's face reflected the tenderness she was feeling and Nerys wondered why she'd not had children herself, she was obviously a born mother. But it was none of her business, Nerys told herself, the way Mona and Ceri arranged their lives was their own concern.

'She's got green eyes just like Siona!' Mona exclaimed. 'Oh, I can't get over her, she's so beautiful!'

Nerys warmed in Mona's praise. 'Siona's so happy that we've got a daughter and I feel I've repaid him for caring for me the way he has. Not many would marry a woman who was expecting another man's child.'

Mona gently returned the baby to the crib. 'Siona loves Emlyn as if the boy was his own. Now, how about a nice cup of tea? I bet you're parched, aren't you?'

Nerys nodded. 'I'd love a cup of tea, how did you know?' She smiled for many was the time she'd sat and gossiped with Mona over endless cups of tea.

'I've made you some pasties filled with good meat and onion, build up your strength again, see?'

'I don't know what I'd do without you, Mona,' Nerys said, her voice soft with gratitude, 'you are always there when you're needed, do you know that?'

'Oh, rubbish.' Mona's colour rose and she hurried from the room, ashamed of the tears in her eyes.

Nerys leaned over the crib. 'You're a lucky little girl, Sian,' she said softly, 'there's so many people around to love you.'

She touched the tiny hand and tenderness surged through her. When she'd known she was expecting Siona's child, she had been fearful at first, worried that she might not love another baby as she loved Emlyn, her first-born. But her fears had been unfounded, for she felt now as though she'd never been without her tiny daughter.

Mona returned with the tray and set it down on the table beside the bed. 'Come on, girl, let me see you eating something for it's been a long hard day, mind.'

Nerys sat up and sighed contentedly. 'Aye, it has that, let's have that tea.'

She watched as Mona busied herself with the cups and noticed that her eyes were shadowed and there were lines of tension around her mouth.

'Is there anything wrong, Mona?' she asked, taking the cup and sipping the hot tea gratefully. 'Don't deny it, you know I can read you like a book. Anyway, you can confide in me.'

Mona shook her head. 'I'm probably being silly but I think Ceri might be seeing another woman.' She sighed softly. 'It could even be Katie Murphy, I know he's never really got over his feelings for her.'

Nerys put down her cup. 'Put that thought right out of your mind,' she said quickly, 'I know Katie and she

24

wouldn't have gone off to Yorkshire that time if she'd really been in love with Ceri. Oh, no, she'd have stayed to fight for him.'

Mona sighed. 'I suppose you're right, but there's something wrong, I just know it.'

'Why not just ask him outright?' Nerys said softly. 'It might be that you're worrying about nothing.'

Mona looked up at her. 'I'm afraid,' she said, 'I couldn't bear it if he admitted there was someone else, I'm just a coward I suppose.' Nerys put down her cup and took Mona's hand.

'Ceri doesn't seem the sort of man to cheat on his wife.'

'What man does seem the sort?' Mona said wisely. 'Perhaps I will pluck up the courage to speak to him about it, it might be easier in the long run than living with my fears.' She moved abruptly. 'Anyway, I shouldn't be burdening you with my problems not at a time like this. I'll go and get the bedding washed for you, the clothes I did earlier have dried nicely in the breeze.'

When she was alone, Nerys lay back against the pillows and closed her eyes, she was so tired and yet so content. It was peaceful and silent in her room and soon she drifted once more into a deep sleep.

'I'm off home then, Siona,' Mona drew on her coat. 'I'll do a bit more washing and ironing in the morning.'

'There's kind of you, Mona.' Siona held the door open for her. 'It's very nice to see you looking after Nerys so well.'

'Nonsense!' Mona smiled. 'This is like my second home after all.' She kissed his cheek that was rough with a day's growth of whiskers. 'You need a shave, man, don't go kissing your new daughter until you've stood close to the razor will you?'

She waved goodbye at the gate and moved up the bank towards the road. The wind was chill coming in off the river, and she hugged her coat closer around her as she stepped out briskly towards home.

This morning Ceri had told her he would be working late and her stomach had turned over with fear and suspicion.

It had done her good talking to Nerys for she spoke sound common sense. Mona decided it would be better to speak to Ceri, challenge him outright about his strange behaviour rather than to let doubt ruin their marriage.

Still, Mona had not been in a hurry to leave the ferry house. The atmosphere there was one of peace and harmony; they were such a lucky couple, even though some people had thought the marriage doomed to failure because of the age difference between Siona and Nerys.

She forced her mind on to more mundane matters, wondering what she could cook for supper. Perhaps something light – poached haddock topped with an egg and some fruit to follow. She was tired after doing all the washing for Nerys and all she longed to do now was kick off her shoes and sit with her feet up in front of the fire. But first she would have to light it.

She was just turning into Market Street when she saw Ceri leaving the fresh fish shop. Mona stopped in consternation, so he had been seeing Katie Murphy!

He caught sight of Mona and waved his hand but anger had begun low in the pit of her stomach, rising up as though to choke her. She turned and ran away from him blind with jealousy, she thought of him holding Katie in his arms, kissing her and she felt physically ill.

Had he always loved her then? Had he been unable to forget that once they were going to be married? Well he was free to go if that's what he wanted.

She found herself on the beach, staring out across the bay to where Mumbles lighthouse sent out its intermittent beacon of warning. Without Ceri, her life would be meaningless.

And then suddenly he was beside her, taking her in his arms. 'What is it, Mona, what on earth is wrong with you?'

She looked up at him and in the dim light he was unfamiliar, a stranger, and she wondered if she had ever known him.

'You, tom-catting after Katie Murphy, that's what's wrong!' The words burst from her lips and once the flow

26

was begun she could not stop it. 'I've known for some time that things weren't right between us,' she said, 'but I didn't want to believe what my senses were telling me!'

Ceri shook her roughly. 'Stop it, Mona!' She began to cry and he cradled her in his arms.

'There's nothing going on between me and Katie or any other woman,' he said firmly.

'Then why were you visiting her shop?' Mona demanded rubbing at her eyes, furious with herself for shedding weak tears.

'I made a special journey to speak to her,' he said gently. 'Her young brother was killed in the accident at the Slant Moira, you know that.' He paused, running his hand through his hair. 'And I wanted to give her my sympathy, that's all.'

'I didn't think of that,' Mona said guiltily, 'I'm sorry, Ceri, but you have been acting strange these past weeks, it all seemed suspicious to me.'

'I've been worried about business, that's all,' Ceri said softly. 'The demand for silver has fallen off recently and I've been wondering if I should move out of the trade.'

Mona put her arms around his waist. 'Why didn't you tell me?' she said. 'I've been imagining all sorts of things.'

'I didn't want to worry you.' He kissed the top of her head, and then taking her hand, led her back towards the road.

'Anyway, what's the news from the ferry house, any further developments?'

Mona smiled. 'Oh, yes, you've got a half-sister, a lovely little thing she is, and your dad is so proud of her.'

She glanced at Ceri. He was only half listening to her, and suddenly all her doubts and suspicions returned tenfold. Whatever Ceri said, there was something going on and she meant to find out just what it was.

3

Luke Proud strode into the bedroom and, pulling at his tie, flung it impatiently to one side, opening the collar of his gleaming white shirt as though it choked him.

'You can't blame yourself, love.' Peta Proud raised herself on one elbow and held out a hand to him. 'Come here, you look fair worn out.'

He sat on the bed and took his wife in his arms, closing his eyes, comforted by the warmth of her. He could still see the funeral procession as though it was imprinted on his memory for ever. Dan y Graig cemetery, swept with wind and rain, the dismal clouds low in the sky and to his left the pewter wash of the sea, bound by the confines of the twin piers jutting from an equally grey beach.

Two modest wooden crosses and a few flowers marked the newness of the graves, the only evidence that his brother-in-law Gronow and Sean Murphy, aged fifteen, had ever lived. Luke felt anger burn his gut.

'Maybe I shouldn't have tried to train Sean to be a fireman, not yet at least.' He brushed back Peta's hair as it lay soft against his cheek. 'My mistake has cost not only a young boy's life but has lost my sister her husband, and Charlotte with two young boys to rear. How can I not blame myself?'

'You can't say that!' Peta was emphatic. 'You know what caused the accident, Rory's carelessness.'

'Rory is not to blame,' Luke said, his voice hard. 'He told me that the powder apparently failed to ignite and that against all his instructions, Sean went up to the heading to see what was happening. He must have been killed by the blast instantly. It was damn awful luck that Gronow entered the heading at that very moment, the men usually keep clear when there's blasting.'

Peta hugged him close. 'I know how sad you are. Because we're expecting our own child it makes you more aware of the feelings of others.'

She was right and yet Luke knew his emotions went deeper than that. This was the first time since he'd started mining that there had been any fatalities at the slant.

He thrust his hands into his pockets recalling the events of that morning. The knowledge that Gronow was beneath the fall had acted like a spur driving him on against all reasonable hope. He felt the pain of his sister's grief as she'd waited at the mouth of the mine and it mingled with his own sorrow, for Charlotte was a widow now, a woman alone.

And he could see the pale beauty of Katie Murphy's face as she'd stood at the graveside of her brother. He sensed the despair that was too deep for tears.

'Come back to me, Luke. I know I'm not so pretty now that I'm carrying a child but you do love me, don't you?' Peta's voice was soft, childlike, trusting, and he turned to her at once.

'You're beautiful,' he said softly. And yet as he looked at her, he noted with sudden concern that she was pale, with dark shadows beneath her eyes and there was a sense of weariness in her that worried him.

'I think I shall have the doctor in to look at you.' He returned to her side and stroked back her silky hair. 'You don't seem to be so strong these days, I should look after you better.'

She smiled and catching his hand kissed his fingertips lightly. 'It takes time, love, and don't forget I'm very young and should be fit enough to bring a bouncing baby into the world without much trouble.'

'You're right,' Luke said reassuringly, 'but there's no need to rub it in that I'm ten years older than you, I know it only too well.'

Peta smiled thoughtfully. 'You were born old, love. I expect you were mature and wise even as a child.'

He rose to his feet. 'I doubt that. I'd better change my clothes and get back to the slant, there's a few things

I want to do.' He moved to the door and Peta looked up at him questioningly.

'But I thought all the men had the day off for the funeral.' There was disappointment in her voice and he forced a smile.

'The horses have to be fed, remember? Old Cal will be pawing the ground in a right mood by now. There are a few other things I want to check on, too. The Slant Moira needs looking after – I'm not a rich man with time to idle away, remember.'

'Oh, all right then off you go, I must be the only woman in all of Sweyn's Eye who has a coal mine as a rival!'

Luke smiled at his wife but as he left her and walked out into the early sunshine, the weight of the disaster seemed to settle once more on his shoulders.

The house seemed silent and empty as Charlotte rubbed at the brass fender mixing ash with water to form an abrasive. The brasses were gleaming and yet she felt compelled to continue to work on them for if she found herself idle, the pain and the guilt would come flooding back.

When at last she had put away her dusters, she moved towards the parlour and stood in the doorway, reluctant to enter the room for it was here that Gronow had been laid out in his coffin. He had looked so peaceful, his face washed clean of coal dust, his hair sparkling with droplets of water as though he had just come from the bath in front of the kitchen fire.

And she missed him so much, more than she would have believed possible, for although she had fallen out of love with her husband she had still felt love for him as a companion and as the father of her sons.

She was about to turn away in despair and return to the warmth of the kitchen when there was a rapid knocking on her front door. She opened it quickly, glad of the diversion and was confronted by a young woman who was nervously clutching a bag in her hands.

'It's about the advert in Murphy's shop window,' the woman said quickly, 'it said that you wanted a lodger.'

'Yes, that's right.' Charlotte stepped back. 'Please come inside.' She didn't want the neighbours learning about her business.

She led the way into the kitchen. 'Sit down,' she said, 'and I'll tell you about the room.'

The young woman sat on the edge of the chair and twisted the strap of her bag between her fingers. 'I would want accommodation for two,' she said, 'there's me and my brother. I'm Sheila O'Conner.'

Charlotte thought quickly. If she put the boys in her room, she would be able to let out the two other bedrooms.

'I think I can manage that,' Charlotte said thoughtfully. 'When would you want to move in?'

Sheila O'Conner smiled nervously. 'As soon as possible, please. We're staying in a terrible boarding house in the Strand at the moment and sure the noise from the other occupants is dreadful, especially on a Saturday night.'

'Well if you give me today to prepare the other bedroom and then you could come in tomorrow morning, how would that suit you?'

'Sure that would be fine.' The young woman's face lit up with pleasure. 'I can see this is a clean, respectable place and speaking for myself I can't wait to move in. Could I just ask, are meals provided?'

'Well, if we negotiate the price, I expect I could cope with two more mouths to feed.' Charlotte smiled warmly as Sheila O'Conner rose to her feet.

'See you in the morning, then,' she said softly.

As she closed the door, Charlotte felt a lightening of her spirits. Having two lodgers would certainly be hard work but at least she would not sit alone in the evening when the boys were in bed, listening to every creak of the floorboards. And if Mr O'Conner was as nice as his sister they would all get along just fine.

Charlotte moved to the kitchen and from under the sink took out her scrubbing brush and a packet of soda. She would start right away on the back bedroom, which could be used more conveniently by Mr O'Conner, as it was separated from the middle and front bedrooms by a small flight of stairs and a passageway.

Charlotte sighed, feeling a flutter of anxiety. Would she be able to cope with two lodgers and one of them a man? She had only anticipated taking in a lady and yet fate seemed to have stepped in and decided matters for her.

Well the bedroom wouldn't be ready if she didn't get a move on, she told herself sternly, it would be just as well to have the beds moved before her sons came home and began to grumble about the new arrangements. Purposefully, she climbed the stairs feeling with a sense of hope that a new phase of her life was just about to begin.

Luke stood outside the door of Murphys' fresh fish shop taking a deep breath before knocking on the door. It was opened at once by Katie and she smiled at him reassuringly.

'Come in, mammy's resting but I know she'll be pleased to see you.'

As he moved into the room where the old woman lay, Luke was shocked by her frail appearance.

'I'm Luke Proud,' he said gently, 'I can't tell you how bad I feel about Sean, Mrs Murphy, he was a good boy.'

She sat up straighter against the pillows. 'Oh, so you're the boss man from the slant, are you?' Her tone was edged with tears and Luke sat beside her and took the thin fingers in his hands.

'I must talk to you about compensation,' he said. 'I know only too well that nothing can make up for the death of your son but I mean to put a sum of money at your disposal which will at least help you financially.'

Luke was unaware that the door to the passageway had opened and two tall, red-haired young men were standing behind him.

'Sure an' isn't that big of you, boss!' The voice was edged with irony, and as Luke turned he saw the men standing behind him.

'These are my sons just come home from up North,' Mrs Murphy said quickly. 'Now, Michael, don't be more

32

of a fool than you can help, there's no call for that sort of talk.' Mrs Murphy raised herself from her pillows.

'Luke Proud is a local man, a good man and he is here to discuss something that is no concern of yours.' She paused a moment to take a breath. 'Accidents happen in the mines,' she continued, 'and no one should understand more about it than you two boys working as you have in many different pits around the country.'

'This man will be paid out by some big insurance company,' Michael Murphy said forcefully, 'none of the compensation will come from his own pocket.'

Mrs Murphy would have replied but Luke held up his hand.

'I'm not here to involve the family in bitterness and anger,' he said, his tone equally as strong as the young Irishman's had been. 'I accept that the accident shouldn't have happened in the first place, but your brother was being trained as a fireman, it was what he wanted. And the position would have given him more wages and some standing in the mine, but the job was a dangerous one, there's no denying that.'

'Look, all your gift of the gab won't wash with me,' Michael said threateningly, 'so take your fancy words and get out of here! You're not wanted in our house.'

'Michael, will you stop it!' Katie said in bewilderment. Events were moving so swiftly she seemed unable to gather her thoughts. 'You're acting like a rabble-rouser. You've only just set foot in our house – you haven't cared in years how we've got on, so why so concerned now?'

'Taking his part, are you?' Michael said suspiciously. 'You're not his side-piece, are you?'

Katie shook her head slowly and Luke could see two spots of bright colour burn against her pale skin.

'Jesus, Mary and Joseph, you take the cake for sheer nerve!' She spoke softly but her anger was evident in the brightness of her eyes. 'I've met Luke for only the second time today. Since when do I have to be a man's side-piece to stick by my principles?'

33

Michael stared at her, his eyes narrowed. 'You are taking the part of a stranger against your own family, then?' he said roughly. 'Haven't you heard of loyalty? And if it's your morals we're talking about here, then by the saints haven't you set the tongues wagging more than once with your carrying on?'

Luke felt anger begin low in the pit of his stomach; he wanted to lash out at the angry face to close the mouth that was insulting Katie Murphy. He made a move forward but Kevin's voice broke the strained silence.

'Hey, come on now, Mike, I think you're being a bit hard on Katie, she's stuck by our mammy all this time which is more than you can say for the two of us.'

Mrs Murphy waved her arms in agitation. 'Sure will you all stop now! Otherwise I'm going to get up out of this bed and take me stick to the lot of you.'

Luke turned to the door. 'I'll call another time,' he said and as he glanced towards Katie, he saw the misery in her eyes and felt as if he'd been struck a body blow.

He drove away from Market Street and down into the town, glad to be away from the hostile atmosphere of the Murphy household. Suddenly he experienced a feeling of inexplicable sadness as though he had lost something he wanted to cherish.

Then he told himself not to be a fool, he would go up to the Slant Moira and forget about the Murphy family.

It had rained in the night and the tramways were covered with mud, and the water washed over the rails. There was a great deal of work to be done which had nothing to do with bringing out coal. It would be a profitless day and money, as always, was tight for the Slant Moira. It was worked on a shoestring and had been since Luke had put into it all he'd saved from his days as a carpenter, but the men would still have to be paid.

Rory was limping a little, arriving at the mine the same time as Tanny. The two younger colliers toiled up the hill behind them.

'I've boiled up the water.' Luke was in the shed, he had the iron stove well alight and the warmth was welcome against the early morning chill. 'Bring your canteens over and we'll have a brew,' he said cheerfully, but the men avoided each other's eyes, for making the tea had been young Sean Murphy's job.

'Look, boys,' Luke continued, 'you know as well as I do that we'll have a cleaning up operation for a day or two. The two falls have to be cleared and then I'll need to cut some timber for new collars and arms to prop up the roof, the old ones are squeezed beyond any salvaging.'

'When do you think we'll get back on the face, boss?' Tanny asked worriedly. 'We've a big order to fill for the Ponty tinplate works. *Daro*! Don't want to lose that contract, mind.'

'We won't.' Luke ran his hand through his hair. If he lost the contract there would be no money to continue working the slant, let alone pay the men. 'We'll get in there right away and start to clear out the debris.' He moved out of the small hut and made his way towards the entrance to the mine with Tanny alongside him, hurrying to keep up.

'Cal is ready,' Tanny said. 'I thought we'd use the biggest of the horses as there's some large stuff to bring out. I've fixed him to the dram though the gun seemed to have been bent a bit and wouldn't fasten properly at first but I managed it in the end.'

'Might have been hit by a piece of rock that bent the metal.' Luke fastened his lamp to his belt. 'We'll have to manage with it for now,' he said. 'There's a lot of rubbish to move before we can get very far in.'

The only way to move the fall was by hauling the pieces of rock along to the opening of the mine and into the dram with brute force. It was hard physical work and yet Luke welcomed it for while his muscles strained and his back ached, he could forget the tragedy that had killed two young men. Forget too the angry feelings aroused in him by the loudmouthed Michael Murphy.

The man was a fanatic, he told himself, as he manhandled a huge rock away from the mouth of the mine. He was the type who would use any means he could to further his own ends, a man not to be underestimated.

The men worked without stopping for several hours and had made little headway. 'Unhitch Cal,' Luke said, 'and push the dram onto the plate ready to tip away the rubbish.' He nodded to Rory. 'We'll move the worst of the outer fall before tonight.'

'Aye, we might but there's no use in killing yourself into the bargain, boss,' Rory said mildly.

Luke lifted his arms to ease the ache in his shoulders and smiled ruefully. 'You're right enough there, man, my back feels split in two.' He walked out onto the gritty dust track that led from the mine to the tip where the rubbish was dumped and stared around him at the folding hills.

They were green and sloping with the ancient rhythms of the land and beneath them was a fortune in coal if only it could be got out. He knew that his methods were out of date, he needed the machinery that the bigger mines could afford. Drills that worked by compression instead of the hand-held, back-breaking augers that were powered by sheer strength and sweat.

And yet he was determined he would make the Slant Moira into a thriving concern. He would perhaps never own a deep pit with a cage that carried men hundreds of feet down into the earth where the rich seams of Peacock, the best coal in the world, lay. He stared out across the rolling hills to the clouds behind and wondered how he was going to raise the compensation that he had spoken so confidently about to Mrs Murphy. It would mean eroding the little savings he had put by in case of difficulties, such as several days of working without profit.

He turned back to the mine. He would not be beaten, he would fill the order for Ponty if he had to work day and night to do it.

'Come on then boys, a cup of tea and a snap break and then let's get our backs into it again.'

Katie sat beside the bed and held the cup of tea laced with gin nearer to her mother's pale lips. 'Now then, mammy, you've let those boys upset you, see how you're trembling?'

'Sure our Michael and Kevin have caused me pain but it's not only that, Katie. I'm missing our Sean so badly.' She paused to rub at her eyes. 'He was my boy, my baby, the last of the family to be born to me and I loved him so much.'

'I know.' Katie smoothed back her mother's sparse grey hair. 'And I miss him too, mammy, but he's gone and we must make our lives go on somehow.' Katie was worried by the lacklustre look in her mother's eyes. Mrs Murphy had never once lost her spirit throughout all the difficulties that had beset her life but this latest tragedy had broken her.

'Shall I freshen your tea with a little drop more gin, sure it can't do you any harm now, can it?' Katie smiled as she poured a liberal measure from the bottle. 'Now don't go pretending to protest, I know it helps keep away the pain of the bone ache.'

'I'm not protestin' my girl, I'm that tired I could sleep for a week.' Mrs Murphy drank from the cup and then fell back against the pillows, her face thin and gaunt, her cheekbones angles of light and shadow in the flickering gas light.

Katie bit her lip as she heard the door slam – her brothers had returned and were letting everybody know it. She wondered how it was that Michael and Kevin had become almost strangers, grown hard and distant in the years they had spent away from home. And now, they had come back as large as life, not making any move away from the house in Market Street.

'You're not to let them boys bully you, for sure as all the saints are in Heaven they will try.' Mrs Murphy was looking earnestly at Katie, her thin shoulders tense, her eyes seemingly too large for her pale face.

'Sure, mammy, you don't have to worry about me!' Katie said fiercely. 'I can handle Michael even though he's become the loudest and bossiest of the boys and acts as though he's my father not my brother.'

Mrs Murphy fell back against the pillows, sighing. 'I still miss Tom, a real man he was, with his red hair and his big tall frame, and wasn't he so good with the business? Though for sure you've run it all well for us these past years and I'm not taking that away from you.' She paused and held out her cup, gesturing with her head towards the gin bottle. Katie obediently poured a measure of the spirit into the cup and replaced the bottle on the table, waiting for her mother to continue speaking. She well knew these moods of nostalgia that sometimes gripped her mother and it didn't do any harm to indulge them even though the truth had been very different to the dreams Mrs Murphy saw now.

Tom Murphy had been hard and unfeeling, a man who had forced himself upon his wife mercilessly, ignoring her protests that she wanted only to be left alone. It had been the constant creaking of the bed in the next room and the swiftly-hushed noises that had made Katie aware, even as a young girl, of affairs of the flesh rather than the heart.

It had been this heightened awareness of things carnal that had led to her love affair with William Owen. She had wanted him with an almost insane desire and without thought of the consequences she had lain with him in the sweet grass of the hillside in the softness of the summer nights.

After he died, she thought she would never fall in love again but of course she had. And yet the intensity of the feelings she'd had for Will had never quite been recaptured.

'Give us a little drop more, Katie love.' Mrs Murphy's voice was slurred. 'And sure enough I'll sleep the night away.'

'All right, mammy, but this one is definitely the last.' Katie smiled. 'Here, you bad woman, take it, you know full well it's mothers' ruin, don't you?'

She plumped up the pillows and left the room quickly for she could hear Michael's voice raised in anger.

'Hush your row, Michael Murphy, your mammy's trying to sleep and you shouting like a fool!'

Her brother turned on her, his face red, his eyes narrowed and angry. 'Shut your gob, woman, or I'll shut it for you!' He staggered and Katie realized with a sinking feeling that he was more than a little drunk.

'Sit down,' she said more softly. 'I'll build up the fire and make us all a nice cup of tea.' She busied herself with the kettle and bit her lip, knowing that for all her fine words to mammy, she did not know this stranger who was her brother at all; and as for handling him, she might as well try to tackle a mad bull.

When she placed the cup before him, Michael looked up at her for a long moment in silence and Katie felt uneasy, as though he was looking inside her head.

'You should be married by now with a brood of children.' He leaned forward, elbows on the table, slopping some of his tea into the saucer and onto the white of the table-cloth.

'I've been married,' Katie said with dignity, 'and you couldn't even come home for my wedding, nor my husband's funeral, so I don't know why you think you should voice an opinion now.'

'That's enough of your lip,' Michael said glancing up at her. 'I demand respect from my sister.' He thumped on the table so that the crockery rattled and Katie moved away towards the stairs without answering him.

He lurched to his feet. 'Listen to me!' he said, his voice low and the bluster gone. 'I've come home and I'm the man around here, and by God you better believe it.'

Katie paused, her hand on the door-knob, knowing there was little point arguing with a drunken man.

'I have come home,' he repeated. 'I run things from now on and you, dear sister, will do as you are told or you'll be out on the streets, do you hear?'

As Katie hurried up the stairs to her room, she felt tears burn her eyes. Michael who could have been a source of strength had become a bully and there would be little help from Kevin, for he was weak.

She stood beside the window and stared out into the darkened street. Her instinct was to pack a bag and put as much distance as she could between herself and Market Street. She sank down onto the bed and put her head in her hands. She would not run away – how could she abandon mammy, sick and weak as she was, to Michael's ill humour?

She undressed, and washed silently in the water from the jug on the table, then climbed into bed. But it was a long time before she could sleep, for she was seeing the angry face of her brother, and within her was growing a feeling of rebellion. Michael had come home sure enough but she would not allow him to boss her about. In the morning, when he was sober, she would give him a piece of her mind and then they would see who ruled the roost in Murphys' fresh fish shop.

4

The streets of Sweyn's Eye were thronged with people, for the working week was almost over and the market stalls were putting out the last of their goods for a cheap and quick sale.

Cockle women cried raucously into the slanting sun, having walked that morning the twelve miles or so from the shellfish beds at Penclawdd, and were now crouched tiredly over almost empty baskets. Deftly, workworn hands scooped up heaps of the small fish plucked from their shells, shovelled them into paper, spiced them with vinegar and salt.

Lava bread, black and pungent, made from seaweed and waiting to be fried into cakes covered with oatmeal, stood in deep bowls on the snowy cloths, and vegetables brought straight from the farmlands of Gower splashed the scene, with the brightness of carrots against the green leaves of cabbage.

Gossip abounded as women stood close together, hair gleaming in the sunlight and the word was that Mary Sutton – Big Mary who once was overseer at the Canal Street Laundry – was home from America and that she was wearing widow-black.

In her room in the Mackworth Hotel Mary Sutton stared out of the long windows into the busy Stryd Fawr overwhelmed by nostalgia. She had come a long way since she'd been born in one of Sweyn's Eye's more seedy backstreets in what was virtually a hovel. She had fought her way out of the poverty, working and striving to make a success of first her humble market stall and later her vast emporium, the first ever seen in Sweyn's Eye. Now she was a wealthy woman in her own right, her fortune increased by the money Brandon had left her after his death.

She rubbed at a fleck of dust on the window-pane and watched the progress of a beggar as he held out a ragged sleeve to passers-by. The haunting tune from the mouth organ he played rose to where she sat and she felt tears burn her eyes.

She missed Brandon dreadfully. Their marriage had survived her one act of unfaithfulness and the ensuing doubts concerning the paternity of her son, and at the last there had been a bond between them that nothing could break. Except death.

She turned from the window and looked towards the bed where her son lay in complete relaxation, his long limbs spread out, his eyes closed as he slept against the covers with the abandon of a young animal. He was dark like Brandon with the leonine head that characterized the men of the Sutton family. He was almost ten years old now, a solemn thoughtful boy with a great intelligence that was leavened by a mischievous sense of humour. Her gaze rested on the white stick that lay propped against the bed and she bit her lip, telling herself not to cry. She still blamed herself for the car accident that had led to her son's blindness.

A soft tapping on the door startled her and she moved quickly from the window. She was tall, an elegant woman with a touch of grey in her glossy hair. Her eyes were fine and bright, her cheekbones prominent, giving her an almost regal appearance.

She opened the door cautiously, not wanting any intrusion into her privacy but then a smile of welcome lit her face and she stepped back, gesturing with her hand for him to enter the room.

'Paul, there's good it was of you to come.' He stood beside her, holding her hand in his and Mary knew in that moment that Paul Soames was still in love with her.

'Mary, you look as beautiful as ever.' He kissed the palm of her hand softly and his lips were warm. 'When I received your letter, I was so delighted that I could be of help.'

'There's a bit of nonsense for you!' She smiled at him. 'Getting to be an old woman I am now, mind; and you as a doctor of medicine ought to know that better than most.'

He closed the door and leaned against it, his head on one side. 'Old? No, not you, Mary, you could never grow old, not in my eyes.'

She moved towards him on an impulse and put her arms around him, resting her head on his shoulder. It was a long time since she had felt the comfort of a man's arms holding her, a long time since she'd had a broad shoulder to cling to, for Brandon had been sick for three weary years and she'd needed to be the strong one.

She moved away from Paul reluctantly and waved her hand towards the chairs near the window. 'It's good to be home, Paul, and yet I feel almost like a stranger here – yours is the first familiar face I've seen since I arrived.'

'You should have got in touch with me sooner.' He leaned forward, his eyes bright. 'Mary, you know how I feel about you, how I've always felt. Can't we . . .?' He stopped speaking as she held up her hand.

'Don't say anything more, Paul, it's too soon.' Too soon to think of any man except Brandon. It was six months since he'd died and the pain was as sharp as it had ever been. She stared at Paul from beneath her lashes. She had lain with him once and once only, more years ago than she cared to remember and for a while she had thought – they both had thought – that the child she carried must be his. But time had proved them wrong, she had been reconciled with Brandon and Paul had stepped out of her life. And yet he had remained faithful: he had never married, he had loved her constantly and she wondered if she could ever live up to his ideal image of her.

'How is Stephan?' Paul asked quietly. 'I see he still has to carry his white stick?' He crossed the rich carpet to the bed and stared down at the sleeping boy almost wistfully. Mary could read his thoughts. Paul was wishing that Stephan was his son so that he would have some tangible bond which would bind him to Mary.

She sighed heavily. 'Some of the finest doctors examined him while we were in America but there was nothing any of them could do.'

Paul rubbed the side of his face thoughtfully. 'Don't ever give up hope, Mary. I've always told you that Stephan's sight could return at any time, haven't I?'

Mary nodded and turned to look through the window, once more wanting only to change the subject, for she had hoped and dreamed many times of her son made whole again, only to wake to the light of day and find him still trapped in his world of darkness.

'As I said in my letter, I need a house, Paul,' she said. 'A nice house, not too big and preferably with a view across the beach.' She glanced up at him. 'You will help me look for one, won't you?'

He returned to her side. 'Of course I will, Mary, I may have just the thing for you, we'll see. Anyway I'm only too glad to be of help.' He pulled at the knees of his trousers before sitting down. 'You'll soon find yourself back in the swing of things.' He leaned towards her. 'What about Mali Richardson, have you been in touch with her yet?'

Mary shook her head. 'No, I've just been taking things easy, Paul, trying to get over the sea voyage and find my bearings again. Of course, I'll be in touch with Mali. Once I'm settled.'

Paul leaned forward. 'Mary I'm so glad you're home, and honoured that you sought my help. You'll never know what your letter did for me, it was like drawing back the curtains in a dark room to have the sunlight flood in.' He coughed, embarrassed at his own rhetoric.

'I've a new surgery now,' he said more briskly, 'I've left Canal Street behind and moved into a property on Mount Pleasant Hill where there's plenty of room for me to conduct my practice and in much more comfort for my patients too.'

Mary looked at him, remembering the old surgery with the leather couch and the skeleton hanging in the corner of the room and the smell of wintergreen oil. It was there

44

that she had gone into Paul's arms and found comfort for her pain and grief.

She coloured at the recollection, wondering if Paul sometimes thought of their brief union – but he was glancing towards the sleeping boy on the bed, staring down at him with compassion written clearly in his face.

'He's fine and strong,' he said to Mary, 'and the image of his father; Brandon will never be dead while his boy is alive.'

Mary felt the tears burn her eyes. She could not fail to hear the hint of wistfulness in Paul's voice. Guilt caught at her and she bit her lip, knowing that she had entered Paul's life as the catalyst that left him alone with only one night of tenderness and love to comfort him in his years of emptiness.

'Why have you never married, Paul?' she asked, her voice tight with emotion, and immediately she regretted speaking her thoughts aloud. He returned to her side and took her hands in his, drawing her to him.

'You know the answer to that already.' He took her face in his hands and she remained motionless, knowing she had precipitated the very scene she had hoped to avoid.

'I love you,' he said softly. 'Not a day has passed without me thinking about you.' He allowed her to draw away from him and Mary stood, staring out of the window, seeing nothing.

'I'll admit I haven't led the life of a monk,' he continued as though now the floodgates were open, he could not stop himself. 'I've had affairs, some of them I considered serious, at the time. But always, Mary, there were comparisons made and you won hands down.'

Mary turned to him. 'But it was only that once, Paul!' she said urgently. 'You have built your life on a dream woman, not the real me.' She shook her head. 'I've more than my share of human frailties, you know that better than anyone.'

'Look, Mary,' he said gently, 'you came to me for comfort when you believed your husband had been killed in battle. That was not wrong, it was only the crying out of a desperately unhappy woman.'

She sighed and rubbed at her eyes with her hand. Perhaps Paul was right for she would never have knowingly been unfaithful to Brandon, but it didn't alter the fact that she had gone so swiftly to the arms of another man.

On the bed, Stephan stirred and in a moment was sitting up, reaching at once for the stick that was almost an extension of himself. Mary felt emotion catch at her throat for her son's affliction was her fault. She had so much to regret in her life.

'Mam –' he turned his head in her direction '– who is here with you?' His perceptions were sharp, his hearing acute, his other senses compensating for the loss of the one of sight.

'It's Doctor Soames, Paul – perhaps you remember him?' Mary spoke matter of factly for Stephan hated nothing more than pity.

He slid from the bed and lifted his head, a tall, well-set young boy, handsome with fine eyes that appeared to see even though they did not.

'Yes,' he said thoughtfully, 'I remember the doctor. How do you do?' He held out his hand and Paul moved quickly to take it.

'I'm delighted to have both you and your mother back in Sweyn's Eye,' Paul said smoothly and Mary was pleased that he did not patronize her son but spoke as one adult to another. 'I hope to assist in finding you a house in the area,' Paul continued.

'That's something I'm looking forward to,' Stephan said in his grave manner, 'I do not like being confined to a hotel room.'

'Why don't we go out this very moment?' Paul said, looking at Mary and searching for a response. She nodded in agreement.

'Yes, why not? Like my son I'm tired of this room.'

Mary ruffled her son's hair. 'You'd better comb that mop of yours and fetch your cap and coat, it might be colder outside than it looks.'

She felt infused with warmth, a sense of purpose that had been missing for too long. She had always been a woman of action and sitting about the place moaning would not cure any of her pains and regrets.

'My car's outside,' Paul said and Mary sensed the pride in him. He had become a man of means, a success in his job, exchanging the old house in Canal Street with its peeling façade and faded paintwork for a new one in the more elite area of Mount Pleasant. She smiled at him, sharing his pride.

'You've done well, Paul, I'm so pleased for you.' She rested her hand on his arm for a moment and the warmth of his fingers covered hers briefly.

Paul led the way into the sunshine of the day and helped Mary into the car. The leather seat crackled coldly beneath her legs as she held Stephan's hand and guided him towards her.

'Shall we go to the pier at Mumbles?' Paul asked turning to look at her with a smile in his eyes. 'There are all sorts of entertainment there these days – you won't know the place.'

'That sounds lovely.' Mary settled back and sighed contentedly as Paul set the car in motion. It was good to have decisions made for her for a change, even ones as simple as where they would spend the day.

A cool breeze drifted in through the open window and Mary touched Stephan on the arm. 'Are you warm enough, *cariad*?' she asked softly and as he nodded, a lock of dark hair fell forward over his eyes. Unconsciously, Mary brushed it back and a pain caught her as she realized anew that Stephan couldn't see anything anyway.

'It feels like a lovely day,' Stephan said, sensing her mood as always. 'I'm so happy to be outdoors, mam, aren't you?'

She swallowed hard. 'It's a lovely day and yes, it's good to get out of that hotel room. The sooner we have our own home the better I'll be pleased.'

Paul glanced back over his shoulder. 'Before we go on to the pier,' he said, resolutely, 'I'm taking you to see just the sort of house you should have.'

Mary raised her eyebrows. Paul had changed, become more forceful and she liked that, it showed character. He had always been a fine man, it was he who had sent for Brandon when Stephan was a baby and it was Paul who had been the means of the reconciliation between them. Paul had always put her happiness before his own.

He drove the car away from the town and up into the soft slopes of Mount Pleasant. The sun dappled the roadway, throwing shadows between the buildings and Mary could not help smiling to herself. She would be happy to live at Mount Pleasant, which was obviously Paul's intention.

He turned the car into a broad street and, glancing back, Mary saw the glittering sea below her and the jutting rocks of Mumbles Head in the distance. At her side, Stephan fidgeted.

'What's it like here, mam? Describe it for me, please.' He leaned towards her and with a rush of love, she kissed his cheek.

'It's as its name suggests, very pleasant,' she said softly. 'The sea is sparkling with sunlight and the sky is clear, it's a very nice day to be viewing houses.'

Paul drew the car to a halt. 'And perhaps this one will be just what you're looking for. I hope so, because I live just a few yards along the road.' He frowned anxiously. 'It's not too small, is it?'

Mary climbed from the car and stood looking up at the tall, elegant house built on three floors, with triangular windows peering out of the roof. She smiled and put her arm around Stephan's shoulder.

'*Duw*, it's quite big enough. I should think there must be more than twelve rooms inside. What do you think I'm going to do, Paul, have a party every night?'

He returned her smile. 'Come along in, I've got the key.' He led her along the short driveway. 'You see I've thought of everything.'

The hall was a modest size but well-proportioned and splashed with light. Mary moved into the largest room and stared with delight at the breathtaking view of the sea.

'It's lovely, Paul!' she said softly. 'I feel as if I belong here already.' She returned to the hallway and Paul flung open another door eagerly.

'Wouldn't this make a fine study?' he asked. 'I expect you'll need one because I can't see you sitting about doing nothing all day.' He smiled. 'You still have business holdings in town, don't you?'

Mary nodded. 'You read me well, Paul. I do indeed have irons in Sweyn's Eye's fires. You may remember Billy Gray who managed my affairs before I went to America? He still works for me. I have a few interests – shares in a couple of small mines on the outskirts of the town, for instance.' She shook her head. 'I couldn't let the old place slip from my grasp, not entirely. I suppose I always knew that some day I would come back.'

She followed Paul up the stairs and looked carefully around the rest of the house. The rooms were large and airy, the bathroom on the first floor adequate (though the heavily-decorated, cumbersome bath was not at all to her taste), but there was nothing that couldn't be altered. She smiled a little grimly; everything was so easy if there was enough money available.

Once she had longed to be rich, to escape from the misery and humiliation of being poor and now she would exchange it all if only her son could regain his sight.

'What do you think, Stephan?' she asked. 'Does the place feel right to you?' She rested her hand on his shoulder and as he turned his thoughtful face to her, her being melted with love for him.

'I like it. I can feel the sun on my face and outside the birds are singing in the trees; it's a friendly house.'

'That's it, then,' Mary said, smiling at Paul, 'we'll have it. Will you see to the arrangements for me?'

He moved towards her and though he didn't touch her she could feel his happiness. 'No sooner said than done.' He smiled. 'I'll drive you and Stephan to the pier and then go into town and sort everything out.'

Mary glanced back at the house and the windows gleamed down at her as though waiting for her to return.

It would be some weeks before she could move in – she would need to buy furniture and carpets and curtains, but all that could be arranged easily enough. She felt a sense of excitement that had been missing in her for too long; she needed a challenge to make her alive again after the shock of losing Brandon.

She sank back in the seat of the car and bit her lip, remembering with bitterness and pain the illness that had drained her husband's great strength. It seemed ironic that he had survived the horrors of the war which had taken so many lives only to fall prey to a sickness that had no cure.

She felt her son's hand slip into hers and stifled a desire to cry. Stephan seemed to know intuitively if she was distressed. She did not lie to him.

'I was thinking of your father,' she said softly, 'but I shall not be sad any longer. We shall go to the pier to smell the sea air and eat some cockles drowned in vinegar out of a paper bag, and enjoy ourselves.'

Paul glanced at her quickly and she smiled at him, grateful that he did not make any comment about the tears in her eyes. He was a good man. Why couldn't she fall in love with him? Life would be so simple, then – he would look after her and comfort her, and always be faithful. He seemed to know her thoughts.

'Give it time, Mary,' he said quietly, 'just give it time.'

The pier was crowded with people. A small girl stepped gingerly over the boards, looking with fascinated horror at the sea, washing far below. Music blared out from beyond the garish roundabout of horses and a cockle woman sat beside her basket, shouting a string of unintelligible words.

'I can smell salt and fish and tar,' Stephan said, lifting his head and removing his cap. The wind ruffled his thick hair and he looked so like Brandon that Mary felt her pulse beat heavily within her.

'Be careful,' she said, 'don't let your stick catch between the planks of wood or you might fall. Come on, there's a seat over there. We'll sit down and then I'll get you some cockles, see how you like our Welsh shellfish.'

She bought two bags of the plump cockles and doused them in vinegar, pinching one between her fingers and sucking on it as she'd done as a child. Then it had been a rare treat, something to savour, and the taste brought back the memories of her childhood when hunger had been so familiar to her.

She laughed as she watched Stephan's reaction to the shellfish: he grimaced at first and then tentatively tried another cockle. 'I suppose I'll get used to them,' he said wryly.

A shadow fell across Mary and she looked up to see a flash of bright red hair surrounding a delicately pale complexion.

'Katie!' she said in delight. 'Katie Murphy, there's lovely to see you.' She stood and hugged the Irish girl in genuine pleasure. 'Come on sit down by here and tell me all about yourself.'

Katie sat obediently beside Mary and took the hand that Stephan gravely held towards her.

'Sure and there's a fine young man your son has become,' Katie said, looking only briefly at the white stick, 'handsome too like his father, God rest him.'

'You've heard, then, that I'm a widow,' Mary said quietly and Katie shook back her bright hair.

''Twas noticed as soon as you returned to the town that you were wearing black, Mary – you should know that nothing gets by the people of Sweyn's Eye.'

Mary sighed. 'I suppose you're right. Anyway, what about you, have you got a man and a brood of children by now?'

Katie smiled ruefully. 'No such luck! Like you I'm still a widow but well used to it by now, it's been a long time since Mark died.'

'I'm a tactless fool!' Mary said. 'I've still not learned to think before I speak, see, Katie girl. I haven't changed much since the days when you used to work with me at the laundry, have I?' She looked more carefully at Katie, noticing the dark shadows beneath her eyes and the lines of strain around her mouth.

'You look peaky.' Mary spoke gently. 'Things not going too well for you?' She saw the darkening of Katie's eyes and waited for her to speak.

'We lost our Sean, my youngest brother.' Her words came out slowly, painfully. 'A mining accident, up at the Slant Moira. Me mammy's taking it badly, of course, him being her baby an' all.'

'I'm sorry,' Mary said, 'though the words are inadequate, I really mean them and if there's anything I can do to help, let me know.' She stared out over the rails of the pier to where the hills of Sweyn's Eye rolled back into the distance. She and Katie had not always been on good terms, there was the time when Katie had condemned her roundly for going to the arms of Paul Soames so soon after the telegram came saying that Brandon was missing, believed killed. The pain was still there, Mary thought, and the guilt, but how could she have known that the news was false and her husband safe?

But for all that, there was an underlying bond of friendship between the two women that could not be broken and Mary reached out and touched Katie's shoulder.

'I'm buying a house on Mount Pleasant,' she said, 'a bus trip will bring you to my door and you'll always be welcome, mind.'

Katie smiled. 'Sure and don't I know that.' She rose to her feet. 'I'd better get off home now, I've left mammy for long enough.' She shrugged. 'But I felt I just had to get away, if only for an hour.'

Mary nodded. 'I understand exactly how you feel. Come and see me soon, don't leave it too long, will you?' She watched Katie's slim figure with the crown of bright hair disappear into the throng of people at the entrance to the pier, and somehow she was comforted by the encounter. It was as though she was becoming part of the fabric of the place once more, fitting into a slot, belonging.

'That lady has a nice voice, mam,' Stephan said, 'all pretty and musical. I think she needs a friend·like you, she's not very happy.'

Mary touched Stephan's arm gently, amazed as always at his perceptiveness. She rose to her feet. 'Come on, let's walk a bit and when Paul comes for us he can take us for tea somewhere nice before we return to the hotel.'

As she stared into the waters of the bay, Mary sighed. There was a new life opening out before her and it was time she grasped at it eagerly. She must put her mourning aside, for hadn't she done most of it whilst Brandon was still alive?

The day suddenly seemed brighter, the sea more brilliant. She slipped her hand through her son's arm and together they walked into the swathe of sunlight that dappled the worn boards of the pier. Mary Sutton had come home.

5

'There's going to be hell to pay!' Michael Murphy, just home from work, stood in the kitchen of the house in Market Street blackened with coal dust, the whites of his eyes appearing to gleam with anger. 'Those blasted pit owners, who do they think they are?' He had come home from Craig Fawr in a foul temper and didn't hesitate to let his anger show. He threw down his snap box and it fell open, spilling leftover bread and cheese onto the floor.

Katie, watching her brother, felt afraid. Michael had become a stranger, a perpetually angry man who had not a good word for anyone, but this time, at least, there seemed to be cause for his fury.

'A fat lot of good it was having Sir Herbert Samuel make out a report; a *cut* in our wages, of thirteen and a half per cent, that's what his proposal is!'

'Sure 'tis a bad day for the mining industry.' Kevin sighed heavily, glancing apologetically at Katie and surreptitiously picking up Michael's snap box. 'We've made our complaints known to the bosses but all they tell us is that the industry has never recovered from the tumble it took in 1925, which is a brazen lie! Well, Cook won't be having any of it – you know what he says, Katie? Not a penny off the pay, not an hour on the day, and we'll back him to the hilt.'

Katie listened, without revealing anything of her thoughts, but the last thing she wished for was to have her brothers bringing disputes and politics into the house. Michael had the power to disturb and upset mammy, making her more nervous and irritable than usual.

'Been on the backs of the miners for years has the Baldwin Government,' Michael said sourly. 'Black Friday, they called it, when that man Thomas decided not to support the miners; marked the end of the triple alliance, so it did, and left us all to the wolves.'

'But that was a long time ago,' Katie said quietly, 'surely nothing could be that bad again? Some mines are making a profit, aren't they?'

Michael stared at her. 'Thinking about fancy-pants small owners like Luke Proud, are you, girl? Well he's nothing, understand me? His mine is a flea-bite compared to the deep pits. No one would care if he went under tomorrow.'

Katie was stung into replying more sharply than she'd intended. 'Well, didn't he give our brother a good living, then, when the big pits wouldn't take him on?'

Michael's lips curled, sweat was running in rivulets through the blackness of the coal dust on his face. 'Have you forgotten that Luke Proud killed our Sean?' He ground the words out and in that moment, Katie realized that it was pointless to talk to him when he was in such a foul temper.

'I have to go and see mammy,' she said quickly and moved away into the kitchen, pushing the kettle onto boil with hands that trembled. She was wary of Michael; he had become arrogant and bullying, and quite obviously had complete domination over his younger brother.

'Katie.' Mrs Murphy's voice was weak and thread-like. 'Bring us a cup of tea, I'm that dry sure I could drink the ocean.'

'All right, mammy, I'll be with you as soon as the kettle boils.' She put out four cups just as Michael came into the room.

'Fetch the bath,' he said abruptly, 'I need to get this filthy coal dust washed off me before I eat a meal. I hope you've cooked something for a man to get his teeth into, I'm ravenous.'

Katie stared at him, longing to give him a piece of her mind. He had gradually become more demanding over the weeks, expecting her to wait on him hand and foot – as it was she already came in from the fish shop to cook the meal for when her brothers returned home from work. She realized quite suddenly that she must not allow Michael to dominate her as he did Kevin.

'I'm busy,' she said and she folded her arms so that he would not see her hands trembling. 'Fetch the bath yourself. I'm not your wife nor your skivvy and sure I've worked a good day in the shop as well as looked after mam.'

Michael's face grew red. He moved towards her. 'Are you daring to talk back to me, girl?' he said in a low voice. 'You just do as you're told.'

Katie stood her ground. 'I'll not give in.' She stared him in the eye. 'And don't threaten me for if I have so much as one little bruise on me I'll go to the constable and have you arrested.'

She knew that she had said just the word to stop him in his tracks. Michael had no liking for the police and Katie guessed that he'd been in trouble with them more than once during the time he'd been away from home.

Suddenly he smiled. 'Sure an' don't go thinking you've bested Michael Murphy, my girl, for you'll learn different and quite soon.' His voice was low but there was so much venom in his tone that Katie trembled.

He went outside and brought in the tin bath taking the kettle full of water and tipping it into the ridged bottom.

'I wanted that water for tea for mammy,' Katie said but Michael filled up the bath with cold water and shook off his clothing, ignoring her presence entirely.

Katie busied herself making the tea and, with a feeling of relief, took the tray into her mother's room.

'That boy been off again, has he?' Mrs Murphy sighed heavily. 'It was a bad day for us when he came back home. Wouldn't have got away with anything if his father had been alive. Sure Tom would have taken his belt to him and after a sound beating, sent him through the door.'

'Perhaps the boys will get tired of it here and go away again,' Katie said soothingly. She didn't believe it for one moment but her mother looked weary and there were lines of pain around her mouth.

'I want you to get one of those solicitors in to see me,' Mrs Murphy said, putting down her cup with hands that shook. 'It's about this compensation. I won't want any money hanging around the place, not with that Michael under our roof.' She sighed heavily and dabbed at the perspiration that beaded her face. 'Wait until the boys are in work – sure I don't want them noseying into my business.'

Katie nodded. 'I'll see to it, mammy, but try to rest now and I'll bring you in a bite of supper after the boys go down the pub.' She moved away from the bed. 'I'm going out for a walk; I can't stay in the same room as Michael for all that's he's my brother.'

'All right, girl.' Mrs Murphy smiled mischievously, 'but put a drop o' gin in my cup before you go and then I'll be sure to have a little sleep.'

Katie let herself out of the back door, hurried along the path and pushed open the gate that sagged tiredly on its hinges. Once Big Jim would have been tethered to the fence, and, beside the animal, would have stood the upturned cart that gleamed silver with fish scales. Now the fish was sold only over the counter and carried to the shop by a shiny lorry.

Mali Llewelyn's mammy had gone to her resting place on the old cart scrubbed clean by Mali and covered with an odd piece of silk. Taken over to Dan y Graig cemetery in the cool of evening was Mrs Llewelyn, and in a real wooden coffin made by her husband.

Katie heard the sound of water washing over the yard and knew that Michael had finished his bath. He would doubtless take some bread and cheese from the pantry, make himself a cup of tea and then go off to the pub. She would make sure she was in bed by the time he came back – he was a brute when he was sober and she would not like to rouse him when he was drunk, for not even the threat of the constable would stop him then.

She moved along the lane and out into Market Street, pausing to look at the shopfront; the paintwork was peeling, the name Murphy, once bold black on white, was faded, almost illegible. The stone slab within the window gleamed dully for she had spent a long time with hot water and soda, washing away the fish scales. She had not wanted to spend her life selling fish but after her father's death there seemed nothing else to do.

She had to look after mammy and somehow make a living for them both, and that she had done very successfully for trade was now brisker than it had ever been. The prosperity and stability her brother had spoken of had been evident in the past months; folk could afford a tasty piece of hake or whiting. Was that all suddenly about to change? she wondered fearfully.

She saw the gleam of sun on the windows of a bus and on an impulse ran towards it, swinging herself onto the platform and sinking thankfully into the nearest seat. She would get right away from Market Street, escape as she'd done when she'd met up with Mary Sutton on the pier.

At least for an hour or two she needed to have a rest from the bullying bluster of her brother, and from the lines of pain etched around her mammy's mouth. She sighed heavily. Why had life suddenly taken on such a grey and depressing aspect? Was she doomed always to be mourning those she loved?

She thought of Sean and tears burned her eyes. She glanced through the window of the bus but saw only her own reflection, distorted and unfamiliar, trapped in the trembling glass. She was tired, she told herself, she did not usually give in to self pity and useless tears.

The bus stopped, jerking her forward in her seat and she rose to her feet, pushing some coins into the conductor's hand without really seeing what she was doing. When the bus roared away along the dusty road, she looked around her and saw that she was within a stone's throw of the Slant Moira, the hill rising upwards, blotting out the sun. Had she really arrived here by chance, she wondered? Or was it more likely that she wanted to be here, to fulfil some hopes of meeting Luke Proud? For he, at least, seemed to be in sympathy with her situation.

She walked over the ragged grass that forced its way through coal-strewn ground and heard the soft whinny of Cal, the biggest of the pit ponies, who seemed never to wander along the hilltop but stood as though on guard at the entrance to the mine.

'Hello, boy,' she said softly, 'sure an' there's no need to nuzzle my hand, I've got nothing for you.' She rubbed the animal's nose and smiled. 'You're a dwarf compared to our Big Jim,' she said softly, 'but you're a nice creature for all that.'

She moved along the tramlines towards the mine and saw that the fall had been completely cleared away. A dram full of Red Vein, good clean anthracite, stood in the cooling evening sun.

She heard a rumble from within the mine and moved quickly from the rails, just as one of the pit ponies trotted out of the entrance, a full dram rocking precariously along the track.

'Slow, damn it!' The voice was commanding and obediently the animal, out in the open, slowed to a walk.

Luke Proud was covered in dust, his eyes appeared brilliantly blue in the sunlight and the muscles on his bare arms were etched in black relief.

'What are you doing here?' Katie said, and then laughed at the absurdity of her question.

'I think I should be asking you that, trespassing you are, mind.' He bent and unhitched the gun from the dram, releasing the pony. She couldn't tell if he was serious or not, she could only see the top of his head and the breadth of his shoulders. He straightened, then, and she saw the glimmer of a smile in his eyes.

'I just wandered up here, though what good I expected it to do me I don't know,' she said honestly. 'I just had to get away from Market Street; I suppose there was nowhere else to go.'

'I was just about to have a much-needed break.' He moved towards the shed that was nothing more than a converted railway waggon, and not knowing what else to do, Katie followed him.

She sat on a stool, watching as he jabbed a poker into the cylindrical cast-iron stove and, replacing the top over the burst of bright flame, pushed a kettle over it.

'Why are you working here alone?' Katie asked, leaning forward, watching Luke's expressive face. She wondered what on earth she was doing here with Luke, who was a married man, owner of the Slant Moira, living in a nice house and driving a car. He was so far removed from her she shouldn't even be talking to him. And yet she could not but admit to herself that he attracted her – more than that, he reached something deep within her.

'I've a large order to fill,' he said, handing her a tin mug of tea and sitting across the chair, his arms resting on the back. 'The roof fall delayed me.' He shrugged. 'I know lives were lost and nothing can make up for that but if I don't deliver the expected load of anthracite on time, then my reputation will go and my orders fall away.' He sighed. 'I can't expect what's left of my team to work all the hours God made but I'm determined not to fail even if I have to work night and day.'

Katie rose. 'Sure an' I'm sitting here taking up your precious time. I'm sorry.' She moved to the open door.

'Don't go.' Luke's voice seemed like a strong thread, holding her, drawing her back towards him. 'Even a workhorse needs a rest sometimes.'

She returned to the stool and took a drink of the strong, sweet tea, her eyes taking in every detail of Luke's appearance. He had removed his hat and there was a white rim around his forehead where the brim had rested. His hair was covered in a sprinkling of dust and yet the life and springiness of it could not be tamed. He smiled wryly and she was aware that she'd been staring.

'You're good to be with, Katie,' he said, 'you're fresh and natural. I don't think I've ever met anyone as honest as you.'

She bent her head and sipped the tea, she didn't answer but she was pleased by his words and behind them she sensed a genuine feeling of friendship.

He rose and the legs of the chair scraped along the ground so that Katie was startled. 'I'd better get back to work,' he said in a level voice and Katie followed him outside to where the sun, glowing orange, was dipping behind the hills.

'Why don't you employ a few men on a temporary basis?' she asked. 'Just until you've filled the order?'

He paused and looked back at her. 'I can't afford to, Katie, not until I've sold this latest load of Red Vein to the Ponty works, it's as simple as that.' He walked away then, his back straight, his tall figure moving purposefully towards the mine.

She sat on the grassy bank, just waiting for what seemed an eternity until Luke emerged with another dram of coal. She somehow felt that her presence was needed and if she could do nothing to help physically, at least she could give him her company. He leaned on the posts at the side of the mine entrance and she could see weariness in every line of his body.

After a moment, he took the reins, led the pony to the edge of the track and unhitched the dram in preparation for tipping the coal onto the lower level.

'Luke.' Katie's voice carried across the open land and he looked up and smiled at her. 'Please give it up and go home, now, you'll kill yourself.' She crossed the distance between them and, disregarding the coal dust, placed her hand on his arm.

His skin was warm and as he looked down at her she removed her hand swiftly.

'*Duw*, I'm all right, girl,' he said smiling, 'I'm used to hard work, mind.'

Katie stared at him thoughtfully. 'This compensation you are giving mammy,' she said, making an effort to sound calm although she was amazed at her own temerity, 'is it coming from an insurance company?'

He stood upright, his hands on his hips, a tall man with a maturity far beyond his years etched into the strong lines of his face.

'I couldn't afford insurances,' he said, softly, 'the premiums would have eaten into what little profit I'm making.' He shook his head. 'I would have come to it, of course, once the slant was making more money.'

'Then how are you going to manage it?' Katie said softly. 'Will you let me help, sure an' haven't I got money put by that's doing nothing?'

He smiled wryly. 'You keep your savings, there's a good girl, and let me worry about my business.'

She stepped back, rebuked, and he reached out a hand as though to touch her before allowing it to fall to his side. 'That was thoughtless of me,' he said, 'I'm sorry.'

'You're right, I'm a nosey old biddy and I should be getting home.' Katie turned and hurried away across the uneven ground.

'Katie.' His voice echoed in the silence. Katie stopped suddenly and glanced over her shoulder. He was smiling. 'Still friends, are we?'

'Sure we are,' Katie walked swiftly down the road towards the town. She felt restlessly that she couldn't return home, not yet. She looked up at the darkening sky.

It was about half an hour later when she heard the sound of a car engine coming towards her. She paused in the roadway and was not surprised when the vehicle pulled up beside her.

'I've decided to take your advice and call it a day,' Luke said cheerfully. 'Jump in if you want a lift but keep well away from me, I've changed my clothes but I'm still covered in coal dust.'

'Sure I don't mind if I do have a lift,' Katie said smiling, 'I was just thinking that the buses have all gone home. I've been waiting here ages.'

The sky was streaked with silver when he drew the car to a halt in Market Street. Katie looked around her fearful of being seen by one of her brothers. The last thing she wanted was to have Michael see her with Luke – he was bound to misconstrue the situation.

She climbed from the car quickly. 'Thank you for bringing me home.' She spoke in a rush, wanting him to go, out of harm's way. She glanced around her and Luke seemed to sense a little of her feelings.

'I'm not afraid of your brothers, Katie.' He spoke softly, without anger but his tone convinced her that he meant what he said.

'Sure, I know that, but I don't like rows.'

She watched until the car had vanished from sight and the sound of the engine had died away into the distance. She felt suddenly drained of energy, knowing that she would like to have called Luke into the house, and would have done if it hadn't been for Michael. She had done nothing wrong, yet her brother would have made her feel guilty, he would somehow have spoiled the friendship that was growing between her and Luke Proud.

She let herself into the house and tiptoed towards her mother's room. Mrs Murphy was wide awake, her face pale beneath the light of the gas lamp, her eyes wide and questioning.

'Jesus, Mary and Joseph, where have you been? You're all dirty, just look at the bottom of your frock!'

Katie looked down, her clothes were indeed streaked with coal dust. She shrugged. 'I went to the mine – I don't know why, mammy, it's just as if I was drawn there.' She sat down on the bed and her mother leaned forward.

'Watch your step, Katie, I don't want you getting hurt. Now just get that frock off before your brother sees you, sure we don't want him asking any awkward questions, now.'

Katie smiled. 'All right, I'll go and get undressed and then we'll have a nice cup of tea, shall we?'

'Forget the tea.' Mrs Murphy picked up the glass from the table beside her. 'This is all I need.'

'Mammy,' Katie said, smiling a little, 'you know you shouldn't drink so much gin, it's not good for you.'

Mrs Murphy took a large gulp of the liquid before pouring more into her glass. 'What harm can it do me now? We both know I'm on my way out.'

Katie winced. 'I wish you wouldn't talk that way, mammy; you're not the sort to give up, are you?'

'It's not a case of giving up, love, I'm just facing reality. I've had my life and now I'm quite ready to slip out of it.'

'Oh, hush!' Katie said. 'I'm going to put on my nightgown then I'll be back, and I don't want any more morbid words from you.'

In her room, she washed her face in the cool water from the jug on the dressing-table and closed her eyes, seeing behind closed lids the strength of Luke Proud's face, and she found herself wondering about his life. No doubt his wife was young, a mere girl and probably very beautiful; they were doubtless very happy together. She drew her cotton nightgown over her head and hurried downstairs, away from the strange sense of uneasiness evoked by her thoughts.

'Mammy, I thought I told you to leave off the gin.' Katie spoke indulgently, for if the spirits kept away the pain then why should her mother not have release?

She sat on the edge of the bed and touched her mother's hand.

'I've been talking to Luke Proud,' she said, her eyes lowered, 'I don't think he can afford the compensation he's promised us.'

Mrs Murphy took another drink. 'That's his worry,' she said, with an edge to her voice. 'My boy died in the Slant Moira and the compensation is necessary to me.'

'By why, mammy? What do you want money for?' Katie asked in surprise. She had imagined her mother would shrug off the compensation, which would doubtless not be very high; the bosses at the lead works gave only the price of a coffin to the relatives of their dead workers.

Mrs Murphy's mouth was folded into lines of stubbornness and Katie shook back her hair in bewilderment.

'Nothing's going to bring him back, mammy,' she said softly, 'and Luke is a good man, an honest man. He'll pay you if it kills him.'

Mrs Murphy rubbed at Katie's fingers. 'Look, my girl, I won't have you beholden to those brothers of yours and this compensation money will help prevent such a thing happening. I'll say no more about the subject and neither will you. Saints alive! What's that noise?'

There was a banging on the shop doorway and Michael's voice calling for Katie to come and let him in.

'He's mad!' Katie said. 'I meant to be in bed by the time he came home but a lot of good it would have done me!' She moved to the door. 'Sure an' you stay in *your* bed now. I'll be off upstairs as soon as I can.'

Michael was banging again, his voice impatient. 'For God's sake, let me in, woman!' he called, thumping the door so hard that the glass in the shop window rattled.

'All right, hush your noise!' Katie held the door wide and in the darkness saw only a jumble of figures. She moved into the kitchen and turned up the light as Michael lurched into the room. Clinging to his arm was a woman in her mid-twenties, her hair was crimped and curled, and she wore too much lipstick. She looked what she was, a woman of the streets.

'Sorry for the noise.' Kevin shrugged off his coat, glancing apologetically at Katie. 'Hope we didn't wake you.'

'The noise was enough to wake the dead,' Katie said tersely. She looked at Michael as he slumped into a chair, his eyes narrowed in amusement.

'Well then, Katie, since you won't cook and clean for me I've brought home someone who will.' He gestured towards the woman who had taken off her coat and seated herself near the dying embers of the fire. 'This is Doffy.'

'You are not staying here,' Katie said quickly. 'Get your coat back on or as the saints are in Heaven above, I'll put you out as you are.'

Doffy looked at her nails. 'I'm not going until Micky tells me to, so there.' She had a childish manner of speaking as though she was a little girl, not a grown woman, and Katie thought she was vaguely familiar.

'I remember you now,' Katie said quietly. 'You're that flossie who tried to get off with Billy Gray, sure and him courting Gina Sinman from Spinner's Wharf.'

Katie smiled. 'The story is that Gina went round your haunts in the public bars telling all who would listen that you had a nasty sickness.' Katie glanced at Michael. 'You're not going to keep a flossie under mammy's roof, not while I'm here.'

His voice was hard, his eyes spiteful as they stared into her face. 'How many men have had their way with you, I wonder.' He looked her up and down. 'Not that you'd be much of a catch the way you look now, covered from head to toe in cotton like a nun.'

'That's enough of that foul talk!' Katie felt fury rise within her. She grasped Doffy's arms and hauled her bodily towards the door. 'Out onto the streets where you belong!'

She swung open the door and pushed the other woman into the darkness. 'Sure if you come back here you'll have a bucket of cold water in your face!' Katie said angrily, then turned back into the room. 'And as for you two, you ought to be ashamed! Holy mother of God what would the priest say, you bringing a sinful woman into mammy's house?'

Michael sank into a chair and ran his hands through his hair. He was silent, hushed by Katie's tirade and she felt a sudden sense of triumph.

Kevin began to apologize, mumbling weakly about Michael only having a bit of fun.

'Shut up, Kevin!' Michael said, his voice hard. He leaned forward his arms on the table, his eyes narrowed. 'Now look here, Katie,' he said, 'I only let you put that flossie out because I didn't care a damn if she went or stayed, but don't go thinking you've bested Michael Murphy, for you haven't. I'm not afraid of any old priest and don't use such threats on me again, understand?'

Katie forced a smile. 'Oh, sure I understand, but you must give as well as take, Michael, and so let's have no more of this bullying and drunkenness, and then perhaps we can all get on all right beneath the one roof.'

Before he could think of anything else to say, Katie moved to the door and turned to look at both her brothers. 'We used to get along just fine and I don't see why we can't do so again.'

As she walked up the stairs, through the shaft of moonlight spilling through the window, she felt a sense of relief. Perhaps Michael wouldn't prove too difficult to handle after all.

6

The evening was mild and full of soft shadows, the sun's
light almost extinguished, leaving a red-streaked sky that
was reflected in the sweep of the sea. Luke stood on the rise
of the hill and stared across the bay to where the lights of
the town hung like fireflies against the dark rising shapes
of Townhill and Kilvey.

He found he was thinking of Katie Murphy, a woman
possessed of beauty as well as sound common sense. What
a pity her brothers should be rabble-rousers.

Impatiently, he moved uphill towards his home, he
should be putting his mind to the task of filling the order
for Ponty Steel Works, not worrying about the Murphy
family.

Matters were growing worse in the coal business. Only
this morning in the paper there was news of another large
pit closing down, over Carmarthen way. The mine owners
were talking about a lock out if the workers refused to
accept the cut in wages and then there would be chaos in
the coalfields.

The Slant Moira would not be adversely affected by the
crisis; on the contrary, orders would probably increase as
businesses found stocks running low. The only problem
Luke would have was the men he employed – would they
wish to come out with their fellow miners as a gesture
of solidarity? As for himself, he could not afford to
stop work: it would take only a few weeks for the
Slant Moira to deteriorate. The earth would begin its
squeeze on the pit-props, snapping them like matchsticks
and the rock and coal would fall, filling up the headings.
Apart from which, if he failed to supply his customers
they would lose faith in him and turn to another
mine.

Up until now, Luke had been able to call on the support of his brother-in-law. Gronow had always stood by him, been a strong right arm, but now he was buried in Dan y Graig cemetery alongside young Sean Murphy.

He walked more hurriedly now towards the lights of his home. The windows were open and he could hear the distant notes of the piano, the melody rushing out into the soft evening, haunting and strangely disturbing.

Peta smiled at him over her shoulder as he entered the room and he stood for a moment, watching her, proud of her beauty and of her skill as her fingers caressed the keys. They no longer caressed him.

The thought came suddenly, a realization that he had forced into the recesses of his mind.

He sat beside her on the stool and put his arm around her waist. His senses alert, he saw her frown and felt the slight withdrawal as she inched away from him. He felt anger rise in him but when he spoke, his voice was level.

'What's wrong, Peta?' He caught her face in his hands so that she could not look away from him. She lowered her eyes.

'I'm so weary since I caught for the baby,' she said gently, 'and I'm afraid of lovemaking, Luke – we might do some harm.'

He drew her closer. 'I wouldn't hurt you, my lovely,' he said, his voice thick with emotion, 'but I need you, Peta.'

'But, Luke, you don't know what it's like for women, what pain we have to go through.' She sighed. 'And it's not only that, it's the indignity of being pregnant, being handled by all sorts of people, it's just awful.'

'I'm trying to understand, Peta,' he said gently. 'I know you've had a difficult time and I'm trying to be patient.' When she didn't reply, he thrust his hands into his pockets.

'I'm not a monk, Peta, and I'm not a leper either, that you have to recoil from my touch.' It was the wrong thing to say and he knew it immediately. He saw the colour come into Peta's face and then she was rising to her feet.

Her eyes were hot with tears, her fingers jabbed at the buttons of her neat dress and she seemed angry and bitter as she stared at him.

'All right, if it's so important then you must have your way. I know my duty as a wife, mind.'

He stared at her, a knot of fury threatening to drown his senses. 'Duty.' His voice was cold. 'You can keep your duty, Peta, I don't need an act of charity from you.'

'Well you make me feel like a flossie from the streets, as though all you want from me you can have in the bedroom.' She began to cry. 'I can't help it if I'm not well. It's your baby I'm carrying, mind.'

He could not argue against tears. He turned and left the room, moving back into the darkness of the night. The sun had completely vanished now and the moon was a shining orb hanging low over the sea. He did not pause when he heard Peta call out his name. Ignoring the car parked outside the house, he strode down the drive out onto the roadway and, after a moment, headed down towards his sister's house in Canal Street.

The kitchen was hot and steamy and Charlotte rubbed at her brow as she bent over the fire warming a large pot of *cawl*. Rich with mutton and vegetables, the soup smelled mouth watering and Charlotte sighed, hoping her lodgers would enjoy the evening meal she had prepared for them.

'Freddie, set the table for mam, there's a love.' She glanced over her shoulder to where her sons were sitting on the rag mat near the fire, reading industriously, or at least making a fine pretence of doing so. 'Come on, you haven't got to pore over those books *all* night,' she said, smiling.

Freddie moved to the dresser and took a cloth from the drawer, shaking out the creases with more vigour than was strictly necessary.

'Why can't Denny do something as well?' he grumbled as he smoothed the cloth over the white-scrubbed table.

Denny looked up. 'I'll cut the bread,' he volunteered and Charlotte hid a smile.

'Oh, aye!' Freddie exploded. 'You're only saying that because you know mam won't let you cut bread.'

'Denny can set out the cutlery,' Charlotte said easily. 'Everyone must do their fair share. I warned you about that when I decided to take in lodgers.'

'Is Miss O'Conner's brother really coming tonight?' Denny clattered the knives and forks into a heap on the table. Charlotte glanced at him and shook her head.

'Well, so she says, though she's been alone here a while now.' She shrugged. 'Mind she's paid the rent right enough and so I'm not grumbling.'

She took the bread from the pantry and cut several thick slices, aware that both her sons were watching her. She paused, hands on her hips. 'I'm just proving to you that I can do things for myself, mind.'

Charlotte ladled the *cawl* into deep bowls placing them on the table. 'Denny, will you knock on Miss O'Conner's door and invite her down to supper?'

Denny hurried to do her bidding. He liked Miss O'Conner, she was so quiet and kind, and sometimes she brought them a bag of assorted sweets from the shop where she worked.

Charlotte sliced the piece of mutton that had earlier been simmered in the *cawl* and placed it on a dish, surrounding it with potatoes and steaming greens. The economical way of making two courses out of one piece of meat had been handed down in the family for generations and Charlotte found it particularly helpful now when money was short. She had not realized at first that widowhood brought financial strains as well as emotional ones, and yet the very need to survive had helped her come to terms with her grief.

Miss O'Conner came shyly into the room and took her usual seat next to Denny. She smiled up at Charlotte, her soft Irish accent more pronounced than usual.

'Sure 'tis kind of you to provide supper,' she said, 'I wouldn't be able to cope if I had to come home from work and cook for myself.'

She did indeed look weary, Charlotte thought, as she took her seat at the head of the table. Miss O'Conner was not a very strong lady and the hours at the shop were long and gruelling.

Charlotte wondered about Miss O'Conner's background. She hadn't liked to question her lodger, and so far little information had been volunteered. Perhaps the brother would be just as diffident and quiet, in which case Charlotte would be in for an easy time of it.

She was just serving the meat and vegetables when there was a knock on the front door. Charlotte looked at her lodger and smiled.

'Go on, you, I expect that's your brother and I'm sure you'll want to greet him in private.'

As she left the room, Fredrick smiled. 'I wonder if he's a mouse like Miss O'Conner?' he said, with a quick look at his mother, expecting and receiving a warning frown of disapproval. 'She's very nice, though,' he added quickly.

Charlotte rose as Miss O'Conner returned to the kitchen. Behind her was a tall man with clear blue eyes and a firm look about him that impressed Charlotte.

'I'll get your meal, Mr O'Conner,' she said but he held up his hand and moved towards the fireplace.

'Sure I can serve myself, I don't want waiting on, Mrs Davies.' He looked at her gravely. 'You've been kind enough as it is from what Sheila tells me.'

Charlotte watched uncomfortably as he ladled *cawl* into the waiting dish and carried it to the table.

'Please,' he said, 'continue with your own meal, I don't want to trouble you at all.'

Charlotte felt flustered. She wasn't used to dealing with a man who was so obviously self-sufficient. She hoped he was not going to interfere in the kitchen: she could not put up with that.

Gronow had always allowed her to preside over her own table; she had cooked the meals and served them and that was how she liked it.

'It's all right for this once, Mr O'Conner,' she said, 'but in future I must be boss in my own kitchen.'

'To be sure.' He smiled easily at her. 'Please call me Jim.' He took a slice of bread from the plate. 'This is excellent soup,' he said and his glance encompassed the boys who were staring at him in curiosity.

'It's *cawl*,' Denny volunteered and Jim nodded his head thoughtfully, taking up a spoonful of the vegetables and tasting them.

'Sure you call it *cawl*, but I call it soup. Tastes fine anyway.' He ate in silence and then pushed away the empty bowl. 'May I take some of that fine-looking mutton there, Mrs Davies?'

'Please help yourself.' Charlotte sat back in her chair wondering if he was making fun of her with his exaggerated politeness. She supposed she had sounded stuffy putting him in his place when all he'd done was try not to be a bother.

She was pleased when he had finished the meal for politeness had kept them all seated while he was eating. She rose and smoothed down her apron.

'You may be excused, boys,' she said to her sons and they looked at her in surprise, wondering how it was she was allowing them to get away without doing their usual chores.

'Miss O'Conner,' Charlotte said softly, 'perhaps you would like to show your brother to his room?'

Jim O'Conner stood up and he seemed to fill the place with his tallness and the breadth of his shoulders.

'Sure, I'd prefer if my landlady would show me the accommodation herself,' he said, pushing his hands into his pockets, emphasizing his unwillingness to follow his flustered sister out of the room.

'Very well.' Charlotte felt her hackles rise. He was being deliberately awkward, so much for her hopes that he would be like Miss O'Conner. She pushed back a strand of hair and moved towards the passageway. 'If you'll follow me,' she said tonelessly.

She cursed herself as she stumbled over a stair in the darkness and then she was aware of his hand under her elbow. She drew away from him at once and led the way to his room.

'I've put you at the back of the house where you'll be more private,' she said, opening the door and lighting the lamp quickly. The gas hissed and popped in the silence as Jim O'Conner looked around him. Charlotte clenched her hands together, biting her tongue. She wanted to tell him to clear off if her house wasn't good enough for him.

'Sure it's a clean and homely room' he said, 'and it does credit to your housekeeping, Mrs Davies.'

Charlotte felt as if the wind had been taken out of her sails. This Jim O'Conner was a strange one all right, not an easy man, but she felt instinctively as though he was someone she could trust.

'That's all right then, Mr O'Conner,' she said. 'I'll leave you now to settle in.'

As she moved downstairs, Charlotte smiled ruefully to herself – there was a man in the house again and with a vengeance!

Luke had almost reached Canal Street. He paused to look down into the water silvered by the light from the moon. He was thinking of his past, how strangely fate had led him to work for himself when his father had died suddenly in a pit accident, leaving him an orphan.

After the funeral Luke had found some money in a tin on the mantelpiece – the entire profits from the years dad had spent underground. Luke had been determined to put it to good use and he left his trade as carpenter and had bought a piece of land up on the hill away from the town, land that held rich coal seams where the coal pushed through the rough grass, waiting like a crop to be harvested.

At eighteen, he'd owned one pit-pony, Old Cal, and a wooden dram Luke had made himself. He had two augers for piercing the coal and his own woodworking tools that served to cut logs for pit-props. He learned how to make collar and arms, one log slotting into another to reinforce the strength of the timber and hold back the press of the land for long enough to work the face. Later he had employed Charlotte's husband and gradually he had built up his business until he could afford a properly-trained fireman and two more colliers.

He had married Peta just a year ago and had provided her with a modest house and a modest living, and at first they had been so happy together. Since she'd conceived the baby, she had changed in some subtle way he could not quite understand.

Briskly, he moved along the road and knocked on Charlotte's door. She smiled when she saw him and reached out to take his hand.

'I've only come,' he said, kissing her cheek, 'to have some of that vile brew you call tea. If you put plenty of sugar in it, it might just be palatable.'

'Cheek!' Charlotte said but she tucked her arm in his as she led him to the kitchen and set a cup before him.

'Do you know I've not yet done the dishes after supper?' she said, smiling. 'There's laziness for you.'

'Never mind the dishes.' He leaned across the table and spoke to her soberly. 'About the compensation, Charlotte.' He held up his hand as she made to interrupt. 'No, you must let me speak. When I have it, there will be money put in the bank to help you bring up the boys, no arguments now.'

Charlotte bit her lip. 'There's a fool I am, Luke, the tears come so easily to me these days. But I'm all right, really, I've got my lodgers now, you see.'

As she finished speaking, there was a knock on the door and Jim O'Conner entered the room.

'I wondered,' he said, 'if you minded me smoking in my room.' He held out his pipe and his eyes rested curiously on Luke.

Luke rose to his feet and the two men regarded each other unblinkingly for a moment.

Charlotte moved forward quickly. '*Duw*, of course I don't mind a pipe. Here take this ashtray with you – I should have thought about putting one in your room for you.' She turned to Luke. 'This is Mr O'Conner, he and his sister are my new lodgers.' She gestured towards Luke. 'Please, Mr O'Conner meet my brother, he owns the Slant Moira up on the hill.'

Once the introductions were made, there seemed to be an easing of the tension and, after speaking a few companionable words, Luke made for the door.

Charlotte rested her hand for a moment on his shoulder. 'Don't try to solve the problems of the world, Luke.' She spoke soberly. 'You do right to pay compensation to the Murphy family but don't worry about me, I'm doing just fine.'

'Clever girl.' Luke touched her cheek. 'In other words, you're telling me to mind my own business. I'll admit I was worried there for a moment, seeing a stranger in your kitchen, but I can see you've got everything under control.'

He left her then and strode quickly along Canal Street, his steps light. He was proud of Charlotte – she had solved her financial problems in the most practical way, for as well as earning a living, she could enjoy adult company and that was very important at a time when she should not be alone.

Jim O'Conner seemed a decent enough man; his presence would offer Charlotte protection and the company of his sister made the situation entirely respectable.

He let himself into the house and stood for a moment, hearing the sounds of the old building as the floorboards settled and the dying embers of the fire shifted in the grate. He took a deep breath and moved towards the study. It was late and yet he was not tired; if he went to bed he would only toss and turn and disturb Peta.

He lit the gas lamp and brought out his books. He must see just what he was able to afford in compensation, and tomorrow he would make the payments both to his sister and to Mrs Murphy. His jaw tightened – that would have to be done very carefully, he didn't want Katie's roughneck brother getting his hands on any of the money.

When he fulfilled the order for the Ponty tinplate works, he would be in a good position financially for this was the biggest order he'd received yet and half the coal was mined already. He would pay the colliers extra to work longer hours and once a further contract with Ponty was secured, he could afford to breathe a bit more easily.

The figures blurred before his eyes, and with a sigh he closed the books. He rested his head on his hands and weariness settled over him. He knew he should go to bed, try to rest, because tomorrow was going to be a busy day.

He must have fallen asleep at his desk because sun was streaking the room, dazzling his eyes, when he became aware of Peta standing beside him, her hand on his shoulder.

'What are you doing down here, my love?' she said softly. 'I waited and waited for you to come to bed and make it up with me.' She wound her arms around him. 'I'm sorry we quarrelled, I didn't mean to hurt you, Luke.'

He sighed and put his arms around her waist, drawing her close until his head was against her breast.

'I'm a bad-tempered boor,' he said softly, 'but a boor who loves his wife.' He drew her down onto his knee and kissed her tenderly. She was little more than a child, he mused, in spite of the fact that she was a married woman who had conceived a baby. But then Peta had not had it hard as he had. She'd been born into a moderately wealthy family, the only child of John Voss who owned a small but elite gents' outfitters. Real kid gloves were displayed in the window of the shop along with hand made shoes and bespoke suits. She'd brought to the marriage a small dowry which Luke had always refused to touch.

'It's an outdated idea,' he'd said often enough, 'like paying to have a daughter taken off your hands and I don't want any part of it.'

Peta didn't know what the fuss was about, but then she had never had to manage money and was not about to start now. Paying the bills, ordering the food, attending to the tradesmen was not part of her life, she left all that to Luke, not realizing that these petty burdens simply added to his already overfilled day. And for the chores around the house she had her faithful Hattie, come with her from mama's house to look after her little darling.

'Perhaps soon we can get back to our usual way of life, Luke darling,' she said softly.

He knew what she meant: she was apologizing for not being a real wife to him and he felt tenderness for her engulf him.

'And I must learn not to be selfish,' he said quietly, then he smiled up into her face. 'But you can't blame me for wanting a girl as lovely as you.'

She released herself from his arms and straightened her dress. She looked neat and clean and utterly wholesome, her cheeks had more colour and her eyes were blue under the curls of baby-fine blonde hair.

'What time is it? I should be at the mine.' He glanced at the clock on the mantelpiece and was surprised to find it was not yet five o'clock. 'God, you're up early, aren't you, Peta?'

A tinge of pink coloured her delicate skin. 'I thought you had stayed out all night,' she said softly. 'I was afraid you were with another woman, there's a fool I am, Luke.'

She paused, her hand on her stomach. 'I've had some pains but I don't think it's anything to worry about.' She looked at him from under her lashes. 'You wouldn't be unfaithful to me, would you, my love?'

'Don't be silly.' He was confused by the workings of her butterfly mind. 'When would I have the time?'

He smiled. 'I'd better get some breakfast before I leave – there's enough work to do today to keep twenty men occupied.' He strode out of the room into the kitchen and was grateful to see that Hattie too had risen early, and had the stove well alight with a pan of bacon sizzling appetisingly on the top.

He sat at the table and took the tea Hattie handed him with a brief nod of thanks, for already his thoughts were on the problems of the day ahead.

It was then that Peta screamed. The sound reverberated through the house and Hattie dropped the teapot to the floor where it smashed into tiny pieces, sending a trail of liquid over the flags.

'My God,' Hattie said, 'she's losing the baby! I was afraid this would happen; she's been poorly for days.'

Luke stood for a moment, looking down at the tea stain spreading slowly over the floor, and fear for his wife and child lay like a stone within him.

Sheila O'Conner woke to the strange room and the sound of children's voices, and for a moment she wondered where she was. Then she remembered she had left the green lands of Ireland behind her and had come to find work in Sweyn's Eye.

She sank back against the pillow wondering what she was going to do with her life. She hated the town where smoke and sulphur hung like a pall over the streets and yet how could she return to the poverty back home? It was all right for Jim – he seemed to settle anywhere, but then men were not such creatures of habit, she supposed.

There was a gentle tapping on the door and Charlotte peered into the room. 'I thought you'd be awake,' she said smiling, 'those boys of mine would wake the dead!'

She turned to her sons, who were both lingering on the landing. 'Go on downstairs now and eat your breakfast; it'll be time for school and you not ready.'

She put a cup of tea on the bedside table. 'Drink that, you'll feel more human then.'

'Sure that's very kind of you,' Sheila said. 'Is my brother up and about yet?'

'Why he's been gone out of the house an hour ago,' Charlotte said, smiling. 'He mentioned he was looking for work and so I sent him up to talk to Luke – my brother may have something at the Slant Moira for him.' She shrugged. 'I don't know if he'll go, mind, he's a hard man to understand is Mr O'Conner.'

Sheila sipped her tea gratefully. Mrs Davies was such a kind lady and in spite of still being in widow-black was so cheerful and so thoughtful of others.

'I don't know if I can stick it in that shop,' Sheila said and was surprised at herself for confiding her feelings to a woman who, though kindly, was a stranger.

'*Duw*, there's no need for you to stay in a job you don't like,' Charlotte said quickly. 'There are other things to do besides standing behind a counter all day. What about one of the manufactories? They pay well.'

Sheila shook her head. Much as she disliked Trustin's Grocery Store, she disliked change more, and she readily acknowledged that she was not a very courageous person.

'I wish I could be more like Jim,' she said softly. 'He's so sure of himself and of his opinions. He's so against this Baldwin government and he's downright furious at the way the miners are being treated. Sure my brother is not afraid to stand up and be counted and I admire him for that even if I sometimes feel afraid that his outspokenness will get him into trouble.'

Sheila couldn't think why she was confiding so much in Charlotte. 'Please excuse me,' she said, looking down into her cup, 'I talk too much sometimes.'

Charlotte smiled. 'Oh, talk away I'm only too glad to have an adult conversation from time to time. All I get out of my boys is moans about the chores they have to do.'

'Sure they're good lads,' Sheila said and meant it. In the time that she'd been lodging in Canal Street, she had come to like Fredrick and Denny very much; nothing was too much trouble for them.

Of course she spoiled them by bringing them home sweets from time to time but for all that, they were so polite and thoughtful.

'You must miss your husband dreadfully,' she said and then she wished she could bite out her tongue. 'Sure that was a tactless thing for me to say.' She put down her cup. 'I'm sorry, Mrs Davies, if I've spoken out of turn.'

Charlotte shook back her hair, pretty dark hair it was, curling naturally around her face. She was a pretty woman, Sheila thought with a trace of envy; Charlotte Davies would not be alone long if she was any judge.

'I don't mind talking about Gronow,' Charlotte said quietly. 'I do miss him, of course I do, and there's the boys – it pains me to think of them growing up without a father's hand to guide them.' She moved to the door. 'But life must go on, though it's hard to believe it will when something dreadful happens, mind.'

When she was alone, Sheila slipped out of bed and began to dress. She had toyed with taking the day off from work but the thought of Mr Trustin's fierce disapproval was too much to bear.

She ate little breakfast and was silent except to wish the boys good morning when they left for school.

'I'm late,' she said when Charlotte returned to the kitchen after sending the boys on their way. 'I should have been in the shop an hour ago.'

'Don't take any nonsense from your boss, mind,' Charlotte said firmly. 'You're a good worker, better than most of the girls I've seen in Trustin's Grocery, so stand up to him – don't let him bully you.'

Sheila laughed without humour. 'You remind me of Jim,' she said, 'he wouldn't take any nonsense and neither would you. I suppose I'm just a coward when it comes down to it.'

'Nonsense!' Charlotte was clearing away the dishes and Sheila envied her. She had her own home and two fine sons, and even though she'd recently been widowed, she was young enough to pick up the pieces again.

'Do you know something?' Sheila spoke her thoughts out loud. 'you've had more experiences in your life than I've had in mine, and I'm sure I must be a few years older than you.'

She'd been left on the shelf: that was her main reason for leaving Ireland to come to Wales with Jim, and now she was here all she wanted to do was go home.

Charlotte had paused and was standing near the sink with the dishes still in her hands, staring thoughtfully around her.

'You're good for me, you know, Sheila,' she said thoughtfully, 'you've made me realize how lucky I've been and still am come to that.'

'I hope I wasn't preaching,' Sheila said, rising to her feet. 'I only meant to say I envy you in the nicest sort of way.'

'I know.' Charlotte followed her into the passageway, waited while Sheila put on her coat and then opened the door for her.

'Now remember, don't take any lip from Mr Trustin, he's just a man, mind.' Charlotte laughed. 'Try to think of him in his nightshirt – that will put him into perspective for you!'

Sheila couldn't help but laugh at the image that sprang to her mind of her fat, balding boss wearing a nightshirt.

And yet even as she waved goodbye to Charlotte, she knew in her heart if Mr Trustin said one wrong word she would simply walk out of her job as shop assistant and catch the next boat home to Ireland.

7

The house was beginning to look something like home. Mary stood back and regarded the heavy drapes at the tall windows with satisfaction. The room was an elegant one, situated at the front of the house and looking out over the sea, it was a good place to sit and think, dream and plan what her future would be. Would it include Paul Soames? She wasn't sure, but last night after dinner he had asked her to marry him.

There was a rapid knocking on the door and Mary moved towards the study, glancing at her watch. Billy was right on time.

The sensible Mrs Bush, the housekeeper Paul had found for her, glided towards the front door, her black dress impeccably neat, her glossy bun arranged at the back of her head with not a hair out of place.

'Show Mr Gray into the study, please,' Mary said and stood near the large desk that glowed with polish in the sunlight streaming in through the open window.

Billy had scarcely changed at all. Mary went towards him her arms outstretched, happy to see him. It was many years since she'd been his childhood sweetheart but there was still a strong bond of affection between them.

'You're still as beautiful as ever, Mary,' he said, taking her hands in his.

She smiled at him ruefully. 'And you are the same old charmer with lies tripping off the end of your tongue like honey. Sit down, Billy. You've brought the books?'

He nodded. 'Aye, that I have and I think you'll be pleased when you see how well Sutton Holdings are doing here in Sweyn's Eye.'

Mary took the red accounting books from him and flicked the first one open. Her mind had always been quick to grasp the meaning of figures. What a great pity that she'd not been as clever when it came to the men in her life, she thought, glancing up covertly at Billy.

The intervening years had made little impression on him. His moustache held a trace of grey as did his hair, but he was still a handsome man – perhaps even more handsome, for now the lines on his face were ones of strength and confidence.

For a time there was silence in the study, and through the open window came the sound of birds calling in the trees at the bottom of the garden. A March breeze drifted through the lace curtain so that it billowed like a cloud of mist. Billy shifted his position once or twice, anxious, Mary knew, for her opinion. But she was nothing if not thorough and took her time, comparing the profits of each year that she had been away. At last, she closed the books and smiled at Billy over the blotting paper on her desk.

'Very good,' she said, leaning back in her chair. 'In spite of the problems of the big pits, our small mines seem to be making a good profit.'

Billy leaned forward eagerly. 'The small mines always benefit when there are strikes,' he said smoothly, 'and there have been plenty of those in the last few years, and more to come, mark my word.'

Mary sighed. 'Yes, well, I'll leave all that in your very capable hands; you've done very well up until now.' She leaned forward. 'But I do think you deserve more money, Billy. I see you haven't had a wage rise for some time.' She allowed herself a small smile.

'There's more than one way of skinning a cat, though, isn't there, Billy?' She reverted to the Welsh idiom as she always did when she was angry or amused. This time she didn't know which to be.

'I don't know what you mean, Mary.' Billy looked all innocence, his eyes meeting hers without a flicker.

'Oh, well, I suppose the odd ton of coal here and there won't be missed, a few pound in the pocket, all part of the job. But you can't put much past me, Billy, boyo, so don't even try.'

Billy ran his fingers through his hair. 'It's no wonder you're the boss and I'm just the henchman,' he said ruefully. 'Spot a splinter in a sow's hindquarters you would, Mary.'

But Mary was nothing if not fair. 'It was on your advice that I put the money into small holdings here in town, so you must take much of the credit.' She rose from the desk. 'Enough of business for now, let's go into the sitting-room and have some coffee and talk about old times.'

Billy seemed quite at ease in the high, elegant room. He sat easily in one of the soft blue chairs and Mary noticed the cut of his suit was good and the shirt-collar above the smart tie was crisp and white.

'Tell me about yourself,' Mary said softly. 'What's been happening to you while I've been away in America, are you married now?'

Billy shook his head. 'No, not married but still I'm walking out with Gina Sinman – you remember her, don't you, Mary? She was widowed in the war and since then has been bringing up my daughter along with her own son.'

'Of course I remember Gina,' Mary said at once, 'do you think America's made me soft in the head?' She shook back her hair. 'And you mean to tell me you haven't married the girl yet, not after all this time?'

Billy shrugged. 'Well, I'm always so busy, travelling around, seeing to the business. I have placed her in a very nice little house, though, and she is well rewarded for looking after Cerianne.'

'I should think so!' Mary said softly. 'Gina's given years of devotion to that child, ever since Cerianne's mother deserted her when she was a baby.' Mary paused thoughtfully. 'Your daughter must be quite a lady, surely into her teens by now.'

'She's a beauty,' Billy said, 'as lovely as her Delmai but with the intelligence of her father.'

Mary laughed. 'And his modesty!' She looked up as the door opened. Mrs Bush glided into the room and placed the tray on the table. There was silence as coffee, fragrant and hot, was poured into delicate cups. Mrs Bush irritated

Mary with her downcast eyes, giving the impression she was totally absorbed in her task when all the time she was bursting with curiosity. After a few moments, Mrs Bush retreated as she'd come, with hardly any sound.

'Drink your coffee, Billy,' Mary said, 'and tell me, do you ever see Delmai these days?' She watched as he took a sip of the liquid before answering her question. She wanted to laugh because she could see his instinct was to tell her to mind her own business and yet expediency restrained him – she was his boss after all.

'I see her,' he said shortly, 'riding about in her fancy car with her three sons like little lords in the back seat.'

'And what of her husband?' Mary asked. 'Is Rickie Richardson still as devious as he always was?'

'Aye, he hasn't changed, he's drinking himself into an early grave if you ask me.' Billy leaned forward. 'But what about you, Mary?' he asked turning the tables neatly. 'How are things with you?'

Mary sighed. 'Well, I suppose I deserved that. I'm a widow as you doubtless have heard. A very rich widow because of the fortune Brandon made in America, but not all the money in the world will make up for losing him.'

'And Stephan?' Billy changed the subject quickly. 'He must be a big boy now, a comfort to you, I'm sure.'

Mary nodded. 'He's wonderful company and selfishly I'd like to keep him with me all the time.' She sighed. 'But I've sent him to a lovely little school near Sketty; they look after him there and they have special teachers for the blind.' Mary rose from her chair and walked to the window. 'If I've done wrong in life, Billy, then I've paid dearly for it.'

He came to her and rested his hands on her shoulders. 'Mary, haven't we all done wrong or foolish things? You can't believe that Stephan's blindness is your fault, it just isn't right.'

She looked up at him and shook her head. 'I can't help the way I feel. I was driving the car when the accident happened and if I hadn't quarrelled with Brandon . . .' Her voice trailed away. 'Oh, I don't know, Billy, I just wish I could put back the clock sometimes.' She moved to the table to refill the coffee cups, and Billy followed her. They sat down again.

'If infidelity is the yardstick well then I should be paying for the rest of my life,' Billy said emphatically. 'I've made more mistakes than most men,' he chuckled. 'Look at the time I was infatuated with that little strumpet Doffy! She really had me twisted around her little finger.' He paused, shaking his head in wonder at his own foolishness.

'And then I heard that she was any man's for a couple of shillings. How dull I was in those days.' He took up the cup and drank from it and Mary thought how absurd it looked in his large hands. Next time he came he'd have a proper cup, not the little doll's china in which Mrs Bush insisted on serving the coffee.

'By the way, talking about Doffy,' Billy said slowly, 'I hear that Michael Murphy took her home with him one night from the public bar of Maggie Dicks and tried to install her in the house in Market Street.'

'Oh?' Mary stared at him in surprise. 'I thought the Murphy boys had gone up north to work in the coal mines there.'

'Aye, well they're back with a vengeance. Michael has turned out to be a proper troublemaker.' Billy set his cup carefully on the silver tray. 'Always spouting about politics, down with the privileged classes. He's a ruddy Commie, if you ask me.'

'I wonder how poor Katie is coping then. I can't see her putting up with any nonsense from her brothers, mind.' She paused. 'I wonder if I should go over to Market Street and see her. I did promise to visit her ages ago.'

'I don't know if it would be wise for you to go anywhere near Market Street, not just now,' Billy said thoughtfully. 'I wouldn't trust Michael not to spit in your eye. I'm telling you he's got a great big grudge against anyone who has more than he does.'

'I won't let him stop me,' Mary said quietly. 'Why I remember when he was little more than a baby playing on the rag mat in the back room of Murphys' fresh fish shop and Mrs Murphy drinking out of a gin bottle to drown out the noise of him.'

'Well, he's no longer a little boy, but if you're determined to go, I shall come with you,' Billy said.

Mary smiled and rested her hand on his arm. 'Look, love, I wasn't the overseer at the Canal Street Laundry for nothing, mind.' She laughed. 'Do you really think that Michael Murphy would get the best of me?'

Billy shook his head doubtfully. 'We're not dealing with an ordinary case of a bad-tempered young man. Michael is irrational – I wouldn't trust him with a dog.'

Mary sighed in resignation. 'All right, then, come with me if it makes you feel any happier. What if you call for me some time this afternoon?'

Billy rose to his feet; a big man, still handsome, but he roused no feelings in her except those of friendship. But then hadn't that always been the problem – that Billy did not touch her emotions in any way? He might have been her brother for all the excitement he awoke in her.

And yet he'd had his share of conquests. Delmai Richardson had for a time given up all for love of Billy – her rich husband, her fine home, her reputation. And then there was Gina Sinman who over the years had given him her utter devotion, caring for his daughter as though Cerianne were her own, showing no favour to her own son but treating Dewi on a par with the little girl she had chosen to rear.

And, of course, as Billy had reminded her, there had been the scandal involving Doffy, the little-girl prostitute who had made such a fool of Billy Gray. He had no doubt been searching for his lost youth, losing himself in the pretty looks and cunning ways that had won Doffy a good following of clients. But he was a mature man now and should be married and settled down – though it was none of her business.

'I'll see you later, then.' Billy picked up the case containing the accounts books and tapped it. 'I'm glad you're happy with the way the business is shaping.'

'I'm more than pleased, Billy.' Mary smiled as she saw him to the door. 'I'm delighted, and to prove it I shall make that rise I mentioned operative from the end of the month.'

When he had gone, she returned to the sitting-room where Mrs Bush was already clearing away the tray. She was efficiency itself but somehow there was no warmth in her. Mary was used to being surrounded by friends rather than employees: Mrs Greenaway had been a gem - 'Old Greenie' who had worked for Mary in the days when the emporium on the Stryd Fawr was her main business concern. It had boasted a fine tearoom and it was there that the pampered women of the town would meet to exchange gossip. But Greenie had died several years ago, working until the last moments, so Mary had heard.

And what had happened to little Nerys Beynon who had looked after Stephan before Brandon took the family to America? Mary had left her well-provided for but since she'd returned to Sweyn's Eye she had heard nothing of the girl.

Mary turned to look over her shoulder. 'Mrs Bush, do you know Nerys Beynon who used to look after Stephan for me?'

The woman inclined her head slightly and sniffed. 'Aye, I do, Mrs Sutton. Married she is now to the man who owns the ferry boat, that Siona Llewelyn.'

'I take it that you disapprove?' Mary asked, concealing a smile.

Mrs Bush lifted her head. 'It's really none of my business, of course, but the man has many sons and he is old enough to be the girl's father. But then, she's no better than she ought to be. Expecting when she got wed, she was, and they say her husband wasn't the true father either.'

'Thank you, Mrs Bush.' Mary sat in her chair and stared out towards where the sea curved in a blue arc against the sky. 'God save me from good women,' she said under her breath.

The spring sunshine splashed the garden outside and yellow daffodils rioted along the edges of the lawn. Yes,

Mary thought to herself, it was high time she involved herself once more in the affairs of Sweyn's Eye.

The hospital corridor was heavily scented with disinfectant and Katie wrinkled her nose as she made her way towards the room where her mother lay. The sound of her footsteps echoed mournfully along the corridor and Katie felt alone and friendless in a hostile world.

It seemed that events had overtaken her. After the shock of losing her brother in the pit accident she'd had to contend with the sudden return of her brothers, Michael in particular, who had upset the smooth running of her life. And now mammy had taken a bad turn and was in hospital. She bit her lip. A great deal of blame for the worsening of mammy's condition lay at Michael's door; he was loud and arrogant and showed no consideration for anyone. He'd even been rude to old Nurse Benson who had come to call, bringing a soothing cordial for mammy.

Katie became aware of a nurse standing before her, a professional, questioning smile on her face. Katie swung back her hair and tried to collect her thoughts.

'I'm here to see Mrs Murphy. I'm her daughter, sure she's taken a bad turn,' she said moving forward.

The nurse held up her hand. 'Just a minute. Mrs Murphy has people with her and she did ask not to be disturbed, but I'm sure she'll see you before too long,' she added encouragingly.

Katie felt her pulse quicken. 'What people?' she asked apprehensively. 'Not my brothers, I hope? Sure an' they'll only upset mammy.'

The nurse leaned forward confidingly. 'There's a legal man in there with her and another gentleman. It all looks very calm and respectable, and it's what your mother wanted.'

Katie retreated to a wooden bench and sat there, feeling bewildered and frightened. Mammy had talked of seeing a solicitor, it was true, and Katie understood that it was all about the compensation to be paid from the Slant Moira, but why the hurry? Suddenly she felt sick – it must mean that mammy was sure she was worse. She rose to her feet, determined not to be kept away from her mother any longer, but just as she approached the door it opened, and she came face to face with Luke Proud.

They stared at each other for a long moment and there was compassion in his eyes.

'I'll wait for you,' he said and Katie scarcely noticed the man with him who carried an imposing-looking case.

Fearfully, she moved towards the bed and stood for a moment, staring down at the whiteness of her mother's face. Mrs Murphy's eyes flickered open, the only sign she was alive. Her lips were tinged with blue and her thin fingers plucked at the covers as though they were too heavy for her to bear the weight of them.

'Katie, my girl, come and sit near me.' Her voice was thread-like and Katie only just made out what her mother was saying.

She sat next to the bed. 'Mammy, there's cold your hands are.' She clutched her mother as though she could keep her alive by sheer force of will. 'Are you feeling worse, mammy?'

Mrs Murphy shook her head. 'My heart, girl, it won't take any more but I must tell you, Mr Proud has handed over the compensation to the solicitor in my presence.' She paused, gasping for breath. 'I've signed all the papers so that the mortgage is paid off and the house and shop are legally yours.'

'Hush, mammy, don't you worry about that now, save your strength.'

'I must speak.' Mrs Murphy tried to lift her head and Katie quickly put her arm around the painfully-thin shoulder.

'The compensation,' Mrs Murphy whispered, 'I had to see to it now for I've not got much time left. Sean would have wanted you to have it, Katie.'

Katie felt tears burn her eyes. 'Oh, mammy, you shouldn't be talking like that, you're going to be just fine, I know you are.'

Mrs Murphy shook her head. 'No, love, don't fool yourself and don't worry about me, for isn't Our Lady waiting for me to come to her? I'll be with Tom again and with my youngest-born son – they'll both be there to welcome me.'

'No, mammy, you'll get well again,' Katie said desperately. 'I need you, mammy, there's no one to care about me but you, please mammy, listen to me, you've got to get better.'

'I can't fight any more, Katie girl.' Her voice was indistinct, the words slurred. 'I'm sorry, my lovely, sorry.' She slumped against Katie's arms, a small shell of a woman, and Katie saw the lines of pain ease away as she looked down at the parchment-white face. She gently put her mother's head back on the pillow and tucked the blankets around the thin frame.

'Oh, mammy!' Katie said brokenly. 'Why did you have to leave me?'

Afterwards, Katie didn't remember how long she'd sat cradling her mother in her arms. She became aware of the nurse leading her outside, handing her a cup of tea and murmuring her sympathy as she sat her down on the wooden bench.

Luke appeared at her side and Katie looked up at him, grateful for his company, drawing from his strength. She didn't know why he had waited, and she didn't care, all she knew was she had a friend at her side.

'Let me take you back to my house for a while,' Luke said gently, taking the untasted tea from her hand and setting it down on the bench. 'Come along, Katie, there's no point in just sitting here.'

She looked up at him. 'I must go home to Market Street,' she said. 'Perhaps in mammy's house, I can begin to clear my thoughts.' She rubbed her hands over her eyes and allowed herself to be helped to her feet.

'If you want to go home then that's where I'll take you.' Luke led her out into the forecourt of the hospital and Katie was surprised to see the sun was still shining, people were laughing and talking, everything appeared normal, as though nothing had happened. She should be used to grief, she told herself, and yet nothing had prepared her for losing mammy. She had seemed enduring, a vital, continuing part of life, someone who was always there with her gin bottle and her sharp wit.

She began to cry. Luke took her in his arms and simply held her, smoothing back her hair, speaking soothingly to her as though she were a child.

'Cry it all out, there's a good girl.' After a time, he led her to where his car was parked and helped her inside.

She turned to him and touched his hand briefly.

'I can never tell you how much it's meant to have you here. I don't know what I'd have done if I'd been alone.' She slumped down in the seat and glanced up at the branches of the trees as they waved gently above her. Mammy was gone, it didn't seem possible. The knowledge of her loss filled her world, she could not think beyond this moment as she allowed herself to be driven through the town, like an inert doll, towards Market Street.

The door to Murphys' Fresh Fish Shop stood open and the sound of raised voices drifted to where Katie stood shivering on the pavement. She glanced at Luke as he slammed the car door shut and then he was taking her arm, leading her along the passage and into the kitchen.

Katie's first thought was that the scene greeting her was unreal, as she took in the group of people gathered around the table. Michael was in the centre of the kitchen and behind him stood Kevin, as always second fiddle to his brother. Facing the brothers was Mary Sutton and with her, Billy Gray.

'This is Katie's home,' Mary said angrily, 'you have no right to it! You've been away from here for years and Katie doing all the donkey-work to keep the place going; the cheek of the devil you've got, Michael Murphy.'

'You're an interfering woman! Why bother coming here when you're not wanted?' Michael said loudly. 'And as for Katie, she can get out of this house for I don't want her here.' His eyes gleamed with anger. 'As far as I'm concerned this is my house now, I'm the eldest son and with my mother in hospital I say what goes on here.'

As Katie moved into the shaft of light from the window, Michael saw her and stopped speaking abruptly.

'Mammy's dead,' she said flatly and Kevin quickly made the sign of the cross. 'You pushed our mother into her grave with your foul temper and your loose women.'

'Don't put the blame on me,' Michael blustered, 'mammy was a sick woman when I came back. If it's anybody's fault then it's yours for not looking after her properly.'

'Oh Katie, there's sorry I am, love.' Mary came to her swiftly, her eyes soft. 'When did it happen?'

'Just a short while ago,' Katie said, gripping Mary's hands. 'She was so sick, Mary, and yet so strong-willed right to the end.'

'Well then,' Michael said with a little less bluster in his voice, 'I'd better find the insurance papers and sort everything out.' He spoke slowly, as though thinking aloud. He became aware then of Katie staring at him.

'You can leave here right away for this is my home now, do you understand?'

He glanced round him.

'And take your fancy friends with you before I have the constable arrest them for trespassing.'

'I don't think you can do that.' Luke moved Katie aside and faced Michael squarely. The men were of equal height but Michael was heavier, his face fuller, his shoulders not so much broad as thick. His jaw jutted out aggressively.

'Why can't I do that, boss?' he said scathingly. 'Who is going to stop me?'

Luke allowed himself a small smile. 'The property has been left to Katie, it's been settled legally, there's nothing you can do about it.'

Michael appeared confused for a moment, his brow furrowed and his dark eyes smouldered. 'But that can't be possible,' he said. 'When the solicitor called here, I sent him away, my mother never saw him.'

'She saw him today,' Luke said, 'at the hospital. I'm afraid there's nothing you can do but go gracefully.'

Michael bunched his fists and slammed them against the table. 'You've arranged this between you!' he shouted at Katie. 'Turned mother's mind while she lay sick! Well, it won't do you any good.' He straightened and stared round him. 'Haven't any of you heard that possession is everything? I'm here and who is going to put me out?'

Kevin touched his arm lightly. 'Perhaps we'd better go, Mike, we don't want any trouble.'

Michael flung his hand away. 'Trouble, there'll be trouble if anyone tries to put me out of my own home.'

He moved forward in a rush only to be stopped by Luke's fist connecting with the point of his jaw. The blow would have felled a weaker man but Michael simply swayed a little and continued to move towards Luke.

Luke clasped his hands together and brought both fists down on the back of the other man's neck. With a groan, Michael folded at the knees and sank to the floor. He shook his head as though to clear it, then scrambled to his feet and charged at Luke. The wild punch caught Luke on the side of his head, his eye began to turn black almost immediately and Katie put her hand to her mouth, stifling a little cry.

Kevin moved to help his brother but Billy Gray blocked his way. 'No need for interference, boyo, is there?' he asked casually, and Kevin fell back a pace, hanging his head.

Michael let out a roar and launched himself towards Luke, who sidestepped him neatly, catching him a sharp blow to his temple.

'Stop it, please stop it,' Katie said, but her words were lost in the commotion. Katie saw Luke grab her brother's arm and twist it painfully behind his back.

'Come on, outside with you.' He pushed Michael towards the door and with a final thrust sent him sprawling into the street. Kevin darted out after him, helping Michael to his feet.

'I'd advise you not to come back here,' Luke said, 'or you'll have to answer to the law as well as me.'

Michael stared threateningly at Luke. 'You've made yourself an enemy this day,' he said fiercely. 'I'd watch your back if I was you for one day there will be a knife in it.'

He lurched away down the street, snarling at the watching neighbours as he wiped the blood from his face, and he was still cursing when Luke closed the door on him.

Katie sank into a chair. She was trembling and Mary patted her arm comfortingly. 'I'll make us all some nice tea, it'll help to take away some of the shock, mind.'

She busied herself with the cups and Katie watched her wearily. 'How can I fulfil mammy's wishes and run the shop, with Michael out to get even with me?' she asked, and Mary clicked her tongue in annoyance.

'That man, though he's kin of yours, needs locking up!' she said angrily. 'Don't let him best you, girl, you put up a fight and you can count on me to help you, for one.' Mary sat opposite her. 'Look, shall I stay here with you for tonight? Billy can always run up to the house for me and fetch my things and let Stephan know where I am.'

Katie shook her head. How could she explain that she wanted to be alone to collect her thoughts, to allow herself to grieve properly over mammy?

'Sure it's kind of you to offer but I've got to get used to being on my own some time, and it might as well be sooner rather than later.'

Luke stood for a moment looking down at her. 'I'm going now,' he said, 'but I'll see Roberts-the-law and ask him to keep an eye on the place so that your brother won't be able to harass you.'

She went to the door with him and looked up at his bruised face. 'Sure you'll have a shiner there tomorrow,' she said. She held out her hands. 'I don't know how to thank you.'

'Don't even bother to try.' He was striding away then, long legs covering the ground quickly. She watched until he reached the car, then went into the kitchen.

'Is there anything at all I can do to help?' Mary asked but Katie shook her head. 'No, thank you, Mary but 'tis good of you to offer.' She paused. 'All I want is to go to bed and close my eyes,' she said softly, 'but I'm very grateful to both of you.' She turned to Billy Gray. 'Kevin would have been sure to put his oar in if you hadn't been here.'

'Any time,' Billy said, moving towards the door. Mary followed him and turned, pausing for a moment.

'Now if there's anything you want, just let me know, mind. I'll be back tomorrow to make sure you're all right.'

When she closed the door, shutting out the world, the silence in the kitchen was a balm to Katie's bruised emotions. She sat in mammy's old chair and stared into the fire, and at last the tears, hot and bitter, ran down her cheeks.

'Mammy, I'm going to miss you so much,' she whispered.

8

Jim O'Conner sat in the smoky snug of the Mexico Fountain listening quietly to the debate taking place around him. He was attending a meeting of the local branch of the FED, the Miners' Federation of Great Britain, and what he was hearing was not encouraging.

'These so-called negotiations are dragging on.' Michael Murphy was holding the floor, his big shoulders hunched, his fists clenched as though to hit out at any one who opposed him. 'Last year we had the TUC firmly with us miners,' he continued, 'but will they stick by us again? If not, we must strike on our own behalf, fight our own battles.'

There was a hubbub of voices and Jim clearly saw that Murphy was a hothead, a man who did not want peace in the coalfields and who was out to cause trouble for the hell of it.

'Wait!' Jim stood up and saw faces turned to him in open-mouthed surprise. 'Before I came to Sweyn's Eye, I was in London for a few days,' he said loudly. 'Serious negotiations *are* taking place between the FED and the TUC. It's proposed that full powers be given to the General Council to go to the government and either conduct fresh talks or in the last resort call a general strike. Nothing can be gained by foolhardy action taken by small pockets of miners.'

'And who gave you the right to shove your oar in?' Michael Murphy said belligerently. 'Sure you've only been in the town for five minutes – you're not even a working miner.'

Jim smiled enigmatically. 'I've been in town almost as long as you have. What's more important, I'm a member of FED and I'm speaking up for common sense,' he said evenly. 'Don't you understand that together we're strong, divided we're weak? Cool heads are what's required now.'

'He's right enough, boys.' Rory, the fireman from the Slant Moira, was on his feet. 'We must keep on working until there's an all-out strike, and only then take action.'

'Ah, but would you come out on strike if there's a union ruling?' Michael Murphy challenged. 'That boss of yours, Luke Proud – don't tell me he'd back us up; he'd be falling over himself to steal custom from the big boys.'

'*Daro*! That's not fair, mind,' Rory called. 'I've worked at the slant since it began mining, along with Timothy Makings and Gerry Parsons who are good colliers. I think I'm speaking for all the men at the slant – old Tanny as well, who has been loyal to his own class through the most difficult times – when I say we'd be true to the cause.

'Remember,' he continued, 'Luke Proud's own brother-in-law gave his life working the coal, as did your young brother, Michael Murphy. I say that our boss would be the first one to down tools if there was a strike.'

'There's not a snowball's chance in hell of that happening, and you lot know it! Luke Proud would look after number one, don't you make any mistake about that.'

Jim intervened. 'I don't think we should concern ourselves about Luke Proud,' he said, 'there are much bigger issues at stake here.'

'He's right,' Rory said with a look of relief, 'I suggest we wait and see what happens. If the government is willing to continue the present subsidy for a few weeks while reorganization of the industry is planned, then we sit tight.'

Michael Murphy tried to object but the men were on their feet, moving towards the door. Jim watched them in silence. On the whole they were a fine bunch of workers, but Michael Murphy would need watching.

Jim downed the rest of his pint. Perhaps it was time he took his landlady's advice and approached her brother, Luke Proud, for a job. He rose to his feet and swung his scarf round his neck, pulling his cap down onto his thick springy hair. It seemed there was going to be trouble brewing in Sweyn's Eye and a strong hand would be needed if there was to be fair play. He left the smoky atmosphere of the Mexico Fountain and moved out into the freshness of the spring day, turning to look at the hills in the direction of Slant Moira.

As Luke drew his car to a halt outside the slant Rory was just emerging from the mine.

'You're early today,' he said conversationally but he was eyeing Luke's bruised face with obvious curiosity. 'Run into a door, did you?' he asked after a moment's silent scrutiny.

'Aye, something like that,' Luke said easily. 'How did the meeting go last night?'

'Mostly the usual hot air, but this chap Jim O'Conner was talking a bit of sense, not that anyone will listen to him.'

'Well, we've got no time for politics,' Luke said, drawing off his coat and rolling up his sleeves, 'if we don't get the Ponty order delivered it won't matter to us if there's a strike or not.'

Rory's jaw dropped. 'Do you mean for us to work on the face with the colliers?' His tone was incredulous. '*Duw*, that's donkey-work, that is, and me a good fireman.'

'Hard luck,' Luke said grimly. 'We're down to two colliers now and for the time being we all haul coal, understand?'

'Aye, all right, boss,' Rory said grudgingly, knocking out his pipe on the side of the shed. 'I'm not afraid of a bit of hard work, mind.'

'Good.' Luke took a lantern and fastened it to his belt. 'Come on then, let's make a start.'

The colliers were hacking away at the coal, each in his own twelve-foot-long seam. The room was limited, not allowing for a man to turn or even sit up straight. The colliers virtually lay along the floor with the coal dust thick around them.

'How's it going there, Gerry?' Luke asked, making his way forward on hands and knees.

'All right, boss. I've just filled the curling box; I'll push it back along the stall now and the coal can be put into the dram.'

'Right, get it to me,' Luke said, 'you carry on working.' He hauled the curling box up onto the dram and clucked soothingly to Old Cal. The horse snorted impatiently, straining towards the light.

'All in good time, boy,' Luke said firmly. 'Now keep still, will you?' He emptied the curling box and returned it to the collier. 'There, Gerry, carry on the good work – we'll have this order for Ponty filled by tonight if it kills us.'

Later, when the men had gathered in the shed for food, Luke sat down with them and accepted a share of the bread and cheese that filled the snap boxes. Usually he drove home and had a meal with Peta, but then he was usually engaged on administration and didn't work on the coal face.

'*Duw*.' Rory lit up his pipe. 'There's going to be murder in the coal trade if Baldwin don't keep the subsidy going a few more weeks.'

'He won't do that, man,' Gerry said, 'hasn't he always claimed that helping out the industry with more money is the last thing he'll do?'

'He'll be forced to pay,' Luke said, 'otherwise the TUC will put a complete embargo on handling coal then Baldwin will have the dockers and the railwaymen against him.'

'You're right there, boss,' Rory said puffing on the pipe contentedly. 'The government will have to do something.'

Luke pushed the kettle onto the stove. He had been given a hard time by Peta when he'd come home bruised and bloody – she'd sworn he'd been fighting over another woman, which was rich. But then he had to make allowances for her; she was still ill after losing the baby.

'That's not a job for you, boss,' Rory said quietly but he didn't move to take over the tea-making and Luke smiled.

101

'These days any man will do any job,' he replied. 'We'll work together or the mine will go under, it's as simple as that.'

'Can you afford another collier?' Gerry asked. 'Tim and me can't work the face alone and, willing as you are, boss, you're too slow to catch a cold.'

Luke allowed himself a smile. 'Thanks a bunch!' he said but he rested his hand on the collier's shoulder, appreciating the man's honesty. 'Aye, we'll have another man, once we get the money for the Ponty load.'

He moved to the door of the shed and looked out over the green hills, beneath which the headings of the Slant Moira wound their way. It was a land rich with coal and would take many years to strip of the black harvest. But survival over the next few weeks was the problem, for the summer months were always the leanest. He rubbed his hand through his hair and dust trickled blackly down his face. The roof fall had been a disaster, killing two men and delaying the mining then, on top of everything, it nagged at the back of his mind that his sister Charlotte was forced to take in lodgers, though he had to admit the O'Conner's seemed nice enough people and the man had plenty of common sense, according to Rory.

'Come on then, boys, let's get back to it,' he said, forcing a note of cheerfulness into his voice. 'The sooner we start the sooner we'll finish.'

He walked along the rails past old Cal who stared at him mournfully and entered the darkness of the mine. It was cold and wet within the headings and not for the first time, Luke wondered if there was not an easier way of making a living.

He could not complain about the quality of the men he'd hired, for during the afternoon they worked at full stretch, the colliers filling the curling boxes and Rory and Luke transporting the glittering Red Vein anthracite to the dram. From there Luke led Cal towards the end of the rails and unhitched the gun.

'Let's get the dram onto the plate,' he said, lending his strength to push the dram so that the front wheels engaged with hooks on the plate, which then tipped forward to drop the coal onto the lower level.

Tomorrow, the lorries from the Ponty works would arrive and the coal would be shovelled aboard. It was hard, back-breaking work for which Luke paid his own men and the men from the Ponty extra money. But he would gradually make improvements in the mine. He would start by having one of the new compressors that powered drills for driving into the coal face. The Slant Moira would be the most profitable of all the small mines in the area, and would lay the ghost of the carpenter he once was. That was his goal and before too long he would reach it.

At last, the final dram was emptied and Luke sat down, rubbing a hand wearily across his face. 'Right, men, get off home with you and there'll be a bit extra in your pay-packets this week.'

He watched Rory, fully recovered now from the blast, stride off down the hill towards home and Tim, his back bent from many years spend underground at the Kilvey Deep, followed him on deceptively spindly legs. A good worker was Tim, in spite of his age.

'See you tomorrow then, boss,' Gerry said, wiping away the sweat that made inroads into the coal dust on his face. 'Knew we'd get the job done, see. Determined lot we are, mind.'

He moved a pace and turned. 'I've worked the deep pits where there's nowhere to have a piss and where you eat your food where you stand if the mice don't get it before you; moving to this job up here in the slant was the best thing I ever did.

'I know the mountain is above you when you work the coal but you are not miles down in the bowels of the earth and the sunlight is only yards away.' He paused. 'What I'm trying to say, boss, is that we all value our jobs here and we'd do anything to keep them.'

'I know, Gerry,' Luke said easily, 'and I've a team of good men I wouldn't exchange for anyone.'

Gerry lifted his hand and strode down the hill, hurrying to catch up with the other men. They would doubtless enjoy a pint of ale in the Colliers public bar before going home and they deserved a drink, for they had worked unstintingly.

He was just about to pull shut the shed door when he heard the sound of horses' hooves and the rumble of wheels on the roadway. He paused, as into sight came the large figure of Big Eddie, legs dangling precariously near the wheels of the cart.

'Luke Proud, there's a sight for sore eyes, you're just the man I want to see.' Eddie slid to the ground and trailed the reins loosely between his fingers. 'Hush, now, Daisy girl.' He patted the animal's nose lovingly. 'We won't be long.' He looked down at Luke from his great height.

'Lovely horse is Daisy, one of the best I've ever worked with; what a character.' He pulled the animal's ears and frowned. 'I got a favour to ask you, a big favour – I need coal urgently, forgot to keep some for my father-in-law and he's not happy, not happy at all.' Eddie grinned. 'And as Bertie-No-Legs owns the coal round it's not surprising he's mad at having to go without a warm stove, is it? What's more my wife's put me in the dog kennel for being unkind to her dear old daddy.'

Luke frowned. 'I've only just brought out enough coal to fill the order for the Ponty works and they are as keen as mustard – they'll be here with the dawn.' He stared at Eddie. The big man had been a good customer, as had Bertie before him and, apart from that, he'd been a willing helper at the scene of the roof-fall, working his guts out to help save the trapped men.

'I tell you what,' Luke said, 'if you'll help me dig out the coal from the face, you can have it half-price. How would that suit you?'

Eddie grinned. 'I've never turned my hand to mining before but, sure as hell, I'm willing to try anything once.'

The two men worked together in the warm womb of the Slant Moira, both of them hacking away at the coal face with lack of expertise but with a good will.

Luke felt weary, his shoulders ached like toothache and his muscles strained against the confines of the low seam in which he worked.

104

Eddie was further handicapped by his bulk. He groaned as he tried to shift his position a little. '*Duw*, you miners deserve all the money you can get,' he said, his voice muffled. 'And if the government would only spend half a day on the coal face they would give the men a rise, not a cut, in wages.'

At last the dram was full. Luke leaned against Old Cal's neck and clucked encouragingly at the horse. 'Come on, boy, let's get out of here, I've had more than enough for today.'

He was surprised to see that it was twilight. The mountain rested in a haze of indigo and the course grass looked as though painted on a landscape in shades of purple. Peta would be wondering what had become of him.

'We'll tip the load right here,' Luke said, 'we won't have the advantage of the incline at the end of the run but, on the other hand, if we mix the coal with the load ready for the Ponty works we won't know where the hell we are.'

'*Duw*, we'll never finish, man,' Eddie said wearily, 'I've got to bag the stuff yet.'

But shovelling the coal was work Eddie was well accustomed to, he had a deftness and economy of movement that augered well for speed. Luke helped but he was much slower, and he paused for a moment, looking up at the darkening sky from which the last of the light was vanishing.

At last Eddie had the cart full of neatly-stacked sacks of coal. 'There then, Luke,' he said, grinning, 'here's the money and with my thanks too, at least Bertie can light the stove and have himself a cooked dinner tonight.'

He took the reins of the horse and the cart jerked into motion. He lifted a hand in farewell and the cartwheels rumbled over the gritty roadway.

Luke went to the shed and placed the lamps on the table. He glanced into the pot-bellied stove but the embers held very little life. He sighed wearily – it was time he went home and had a damn good bath. He felt as though the coal dust had found every fold of his clothes and lodged there to chafe and scratch.

He was walking the short distance to the car when he heard a loud crashing noise. For a moment he thought it was a roof fall inside the mine, but as the echoes died away he knew it was an explosion from somewhere along the road that led towards the town.

He ran to the car and started the engine quickly. There were no mines blasting this late in the night, and in any case the explosion had been too close to the Slant Moira.

He drove down the road and saw the leap of flames against the darkness of the sky. Coal lay scattered in a large area along the road, and as Luke drew the car to a halt, he saw the remains of a cart crackle and burn against the roadway.

'Eddie!' He jumped from the car and hurried to the source of the fire. The horse lay still, unmoving, and a quick glance told Luke that the animal was dead.

'Eddie, where are you, man?' Luke heard a groan and he saw a figure sprawled at an awkward angle against the verge of grass. 'Eddie!' Luke knelt beside him and quickly ran his hands over the large man's limbs. Nothing seemed to be broken. Eddie sat up and shook his head like a boxer recovering from a knock-out blow.

'*Iesu grist*, what happened?' he said, staring around him in bewilderment. He struggled to sit up and rubbed at his coal-streaked face.

'There's been an explosion,' Luke said grimly. 'Someone must have placed a charge in the roadway and waited in the darkness, lighting the fuse when they heard you approach.'

Eddie got to his knees and shook his head, still groggy. 'But why would anyone want to harm me?' he asked slowly, struggling to rise to his feet.

'It wasn't meant for you,' Luke said. 'It was me they were after and I've got a very good idea who is behind it.'

'*Duw*.' Eddie lumbered to his feet and stared at the wreckage with horror. 'Daisy, what about Daisy?'

He moved to the centre of the road and knelt by the unmoving animal. 'Poor girl,' he whispered, rubbing the tangled mane, 'my poor old girl.' Tears made rivulets in the coal dust as the big man cried over the dead horse. His shoulders were bent and he remained kneeling on the ground for a long time.

Luke understood how he felt: a working animal became a friend, a constant companion who gave loyalty unquestioningly. He moved towards Eddie and put a hand on his shoulder.

'Come on, let me take you home; there's nothing more can be done here tonight. I'll get my men to bury Daisy in the morning.'

'Who did this thing?' Eddie asked pleadingly. 'Just tell me, Luke, and I'll take him apart with my bare hands.'

Luke pressed Eddie's arm. 'Come on, just think about yourself now and your wife and Bertie–No-Legs, they'll be waiting for you to come home. It's getting late, man, they'll have the constable out soon.'

'All right,' Eddie said dully. 'Some man must really hate you, Luke. Watch out for your back, boyo. And me, I won't forget this, mind. I'll get the bastard who did it, you'll see if I don't.'

Luke led him to the car. 'Aye, I know you will, Eddie,' he said soothingly, and added under his breath, 'but not if I get there first.'

It seemed to Luke he would never get home, but, at last, he turned the car into the driveway of his house with a sigh of relief. He let himself in with his key and the house around him breathed and creaked in the darkness, all seemed peaceful.

He went into the kitchen, still warm with the residue of heat from the stove. Luke stripped off his clothes and left them in a pile on the floor.

In the bathroom, he ran the water, feeling almost too weary to wash the clinging coal dust from his body. God, what a day it had been. He'd worked from early light until dusk, breaking his back to fill the order for Ponty.

He thought with a burning, searing anger of the explosion that had ripped through Big Eddie's cart, killing his horse. It had been meant not for Eddie but for him, that much was obvious. It was fortunate Eddie had been thrown clear or Luke would have had yet another death on his conscience.

He scrubbed at his arms and chest. 'It's got to be Michael Murphy's doing,' he muttered as he sluiced the residue of dust from his body. 'Surely no one else would be so insane?'

He left the bathroom as it was, too weary to clean up the place. He would doubtless feel the sharp edge of Peta's tongue in the morning but all he needed now was sleep.

He went into the spare bedroom – it would be pointless to disturb his wife. He fell into the bed and closed his eyes and the darkness folded around him, warm and soothing.

The door opened abruptly and the lamp was lit quickly so that the pale light penetrated the room. Luke looked up to see Peta standing over him, her face white with anger.

'So you creep home like a thief in the night and without even the decency to let me know you're safe?' she said, her voice rising.

'Peta.' He sat up. 'I've had a hard day – let's talk in the morning, shall we?' He tried to keep the edge of irritation out of his tone but Peta moved closer and stared down at him.

'There's daft you must think me, Luke Proud! No man stays out to this sort of hour unless he is up to no good.' Her eyes roamed over him scornfully. 'And it's clear as daylight that you've had no accident, so there must be another woman, mustn't there, and we both know who it is, don't we?'

'Peta!' His voice was hard. 'I said we'll talk about it in the morning.' Weariness lay like a cloak over him, his eyes refused to focus and the tortured muscles burned in his back.

She reached out suddenly and slapped him hard across the face. 'Don't take that tone with me. I'm not a child and

108

I won't have it, understand?' She stepped back a pace as though afraid of the consequences of her action.

'Go to bed,' Luke said tiredly and turned out the light. He could hear her harsh, angry breathing but he could do nothing about it. He was being dragged down into a pit of weariness and all he wanted was to sleep.

In the morning, he was up early before the rest of the household. He didn't bother with breakfast but made his way quickly to the front of the house and climbed into his car. His eyes still felt gritty as though he'd not had sufficient sleep, and every part of his body seemed to ache; but at least the order for the Ponty works was ready and he'd have some money to add to his sadly diminished capital.

As he drove along the road to the Slant Moira and saw the scattered coal and the body of the dead horse, he felt anger burn in his gut. Whoever had planted the charge was a maniac and should be placed behind bars where he could do no harm.

Rory was at the shed before him. He had the stove burning well and a kettle issuing steam bubbled and danced on the top of the metal plate. 'What happened down the road, boss?' he asked, frowning. 'Some explosion that was. Stolen from my box the stuff was, mind.'

'I don't know who was responsible,' Luke said quickly, 'but it was lucky no one was killed.' He changed the subject adroitly. 'That's a welcome sight,' he said, taking a mug of tea. 'I'm parched.'

He took off his coat and hung it on the back of the door. 'I'm glad you're in early, Rory, at least we'll be ready for the men from the Ponty.'

'Ah,' Rory said hesitantly. 'There's been a man up here, said the Ponty lorries might not be able to get here today after all.'

'Blast!' Luke said angrily. 'After us working our guts out to have the order ready, what are they playing at?'

'The bloke didn't seem to know much, said something about an embargo on handling the coal, bloody politics be the ruin of us, they will.'

Rory made fresh tea and placed the can on the table. 'Here, have another cup, boss, you look as though you need it.'

'Aye, thanks.' Luke stared into the distance, trying to sort out his thoughts. How could he get the coal down to Ponty tinplate works? Could he hire some lorries himself? But then that would take money and there wasn't very much of that available at the moment.

'About what happened up here last night, boss,' Rory said quietly, 'it must be someone who's got it in for you. The explosives were handled by amateurs – wonder they didn't blast themselves to kingdom come from what I could see.'

'Pity they hadn't,' Luke said. 'It's what they deserve.' He put down his can. 'Eddie Llewelyn came up here for a load of coal last night, it was when Eddie was driving back down the road that all hell broke loose.' He glanced at Rory. 'Eddie was just an innocent victim.'

'*Duw*, who'd want you dead, Luke? You must have made some terrible enemies.'

'Aye, but I'm not a good man to cross, Rory, as the ones who did this will find out to their cost.' He rose to his feet. 'Look, help me load a bag of coal onto my car and when the other men get here, tell them to bury the horse and then tidy up a little, after that they might as well go home – no good bringing out any more coal until we know what's going to happen to the load we mined already.' He moved out of the shed. 'See you later, Rory.'

He drove downhill towards Sweyn's Eye, hardly seeing the flurry of sparks from the tinplate works or the huddle of houses that crouched against the hillside. Or that Stryd Fawr was busy. The big emporium once owned by Mary Sutton thronged with people for it was the fashionable place for the rich to gossip over tea and cakes.

The smaller shops seemed to be empty. The dismal lines of boots and shoes were hanging outside the leather shop with apparently no one to buy them. It seemed the prosperity of the early part of the year had been a spurious one and that bad times were coming again to Sweyn's Eye.

Luke drove the car towards St Thomas, his hands more purposeful on the wheel. He had considered the problem of transporting the coal to the Ponty works and he thought he just might have the answer.

He drew the car to a halt on the hillside overlooking the docks. A tall sailing ship stood, masts high, an unusual sight now among the many packet-steamers that jostled in the water.

It was Eddie who opened the door and smiled as he waited for Luke to step inside.

'I've brought you some coal, enough to be getting on with anyway,' Luke said pointing towards the car. Eddie moved forward.

'There's good of you. Bertie–No-Legs has been complaining bitterly because he's had no breakfast yet, there being no coal for the stove.'

Luke followed Eddie inside and, in the neat parlour of the house, sat Bertie, a rug around his middle, his face long with misery.

'Luke has brought us some coal,' Eddie said over his shoulder as he heaved the sack through the narrow passageway towards the kitchen. 'There'll soon be a lovely breakfast for you, Bertie, don't you worry – my little wife will see to that.'

Bertie's expression lightened a little. 'Sit down, Luke,' he said warmly, 'and many thanks for coming down here yourself.'

Luke smiled. 'I've got an ulterior motive,' he said openly. 'I need your help, Bertie.'

'Aye, well if there's anything I can do, just let me know, except if it's a plea for money, mind, for I've got very little of that these days.'

'How many carts do you use on your coal round?' Luke asked, sitting back in his chair. He glanced up as Eddie entered the room and stood near the door, listening.

'I did have half a dozen before last night,' Bertie said, the frown of gloom returning to his brow. 'I've only five horses now.' He stroked his chin. 'That was a rum do – some fool blowing up the place.

111

Have you been to the police station to report it, man?'

Luke shook his head. 'I'll see to it myself. But about your carts. I want them for today to take coal from my mine to the Ponty tinplate works: it's not a long trip so it shouldn't take too much time.'

'*Duw*, what's happened to the Ponty lorries?' Bertie asked. 'They can't all have broken down.' His scorn of the mechanical was evident in his tone and Luke concealed a smile.

'No, they haven't broken down but there's an embargo on the handling of coal from the big pits and the Ponty drivers seem to have downed tools.'

'Well, I don't know, tying up my carts for even a couple of hours will lose me some profit.' Bertie rubbed his chin.

'No,' Luke said, 'for every load you take to Ponty I'll supply you with a ton of coal. How does that sound?'

Bertie appeared to consider the matter and glancing at Big Eddie, Luke saw him winking. The round had been completed yesterday and it was hardly likely any customers would be desperate for coal for another day or two.

'All right then,' Bertie said at last, 'providing you feed the animals as well, it's a deal.' He looked up at Eddie. 'You get everything sorted out, boyo, and for God's sake tell that girl of mine to get me breakfast, I'm starving.'

Outside, Eddie rested a hand on Luke's shoulder. 'I'll get the men together and I'll be up at the mine with them to help load the coal.' He ambled off along the street and as Luke watched him he felt a deep gratitude to the big man.

He drove back to the mine at top-speed and caught Rory just as he was leaving. 'Get the men together,' Luke said cheerfully. 'We are going to get that load of coal to Ponty if it kills us.'

9

Market Street was warm with spring sunshine and the tall windowed shops were doing a good trade, for the fine weather brought the shoppers out of their houses. But Murphys' Fresh Fish Shop was the exception and had no customers. The glistening marble slab was empty, for the delivery of fish was late.

Katie stood in the doorway, staring anxiously down the hill, hoping for a sight of the familiar red-painted lorry that came from the fish market at the docks. But the road was deserted, only a lone bicyclist laboured along the steep roadway. At last she returned indoors and, hanging up her apron, pulled on a cardigan and took up her keys. This was the fourth time this week there had been no delivery and, one way or another, she meant to sort it out.

She glanced around the dim living-room. The sun did not penetrate to the back of the house and in the shadows the heavy, good furniture crouched like beasts waiting to pounce.

'Mammy,' Katie whispered and it seemed that the silence grew more profound for her mother had been laid to rest some weeks now and still Katie expected to see her, to hear her thin voice calling. Even the lightest scent of gin brought mammy to mind, for she had loved her drink and no harm in it.

She left the house, locking the doors securely – in the back of her mind was the ever-present fear of Michael returning and taking over the house and shop in his usual belligerent way. Legally he had no rights, but Michael believed himself above the law.

How he had changed from the little brother who had lain side by side with Kevin in the old pram. Then the boys had been so alike, two peas in a pod, people had

113

said. Now Michael was a bully and Kevin a coward, and Katie felt she was left alone in the world with no one who cared a fig for her.

But she must stop feeling sorry for herself. Self-pity was so destructive, it was weak and absurd, and she would not give in to it.

She walked down the hill into the Strand and from there it was only a short distance to the docks where the fish market stood at the side of the water. It was a beautiful day, cloudless and fresh, and people around her all seemed to be in pairs. She felt invisible almost, as though she had no more substance than a shadow, but there she was again, wallowing in self-pity.

She moved into the market where the smell of fish was overpowering, but Katie was used to it – it had been her livelihood for some years now and her father's before her. She could gut a fish swiftly and fillet it just as neatly, cutting the bones from the flesh in deft movements of her knife. Sometimes the scales cut and burned the skin, but Katie could put up with that so long as she had honest work that would earn her daily bread.

In the market, she stood for a moment looking round her. Men walked about in oilskins and the chink of ice in boxes was an accompaniment to their task of weighing and stacking the catch.

She approached one of the men. 'Excuse me, but have you seen Sammy, the delivery boy?' she asked and, without pausing in his task, the man shook his head.

'Off sick,' he said abruptly. When she didn't move away, he glanced up at her and straightened. 'Not his girlfriend, are you?'

Katie smile coquettishly. It seemed guile was needed to get any information out of the taciturn man. 'Sure and why not? Will you tell me where he lives?'

The man pushed his cap back with the heel of his hand. 'Well, can't do no harm, I suppose. He lives in one of them old houses in Green Hill.' He bent over the box of fish once more and Katie felt as though she were dismissed.

She turned, leaving the docks and the buzz of the market behind her, and made her way back up the hill, away from the town. She was angry with Sammy. She had made inquiries and he seemed to be able to make his deliveries to other shops quite well – it was when it came to Market Street that he suddenly took sick.

The canal was turgid and the fronds of grass beneath the surface of the water moved and twisted as though trying to escape from a watery grave. Katie shuddered and moved along the street, wondering which house was Sammy's. She decided to knock on the door of Luke Proud's sister's house and she smiled as Charlotte looked at her in surprise.

'Sure I'm sorry to be troubling you but I'm looking for Sammy – he drives the big lorry from the fish market.'

'Oh, Sammy lives two doors down, Katie – that's right, the house with the brown door. But won't you come in a minute?'

Katie shook her head. 'Sure another day I'd be only too glad but I've got to get back to the shop.' She moved to the house Charlotte had indicated and knocked loudly on the door. The barking of a dog could be heard somewhere in the back regions of the house.

The woman who stood in the open doorway looked at Katie with suspicion, her face was pale and she looked as though she'd been crying. 'What do you want?' she asked abruptly.

'I would like a word with Sammy if it's possible,' Katie said, 'but sure I don't want to go bothering him if he's too sick.'

'I'm Sammy's wife,' the woman said more easily, 'who shall I say wants him?' She was stepping back into the passageway as she spoke.

'I'm Katie Murphy from the fresh fish shop . . .' Katie began but before she could go any further the woman moved towards her menacingly.

'You got a nerve coming here!' Her voice rose hysterically. 'After what your brothers did to my Sammy and all, should be locked up, the lot of you. Crazy Irish peasants that's what you are.'

'I don't understand,' Katie said in bewilderment, 'what have my brothers got to do with this?'

'Sammy, you just come out by here and show this creature what's happened to you.'

From the dimness of the passage a figure loomed into view. Sammy was a small man, with a thin face and gaunt cheekbones. Katie gasped when he came into the light of the open doorway for he had two black eyes and a badly-cut lip and he moved as though he ached all over.

'Mother of God!' Katie exclaimed. 'Did my brothers do this to you?' She knew the answer even before he nodded his head. 'By all the saints I'm sorry,' Katie said, 'It was none of my doing, I promise you.'

'That's as may be.' Sammy's wife slipped her arm through his. 'But my husband is not taking any more beatings, you'll have to just get someone else to deliver your fish.' The door was shut with a click of finality and Katie stepped back into the sunlit road feeling sick and angry. Would her brother stop at nothing to get back at her?

She walked home slowly, feeling defeated and lost. Why had Michael ever come back to Sweyn's Eye? He was a ruthless man who would do anything to get his own way.

She turned into Market Street and stopped suddenly, the colour draining from her face. The shop was open, the slab full of fish and behind the counter, wearing a white apron, was Kevin. He looked sheepish when he saw her approach, but he continued to serve the customers without a word.

'What's happening here?' Katie said to him in a fierce whisper and he jerked his head towards the kitchen.

'Michael is in there, you'd better go and ask him.' He had the grace to blush but Katie knew that Kevin was much too weak to cope with his older brother.

'It's not your fault,' she said softly. Taking a deep breath, she moved along the passage and into the kitchen. Michael was seated in mammy's chair, a glass beside him, a pipe resting on the table. He had made himself at home.

116

'Well, Katie, you've come home,' he said. 'You should be running the shop – can't make a living by gallivanting around town, you know.'

'Don't talk such rubbish!' Katie said angrily. 'I've been down to Canal Street and seen what you did to intimidate poor Sammy. He's black and blue - no wonder he won't deliver any fish to the shop. And anyway, how did you get in here?'

'Sammy? Never heard of him,' Michael said. 'He should make a complaint to the police if someone has done him harm.' He leaned forward. 'You didn't really think a few bolts would keep me out did you?'

Katie sank into a chair. 'What do you want, Michael?' she asked quietly. 'What do you really want?'

His easy manner suddenly disappeared. 'I want my rights. I am the eldest son – I should have the house, and the shop an' all.'

Katie sighed. 'Mammy made a point of leaving the place to me. What did you care about us, or the shop, all those years when you chose to stay away?' She rose to her feet and pushed the kettle onto the fire. Suddenly she was angry, angry with herself and with Michael for making her afraid.

'If Sammy won't make a complaint to the police, then I will,' she said decisively. 'I'll have you put out of here, if you don't go of your own accord.'

Michael smiled and relaxed in his chair. 'What would the police act upon?' he asked reasonably. 'There's not a mark on you, my dear sweet sister and all Kevin and me are doing is helping you in the shop. There's no law against that, is there?'

'But I want you out of here,' Katie said edgily. 'I've run this shop alone for too many years, I don't want you or need you, do you understand?'

He rose to his feet. 'Well I'm going for now, but wait until you can't get any deliveries and there's no money coming in to pay the bills – you'll come to me on your hands and knees then.'

When she was alone, Katie found that she was trembling. She made a cup of tea and sat with it beside her, too shaken to drink it. She heard footsteps along the passage and her shoulders grew tense, but it was Kevin who entered the room.

'All sold out!' He spoke cheerfully and then his gaze rested on her pale face and shadowed eyes. 'Why don't you let him have what he wants?' he said softly. 'He's changed – he's violent and vicious and he'll keep at it like a terrier with a rat until you give in.'

'No!' Katie said. 'I won't give in to him. Michael has to be stopped, can't you see that, Kev?'

He sat beside her. 'I am afraid of him Katie, love, I can't stand up to him any more than you can, though there's been times when I long to put one right on the point of his jaw, believe me.'

'Well, I'm going to the police,' Katie said and she saw Kevin shake his head sadly.

'It won't do no good, love, he hasn't done anything to you and he won't – he's not stupid.'

Katie took a sip from her cup, almost spilling the tea in her lap. 'What about Sammy? He did something to him sure enough.'

Kevin rose to his feet and took off the apron that glittered with fish scales. 'Forget it! Sammy knows there'd be more of the same if he made charges against Michael. I'm going to have a wash and get off home now.' He grinned ruefully. 'If you can call the boarding house home, that is.'

Katie closed her eyes. 'I'm sorry, Kev. If only things were different, if only Michael . . .' Her voice trailed away and Kevin, drying his hands, smiled at her.

'Sell up, that's the answer,' he said. 'It's the only way you'll best that brother of ours because he'll ruin the business if he doesn't get a share of it.'

Katie poured herself more tea and stared down into the swirling liquid. It was a solution she herself had thought of, but what would she do then? Even if she started up some other business Michael would be there in the background doing his best to ruin her.

'I'd have to move out of the district,' she said, 'and even then how do I know he wouldn't find me? No, I'll take my chances here; I'll sort something out. Don't you worry about me, Kev.'

When he'd gone, she took a bucket of water into the shop and began to scrub down the slab methodically. It was a tedious, back-breaking job and yet the activity was somehow a relief because she at least had something to occupy herself with. But her mind continued to race with questions: how could she get stock delivered in spite of Michael? Another thing – did she really want to continue in the trade that was hard and sometimes unpleasant?

Sighing, she put up the shutters and locked the front door. She was weary and longed for a hot bath. She would put the large pan on the fire and boil up some water. She would wash her hair too and then when it was dry she would go to bed and rest; perhaps if she was less tired, she could think more clearly about her future.

It was good to luxuriate in the hot water even in the confines of the long, narrow tin bath and to Katie it was worth all the effort of boiling the water. She washed her collar-length hair and wrapped a towel around her head, and slowly she began to relax. She deliberately cleared her mind of all her problems – there was time enough to sort out her muddled thoughts later, when she was rested.

The worst part of bathing was when she had to drag the tin bath towards the back door and tip the water down the gully leading to the drain. It was heavy and difficult and she was panting by the time she'd finished.

She walked back slowly into the house and sank into a chair, still wrapped in the towels. It was silent and oppressively hot in the kitchen, and Katie moved to the stairway. Perhaps if she rested on the bed for a while she would be able to shake off the lethargy that seemed to envelop her.

Her bedroom was neat, and though the furniture was not plentiful, what there was of it was good, a far cry from the days when Mary Sutton had come to stay with her and they'd shared the one room with only a blanket strung between them for privacy.

She sank down onto the brightly-patterned quilt and sighed with relief: it was good to be comfortable and cool.

She closed her eyes, she was so tired. She must have slept a little for she became aware only slowly of the sound of knocking on the door and a voice calling her name.

'Katie! It's Luke Proud, are you all right?'

She slipped from the bed and went to the head of the stairs. 'Come on in, I'll be with you in a minute,' she called, looking around quickly for her clothes. 'Go on into the kitchen,' she added, 'sure I'll be down in two ticks.'

Flustered, she pulled on a skirt and blouse and buttoned the neck while she hurried down the stairs. Luke was in the kitchen, staring into the fire and when he looked up at her there was a strange expression on his face.

'What's wrong?' she asked, aware that her cheeks were hot and her hair dishevelled. 'Sure I suppose I look a real sight!'

'You look lovely,' he said slowly. He moved away from the fire and stood at the window looking out, hands thrust into his pockets. 'I'm looking for Michael. Do you know where he is, Katie?'

'Sure he was here earlier and our Kev said they were staying in some boarding house but I don't know the address. Why, what has he done this time?'

'There was an explosion on the roadway leading to the Slant Moira some days ago.' He held up his hand when Katie tried to speak. 'No one was hurt, though big Eddie Llewelyn was shaken up and his horse killed. Not taking that lightly, is Eddie, and if he finds any proof that your Michael was involved he'll take him apart.' Luke stared directly into her eyes. 'And I'm sure your brother was involved. I believe he was after me, not Eddie.'

'Oh, God, what will Michael do next?' Katie felt a sense of despair wash over her. Her brother was bad – she couldn't believe they were of the same blood.

'Michael attacked Sammy,' she said softly, 'the man who makes the deliveries of fish to the shop. He won't come here any more, I don't know how I'm going to carry on.'

'Are you afraid he'll attack you?' Luke came to stand close to her and she glanced up at him feeling somehow awkward in his company.

'He won't do me any harm,' she said quickly, 'not physically, he's too cunning for that, sure he knows I could go to the police if he hurt me.' She looked at him from under her lashes. He was very handsome, with his dark hair and fine eyes.

Luke touched a damp curl at the side of her face. 'I'd give him the hiding he deserved if he harmed you.' His tone was level but Katie had no doubt that he meant every word he said. She was aware of his nearness but she did not want to draw away from him.

His touch and his closeness were attempts to comfort and reassure her, and yet somehow, intangibly, the atmosphere was charged. Luke's hand was beneath her chin, forcing her to look up at him. His eyes were clear and blue, and the crispness of his hair curling against his forehead made her want to reach out and touch it.

'Katie,' he said softly and for a long moment they remained unmoving, looking into each other's eyes. Very slowly, his mouth came closer to hers and Katie, fearful of destroying the magical feeling, remained still, waiting.

When their lips touched it was though a fire had reached into her heart and as she clung to him, she felt a re-awakening of all the feelings of tenderness, so long suppressed.

But at last, Luke turned away from her, 'I have never seen such beauty,' he said softly. 'But as much as I find myself drawn to you, I have no right to touch you, we both know that.'

He moved to the window and stared out into the street and as she watched him, Katie wondered what he was thinking. Were his words merely kindly lies, or did he really feel something more than passion for her?

Suddenly she felt uncertain and experienced an almost child-like need to be reassured. 'Luke?' She looked towards him pleadingly.

'I mean what I say, Katie.' It was as though he sensed her need. 'I'm not a womanizer and not given to lies, believe me, *cariad*,'

Katie felt the tears burn her eyes and was ashamed of her weakness, but Luke came towards her, and after a moment's hesitation, he held her close with infinite tenderness.

'You are too much of a woman to take second-best.' He moved away from her abruptly and she knew he felt he was being disloyal to his wife. It hurt and yet she understood it – Luke was a man with a conscience, he would not willingly betray anyone.

He moved to the door and looked back at her. 'Lock up securely once I've gone, Katie. I don't want that brother of yours getting in here again.'

With the mention of Michael, Katie's spirits sank. She nodded her head, making an attempt to smile. 'Don't you worry about me, I've been taking care of myself for a long time.'

She watched from the window as he made his way towards the car. He glanced towards her and lifted his hand, then disappeared from sight – and Katie was alone with her thoughts.

She forced herself into action, pushing the kettle onto the flames and poking life into the coals. She stared around her at the empty, silent room, darkened with a myriad shadows that wrapped themselves around her as though with friendly arms. This was her home and she knew with certainty that she must continue to work and live here, whatever Michael did.

She sat with a cup of tea untasted on the table beside her. She had longed for a few foolish moments to change her life drastically, to take Luke as her lover. As his hand had touched her hair, she'd selfishly wanted to grasp at any happiness that came her way.

But to be realistic, as Luke's fancy-woman she would only have the crumbs that fell from his wife's table. And yet she knew in her heart she would be grateful for them because now, for the first time in years, she felt alive again, a woman with senses and desires.

She heard a sound at the back door and realized she had not locked up as Luke had instructed her. She rose to her feet, her hand to her throat as footsteps drew nearer the kitchen.

'On the name of the Blessed Virgin, Kevin, you frightened me!' Katie sank into a chair and pointed to the teapot with its brightly knitted cosy. 'Help yourself, for my hands are shaking too much to pour you any tea.'

He sat in the chair and stared at her worriedly. 'Michael told me to watch the house and report on any visitors you might have,' he said. 'I saw Luke Proud come here – and stay for a long time too. What's going on, Katie?'

She leaned forward, her hands stretched out to grasp his. 'Don't say anything to our Michael, Kev – he's dangerous, sure, an' don't you know that without me telling you?'

'I know he's hot-tempered, mad even,' Kevin said. 'He has many faults, but he's my brother after all and I owe him something. I should tell him about Proud's visit; he'll find out anyway.'

Katie sighed. 'There's nothing but friendship between me and Luke, I promise you that, but even if there weren't it wouldn't be anything to do with Michael.'

'But don't you understand?' Kevin said softly. 'He feels he's been cheated of his heritage: the house and the shop should be his by rights, he is the eldest son, after all.'

'Look, what if I gave him a share of the profits?' she said at last. 'I know it's giving in to him, Kev, but I just don't want anyone else getting hurt – I've got poor Sammy on my conscience as it is. Tell Michael I'll split the proceeds between us, perhaps that will satisfy him.'

Kevin rose, then brought a cup from the pantry and poured some tea. 'I'll tell him, but don't count on anything, will you?'

'What do you mean?' Katie asked, frowning. 'What more could he want?' She was biting her lip worriedly as she watched the amber liquid flow from the teapot.

'He's got it in for Luke Proud. Sure he needs to pay him back for manhandling him out of his own home – he's got to save face, hasn't he?' He replaced the cosy over the pot and sat down. 'Don't *you* think that as the eldest son, everything should be Michael's, then?'

Katie felt anger flower within her. She rose to her feet, the blood rushing into her cheeks. 'No I do not!' she said angrily. 'It was me who took over when daddy died, me that kept things going. If it wasn't for me there would be no business, can't *you* understand that?'

Kevin sighed. 'I suppose I can see your side of it just a little, but Michael's ideas will never change.'

'Well,' Katie said fiercely, 'in that case you can just tell him to go to hell!' She spun round to look at Kevin. 'Tell him I won't give him anything now, why should I? If it wasn't for my hard work the house would have been sold from under me and mammy a long time ago. It was me who paid the bills and me who slaved to keep mammy and me with a roof over our heads, and if Michael thinks he can just come back and take it all away from me then he's sadly mistaken.'

Kevin sighed. 'I know, Katie, love, I know.' He touched her shoulder lightly. 'Trouble is I can see both sides of the question.'

Katie followed him to the back door. 'No, Kev, you're frightened to cross our brother, that's what it is, if the truth be known. Well you just go and tell him anything you like, but from now on neither of you are welcome here, do you understand?'

Kevin sloped away down the back lane and Katie closed the door, shooting home the bolt yet knowing at the same time that if any of her brothers chose to break in, no bolts would keep them out.

She sat in the kitchen and put her head on her hands and the tears flowed between her fingers. Her emotions had been through the wringer in the past few hours – there had been too much for her spirit to cope with.

'Luke,' she whispered, 'why can't you be with me?' This then was to be her future. She had fallen in love with a man she could not have and she would be condemned to spend a lifetime alone without the comfort of a loved one's arms. It was a bleak outlook indeed and, in that moment, Katie wondered if she was strong enough to face it.

10

'When are we going to get out of here, Micky?' Doffy was seated in the bay window, staring down into the street, her distaste at her surroundings reflected in her face. 'It's such a dump,' she continued, 'I hate living in one room in grumpy old Griffith's boarding house – thought I was going to keep house for you proper-like.'

'Oh, shut up, woman! Sure can't you see I'm trying to sort something out here?' Michael sat with paper and pencil, writing down figures and then crossing them out savagely. 'Blast, it'll take me months to get Katie out of the shop and by my reckoning, she's earning a nice little fortune. But I'll beat her, I want that house and the business – 'tis my right as eldest son.' He rose to his feet, screwing up the paper and threw it into the fire. 'If she hadn't turned my sick mammy's head I'd be sitting pretty right now.'

Doffy eyed him warily. Michael had to be treated gently when he was in a bad mood, she'd learned that much about him. But there was no denying that he was a handsome devil – he had lovely, red-gold hair and such fine eyes that seemed to look right inside a girl. Dimly, she recognized that with a man like Michael she would be happy to give up the streets and simply work in the house, waiting for him to come home to her each evening. And if Michael had set his heart on having the house in Market Street then she would do all she could to help him.

She chewed at her fingernail. Why he would want to live in a fresh fish shop she couldn't imagine – it smelled awful and she just hated the sight of the dead fish-eyes that stared up at her from the slab. What she would like was for him to sell the business and buy somewhere nice, up on the hill.

'There's nothing to do in by here, I think I'll go into town,' she said doubtfully, and Michael stared at her for a long time without answering.

'Go ahead, then, get out of my sight. You make me sick anyway with all the scent you drench yourself in.'

Doffy snatched up her cardigan and hurried down the stairs out into the sunlit street before Michael could change his mind. There was no knowing which way he would turn; he was like a mad bull at times and yet he was a real man when he was between the sheets.

She walked slowly along the roadway, staring into shop windows, not knowing what to do with herself. She saw a red silk blouse, cut low at the neck in a V, and with a sash low on the hips. She put her head on one side. She would look really appealing in that; Michael would surely find her irresistible and might it not put him in a good mood again? But she had no money. Michael worked hard in the pit and brought home good pay, but he gave none of it to her.

It was true that he kept her in food and put a roof of sorts over her head, but she wasn't paid anything for all her slaving in the tiny kitchen shared with the people downstairs. But there was one sure way she could earn money: one customer – just one – meant she could have the blouse and Michael would never know.

Looking over her shoulder, she made her way quickly into the narrow dark passageway of the Lamb and Flag, where some of her regulars often met. The public bar was quiet with just a few men seated at a table playing cards, and one – a well dressed man – standing at the bar. She quickly summed up the situation. The card players had too much money on the table to abandon the game, so she was not left a great deal of choice.

''Scuse me,' she said in her little girl voice, 'would you have the time on you, please?' It was a lame excuse to make contact, but Doffy had found that the opening gambit didn't matter very much when a man was hungry for a woman.

He turned then and she stepped back in surprise. 'Billy Gray. *Duw*, I didn't know it was you or I'd

127

. . .' Her voice trailed away as he smiled down at her.

'Or you'd not have bothered to approach me, is that it?' he said. He put some money on the bar and Doffy looked at it eagerly. 'Have a drink?' Billy said. 'And that's the only thing you're getting.'

'Oh, all right, a sweet sherry, please.' Doffy didn't like to drink – she begrudged the money spent on it – but a sweet sherry sounded lady-like and it might lead to something more.

'Come and sit down,' she coaxed and slipped her arm though his, drawing him towards a corner table. 'There's posh you are now. Gone up in the world, haven't you?'

'I've got a reasonable job,' he agreed. He leaned towards her. 'And why are you mixed up with the like of Michael Murphy? Don't you know he's dangerous?'

'Michael is all right,' Doffy said quickly. 'You can't blame him for losing his temper like he did that day up at the fish shop; the place should have been his by rights.'

'Silly, silly little Doffy,' Billy said, shaking his head.

Sensing a softening in him, Doffy put her hand on his. 'Don't let's talk about Michael.' Her eyes were warm. 'Let's talk about the old days when you and me had such sweet times together. Oh, you were a man and a half, Billy Gray, the finest lover in the land.' She tiptoed her fingers across his palm. 'Been hiding yourself away these last few years. Haven't gone all respectable and got married, have you?'

'I'm not married,' Billy said, 'but I've got a good job that keeps me busy.' He smiled. 'I've seen you around, mind, even though you haven't seen me.'

She dimpled prettily. 'Oh, Billy, you haven't forgotten all about Doffy then?' She leaned closer, allowing her breast to touch his arm. He looked down at her and deliberately moved away.

'We're having a drink for old times' sake,' he said gently, 'but if it's custom you're after then go and find someone else.'

128

She pouted at him. 'Don't be so horrible to me, Billy,' she said, 'I can't help being affectionate, can I?' She paused for a moment, staring down into her drink. 'There's different our lives are, Billy.' She thought she'd try a new tack, if he wasn't to be tempted into bed perhaps she could get money out of him some other way. 'You're posh now with a good suit and a lovely white shirt and me, well I've not even got the money to buy myself a new blouse.'

He leaned back in his chair, a smile on his face. 'How much?' he asked, and she smiled warmly.

'Oh, I wasn't meaning to hint or anything like that.' Doffy paused, wondering how much she could get away with. 'One and six pence, that's all.'

He put his hand in his pocket and placed some coins on the table. 'Here's five shillings, now be a good girl and get off home.' He glanced at his pocket watch and she realized that he must be meeting someone. She picked up the money quickly and rose to her feet.

'You're a good friend, Billy,' she said, 'and I'll never forget you. If ever you're lonely just look me up.'

She left the public bar but did not move very far away from the doorway of the Lamb and Flag; she was curious to know who Billy could be meeting in such a seedy, out-of-the-way place. She did not have to wait long. A cab drew up a short distance away and a well-groomed woman alighted, staring round her as though worried about being seen. She passed by in a cloud of perfume without noticing Doffy and disappeared into the dim passageway. Doffy's eyebrows were raised as she digested the fact that Mrs Delmai Richardson, wife of one of Sweyn's Eye's richest men, had an assignation with Billy Gray. 'That's one affair that's not dead and finished, then,' Doffy muttered to herself. She would store away that piece of intelligence, it might one day come in useful.

The red silk blouse looked every bit as good as she thought it would but the trouble was how to explain its purchase to Michael. What if she were to say that her friend gave it to her? Not that Rosa was given to being generous very often, but Michael didn't know that. To make her excuse more believable, she would go round to Rosa's lodging house and have a little chat to her, perhaps she would come back to see Michael with her and together they could spin him a line.

Rosa had been the one who had brought Doffy into the trade. She was much older than Doffy and very experienced in the ways of men. Her advice had been to catch a good one and stick with him but she herself had never managed that – she was nothing more than a shilling stand-up job in a back alley. Doffy prided herself that she would never come to that. She had the looks to attract a better sort of man, while Rosa would take a miner straight out of the pit if there was money in it.

In the mean court where Rosa lodged Doffy paused, uncertain which door to knock on. Some young lads stood on the corner, eyeing her up and down and after a moment one of them whistled through his teeth at her. She flounced up to them, smiling.

'Get away with you – not more than thirteen years old, any of you; wouldn't know what to do with a woman if you had one.' She put her hands on her hips. 'Now which clever boyo can tell me where Rosa lives?'

One of the boys leaned forward and spat into the road. 'That tramp?' he said. 'If I was you I'd keep right away from her; got the pox she has.'

For a moment Doffy was silent with shock. 'She's sick?' she asked uncertainly and laughter broke out among the group.

'That house by there with the black curtains, that's where the old whore lives.' The same boy spoke, his eyes curious. 'You're no do-gooder, though, not dressed quiet enough – must be like Rosa then, one of the street-women.'

Doffy found her voice. 'Mind your tongue! And if you don't shut your mouth I'll shut it for you, you little runt.'

She moved towards the house and saw that the door was ajar. Cautiously, she pushed it open. 'Rosa, it's me, Doffy, are you in?'

A thin voice answered her and Doffy, encouraged, walked into the room. The stale smell of sweat drifted towards her and she paused for a moment, not knowing if she should go forward or turn and run.

'Fetch me a drink of water, there's a good girl; that's not asking much, is it?' The querulous voice now entreated.

Doffy went into the kitchen and wrinkled up her nose. There were dirty dishes everywhere and the sanded floor had not been swept in weeks. A mouse scurried away as she crossed the room and she gave a little scream of fright. Quickly, she rinsed out a glass that held stale beer and filled it with water. She hurried back into the parlour and pulled back the curtain to allow a little light into the room.

Rosa was almost unrecognizable. Her face was drawn and pale and her eyes were practically closed. Her thin hair was plastered to her scalp and it was clear she'd never work again, but that was none of Doffy's business.

'Here's your water,' she said, drawing back her hand quickly for fear of being touched. 'Have you had the doctor in to look at you?'

Rosa gave a croak that might have been a laugh. 'Doctors cost money and I haven't got any . . . can't get any now, can I, not sick as I am? You haven't got any, have you, Doffy, for old times' sake?'

Doffy took a shilling from the money Billy Gray had given her and dropped it on the cluttered table. 'Can't stop,' she said with forced brightness, 'in a terrible hurry, see.'

Outside, she took great gulps of air. God forbid she should end up like Rosa – the woman was near death's door, anyone could see that. She hurried away from the dingy court and back towards the town, unable to forget the sights and smells she had just experienced. She felt a twinge of conscience; she should really try to help Rosa, but then she had given her some of her precious money, what more could she do?

She shuddered, thinking of the phrase from the Bible she'd seen on a picture once: 'The wages of sin are death.' Well, she would try not to sin any more; she would not walk the streets again however much she wanted money. She would just have to cling to Michael Murphy, make him her one and only man, persuade him somehow to keep her – for if a life on the streets brought a girl to such an end then that wasn't for her, no fear.

When she entered the house, Michael was nowhere to be seen and Doffy was grateful for that. She brought up water from the kitchen and after taking off her clothes washed thoroughly, as though somehow the contact with the sick woman had contaminated her. She dressed in the new red blouse and a black skirt, and then brushed her hair until it curled around her face, then she peered into the cracked mirror on the high mantelpiece and congratulated herself that she looked good.

It might have been an hour later when Michael returned. He glance at her carelessly and then took a second look.

'Am I pretty, Michael?' Doffy asked, putting on her babyish voice. 'I visited an old friend of mine and because I did a bit of work for her in the house, she gave me this blouse.'

Michael wasn't even remotely interested in her story. 'You know,' he said, his eyes lighting up, 'I just might be kind to you if you treat me right.' He crossed the room in quick strides and lifted her into his arms. She squealed excitedly, clinging to his broad shoulders. 'Careful, Michael, mind my new blouse.' He tore at the buttons and she pouted up at him. 'That's all you think I'm good for, isn't it, Michael? A bit of fun, that's all I am to you.'

Michael's hand was on his belt; he didn't bother to reply. He buried his head in her neck and pushed at her skirt, jerking it up in a bunch behind her. She gasped as the full weight of him pressed her into the bed and then he was fumbling with her underclothes.

Why just for once couldn't a man treat her kindly and with a little bit of loving? she thought desperately.

'Wait!' she said in his ear. 'There's no train to catch, boyo, let me show you how lovely it all can be if you only take your time.' She smoothed his strong shoulders and then allowed her hands to travel over his body, slowly and sensuously.

'I've learned a few tricks of the trade in my time,' she said, smiling up at him invitingly. 'If you'll only let me, I'll show you some of them.' If she couldn't capture his heart, perhaps she could make herself indispensable to him in other ways.

'Sure,' Michael said roughly, 'do your damnedest but don't forget that I'm not paying for it.'

Doffy wanted to cry – just a little tenderness, that's all she wanted. Was it asking too much of life? She swallowed her tears and pushed him over until he lay on his back.

'Nobody could buy what I'm going to give you, my lovely,' she said and her voice was hoarse not, as he imagined, with passion but with tears. Well, she would make him remember Doffy, she told herself: whoever he had in the future, no woman would give him the pleasure that she would give him.

Kevin, running up the stairs, paused, hearing sounds of obvious passion from within the room. He grinned to himself. He had to hand it to Michael – he never went without a woman; he didn't have to, they seemed to love the aggression that was so much a part of him. Quietly, Kevin retraced his steps. He would walk around the streets for half an hour, perhaps have a pint at the Mexico Fountain and then he would go back and tell Michael that Luke Proud seemed bent on making Katie his fancy-piece.

Billy couldn't wait to get Delmai out of the grubby public bar of the Lamb and Flag and into the suite of rooms he'd reserved at the Mackworth Hotel in the Stryd Fawr. The appearance of Doffy had made him uneasy; his past was littered with mistakes and she was one of them.

Delmai sat at the little table in the window and stared at him in a way she had, as though he were a butterfly she had trapped with a pin.

'Why haven't you brought my daughter to see me?' she asked coldly. 'You've been promising me a meeting with Cerianne for weeks.'

He sighed and thrust his hands into his pockets. He didn't know why he'd renewed this clandestine relationship with

133

Delmai – he'd suspected that she was warm and loving to him only because he was a means to an end, and now it appeared he had been right.

'It's very difficult,' he said quickly, 'she's not a child any more, she's a young lady now, and what's she going to think if I bring her to an hotel room?'

Delmai sighed heavily. 'Order some lemon tea, Billy, I'm parched.' She took off her hat. 'Why is it that I have to do all the thinking?'

He pressed the button above the large, heavily-draped bed. There was a fat chance of getting Delmai between the sheets – not today, at least, – she was in her Mrs Rickie Richardson role and would enjoy keeping him at a distance.

There was a knock at the door and with an exasperated glance at Delmai, who sat quite unconcerned in the window seat, Billy spoke to the maid and gave her the order. He was becoming slowly disillusioned with Delmai Richardson, he'd been a fool to take up with her again after the way she had walked out of his life all those years ago, abandoning both him and their baby daughter.

'Delmai,' he said in irritation, 'why exactly did you take up with me again? Was it because you wanted me or Cerianne?'

Gauging his mood correctly, Delmai's attitude changed. 'Billy, my love, you know that no man means as much to me as you do,' she said, leaning across the table and touching his hand. 'It's just that I'm tired and I haven't been feeling too well lately.' She glanced up at him from beneath lowered lashes. 'A lady doesn't always feel in the mood for loving. If you were married, you'd have known that, Billy.'

He smiled knowingly. He may not be legally married but he'd cohabited with Gina for many years now and was quite capable of assessing a woman's moods. Delmai's initial ardour had been a lift to his pride, for any relationship could grow comfortable, if not stale, and the return into his life of the woman who had once given up all for a passion she could not control was exciting, he could not deny it.

'How are your sons?' he asked and Delmai brushed back a curl from her forehead before replying.

'Just fine, well and hearty and noisy as can be expected from boys of their age.' She sighed. 'I'm always grateful when they return to boarding school after the summer holidays.'

There was a discreet tapping on the door and Billy went forward to take the tray from the maid. He pressed a coin into her willing hand and she bobbed him a small curtsey. How money talked, Billy thought wryly. Once he'd been reviled by the people of Sweyn's Eye, a womanizer and – worse – a jailbird. But all that was behind him now; he must look forward to the future and he wasn't sure at this point he wanted it to include Delmai Richardson.

'Let's have our tea,' Delmai said, 'and then I really must be getting back home, I've got the most dreadful headache coming on.'

'I'm sure you have,' Billy said softly but his sarcasm was lost on Delmai, who merely sat back in her chair waiting for him to hand her the cup of tea. He must be crazy, he told himself. He was allowing himself to be manipulated by this woman, who wanted something from him, and it wasn't passion.

'About Cerianne,' she said casually. 'Bring her to Victoria Park next week sometime, during the afternoon at, say, about three-ish. We can meet then as if by chance.'

Billy stretched his long legs before him. 'No can do,' he said. 'I do have to work for a living, you know.'

She waved a delicate white hand at him and he noticed her nails were painted with vermilion varnish. In a poorly-dressed woman such an affectation would be considered sluttish but with Delmai, in her fine, expensive clothes and handmade shoes, it appeared to be smart and modern.

'We both know you work to suit yourself, Billy,' Delmai said petulantly, 'so I'll see you a week today in the park, all right?'

Billy nodded. 'All right, I'll try to square it with Gina – but don't forget Cerianne has to work for a living; she

135

doesn't go to a posh boarding school like your kids, either.'

Delmai wagged a finger at him. 'Now, now Billy, your prejudices are showing.' She rose to her feet. 'I must be off home now, especially as I shall be out tomorrow afternoon; I'm very busy, you know.'

Billy felt the old creeping feeling of being inferior to Delmai, needing to please her, keep her happy. When they'd lived together in the small house in the mining village of Carig Fach, she had tried to adapt to his way of life. She'd washed dishes, cooked his meals, she even began to look like a miner's wife, but somehow she'd always retained her air of aloofness, a cut above the rest of the community.

Well, he didn't have to put up with that sort of attitude now. He was successful in his own right, well-thought-of in the business world and trusted by Mary Sutton to handle her not inconsiderable investments in Sweyn's Eye.

'I'm sure you are busy,' he said smoothly, 'though not too busy to put in an appearance next week, I trust?' His voice was edged with sarcasm and Delmai glanced at him uncertainly.

'Oh, Billy, don't be an old grouch.' She moved towards him and touched his cheek. 'You know I didn't mean it that way. I love being with you but this week there's just so much happening in my life.'

'I suppose you have a fitting with your dressmaker and an appointment with your hairdresser – all important events in your calendar, I expect.' He grasped her wrist. 'What exactly do you want, Delmai? A lover, or are you just using me as a means of access to our daughter?'

She drew away from him. 'If you must know I have to go along to the doctor's with my husband in the morning,' she said sharply. 'Rickie has been having some trouble with his breathing and, naturally enough, I'm concerned about him.'

Billy shook his head. 'So concerned that you slipped out to meet me. Yes, I can see you are trying hard to play the role of a good wife but that isn't exactly your scene, Delmai. How long will it take you to understand yourself?'

He picked up his coat. 'I'm leaving now – it wouldn't be good for us to be seen out in the street together, would it?' He paused at the door. 'I'll leave you to pay the hotel bill.'

He chuckled as he descended the thickly-carpeted stairs – Delmai had been outraged at the prospect of having to demean herself and go to the desk-clerk. Well, it would teach her not to be so high and mighty.

As he drove home, Billy was thoughtful. Had he been foolish getting caught up again with Delmai, beginning a relationship that could go nowhere? But she had been so sweet at first and it had been she who had taken the initiative, approaching him in the street, making love to him with her eyes, whispering innuendoes in his ear. She had been exciting, making him feel youthful again but now, after only a few months, she was changing her tune, calling meetings off and, when they did meet, making excuses not to go to bed with him.

At Spinner's Wharf he stopped the car and stepped into the roadway. Down below him the stream that drove the mill meandered through the trees, making a rushing sound he found distinctly soothing.

He had spent some happy days at the mill keeping company with Gina, learning to know her. During the war she had been his life-line, his link with home, writing him letters, sending him parcels. She deserved faithfulness and he'd given her nothing but betrayal.

It was some years now since the mill had been sold and Gina had moved quite happily to the small house at the foot of Constitution Hill. She had expected they would be married then, but somehow Billy was fearful of taking the final step.

He returned to the car and drove towards town. He would go to Gina, stay the night, talk to her, make plans – she deserved to be his wife and it was about time he forgot about living on his own and married her.

She was sitting in the sun-filled parlour. She had changed very little in the past few years: her hair was still glossy, her eyes bright – she was a wonderful, wholesome woman and he should be going down on his knees and thanking God for her love. Perhaps, though, it was her very wholesomeness that he feared. Was it only to tramps he could give his passion?

'Hello, Billy love.' Gina rose and kissed him, just like a wife. 'You've just missed Cerianne, she's gone out to a concert at the church hall.' She smiled. 'Don't worry, our Dewi's gone with her, he'll see she comes to no harm.'

'He's a good boy,' Billy said, 'he's like a brother to Cerianne.' He sat in a chair and stretched his feet out to the fire. 'But I swear that Dewi grows more like his father every day.'

Gina nodded. 'Aye, Heinz will never be dead while Dewi's alive.' She smiled somewhat sadly. 'The only thing missing is the strings of brightly coloured wool in the boy's springy hair. A big clown Heinz used to look some days, mind, with his apron all covered in dye; at least that's what your sister used to say.'

She moved to the mantelpiece. 'Oh, while I remember, there's a letter from your Rhian.' Gina slipped the pages of notepaper from the envelope. 'She and Mansel Jack are doing fine, there's another baby on the way to keep their little girl company and the spinning business is booming.' She handed him the letter. 'Here, read it while I go and make us a cup of tea.'

He sat looking at his sister's handwriting, remembering how radiant Rhian had been when she had married her Yorkshire mill owner. She was a lucky girl; love such as that didn't come to many.

Gina brought in a tray and set it on the table. 'Here, have a cup, Billy and a Welsh cake; I made them fresh this morning.' She glanced at him playfully. 'Make someone a good wife I would, boyo.'

He got to his feet. 'I was going to talk about just that subject.' He smiled and no one would have guessed his enthusiasm was a little forced. 'I want us to name the

138

day. It's long since overdue and I should be whipped for keeping such a fine woman as you waiting.'

She looked up at him in surprise. 'I was only joking, mind,' she said, 'but if it's naming-the-day time then I'm glad; I can't say I've relished the role of being a kept woman.'

Billy took her in his arms. 'You know you've always been much more than that to me,' he said softly. He kissed her and there was warmth and love – but where was the passion? Somehow it had always been an element lacking in their relationship. But then most married couples could say the same thing, he thought ruefully.

She leaned back in the circle of his arms. 'Yes, I know you love me, Billy, and yet you've always gone back home to your own house in the nights. I haven't known much about the happiness of waking beside you in the mornings.'

'Well, we'll alter that soon, very soon.' He released her. 'Let's have this tea then, shall we?'

She smiled and ruffled his hair as she passed his chair. 'You've been a bad man in your time, Billy Gray: going to jail, running around after women. I don't know why I fell in love with such a tom cat.' She returned to her seat, cup in hand. 'Remember that little flossie you once had – Doffy, wasn't it?' She smiled. 'You were a fool being taken in by such a one.'

He fidgeted self-consciously. It was as though Gina could read through him and knew that he'd seen the girl only this afternoon. Women were strange intuitive creatures.

'Aye,' Gina continued, 'I paid her back, though – went round all the pubs telling the men she had a bad sickness. I bet it was a long time before she had any customers after that.' Gina giggled like a young girl at the memory of her own daring.

'How could I ever forget?' Billy said drily and, setting down his empty cup, he got to his feet.

'I want to take Cerianne out with me, say, this time next week,' he said. 'I can let her know we're going to get wed at last.' He moved to the door. 'Tell her I'll call for her.'

Gina followed him to the front step. 'That'll mean her missing her afternoon at work, but then I don't suppose it matters for once.'

Billy kissed her and slid into the driving seat of his car. 'See you then,' he said but Gina remained silent, watching him as he drove away. He wondered just what was going on in her mind.

11

Dawn stretched rosy fingers over the town of Sweyn's Eye; the calm sea in the curve of the shore shone redly in the spring sunshine. It was a clear, sparkling day and Luke told himself he should be feeling on top of the world.

Last night, Peta had received him with open arms, all her ill humour vanished.

'There's a silly goose, I am.' She had hugged him close. 'Me being all horrid and you working so hard to make a living for us, ashamed of myself I am, mind.'

Ironically, Luke's thoughts had centred not on his wife but on Katie Murphy. He recalled vividly the look of her, the scent of her and more, her vulnerability in the face of her brother's aggression, a vulnerability that was so appealing because basically Katie was so strong.

He stared out at the grassy lawns and the ancient trees surrounding his house and instead of his usual feeling of satisfaction there was a sense of anxiety; to keep up his standard of living he needed to produce coal and that was becoming more of a problem as the talk of strikes increased. And yet Luke was determined that he would employ not only a new haulier but a young boy as well. The coal was there, it only needed bringing out of the ground.

Behind him in the bed, Peta stirred, her arms stretched out as though she were a small kitten. Luke smiled at her, noticing with a feeling of sadness that she was still pale and much too thin. The loss of the baby had taken its toll on her health.

'You look tired,' he said moving towards her. 'It wouldn't be a bad idea if I asked Doctor Soames to call and see you.'

'Men!' Peta said scornfully. 'Always fussing. I'm right as rain! Go on you, off to work, and don't worry about me.'

He bent forward to kiss her brow and for a moment she put her arms around his neck, and clung to him.

The kitchen was cool, the flagged stone floor reluctant to absorb the sun's early rays. Hattie was still in bed, though usually she was up and about long before Luke.

He bent over the stove. The embers were still burning beneath the dampening of small coal he'd added the previous night and, sighing with relief, he stoked it into life. At least he could make himself some tea before he left for work.

He cut some rounds of bread and a piece of cheese and put them into his snap box. He supposed he should feel aggrieved, for when Hattie was abroad she cooked him slices of bacon or cut into one of her meat and potato pies, but he did not begrudge her morning in bed for she was often awake in the nights seeing to Peta.

His wife called unmercifully on the good nature of the woman who had come with her from her parental home and Hattie, it seemed, was only too willing to be used, for she loved Peta as though she were her own daughter.

When he left the house the sun was warming the landscape, turning the sea from red to gold and casting dappled patterns through the trees onto the roadway. It was a good day, a fine sunny morning and why was it he thought of Katie as he climbed into his car? Did the red-gold of the sea remind him of her hair?

He drove uphill towards the Slant Moira, turning his mind to matters of business. With orders now coming in from all sides there was enough work to keep the mine in production for many months to come.

Now at last he was able to pay Charlotte the compensation he'd been promising her. His sister had borne her bereavement with dignity; she had been a provident housewife putting away money for a rainy day. Had she a premonition that she would lose her husband to the mine? he wondered, then dismissed the idea as fanciful.

Charlotte was essentially a sensible woman – look how she subsidized her savings by taking in lodgers. It pleased Luke to know his sister had found not only a source of income but a way of alleviating her loneliness.

Rory greeted him with a wave when Luke drove up the dusty, coal-strewn roadway towards the slant.

'*Duw*, boss, you're early enough. Couldn't you sleep?' He laughed good-naturedly. 'I expect that pretty young wife kept you going; I told you women were a mixed blessing, didn't I?'

Luke shrugged off his coat and pulled on his moleskin trousers then buckled the wide belt firmly around his waist. He had become more adept at mining the coal, priding himself that he would not ask his men to tackle anything he could not do himself.

Rory was suddenly serious. 'Things are looking bad, boss,' he said. 'The negotiations with the government are breaking down. We might see an all out strike in the next few weeks and if it comes it will be a beauty, the town will come to a halt.'

Luke made for the slant, the diamonds of coal crunching beneath his feet. He paused at the blackness of the mine entrance.

'Well it's not going to affect me too much,' he said firmly. 'I've not worked myself to a standstill making a good name for myself to see it all go down the drain with a capful of politics.'

Rory looked doubtful. 'I don't see how we can keep out of it, boss,' he said slowly, 'we'd be branded as blacklegs if we carried on working.'

Luke smiled. 'That's just too bad,' he said easily.

Rory shrugged and it was apparent he meant to say no more on the subject. 'Colliers have dug out a good few drams this morning,' he said after a moment, 'but we need another haulier, boss. The moving out of the coal is slowing the boys down, mind.'

'Anyone in mind?' Luke asked, knowing Rory well. The fireman pushed back his cap.

'*Duw*, I know just the man – a big Irish fella by the name of Jim O'Conner. Do us all right, he would, in spite of him not being Welsh.'

Luke smiled into the darkness. 'All right, then. You ask him to come up and see me,' Luke said and Rory's reply was swift.

'Done that, Luke. Told the chap to come round here about eight o'clock when we're having a bit of grub.'

There was a brief silence in the womb of the mine, a silence that suddenly falls upon a group of people in a crowded place, and then there followed the continuation of everyday sounds: steel upon coal, voices calling to each other, and the steady slap of water on boot as Luke walked.

The heading was a long road of darkness illuminated only by tiny shafts of light from the lamps the men carried. When he reached the seam, Luke paused and clipped his lamp to his belt; his muscle would be needed for helping to carry coal to the dram. Luke worked in silence, loading the coal, pausing now and then to pat the dust-caked neck of the pony and speak soothingly as the slabs of coal hit the wooden sides rocking the dram on the rails. But his thoughts were again of Katie – her silky gold hair, the scent of her. He couldn't seem to shake the sweetness of her from his mind. Luke worked mechanically, disregarding the ache in his back and the veins standing proud on his forearms. Mining was a man's job and there was no place for the weak or faint-hearted.

'Got to do a bit of blasting, Luke.' Rory's voice broke into his thoughts. 'Make a new seam up ahead.'

'Aye, right,' Luke replied, straightening to look around him. The Slant Moira was well organized, using the pillar and stall method of mining which involved a main heading which had seams turning off it at intersections like a network of streets. After each blasting, every corner turned towards a new seam needed to be shored up with waste and timber to support the roof. It was the collier who, with a prized axe sharpened and honed, lovingly cut the grooves in the timber, bound together to form a resistance to the weight of the rock above.

Luke squeezed past the dram and, talking softly rubbed the nose of the young pit pony. 'Good boy, Nappa, quietly now.' The pony was still spirited, nervous, fearing the stones and coal that sometimes rattled down from above. Unlike Cal, the big black horse who had worked in the mine for many years, accustomed to the gloom and the shouts of the men and the darkness that was all around, Nappa was still inclined to bolt at the least fright.

The colliers were hacking at the face, Gerry adding another slab of coal to the already-full curling box. The anthracite slipped, dislodging other pieces that fell back to the ground and Gerry cursed soundly.

'Lazy man's load,' Rory said laconically. Gerry, pushing the box before him, edged towards the opening of the two-foot seam and was delivered into the main heading like a baby coming into the world.

'Shut your mouth,' he said but there was no hostility in his voice. The men had worked together since they were boys and the mine was a close community where trust and respect played a large part in the safety of the working day.

'*Bore da*, boss,' Gerry said amiably, 'you only been here half-hour and I've done a day's work, and you not yet dirty. *Duw*, it must be good to be an owner instead of a worker.' His teeth gleamed in the light from Luke's lantern as Luke unhooked it from his belt and held the light higher.

'Aye, and you work for the money I pay you, not for love,' he said drily. 'How's the seam, looks rich enough?'

'Good seam, excellent, but then it's a fine mine this, boss,' Gerry replied. 'You had brains when you bought this piece of the mountain, coal just about falls out of the rock!'

Luke watched the collier heave the coal into the dram and waited until he had straightened up, hands on the small of his back, face creased with sweat.

'In that case, if getting coal is so simple, perhaps I should be paying you less wages,' he said, hiding a smile.

'*Duw*, only giving us one shilling and tenpence a ton now, boss, any less and we'd be on starvation wages.'

'Which is better than you'd have if you went on strike,' Rory said, looking over his shoulder. He had been boring a hole in the rock at the end of the heading in preparation for blasting, and was breathing heavily. 'Soup kitchens and thin bellies is all you could look forward to then.'

'Everything would be all right if that old buffer Baldwin boosts up the pay and profits,' Gerry said, 'but, watch you, there'll be another royal commission which will find in favour of pay-cuts – they always do,' he added thoughtfully.

'I'm ready for blasting, Luke,' Rory said, wiping the dust from his face. 'Why don't you all go and have a bit of breakfast?'

Luke sat at the door of the shed and stared out across the hillside. In the distance, he could see a figure toiling up the dusty road. The man's hair gleamed red in the sunlight and his shoulders revealed the straightness and easy movements of the young. He was probably the man who had spoken to Rory last night, Luke concluded.

He watched as the figure drew nearer, appearing to increase in size. There was something about him that puzzled Luke, as though he were vaguely familiar. The man crossed the rough ground and paused before Luke, smiling amiably.

'Good day, Luke,' he said, his tone easy. His manner, though respectful, was in no way subservient.

'It's you, Jim,' Luke said pleasantly, 'I thought there was something familiar about you when I saw you coming up the hill. Rory said you were looking for a job and I'll be glad to give you one, but have you any experience in the coal mining?'

'I've worked deep pits though not in a slant.' Jim thrust his hands into his pockets. 'I worked with the Murphy boys in a pit up north but I expect coal dust tastes the same wherever it comes from.'

Luke eyed Jim O'Conner thoughtfully. 'I hope Michael Murphy is not a pal of yours,' he said evenly.

Jim shrugged his big shoulders. 'I don't give a damn about him one way or another.' His tone was equally smooth and Luke stared at him for a long moment. The man was an enigma; it was difficult to read him but then he was only asking for the job of haulier which required only strength of muscle and a willingness to work. And there was something essentially trustworthy about the man. Luke nodded.

'The pay is four and sixpence a day; if you are willing and can put your back into a job you can start tomorrow.'

'That sounds fair enough, Luke,' Jim said, touching his cap. 'I'll sort out some working clothes by tomorrow.'

He made to move away but Luke stopped him. 'Jim, give my regards to Charlotte, tell her I'll be visiting her soon.'

Jim nodded and moved away easily down the hill without looking back.

From behind Luke, Gerry slipped over the loose stones, cursing a little. 'Rum sort of chap; here, take your tea, boss,' Gerry said and, turning, Luke took the cup the collier held towards him. 'Seen him before somewhere, but can't quite place him,' Gerry continued.

'Don't worry, he's all right.' Luke drank from the cup and the tea was hot and strong. 'That'll lay the dust, boss,' Gerry said, squatting beside Luke on the ground.

From within the bowels of the mine came the sound of blasting and the rumbling noise was like thunder echoing on the sunlit air. The pit-pony moved in agitation, hooves ringing against the rails.

'Take it easy, Nappa,' Luke said softly, 'you should be used to it all by now.' He patted the animal's neck that strained against the reins as Nappa shunted backwards, eyes rolling, pushing the empty dram almost off the rails.

'Get that beast down to the knackers' yard, boss,' Gerry said slowly. 'His sort causes accidents in the mine – nervous, like he is. *Duw*, I remember one horse – big grey, he was, kicked the sprags from the dram in the deep pit and the weight of the coal running into him broke his back. Odd creatures are horses, some of them without enough guts for facing danger.'

Rory approached Luke from the mouth of the mine. He was covered in dust but his eyes gleamed with the satisfaction of a job well done. 'Safe to go back in, now, Luke.' He wiped his brow with a scarlet handkerchief, le ving streaks of white against his skin. 'Get some good coal out of that seam, I should think.' Rory moved inside the shed. '*Daro*, I could murder a cup of tea. Shove over, boys, let the dog see the bone.'

Luke thrust his hands into his pockets. 'Right, boys, the dust should have settled by now so it's back to work. There's a lot of clearing out to be done before we can get at the coal.' As he moved towards the Slant Moira, Luke took a deep breath. In spite of all the hardships, it was a good feeling being his own boss.

Michael Murphy lifted the foaming glass of ale to his lips and stared over the rim at the man seated opposite him. It seemed that Jim O'Conner had wormed his way into the Slant Moira and got himself a job as haulier – which was exactly what Michael wanted.

'Sure you did well, Jim, you won't be sorry.' Michael was not altogether sure of the man; he was a bit of an enigma, newly-come from Ireland. He was related to the O'Conners from Emerald Court – Stella O'Conner was a fine old woman, a matriarch, who, in spite of her widowhood, remained calm and serene, holding sway over her daughters in the close-knit community they formed with their husbands. This man, Jim, though he had the golden hair of the O'Conners, had too a certain hardness, a steely quality in the eye that told Michael he could not intimidate him as he did most other men with whom he came in contact. Michael was hoping to learn something more about Luke Proud from Jim – it would be useful to have a man on the inside. There was no doubt Jim needed the job. He had very little money and what he had in his pocket Michael suspected came from the largesse of the loyal Stella. But Jim had taken up the idea of working at the Slant Moira perhaps a little too readily and Michael told himself he would have to be wary of this one. Nevertheless, he smiled at Jim as he congratulated him.

'Sure an' you must be happy to have got the job at the slant. Good thing for you that they needed men,' he said, and the unspoken inference was that Michael might need information from Jim sometime.

'It's work,' Jim said evenly and there was little gratitude in his tone. Michael settled back in his chair. Perhaps it was time he took matters a stage further.

'I'd like you to do something for me,' he said. 'Just keep your eye on this character Luke Proud.' He saw Jim's eyes half close and felt faintly uneasy. 'I have suspicions about him. He's hot-footing it after my sister and he's a married man.' It sounded feeble even to Michael's own ears and he added quickly, 'and he's a Protestant to boot.'

'Sure is that a fact?' Jim said but there was something in his voice that gave Michael cause to suspect any information forthcoming would be charged for; it certainly wouldn't come as a favour.'

'Another pint of ale?' Michael asked. He found himself for once in the position of trying to ingratiate himself with a man, and he didn't like the feeling one little bit. Jim emptied his glass with one long swallow and placed it on the table.

'You please yourself.' He didn't look at Michael but stared around the room, his clear eyes alert as though taking everything in. Michael moved to the bar, clenching his teeth in anger. Jim O'Conner might think he was a big man, a hard man even, but he had not yet seen the length and breadth of Michael Murphy. Let him once step out of line, be a little too clever and he would soon learn he was not dealing with a weakling.

In some ways, Michael was sorry he'd befriended the man. He'd been sitting on his own in the public bar of the Dublin when Michael had first approached him. He'd recognized Jim at once for they had worked together in one of the big pits up north. He'd kept the man company in spite of a certain lack of response and he'd even gone so far as to suggest a job up at the Slant Moira. Yet today, when he'd seen Jim again in the bar of the Mexico Fountain there had been no air of gratitude – indeed, there was almost a feeling of hostility about the man.

Still, he was a better friend than enemy and could prove useful, so Michael carried the foaming glasses of ale back across the room. But the chair where Jim O'Conner had been sitting was empty and, in a fury, Michael slammed the glasses onto the table sending eddies of ale running across it to spill in a cascade on the sawdust-covered floor.

He left the bar in a temper, his hands clenched into fists and looming large in the forefront of his mind was the fear that in Jim O'Conner he had not made the friend he'd wanted but the enemy he dreaded.

Jim walked back quickly towards Canal Street, his hands thrust into his pockets. He disliked Murphy intensely, had never liked him, but tonight the man had proved what a miserable creature he really was. Jim had almost laughed in the man's face as it became clear that Murphy expected him to act as an informer, spying on Luke Proud's activities.

Jim had not bothered to correct Murphy's assumption that it was he who had pointed him in the direction of the job at the Slant Moira. The man clearly had no idea Jim was actually lodging with Luke Proud's sister.

As Jim let himself into the house on Canal Street, the warmth of the atmosphere closed in around him like welcoming arms. He felt completely at home there and Charlotte's young boys seemed to accept both him and Sheila. Yet, sadly, his sister had not been entirely happy since she had left the green fields of Ireland behind her.

In the kitchen, Charlotte was alone. She glanced up and smiled as she took another cup from the pantry. 'You must have smelled the teapot,' she said warmly.

'Sure 'tis quiet in here – the boys in bed, are they?' Jim seated himself at the table, stretching out his legs to the warmth of the fire.

'Aye.' Charlotte grimaced. 'I'm having some peace at last and that's only because Sheila volunteered to tell my sons a story. Talk about bribery and corruption!'

Jim leaned forward, elbows resting on the red and white gingham table-cloth. 'She's very fond of Fred and Denny,' he said thoughtfully. 'I sometimes think if it wasn't for them she'd have gone off home by now.'

Charlotte sat opposite him and he couldn't help noticing the shapeliness of her breasts beneath the neat blouse. He looked away quickly as she spoke.

'I sense she's not happy here but I hope she'll stay – I hope both of you will stay, Jim.' She said his name shyly, he noticed, and there was a rosiness in her cheeks as her eyes met his.

'I'll not budge from here,' he said reassuringly. 'I know when I've got a good home, don't you worry.' He paused as she poured him a second cup of tea.

'I took your advice, Charlotte,' he said. 'I've been to the Slant Moira to see your brother and he's given me the job of haulier. I'm to start tomorrow.'

Charlotte's eyes gleamed. 'There's good news! I think you and our Luke should get on well together, though working the coal doesn't suit everyone, mind.'

'It suits me well enough,' Jim said slowly. But for how long would Luke Proud keep the slant open, he wondered? One of the TUC boys had come down from London and he was convinced that trouble, big trouble, was brewing in the coal field. Later tonight there was a meeting of the

151

FED and the TUC members to discuss whether to support an all-out strike. But he kept his thoughts to himself; it was pointless to give Charlotte cause to worry about her brother at this stage.

'I shall have to go out again,' he said. 'I might be late so if you would be so kind as to leave me the door-key I shall lock everything up when I get in.'

'Don't worry about that,' Charlotte said quickly. 'There' no cause to lock doors around these parts.'

Jim frowned. 'You are too trusting, Charlotte. Perhaps you'd humour me by allowing me to slip the bolts across when I come in.'

Before Charlotte could reply, Sheila entered the kitchen, her usually-pale face animated and warm with colour.

'Those boys of yours are real comic-turns!' she said. 'Especially that little Denny – corrects me if I dare to tell a story wrong, so he does.'

Charlotte rose to her feet. 'You're too good to them, Sheila. They'll wear you out if you're not careful.' She moved to the hob where an enamel casserole dish simmered at the edges of the fire along with several saucepans.

'I think we're all in need of a good dinner,' she said and as she lifted the lid of the casserole dish, the appetizing smell of lamb permeated the room.

Jim watched Charlotte's neat movements with appreciation. It was a lucky day for both himself and his sister when Sheila had found them lodgings in the little house in Canal Street.

Later, when Jim made his way down to the snug of the Mexico Fountain, he found himself thinking of Charlotte's face, flushed from the heat of the fire, her hair curling around her fine cheekbones. She was a beautiful woman, but he must not allow himself to forget that she had only recently been widowed.

*

The hubbub of voices reached Jim even before he entered the smoky atmosphere of the snug.

'Wait a minute, men.' Rory the fireman from the Slant Moira was on his feet. 'Don't be hasty now.'

'Hasty, he says – hasty! Why, man, if we go any slower we'll come to a full stop.' The voice from the crowd was familiar and Jim caught sight of Gerry, one of the colliers from the slant, who was smiling wryly, a pint of ale in his hand.

'Yes, but we can't just down tools on our own, mind,' Rory said. 'We'd look soft if nobody else got involved in the strike.'

Rory caught sight of Jim and waved at him frantically. 'You're a sensible man, Jim O'Conner – what do you say about us men of the town going out on a limb by ourselves, then?'

Jim moved to the centre of the room. 'Sure Rory is right, if we act now we'll act alone,' he said. 'I've made a point of finding out what's going on in London and the latest is that the *Daily Mail* was going to put out an article condemning the idea of a general strike.' He held up his hand as Rory attempted to speak. 'Wait. The print workers are standing by the working man and refusing to go to set up the type.'

A cheer went up from the men and Jim held up his hand. 'We'll be on strike soon enough but until it's official, stick by your jobs, men.'

'Sure an' who do you think you are to tell us what to do, O'Conner?' Michael Murphy swaggered up to Jim. 'How is it you know so much about what's going on? Could it be that you're a government man yourself?'

Jim thrust his hands into his pockets. 'If you can't talk sense then button your mouth,' he said, his eyes never leaving Murphy's face. 'If I was a government man I would be living in a fine house up on the hill not boarding in rooms in Canal Street.'

'That could all be a cover.' Michael raised his voice against the jeers of the men. 'All right, then, be fools if that's what you want.' He gave Jim a venomous look, then turned and pushed his way through the crowd.

'I'd be careful of that Murphy fella.' Rory, who had moved towards Jim, tapped his forehead meaningfully. 'When the drinks in with Michael Murphy the sense is out,' he said.

'I can handle Murphy,' Jim said easily. He raised his voice. 'Enjoy your beer for tonight, men,' he said, 'because next week you might not be able to dip your hand into your pocket and bring out any money.'

As he walked up to the bar, Jim felt a sense of sadness. The men were all set to stick by their rights, to fight for what they believed in, but nothing was achieved easily. This strike could spread out of all proportions, and should that happen it could alter the lives of every man, woman and child in Sweyn's Eye.

12

Mali Richardson sat near the open window staring down into the garden where her two children played. Their voices – young, eager – rose and fell on the soft air and Mali sighed contentedly. Life had treated her kindly: she had a fine family and a husband she loved as much now as when they'd first met. She could see him in her memory so clearly, standing tall against the backdrop of green earth and ageing headstones in the grounds of Dan y Graig cemetery. He had stared down at her, his violet-blue eyes taking in every detail of her appearance. She was sixteen, with a cloud of dark hair hanging to the shoulders of her plain dress and she had been tearful, in mourning for her mother. He too had come to bury his dead and grief had seemed an instant bond between them.

And then she had heard his name called loud and cutting on the still evening air and anger poured through her. He was Sterling Richardson, owner of the copper company, the man responsible for dismissing her father, Davie, so heartlessly. She had flung accusations at Sterling, told him that Davie had stayed off work only to look after his sick wife. Sterling had not commented on her wild words but, later, her father had been reinstated at his old job of ladler in the copper sheds.

Mali brushed back a stray hair and tucked it behind her ears, smiling at her memories. She had stunned the town by marrying the copper boss and she had regretted none of it since.

They were both now caught up in the affairs of the town – Sterling had become a councillor and she served on more than one charitable committee. Mali found she had become something of a do-gooder, and she smiled ruefully at the thought. She had never imagined in those far-off days when she lived at Copperman's Row that she would be in a position to help the less fortunate people of the town – indeed, she had thought herself one of them once. But now she was able and most willing to give practical help at the home for unmarried mothers on the wooded outskirts of Sweyn's Eye. She rose from her chair and glanced at the ornate clock on the mantelpiece. She was meeting Mary Sutton in town in just over half an hour and here she was, dreaming her life away. But it had been the return to Sweyn's Eye of her old friend Mary that had invoked thoughts of the past.

She hurried upstairs to the bathroom and quickly dashed water over her face and wrists. She paused to stare at her reflection in the mirrored walls and saw a woman of thirty-two with the same cloud of black hair (cut short now) and the green eyes a little more lined, perhaps – the progress of time was so difficult to analyse and yet she was so very different to the young girl who had first fallen in love.

There she was, day-dreaming again. She brushed her hair and swung away from the mirror, walking over the soft carpeting of the large landing into the bedroom she shared with Sterling. It was a high-ceilinged, gracious room with large windows that looked over the sea far below. Mali loved the house and yet she knew it was not bricks and mortar that made a home but people bound together in love.

'There's soft I'm getting in my old age.' Her thoughts spoken out loud jolted her into movement. She picked up a light cashmere cardigan from the bed and hurried down the stairs; she would be late if she didn't put a move on, she chided herself.

She stepped into the Austin that was Sterling's latest gift and wondered at her own temerity in driving such a gleaming monster. She had found a ready response to handling the car, a natural facility for conquering the intricacies of driving, which surprised her. She was not, like Mary, a naturally independent, ambitious woman but the thought of the freedom the car afforded her was incentive enough to make her try to master it.

She drove down into the town and felt the sun warm on her face through the glass of the windscreen. It was a good day to be out, a fine spring day and she would enjoy taking tea with Mary in the emporium her friend once owned. When she drew the Austin to a stop at the kerb, the doorman approached and assisted her onto the pavement. She felt the hard stones beneath her feet and stepped quickly into the smart foyer of the emporium. It had all changed now – the green leafy plants in china jardinières were gone and a trelliswork covered in creeping plants had taken their place. The tearooms were different too – now there were no snowy linen cloths and vases of flowers; instead, the rooms were furnished with functional wrought-iron tables and hard iron chairs, offering no inducement to linger over a pot of tea or a cup of coffee, which was perhaps the reason why the rooms were half-empty.

She saw Mary at once. She had scarcely changed – still the same regal bearing; and there was little, if any, grey in the glossy sweep of her hair. Mali raised her hand in welcome and moved forward quickly into her friend's embrace.

'There's lovely to see you again,' Mali said softly, 'and you still looking like the same Mary I knew when I was sixteen.'

They seated themselves and Mary smiled a little wryly. 'Perhaps not quite the same,' she said and her voice now held a slight trace of an American accent. 'When I met you in the laundry, I was plumper and my hair was straightened with all that steam.' She smiled. 'And I was a dragon – Big Mary you all used to call me, don't think I didn't know!'

Mali leaned across the table and touched Mary's hand. 'Yes, but it was an affectionate name,' she said defensively, 'we all respected and admired you, Mary; and with good cause – you certainly made a success of your life. Look how rich you have become.'

Mary lifted her hand, attracting at once the attention of a waitress. She had always carried an air of authority, Mali remembered, and the years had not diminished it. She looked more closely at Mary. There were faint lines of strain around her generous mouth and the black dress she was wearing took something from her pale complexion, so that it appeared almost sallow. Widow-black did not suit her.

'There's sorry I am about Brandon,' Mali said softly, 'I hope I'm not rushing in where angels fear to tread, but I can imagine how devastated you must be.'

Mary sighed. 'It was a relief in the end, Mali. We had mourned together for a long time and when he went I was glad for him to be at peace.' She turned to the waitress with something of her usual briskness.

'We'll have a pot of tea for two and I think some Welsh cakes. Will that suit you?' She paused, waiting until the woman with her black dress and tiny crisp apron had disappeared, then she looked directly at Mali.

'You're as much in love as ever.' It was almost an accusation. 'You don't have to tell me, I can see it in your face.' She leaned closer. 'Yours is a marriage that has never faltered – not for you and Sterling doubts and infidelities.' She smiled. 'It restores my faith in human nature.'

'Don't talk soft,' Mali said quickly, 'Sterling and I are as human as the next person. We shout and quarrel, and I have been known to storm out on him, threatening to leave him forever. We're ordinary, Mary, just people.' She didn't want Mary to think of her as above reproach; it somehow placed a barrier between them. 'We've been lucky,' she said, 'Sterling and I have been strong enough to survive our differences, but there's not magical mystery abut our relationship, I assure you.'

The waitress placed the tea on the table. The Welsh cakes were still hot from the griddle, smelling spicy and rich and evoked for Mali vivid memories of life at home in Copperman's Row with her mam baking cakes over the fire. But that was when life was good before her mother became ill.

'I must be getting old,' Mali said softly, 'that's all I seem to be thinking of today is my childhood.' She sighed. 'We had our good times, Mary, didn't we?' If Mali's voice was a little wistful, Mary appeared not to notice it.

'Good times and bad, as always,' she said practically. 'You came from a respectable home, mind, with a mother and father who loved you.' Mary's gaze was direct. 'I was born in a hovel, Mali, with a mother too dazed by drink to care about me or my little brother. It was me who brought Heath up, who bought us the first real home we ever had, me who nursed him when he was sick.' Mary frowned suddenly. '*Duw*, you've got me at it now Mali Richardson, thinking about the past doesn't do any good, and we're like two clacking old women biting our gums over our memories. Let's hope there's a lot of living for both of us still to come yet!'

There was a silence except for the tinkling of cups as Mary poured the tea. It was a strange day, Mali thought, a day for looking back. But Mary was right, it did no good; looking forward was the only way to live.

'My children are quite grown up now, Mary.' Mali tried to bring the conversation back to life, for both she and Mary seemed to be in the grip of past tragedies. 'I suppose your Stephan will have grown beyond recognition by now.'

Mary glanced at her. 'He's still blind,' she said abruptly. 'I suppose I'll always blame myself for the accident. If I hadn't been driving along in such a hurry, I might have taken more care.'

Mali felt a sense of shock – she had forgotten that the boy was blind. How could she have been so insensitive?

'I'm sorry, Mary,' she said quickly, 'but don't take on all the guilt, things are never that simple.' Why did her words sound so trite and shallow? 'Is there any hope that Stephan might one day recover?' she asked.

'According to Paul Soames there is,' Mary replied. 'He thinks Stephan could regain his sight just as suddenly as he lost it.' Her shoulders drooped. 'But I've almost given up hope. Do you know the pain of seeing your son stumble about in a world of blackness? How can I not blame myself?'

Mali bit her lip, the reunion with Mary was not turning out very well. Why was it that the wrong words were spoken, ill memories revived? She had meant the meeting to be so happy but then, she admitted to herself, she had always been a little naïve. People changed – life forced them to change – and somewhere along the line a little bitterness must creep in. She had wanted to tell Mary all about her work with unmarried mothers, the joy she found in helping to bring families together, but it seemed now that such talk would sound smug and a little boastful.

'Have you seen anything of Katie Murphy?' Mali asked in an effort to break the strained silence. 'Her mother has only recently passed away but I believe Katie's brothers have returned home and are helping in the fish shop.' She did not add that in Sterling's opinion Michael Murphy had turned out to be a thoroughly unpleasant man, it didn't somehow seem the tactful thing to say.

'I saw Katie some weeks back, just briefly,' Mary said. 'She's looking a little bit pinched and under the weather but just as pretty as she always was, mind.'

Mali sighed with relief, it seemed the awkward hiatus in their conversation was over. 'Katie's had such sadness in her life,' Mali continued. 'She lost Will Owen all those years ago when she was a young girl and then when she married Mark she lost him too.' She sighed softly. 'Now with Mrs Murphy gone it seems to me to be the end of an era; the old woman appeared indestructible somehow.'

Mary poured more tea and helped herself to a Welsh cake. 'Wasn't there talk about Katie and Ceri Llewelyn getting married?' she asked, breaking into the soft pastry with her finger tips.

'Yes, they were promised. There was a lovely party with a fiddler playing fine music in the street,' Mali said, 'but it all came to nothing. Ceri married Mona, a little mousy girl who used to help out in the ferry house. Katie went away for a time then to stay with Rhian Gray and her husband in Yorkshire.'

Mary leaned back in her chair, brushing the crumbs from her skirt. 'Perhaps Katie, like me, is not destined to find happiness with a man,' she said quietly.

Mali suddenly felt impatience burgeon and grow within her, she was weary of tiptoeing round subjects that might hurt or offend Mary. 'Rubbish!' she said abruptly. 'We make our own destinies and you above all people should know that. Just look around you – you built up this emporium alone and you chose to sell it off and go abroad.' She paused for breath. 'I'm sorry, Mary,' she continued, her voice falling into the astonished silence, 'but you are turning into a difficult, moody woman and I've been afraid to open my mouth in case I offend you. Wake up and see what you've got instead of moaning over what you think you've missed in life. I think you've been blessed – you've had a fine husband and you still have his son to love; you are wealthy; able to afford a lovely home and all the comforts, which is a lot more than most people have, including our friend Katie.'

She leaned back breathlessly, expecting Mary to turn and berate her. Mary said nothing, staring down at the wrought-iron table-top for a long time and then her eyes, clear and direct, met Mali's.

'You're right, mind,' she said softly, 'I'm filled with self-pity and I should be ashamed of myself.' She smiled then a little wickedly. 'But you have changed too. You've become a little complacent – so sure of your love for Sterling and his for you that it blinds you to the problems women like me have to face. But underneath it all, we're still the same, insecure girls we once were, straining to prove something to the world.' She reached forward and clasped Mali's hand. 'It's a true friend who speaks the truth, Mali, and I'm glad you've done that for me today.' She rose to her feet. 'I'm going home now to my son, to look on his face so like that of his father and thank God for what I still have.'

Mali watched Mary sweep gracefully from the room. Her head was high, her shoulders straight: she was regal and lovely; and there was not a shadow of doubt in Mali's mind that if she wanted, Mary could find herself a husband tomorrow.

Sighing she left some coins on the table and moved to the door. It was about time she was leaving, too, for she had made up her mind to visit Katie Murphy. After her strong protest to Mary, she was aware of how little she herself had done to keep in contact; it was all well and good to give help to strangers but there was a lot to be said for keeping up with old friends as well.

Within the dim kitchen of Murphys' fresh fish shop, at the back of the house and away from the warm spring sunshine, Katie sat as though transfixed, staring up at her brother Michael.

'I know Luke Proud's chasing after you!' he said. 'It's the usual story – a boss man after a bit of skirt on the side, and you, my girl, are fool enough to fall for all his claptrap.'

'I've told you,' Katie said at once, 'there is nothing wrong happened at all between Luke Proud and me, sure and I'll swear that on my mother's grave.'

'Don't take me for a fool!' Michael said sourly. 'He creeps up here like a thief in the night and you say there's nothing going on? Well, I'll have my own back on that rattlesnake and I can start by telling his wife about his little side-piece.'

Katie rose to her feet in sudden anger. 'Have you no shame, Michael Murphy? Our mammy would turn in her grave if she could hear you now! Get out and leave me alone or I'll run for the constable, so I will.'

'Just you think over what I've said. I want this shop and I mean to have it one way or another.'

The door slammed behind him and Katie sighed in relief. Michael had gone for the moment but he would be back, there was nothing surer than that.

She moved from the kitchen along the passageway towards the shop, staring round her with an undeniable feeling of pride. She had called the carpenter to build shelves along both sides of the room; the old slab had

162

been torn out to be replaced by a fine wooden counter and the shop was ready now for her new venture: from now on, Murphys' would be selling anything and everything except fish.

Soft sunlight filtered in through the window and the shop looked pleasant and welcoming. The smell of fish that had pervaded the premises for as long as Katie could remember was gone. She had scrubbed the place vigorously with hot water and soda and placed fresh sand on the floor. All was ready for the new stock of tinned foods, bacon and coffee and there was even a cabinet for the display of wool and knitting-needles.

Katie opened the door and a cooling breeze drifted towards her, lifting her hair from her brow. If only Michael would go away and leave her in peace, she would be happy.

Along the pavement, just rounding the corner, she saw a slight figure with dark hair bobbing silkily in the soft air. Katie smiled to herself – Mali was coming to visit. Perhaps company would help eradicate from her mind the unpleasant memories of Michael's threats.

'Sure there's fine you're looking, Mrs Richardson,' she said with mock formality, 'come to view my new shop, have you? Well you just wait, I might even rival Mary Sutton before I'm through.'

The two women embraced and then Katie led the way back towards the kitchen.

'I've not lit the fire today,' Katie apologized, 'so there's no hope of us having a quiet cup of tea.' She smiled. 'What I can offer you, though, is some dandelion and burdock cordial, cool from the pantry.'

She watched as Mali sat in a chair, crossing silk-stockinged legs as elegantly as any high-society women.

'I've been meaning to come and see you for ages,' Mali said in her soft, musical voice. 'I had tea with Mary the other day and realized suddenly that I was losing touch with my old friends.'

'Sure, you needn't worry about that,' Katie said, 'we used to live in each other's pockets – grew up together we did, nothing can destroy all that. And I got you your first job in the laundry. Remember how thrilled you were that morning, trotting along Canal Street, longing to start the day's work?'

Mali laughed. 'It's catching,' she said and Katie raised her eyebrows questioningly.

'What's catching? Sure, Mali, you are talking in riddles.'

Mali placed her glass on the table. 'When I was with Mary, all we could think about was the old days – became quite maudlin, we did, and now I've got you at it.'

'Well, sure sometimes it's an escape from the difficulties of the moment to talk about the past.' She was not aware that she was sighing heavily until Mali leaned forward.

'Want to tell me what's wrong?' Mali's face was full of warmth and sympathy and Katie relaxed, smiling a little.

'Sure there's nothing anyone can do to solve my problems.' She smiled. 'Let's talk about more pleasant things. Tell me about your work with unmarried mothers, sure it must suit you down to the ground, you loving babies as you do.'

'I like it well enough,' Mali said softly, 'but there's sorry I am for the girls who have been let down by the man they love. Most of them have been put out by stern, unforgiving fathers. On the other hand, times are hard enough for working men trying to keep a family going – I can see that the thought of an extra mouth to feed would be frightening.'

'Sure things are not all that bad, are they, Mali?' Katie asked, leaning forward earnestly. 'This strike that everyone's on about – it will never come about; it's too big. It would involve all the country.'

Mali sighed. 'There's every chance of a strike, lovely,' she said wistfully. 'I know by the things I hear from the girls in the home that the menfolk are standing firm, this time there'll be no giving in to the bosses. The pits and everything else would come to a complete halt in the event of a general strike.'

'Sure it's a frightening thought,' Katie said, speaking her fears out loud, 'and our Michael will be in the middle of things.'

Mali looked at her in concern. 'You're very worried about him, aren't you?'

'Sure I'm worried,' Katie said. ''Tis not that Michael is on the side of the worker so much as he wants personal revenge on Luke Proud.'

'But why?' Mali asked. 'What has Mr Proud done?'

Katie shrugged. 'Our Michael got a bit rough with me one time and Luke put him out into the street. Michael is saying now that me and Luke are carrying on together and Michael is threatening to go to Mrs Proud and tell her.'

'Call his bluff!' Mali said. 'You have to otherwise you'll never be free of him.'

Katie saw the wisdom in her friend's words. Michael was a blustering bully, no one would ever believe him even if he did carry out his threat and tell Luke's wife a pack of lies about her husband.

'You're right sure enough. I can't give in to our Michael: not now, not ever, but how I wish he'd never come back to Sweyn's Eye.'

Katie watched as Mali put down her glass of cordial. 'Well, I suppose I'd better be going,' she said. 'I promised I'd visit my uncle Siona, he and his wife are so pleased to have a little sister for their boy Emlyn.'

It was strange, Katie thought, how everyone else's life seemed to run on a straight course – love, marriage and children – while she seemed destined to spend her life alone.

Mali, as always, seemed to sense her feelings. She reached out and touched Katie's arm. 'There'll be happiness ahead for you, I just know it in my bones,' she said smiling. 'Someone as beautiful as you won't be alone for ever.'

'I hope you're right!' Katie said. 'Though I don't know about being beautiful, I feel quite old and haggard these days.'

And yet that wasn't quite true. Lately, Katie had been feeling more vibrant and alive than for some time and she wouldn't admit the reason even to herself.

She went to the door with Mali and watched her depart along Market Street, a small-boned, elegant woman, and so warm a friend. Katie paused in the doorway, looking at the familiar sights around her, so familiar indeed that she'd almost ceased to see them. The end house where Dai used to sit playing his music was a saddler's now, with saddles and bridles hanging around the door. The smell of the leather reminded Katie of the days when Big Jim, the Murphys' old horse used to pull the cart around the streets.

She caught her breath in dismay as she saw the familiar figure of her brother striding towards her. Why was he returning so soon?

'I need money.' He spoke without preamble, pushing past her into the passageway and striding towards the kitchen.

Katie followed him. 'Sure an' what do you need money for, you're earning a good wage at the pit, aren't you?'

'I've been sacked,' he said, 'and I put the blame at the door of that bastard Proud. Thick as thieves with my boss he is and I can see him now putting in the poison about me.'

'That's silly!' Katie said at once. 'Why should Luke want you to get the sack?'

Michael caught her arm and twisted it suddenly. 'Don't back-talk me. I want some money to pay for my digs otherwise I'll have to come back here to live and I know you wouldn't like that.'

Katie stared at him without flinching. 'Just let me go, Michael, or by all the saints I'll have the police after you.'

He released her and stepped back. 'Aye, you would too – anything to stand by your lover. Well, you won't get away with it, either of you.'

He went to the teapot where Katie kept some loose change and shook out the contents onto the table.

'You'd better pray that I get a job and soon!' he said viciously as he turned, stamped along the passage and slammed the front door behind him.

Katie sank into a chair and realized her hands were shaking. It was one thing to decide to be brave but when confronted, as she'd been, with Michael's anger, she felt defenceless and afraid.

13

The sun was rising over the bay, streaking sea and sand with warm gold that became phosphorescent at the water's edge. The early morning air was fresh and clean and the only sound was the rushing of the waves against the shore and the calling of gulls wheeling high above the town.

Gina Sinman stepped cautiously along the watermark line of seaweed and flotsam, her head high, a bloom to her cheeks that had nothing to do with the fine morning air. At last, she thought, hugging her joy like a precious jewel, at last Billy had named the day – they would be married in September at St Jude's Church, poised near the top of Constitution Hill. It was not before time that Billy was proposing to make their union official, Gina conceded to herself; they were not bright eyed youngsters but folk fast approaching the middle years of life.

Her feet sank into the soft sand and she made her way towards the rippling sea where the outgoing tide left a harder, firmer sand. She paused and stared across the water to where Mumbles Head jutted outwards, grey rocks and green grass forming a patchwork of colour, and on the outer mound was the lighthouse that bravely faced the channel between Wales and Devon.

There had been many shipwrecks around the rugged coastline of Gower; some said there was a fortune in Spanish gold lying on the sea beds beyond Port Eynon and Rhosili. Gina sighed contentedly, she would forego all the Spanish gold, and settle for a small gold ring on her finger.

She turned and retraced her steps. The sun was rising higher in the sky and the youngsters would be awake and expecting breakfast. She warmed with pride, for her son Dewi was studying at the art college, doubtless following his father's love of colour and craftmanship. He was a handsome boy, tall like Heinz had been and at almost sixteen years of age, strongly built. Soon he would set up his own studio for taking photographs, an art of which Gina knew little and understood less, but then her son was a clever intelligent boy.

She was equally proud of Cerianne, who had recently begun working in a solicitor's office in town, her dainty fingers tapping away at a machine that produced a type-written sheet so neat and tidy Gina thought it quite magical. They were settled, both of them, and now was the time for Gina to begin thinking about herself.

The streets were coming alive, the shops opening their doors and the green grocer in Oxford Street was carrying his boxes of fresh fruit and vegetables onto the pavement. Gina, hurrying now, made her way through the small streets and towards the steep rise of Constitution Hill. Breathless, she let herself into the dimness of the passageway, coming face to face with Billy's daughter.

'There you are, Gina!' Cerianne kissed her cheek. 'I was worried about you, it's not like you to go out so early.' Gina took her arm. 'Come back to the kitchen – have a little cup of tea with me; you don't have to run off to work yet.' She opened the door and blinked in the shaft of sun slanting through the window. 'Dewi gone to the the college, has he?' Her question was unnecessary for it was obvious by the silence that her boisterous son was no longer in the house.

When she'd made the tea, Gina sat opposite Cerianne and smiled. 'You look so pretty,' she said softly. 'Have I ever told you how proud I am of you?' She leaned forward and took the young girl's hand. 'You're as dear to me as if you were my own daughter, you know that, don't you?'

Cerianne kissed her cheek. 'Of course I do, Gina, and I love you much more than I could ever love my real mother, whoever she is.' She frowned. 'Why has daddy never told me about her – is she so awful that he can't bring himself to speak of her?'

Gina took a deep breath, wondering at her foolishness in opening a subject that should have been left well alone. 'You talk to him about it, *merchi*,' she said. 'Perhaps it's about time he explained a few things to you.' She smiled suddenly. 'Come along now, you'd better be going – don't want to be late for work, do you?'

Cerianne rose quickly, glancing at the clock. 'Gosh, is that the time?' She smiled. 'I'll have to run all the way into town or I will be late.'

When Gina was alone, she stared at the clock ticking away on the mantelpiece and suddenly shivered. 'A goose walking over your grave, Gina girl,' she said to herself. 'Time you shook yourself out of your laziness and did some work.'

She carried the breakfast dishes to the sink and poured the steaming water from the kettle into an enamel bowl. She stood for a time, staring unseeingly at the congealed grease on the plates and wondering why, suddenly, when everything seemed to be going her way, she felt uneasy.

Later, she left the house and with a basket over her arm, made her way to the butcher's shop on the corner. She would buy a nice piece of topside of beef, cook it slowly until it was tender and serve it with cabbage and carrots. It would be a special treat for tonight, when she would announce her wedding plans. Not that any of it would come as a surprise – the children had grown used to discussions about marriage but now, Gina thought warmly, it was going to be more than talk.

She raised her hand in greeting to Big Eddie as he led his horse along the road. 'Leave me two hundredweight, there's a good man,' she called, and he lifted his cap in acknowledgement.

The floor of the butcher's shop was spread with sawdust and above the wooden slab hung great sides of beef. Gina, hearing a step behind her, turned, the polite smile vanishing from her face as she was confronted unexpectedly by Doffy. The girl looked as sluttish as ever in a brilliant red silk blouse and a dusty skirt. Her close proximity aroused emotions Gina would rather have forgotten.

She turned away, deciding to ignore the girl's presence, surprised to find that the pain of jealousy was still sharp after all this time.

It was some years since Billy had indulged in a fling with the girl; a foolish thing to do, to be taken in by a flossie, but then men had no sense when it came to women of that sort. She felt a touch on her shoulder and turned indignantly.

'Take your hands off me,' she said sharply, drawing back from the smell of gin on Doffy's breath.

'There's something I've got to say to you, Miss Hoity Toity.' Doffy's heavily-rouged cheeks and lipstick-coated mouth were garish in the morning sunlight.

'Well, I'm sure there's nothing I want to hear,' Gina replied, 'so I'll be obliged if you would just let me alone.'

Doffy sniggered and waited while Gina, hands shaking, bought a large piece of beef, scarcely glancing at it as she thrust it into her basket. She followed Gina from the shop and fell into step beside her.

'You'd better listen for what I want to tell is for your own good,' Doffy insisted, the feather in her hat dancing to and fro above her brow. She looked what she was – a cheap bawd and Gina suddenly felt sorry for her.

'Anything unpleasant usually is.' She sighed in resignation. 'Do you want money from me, is that it?' She edged the basket into a more comfortable position on her arm and waited.

'I want to tell you about Billy boy,' Doffy said leaning closer. 'He's not being straight with you – up to his old tricks he is, mind.'

Gina shook her head. 'It's no use, I don't believe a word of it. He had his fling with you and I don't think he'd be such a fool again.' She would have walked away but Doffy's next words stopped her in her tracks.

'Oh, it's not me you have to worry about – it's Miss Fancy Knickers, Delmai Richardson.' The name fell into the air like stones and Gina almost dropped her basket.

'I hope you can back up what you're saying.' Her voice was low. 'Otherwise you'll find yourself in trouble with the police, you flossie.'

Doffy smiled. 'Been taking Delmai Richardson to the Mackworth Hotel has Billy, lovely private suite of rooms too, mind, nothing but the best for such a rich lady.'

Gina fought back the waves of shock and faced Doffy stolidly though her knees were trembling. 'How do you know?'

'I saw them meet in the Lamb and Flag and then they went on to better things.' Doffy's laugh tinkled musically on the soft air. 'Seems she still hankers after Billy's manly charms. He is good in between the blankets, which I can testify to.'

Gina shook her head. The girl was simply trying to cause trouble. 'I don't believe you,' she said calmly, 'you've doubtless heard that Billy and I are to be married and you want to do your damnedest to hurt us – well, it won't work, sorry.'

Gina began to walk away but Doffy followed her. 'Don't take my word for it,' she said quietly, 'just go to Victoria Park this afternoon and you'll see them there, large as life.' Doffy's eyes were narrow slits of spite. 'And consider yourself paid back for what you did to me in the past, going round to my customers telling them I had a nasty disease. Thought you were so clever then, didn't you? But you are not looking so clever now, madam.'

Gina couldn't bear to look at the triumph in Doffy's face any longer. She hurried away back to the quietness of the house at the bottom of the hill. She sank into a chair and stared down at her hands and saw that they were trembling. Doffy was speaking the truth, she had to be, for there was such a look of gloating satisfaction in her eyes. Well, there was only one way to find out – she would go to the park and wait and watch, and she would find out if Billy was betraying her yet again.

Delmai Richardson stared at her reflection in the coolness of the hall mirror and smiled. She was still a sensuous, beautiful woman even though she had a teenage daughter and three strapping sons. Her hair was untinged with grey, her eyes bright, her smile an invitation.

Yet once she had dreaded the marriage bed, had been fearful of a man's embrace and it had been Billy Gray who had changed all that. Her eyes grew soft. It had been in the prison grounds that she had met him, a man with his hair just beginning to grow after being shaved to the bone. A handsome yet vulnerable man and something in him had reached out to touch her.

It was for Billy Gray that she had left her husband and home, discarded all the trappings of the rich and exchanged them for a spartan existence in a miner's cottage. She had known what it was to be poverty-stricken, a salutary experience which she did not propose to repeat.

She moved into the sitting-room where Rickie sat before a roaring fire, even on this warm morning. He held a glass of brandy in his hand and she noticed he was pale and sweating. He began to cough and she moved towards him with simulated concern.

'Still feeling under the weather, are you, darling? Shall I call the doctor for you?' Inwardly she was impatient with him. Rickie was such a baby when it came to sickness.

'Yes, call him in.' His voice was surprisingly weak and Delmai looked more closely at him. He was unusually pallid – his cheeks fallen into hollows – and beneath his eyes there were violet shadows. Perhaps this time he really was ill.

'I'm going into town; I'll call into the surgery and see Doctor Soames myself,' she said decisively, drawing on her gloves. 'We'll have him to look at you this evening.'

She dropped a kiss lightly on his forehead, and for a moment he clutched at her hand. 'Stay with me, Delmai,' he asked and in his eyes was a look of fear.

She disentangled herself. 'I shan't be long, darling,' she said gently. 'I wouldn't go out but it really is important.'

He hunched his shoulders and gazed into the fire, and she knew she was dismissed.

As she stepped out into the sunshine, she told herself she really wouldn't be long, but how could she give up what might be her only chance of meeting with her daughter? If she let Billy down this time, he would assume she had been merely acting on a whim and she knew him – he would not forgive her easily.

Her footsteps were light as she made her way towards the car. She would drive across to Mount Pleasant, speak to the doctor and then she could enjoy her afternoon with Cerianne without feeling a guilt hanging over her.

The doctor was out and Delmai hastily scribbled a note, handing it to the old woman who kept house for him. 'Make sure the doctor reads it,' she said imperiously and she was oblivious to the woman's sniff of derision as she closed the door and placed the note on the hall-table along with the rest of the mail.

The park was dappled with sunshine and a slightly tangy salt air drifted across the road from the bay. Delmai stood near the gate, staring anxiously, trying not to look too conspicuous. She wished Billy would hurry up and put in an appearance, for the last thing she wanted was to be spotted by a neighbour or someone who would quickly report back to Rickie.

And then she saw his tall frame as he moved between the crowds heading towards the slip. She held her breath, watching intently, waiting for a glimpse of her daughter. She was not disappointed. Cerianne was so very much like her – the eyes, the line of the cheekbone, the tilt of the head – Delmai would know her daughter anywhere.

She resisted the urge to dash forward and clasp Cerianne in her arms, instead she stood her ground, smiling politely as the couple drew near.

'Good afternoon, Billy,' she said softly, 'it's lovely meeting you again, and this charming young lady is your daughter?'

'I've told her,' Billy said gently. 'I saw no point in beating around the bush. Cerianne knows who you are.'

Delmai was taken aback. She longed for a sign from the girl, any sort of recognition but there was only a polite smile, such as would be offered to any stranger.

'I must sit down.' She moved to a bench and fanned herself with her gloves. She glanced covertly at Cerianne and was pleased to see the girl sit beside her, a look of concern in her eyes.

'I don't know what to say,' Delmai began breathlessly, 'it's just that I've wanted to see you so many times, longed to speak to you to explain how it was we were parted – oh, sweetheart, you're so like me. You are the daughter I've longed for every day since I was forced to leave you with your Aunt Rhian.' She thought she saw a softening in Cerianne's face and pressed home her advantage. 'I never wanted to be separated from you, it was all beyond my control, you see.' She doubted if Billy or Gina would have spoken ill of her, they would be too considerate of the girl's feelings for that.

Cerianne was studying her, head on one side, a smile lighting up her eyes. 'Yes, we are alike, even I can see that.' She leaned back against the wooden slats of the bench. 'And don't worry, I've been well-cared for. I couldn't have asked for a more loving home than the one I've had with Gina and Dewi.'

Delmai felt a small pang. This wasn't what she wanted to hear; she would have liked Cerianne to beg for Delmai's affection, to declare a wish to make a life with her natural mother. She sighed.

'I know your father has always provided for your every need,' she said, her eyes drinking in each detail of Cerianne's appearance. She longed to reach and touch the girl's hands, to kiss the young bloom of her cheek but she sensed that her daughter would shy away from such overt displays of affection.

'I hear you work in an office?' Delmai said, twisting her fingers together. 'I think you must be terribly clever.'

Cerianne smiled deprecatingly. 'No, it just needs training, that's all – it's something anyone could do.'

Delmai looked up at Billy, wishing he would go away and leave her alone with her daughter but he stood his

175

ground, a solid figure in the sunlight, and even if he sensed her thoughts it was clear he had no intention of acceding to them.

'Shall we take tea together?' Delmai asked. She had become suddenly aware that it was not wise to be seated out in the open with a man who had been her lover and with the girl who in anybody's eyes was clearly her daughter. Such a scandal there had been when Delmai had run away to live with Billy, who could offer her nothing but a bad reputation and a life of poverty in a mining village.

But their lovemaking had been beautiful. Billy had taught Delmai how to glory in the pleasure of the flesh but in the end even that had not compensated for the grinding, harsh poverty he had brought her.

'We'll go to the little coffee-shop near the beach.' Delmai rose to her feet, feeling secure in the knowledge that no one of her class would patronize such an unfashionable establishment. She glanced at Billy and had the grace to blush, for he read her well as was apparent by the derisive smile on his strong mouth.

It was dim in the coffee-shop after the bright sunlight outside and Delmai failed at first to see the man seated near the window. She took her seat and gestured for Cerianne to sit near her as she clasped the girl's hands lightly in her own.

'It's so good to meet you like this,' Delmai said breathlessly, 'I do wish I'd plucked up the courage to approach you before but I was afraid of being rejected, you see.' There was a little truth in her words but what she did not say was how busy she had been, how wrapped up in her coffee-mornings and afternoon teas and the minutiae of life as the wife of a respected businessman.

Cerianne smiled but made no comment and Delmai, a little discomfited, ordered mint tea and sat back in her chair, staring around; barely able to conceal her distaste. The place had sand on the floor and spartan wooden tables with ugly cast-iron legs. The window was streaked with grime and the entire establishment smelled of salt and tar.

She glanced towards the figure in the window and stiffened – it was the horrible little man from the Cooperative Movement, a sneak and a troublemaker if ever there was one. He had approached her recently requesting a donation for some scheme of his and she had sent him away at once, her manner abrupt, almost rude. He saw her glance and inclined his head. She looked away, dabbing at her forehead with a lace handkerchief. What harm could he do her? After all, she was in a public place taking tea, how could that be wrongly construed? And yet she felt uneasy as she turned her attention once more to her daughter.

'And tell me, are you walking out with a young man yet?' she asked and was pleased when Cerianne shook her head.

'No, I have to concentrate on my work, at least for the time being.' The girl seemed to have a maturity beyond her years. 'In any case, I hardly get out to meet any young men – Gina cares for me too well for that.'

The reply pleased Delmai. She didn't want Cerianne to be farmed out with any dullard; the girl was dainty and clever – in short, her mother's daughter. She would somehow see to it that the right young men were introduced to Cerianne. A great happiness encompassed Delmai. This, then, would be her great role, to place her daughter in a fine home with a rich husband to care for her. In this way she would mitigate the wrong she had done by abandoning the child in the first place. Not that she had wilfully done so, she told herself hurriedly; it had been a matter taken out of her hands completely, the act of a cruel fate, but she would make up for it. So enamoured was she with her plans that she did not see Alfred Phillpot slip out of his seat in the window.

'We'd better be going now,' Billy said, sitting uneasily on the wooden bench, glancing at the watch hanging on the thick gold chain across his waistcoat.

'Oh, no, I've not yet learned half of what I want to know about our daughter,' Delmai said softly. 'Please, Billy, just a little longer.'

'Well, all right, but let's get out of here,' Billy said impatiently, 'it's stifling.' He ran his hand around his collar and Cerianne leaned towards him in concern.

'Are you all right, daddy?' she asked, resting a small hand on his shoulder and in that moment, Delmai felt tears burn her eyes. There was such love between father and daughter and she wanted – no, was determined to share in it.

'Aye, there's nothing wrong with me, *merchi*,' Billy said, 'at least nothing a bit of fresh air won't remedy.'

Delmai followed Billy outside and caught Cerianne's arm as they crossed the busy Oystermouth Road towards the beach. Billy stood on a grassy dune and took deep breaths, watching his daughter walk down towards the sea, and there was a worried frown between his eyes.

'It's all right,' Delmai said gently, 'I know you so well. You are feeling you've been disloyal in bringing my daughter to see me but Gina would have been the first to agree to it, had you asked her.'

'Maybe,' Billy said, 'but I didn't ask her, I've deceived her, and you're right – I can't help feeling nothing but bad will come of it.'

Cerianne was retracing her steps, her eyes shining, and she had the bloom of youth in her cheeks. She was beautiful, Delmai decided, with a feeling of pride. Delmai moved towards her daughter and smiled warmly.

'Come along, let us talk just for a while.' They moved along the damp sand beside the sea and Delmai encouraged the girl to talk about herself, and listened, entranced, to the soft lilting voice, her resolve hardening. She would have a hand in her daughter's future, whatever it cost her. But after a time, Cerianne turned towards the spot where Billy stood waiting.

'We should get back, daddy,' she said softly. She smiled at Delmai. 'Perhaps we can meet again another time.' She was so gravely mature, so in control of her feelings that Delmai longed to hug her.

'I'm so proud of you,' she said instinctively, knowing the right thing to say. 'You are a credit to Gina and your father.' She turned and left the beach and made her way back to the road near the park where she had left her car, sighing softly as she started the engine. She had her daughter in her sights and catch her she would.

It didn't take her long to drive home. She parked the car and made her way into the coolness of the hall, her head spinning with plans for further meetings with her daughter and without Billy's dour presence if possible.

Rickie was in bed when she arrived home. She hurried up to his room and paused in the doorway, half hoping he was asleep but he raised his head when he heard her step.

'Why didn't you get the doctor as you promised?' he said, propping himself up on the pillow.

'Oh, darling, didn't he come?' She swept towards him, peeling off her gloves. 'I called at his surgery but he was out so I left a note.' She sat on the bed beside him. 'That woman I saw obviously didn't give Paul Soames my message.' She rested the back of her hand against his forehead. 'But you don't feel as though you've a fever, darling, so perhaps tomorrow will be time enough to call the doctor in.'

He seemed pale. His breathing was shallow and difficult, and there were deep lines running from nose to mouth. He stared at her almost malevolently.

'What have you been doing with yourself for the rest of the afternoon?' he asked, his voice thready and weak.

'Oh, nothing really, darling.' Her eyes flickered across his face and she sensed somehow that he knew exactly what she'd been doing. 'I had tea in some little coffee-house near the beach and walked a bit and then returned home. Is there anything wrong, Rickie?'

He grasped her wrist suddenly. 'Liar!' He tried to shout but he hadn't the strength. 'You've been with your lover, don't deny it!' He twisted her arm and she gave a small scream.

'Don't be silly, let me go – you're hurting me.' She tore her hand away from his grip and stood up, panting, trying to quell the rising panic that threatened to escalate into hysteria.

'You were seen,' he said. 'Alfred Phillpot took the trouble to come and tell me all about it – how you sat there with your lover and the bastard child you conceived by him. Have you no sense of decency, Delmai? Are you so stupid that you believed I'd never know?'

He struggled to raise himself from the bed, the veins standing out on his neck. 'I could kill you! I forgave you once and took you back but I'll not be cuckolded a second time.' He shook his fist at her. 'I won't let you get away with it, do you hear me?'

'Rickie, for God's sake control yourself; you're not well, you don't know what you're saying.'

He sat on the edge of the bed, glowering at her, his eyebrows drawn together and a line of blue appearing around his lips. 'I know what I'm saying,' he replied, breathlessly, 'I'm saying that my wife is a whore! But you shan't beat me. I'll change my will, I shan't leave you a penny of my money.'

'Rickie, please don't distress yourself.' She moved forward. 'Let me help you back into bed and then I'll send for the doctor, you look dreadful.'

'Get away from me, slut!' He pushed at her with all his strength and Delmai fell against the dressing-table, sending bottles scattering to the floor. The heavy perfume filled the air as Delmai tried to regain her balance.

Rickie gave a sudden, strangled moan and slid gently back against the covers. Slowly, with a feeling of dread, Delmai pushed herself to her feet. She stood quite still for a long time, afraid to move or think. She covered her face with her hands, wondering if she was trapped in some nightmare world from which she would shortly awake. At last, she forced herself to go to the bedside and she clenched her hands into fists, fighting the urge to run. After a time, she sighed softly and turned away, walking slowly towards the door. It had taken only one swift glimpse of her husband's ashen face to know that he was dead.

14

Jim O'Conner stood near the entrance to the Slant Moira, his hair gleaming in the sunlight. His shirt-sleeves were rolled above his elbows and from the belt of his moleskin trousers hung his miner's lamp. His expression was grave.

'Well, that's it, lads,' he said, his words falling harsh into the balmy morning air. 'It's a lock-out, a million men are out of work on this fine morning. Mark it well, for the first of May 1926 is a day to go down in history. Treachery by government, that's what we're facing, and will we sit down like tame cats under the iron fist, or will we fight like tigers for our rights?'

Rory was the first of the listening men to break the silence. He moved forward, pushing back his cap and scratching his head.

'But we don't work for no government, man,' he protested, 'we work for Luke Proud.' He gestured around him. 'What good would it do for a handful of miners like us to come out on strike, I ask you?'

Jim looked at him long and hard and Rory shifted uncomfortably. 'In a few days' time the TUC will bring out on strike another two and a half million workers – that's if the government will not see sense,' Jim said forcefully. 'It's true that Bevin and Thomas are moderate men but they will not simply stand aside and watch the Baldwin government make mincemeat out of the working man. We must all make a stand to protect our rights.' Jim looked around him and Gerry thrust his hands into his pockets, turning away. 'Or is it going to be every man for himself?'

Gerry glanced up, almost apologetically. 'We've got families to think of, Jim,' he said. 'Principles don't put food in children's bellies, mind.'

'But don't you understand?' Jim said, his eyes alight. 'The government wants to cut your pay, man! They want you to sweat and toil more hours and bring out more coal for less money.'

'It's all right for you, Jim.' Gerry spoke almost inaudibly. 'You are a man alone, you have only yourself to think about.'

'I know that's true,' Jim agreed, 'but think back to the past, man, remember what has been done to you by the governments in 1921 and '25.'

'There's the boss's car,' Rory said and the relief was evident in his voice. 'You talk to him, Jim – see if you can convince Luke Proud that a strike is what we need.'

Jim watched as Luke drove towards the mine entrance and jerked on the brake of his car. He slipped easily from the seat and stood facing his men, his shoulders hunched as though he was ready for a fight. Jim admired the man; he was good and honest; but he was a boss, and as such was on the other side of the fence.

'Well, what's going on?' Luke said. 'Are you going to work like sensible men or are you going to let the madness of strike-fever go to your heads?'

'We don't know what to do, boss, and that's the truth,' Rory said sheepishly.

'Listen,' Luke spoke easily, 'I'm not with the government. I'm not asking *my* workers to take a cut in pay – indeed, haven't you all been sharing the profits we've made out of the slant in recent months? And better times are coming, so long as we all keep calm.'

'The boss is right, mind,' Gerry said quickly, 'what good will it do the country if we few men stop cutting coal?'

Jim didn't move but his eyes were shrewd as he stared at the men around him. 'It's a question of sticking together,' he said, 'there's strength in numbers. Look, what if other men all over the country divided up into little pockets of workers? The strike would be defeated before it was begun. Sure there's more at stake here than a few weeks' pay in our pockets.'

Luke faced Jim squarely. 'Learn from the past, men,' he said. 'Haven't we all been losers after a strike? We go for weeks or months on empty pockets with the pale faces of our wives and children as a reproach and then at the end we are punished for our efforts with longer hours and less pay. It's always the way.'

'Aye,' Gerry said, 'the boss is right – we can't win against the might of the government.'

'That's defeatist talk!' Jim said angrily. 'The miners who cut coal are men, not frightened chickens to bend under the whip of a merciless, demanding government. Shall we accept every injustice, every betrayal without protest, then? If so, we might as well give in here and now and don women's petticoats!'

'Hear, hear!' Rory stepped forward and stood beside Jim. 'Sorry, boss,' he said. 'There's nothing personal against you, mind, but it's not right to give in so easily without even a fight.'

Luke lifted his head. 'I shall run the slant whatever you men choose to do. I shall employ more men – there's many will be willing to work the coal. I'll do it on my own if necessary.'

Tim moved towards Luke. 'I'm with the boss,' he said. 'I'm too old to care about principles. I've found they bring a man nothing but grief.'

After a moment, Tanny joined Luke, avoiding Jim's eyes, and hitched his lamp to his belt with a click of finality.

'Sorry, Luke,' Jim said. 'I hope you know that I've got nothing against you – sure you're a good man – but we must put up a fight, we must show Baldwin that we are not simple-minded peasants willing to slave for next to nothing. I wish you could understand that.'

'Oh, I understand, all right,' Luke said slowly. 'I understand that if I leave my mine for a few days, the water will rush in, the headings will snap beneath the squeeze of the land and all my work of the past few years will come to nothing.'

Jim sighed softly. 'There are always casualties in a fight of this sort,' he said, almost gently, 'and I'm not willing that the working man should have his face ground yet again into the dust. I can only hope that when you see what is happening to the country you will change your mind and put aside your own interests for the greater benefit of the workers.'

'What are you putting aside?' Luke asked. 'Not a great deal, as I see it. You have no holdings, no property; you can move on any time you like, pick up the threads of a new life if you choose.'

Jim shook his head. 'If I can't make you see what's right then I'm sorry.' He turned away and led the men along the dusty road towards the town.

Peta sat beside the window, staring out at the dismal rain. The sky was overcast and the budding leaves on the trees dripped dismally. She could hardly believe it was early May.

The front door slammed and as Peta looked up she saw Luke enter the room in a flurry of fresh air and raindrops. She smiled at him, feeling a sudden pride that this tall, handsome man was her husband. It was true she was seeing very little of him lately but then he needed to work hard at the mine to keep up the increased orders that had come his way. Money was easier and she was pleased she no longer needed to penny-pinch quite so drastically.

Only last week, Luke had given her money for new curtains and she had spent a long time in town choosing a good, heavyweight cloth suitable for winter drapes.

'How are you feeling?' Luke came to her and kissed her cheek and she smiled up at him happily. He was an ideal husband, no longer pestering her with his attentions, for in the nights when he was home he slept in his own room. She was pleased with him for he was obviously aware of her delicate health.

'I've scarcely any pain today, love,' she said, rising to her feet. She saw his glance run over her and an anxious frown appeared on his brow.

'You're too thin,' he said. 'I must have Doctor Soames to call. I think by now you should be over the loss of the baby and recovering your strength.'

Some of her contentment trickled away. She put her hand onto his shoulder and looked up at him pleadingly. 'I know I'm not being a wife to you, Luke,' she said softly, 'but I do worry about you, you're the one who's got thin from working too hard.'

He took her hand and kissed the tips of her fingers and she thought she saw pity darken his eyes. 'I'm all right,' he said gently. 'It's you we have to worry about.' Luke smiled and his hand brushed a strand of her hair into place. Peta moved a little uneasily, hoping he wasn't becoming amorous. As though sensing her withdrawal, Luke moved away from her and thrust his hands into his pockets.

'If only I could get more men,' he said. 'The orders are there but I can't fill them, not without the colliers to cut the coal.' He moved to the door. 'I'm going out,' he said. 'Don't wait up for me, I could be late.'

He avoided her eyes and Peta sighed with relief. He might be a little angry with her but at least he wasn't going to make an issue of this thing men and women did together in bed. Perhaps when the time came that they both wanted another baby, she would go to him, but until then she would prefer to refrain from such contact.

'That's all right, love,' she said warmly, 'I know you have a lot of things to see to.' She smiled. 'I think I'll have a hot drink and go to bed early, I've got a bit of a headache coming on.'

She went with him to the door and accepted his kiss on her cheek with cheerfulness. 'Now don't get yourself a cold in this awful rain,' she said solicitously. 'I don't want you bringing coughs and colds home, mind.'

She returned then to the warmth of the fire and before Luke's car had left the drive she had drawn the curtains against the pattering rain. It was cosy and safe in her little world, and Peta was content.

A little while later, Hattie came into the room balancing a tray on her arm. 'Some hot milk for you, Miss Peta,' she

185

said. 'Put a bit of meat on your bones, it will, for you don't eat enough to keep a bird alive.'

Peta smiled. 'Now you know I've always been delicate. I'm no different now than I always have been, so don't worry yourself – you and Luke both go on about my health far too much.'

She saw Hattie bite her lip and looked up at her in concern. 'What's wrong? You look as if you've swallowed a sour plum.'

'I don't know how to say this, miss, but speak I must whatever . . .' She glanced towards the door. 'It's Mr Luke; the gossip is he's seeing another woman, Katie Murphy from Market Street. I blame this strike business, myself, turning men strange, it is.'

Peta felt a pain thrusting deep within her. She stared at Hattie with wide eyes and shook her head.

'It's true, miss,' Hattie said pleadingly. 'I didn't want to tell you but he visits her at the house often, so I've heard, mind.'

Peta put her hands to her face. She hated Hattie in that moment for tearing aside the veil. She had known, deep down inside herself that Luke was far too much of a man to be without love and she had deliberately put the thought from her mind. Now Hattie, with her sincerity and loyalty, had stirred up a whirlpool of emotions within her.

She clasped her hands together and stared down at the slim white fingers. She didn't want ruffles on the smooth surface of her life; why hadn't Hattie kept her gossip to herself? 'What should I do?' she asked, without looking up.

'It isn't for me to say, miss,' Hattie's voice was edged with indignation. 'But if it was my husband, I'd go there to that very house and confront him with his sin.' Peta stared into the fire, the rain outside was beating against the windows and she was tired. Couldn't she put off the confrontation until the morning? She glanced at Hattie's rosy face and knew she could not.

'Fetch my coat, then,' she said in resignation, 'and my good walking shoes and you'd better tell me exactly where this woman lives.'

She dressed reluctantly and pulled on the heavy shoes. She really shouldn't be going out in such dreadful weather, and yet what sort of woman would she be if she didn't make some effort, at least, to salvage something from her marriage? She had no doubt that, once confronted, Luke would drop this woman, whoever she was, and come running back home. He loved her, she knew he did, and a tiny flame of anger kindled in her at the thought of another woman in his arms.

It was growing dark outside and the rain fell relentlessly from grey, wraith-like clouds. She paused on the step and looked back longingly at the light cast from the warmth of the hallway. 'Keep a good fire for when I return, mind,' she said and then, unable to linger further, strode out into the night.

She wasn't used to walking very far and she soon felt breathless. She paused and looked down the wet shiny road, and wondered if she should return home with the excuse that she had found no one at home in the house in Market Street. But, she told herself, she mustn't be spineless – she was a woman fighting for her marriage and surely a little discomfort was not too great a price to pay?

The house on Market Street was easily located. Above the large window was the name of Katie Murphy in black lettering. Peta sighed and stared upwards, not knowing what she was going to say to this harlot who was chasing her husband.

A light shone from between a crack in the curtains; cheap curtains without the advantage of a lining, she thought with distaste – the woman obviously had no breeding. She paused on the step, wondering what she was going to say and then rang the bell before she could change her mind and run away.

The door was opened quickly by a smiling woman with a cloud of red-gold hair. The smile vanished as the woman stepped aside for her to enter. She obviously knew who Peta was.

'Is my husband here?' Peta stepped into the small passageway that ran the length of the house and was ushered into the parlour.

She stood, staring down at the rain dripping from her coat and searched her mind for a clever, cutting remark but then it was difficult to think with this strange, beautiful woman staring at her.

'Luke's not here.' Her voice was soft with Irish intonations and there was something like pity in her eyes. 'I'm Katie,' she said, 'you must be Peta.'

'I'm Mrs Luke Proud,' Peta said, disliking the familiarity.

'Of course,' the woman said softly. 'What can I do for you? Would you like to sit down? You seem tired.'

Peta squared her shoulders. 'What time do you expect my husband to put in an appearance?' she asked. 'I'd like to wait for him.'

Katie glanced at the clock. 'I happen to know that he has gone to a meeting in the town tonight,' she said softly, almost apologetically. 'If he calls to see me it will be after the meeting's over. Sure, I'm forgetting my manners, won't you take some tea?'

Peta took a seat without a word, her legs trembling. She felt she had no control over herself or her emotions. She was at a loss, not knowing how she should handle the situation. Katie Murphy, on the other hand, appeared so calm, so sure of herself.

Suddenly Peta was angry. She leaned forward, chin jutting defiantly upwards. 'Why did you have to take him?' she asked. 'You must have known he was a married man. I've carried his child, I've cared for him . . .' Her voice trailed away as her eyes met Katie's.

'Sure I haven't taken him away from you.' The woman's voice was soft, conciliatory and Peta felt a blush rise to her cheeks.

'If he's been discussing me with you, I'll . . .' She clenched her hands into fists but Katie was shaking back her lovely hair.

'He hasn't, I promise.' The words hung in the air, kind words spoken with anger and Peta began to cry.

'I need him,' she said, 'he's my husband, he must look after me.' She took out a handkerchief and impatiently wiped the tears from her face as the woman stared at her with large eyes.

'Go home,' Katie said softly, 'Luke and me have done nothing wrong. Please don't upset yourself. I'll send him straight to you when he comes in.'

Anger returned along with the last shreds of Peta's pride. This woman wasn't going to patronize her! Offering Luke back to her as though he were a toy at her disposal.

'I'll wait for him,' she said obstinately. She glanced round her. 'No doubt he pays for all this and I have to beg for new curtains – to think I was actually grateful to him for allowing me to have them!'

The silence seemed to go on and on and Peta realized how petty she must have sounded. She clasped her hands together, determined not to be driven away from the house where Luke's harlot lived, not until some questions were answered.

There was the sound of a key in the lock and as the door opened, Peta sat, staring fixedly ahead. She was tense with apprehension but then she told herself she was the injured party, and Luke had some explaining to do.

He paused when he saw her sitting there and his gaze moved quickly to Katie who shrugged and rose to her feet.

'Sure, I'd better leave you alone to talk,' she said, but Luke held out his hand.

'No, stay, I'd prefer it.' He turned to where Peta was sitting and frowned. 'You shouldn't have come out in this weather,' he said gently and she realized that to him she was not a full-blooded woman but a child.

'How could you do this to me?' she asked, colour flooding into her face. 'You've made a fool of me with this woman and everyone knows, everyone!'

He thrust his hands into his pockets. 'Is that what worries you?' he asked slowly. 'Well, no one has made a fool of you. Katie and I are friends.'

Peta stood up. 'What sort of simpleton do you take me for?' She faced him squarely, her colour high. 'Tell me, come on, tell me to my face that you care nothing for this woman.'

'Peta, we both know you don't want me as a husband,' he said softly. 'I'm just someone to take care of you.' He touched her arm. 'Let me take you home – you look tired, we'll talk about this tomorrow.'

She shook him away. 'You haven't answered my question. Well, you must choose – it's her or me. I'm not going to be the laughing-stock of the town any longer.'

'Don't be foolish, Peta.' His voice had an edge to it. 'No one is laughing at you. Come on, I'll take you home, see you safely into bed.'

She flung herself away from his outstretched hand. 'And then what? You'll come back here to this woman; I'm right, aren't I?'

'Yes,' he said angrily, 'you're right; I'll be coming back here to talk to Katie once I've seen you home.'

She pushed past him. 'You've made your choice, then – it's her!' She moved quickly to the door. 'I'll get home under my own steam, don't you worry.'

He caught her arm tightly. 'I'm taking you home.' He guided her almost roughly outside and the rain was falling like tears along Peta's cheeks. She had lost him, then; he wanted this Katie more than he wanted her. She sat stiffly beside him as he drove along the wet road and she huddled into her seat in silent misery.

'I'm sorry, Peta.' His voice was low. 'I don't want to hurt you but Katie is someone I can talk, really talk to.' He drove carefully beneath the pools of light from the streetlamps and she almost laughed in his face.

'"Talk to", that's rich! You must think me stupid!' She paused, drawing a deep breath. 'You don't want to hurt me, that's why you're carrying on with that woman. You must have wanted me to know or did you think I was so dull I wouldn't find out?'

'There's nothing to find out,' he said firmly. 'If my guess is right, Hattie's been gossiping to you.'

She didn't reply, she just wished Hattie had remained silent about the other woman then Peta could have been happy.

'Why did you have to be so open about it?' she asked in a small voice. 'Why couldn't you be like other unfaithful husbands and hide the truth from me?'

'Poor Peta,' he said softly, 'determined to believe the worst.' He helped her from the car and went with her to the door, waiting for her to go inside. She paused on the threshold and stared back at him.

'I shall go home to my father,' she said with dignity. 'It's impossible for me to stay here with you now, you realize that.'

'If that's what you want I shan't stop you,' he said. 'Our marriage has been nothing but a sham. But I shall take care of you financially, of course.'

'Keep your money!' She flung the words at him. 'If that was what I wanted I would have married someone far richer than you. I had my chances, mind, there was more than one suitor after my hand.'

'Yes, of course,' he said and his manner was placating, like an adult talking to a fractious child.

'Oh, go to hell!' She hurriedly opened the door and almost before she had stepped into the hall, she heard the car drive away.

Hattie appeared in the doorway, her face creased into lines of concern. 'Oh, Miss Peta, there's glad I am you're back, I was that worried about you. Come on, let me take your coat, it's damp, look. *Duw*, you're trembling, come on and sit down and I'll make you a nice hot cup of tea.'

Peta sat before the fire and stared into the flames, wondering how in the space of a short hour her life had fallen apart.

'I'm leaving him,' she said as Hattie placed the tray on the table. 'We'll go back to daddy, he'll know what I should do.'

Hattie began to cry. 'Oh, miss, I did right telling you, didn't I?' She rubbed at her eyes. 'I couldn't bear it, you not knowing and that awful Michael Murphy talking about it to anyone who would listen. They say the wife is the last one to know, don't they?'

'Oh shut up, Hattie,' Peta said irritably. 'Go and put a hot water-bottle in my bed. I'll turn in early and then tomorrow you can go over to daddy's house and tell him to come and fetch me. I shan't stay here a moment longer than I can help.'

The bedroom was cheerful with a good fire blazing in the grate, and Peta undressed quickly before going into the bathroom to wash. She was so tired she could hardly keep her eyes open; all she wanted was to fall into bed and sleep. Her nightgown crackled as she pulled it over her head, the cotton cold against her skin. Sighing, she slipped beneath the quilts, warmed at once and comforted. Let Luke have his woman: she had lived without him before and she could do so again. And yet there were tears in her eyes as she closed them and tried to sleep.

In the morning, she woke early and knew at once the feeling of dread and hopelessness that had been with her in the night. Luke had another woman; the knowledge was like a stone within her.

'Hattie!' she called as she rose from the bed. 'Hattie, bring me some tea, there's a good girl.'

Hattie appeared at once, carrying a tray in her arms. Her face was shining with the sting of cold water and she was smiling.

'I've packed some clothes ready,' she said, 'and if you like, I'll go on the bus to your father's house and ask him to fetch you in his car.'

Peta sank into a chair. 'Oh, Hattie, could you?' she said appealingly. 'I'm so tired this morning, I feel positively ill.'

'All right, then,' Hattie said cheerfully, as she hurried from the room. A little later the front door slammed and Peta sighed. She'd teach Luke to fool with another woman.

By the time Peta had finished her tea the fire in the bedroom had almost burned itself out. Sighing, Peta wandered downstairs, shivering a little in the cool of the morning. She clucked her tongue in annoyance to find that the fire in the kitchen had not even been lit, no doubt Hattie felt she was economizing on coal, but what a ridiculous thought when Luke owned a whole mine full of the stuff.

The door opened and Peta looked up in surprise, expecting Hattie to appear. Silly girl must have forgotten something. But it was a strange man with red hair who stood smiling down at her.

'Sorry to trouble you, missis,' he said pleasantly, 'but could I get some water for my lorry? It seems to be overheating.'

'Oh all right,' Peta said, waving her hand towards the sink. 'Help yourself.' He came closer to her and she wondered why he looked somehow familiar.

'Luke Proud's wife, aren't you?' he said, looking her up and down, and she stepped back a pace, suddenly wary.

'What if I am? Is that any of your business?' she asked curtly. 'Just take your water and leave my house.'

To her surprise, he caught her arm and drew her roughly towards him. 'Not until I'm good and ready,' he said.

'How dare you!' Outrage made her voice tremble. 'Take your hands off me, you ruffian!'

He lifted her and the breath was knocked out of her as she fell across his shoulder. She could not believe this was happening to her; she was being attacked in her own house.

She beat at his back with her fists but he simply took no notice. He mounted the stairs quickly and easily and once in the bedroom threw her down roughly.

She sat up and stared at him, panting with fear. 'My father will be here soon,' she said desperately, 'my woman has gone to fetch him.'

'Aye, I know,' he said smiling, 'my brother has offered her a lift in a little car he's borrowed just for the occasion. Charming man is Kevin Murphy – good with the ladies; he'll take her the long way around, you see.'

'What do you want?' Peta asked in dread, already knowing the answer as the man's eyes moved from her face to her shoulders and breasts, revealed by the thin nightgown she was wearing.

He tore the cotton easily and she pulled away from him, her mouth dry. 'Please,' she said, 'I'm not very well. Just leave me alone and I'll give you money, anything.'

'What I want is revenge,' the man said softly. He was upon her then, his rough hands bruising her flesh. She moaned, closing her eyes as though by not seeing him she could make him go away. He jerked at her gown, tearing the soft cotton, bearing her down so that she could not move. She tried to scream but there was only a low strangled moan as he pressed his mouth upon hers.

Then there was pain, unbearable pain. She tried to raise her mind above what was taking place on the bed but he was savage and punishing and she was helpless against his great strength. It seemed to go on and on, the hurt and degradation. He thrust at her, again and again, his cruel laugh the final humiliation.

When he moved away from her, she could not move, not even to cover her nakedness. He stood above her doing up his clothing, looking at her without a trace of compassion.

He moved towards the door and she held her breath, half expecting him to return and attack her again. But he moved out towards the landing, calling back over his shoulder.

'When you tell your husband about this, you can explain that the man who's had his pleasure with you was Michael Murphy.' He went out and after a few moments she heard his footsteps on the stairs.

Peta didn't know how long she lay dry-eyed and tearless, but at last she forced herself to rise and go into the bathroom and the name ringing around in her mind, driving out all sane thought, was Michael Murphy.

She was sick then and dizzy. She staggered into the bathroom and began to wash. She wrapped her torn gown into a bundle and pushed it into the deep recesses of the cupboard. Then she stood and stared at the white face that looked back at her from the mirror. Her mind was falling away into some limbo of darkness that had no sense or meaning, and then there was only a deep blackness.

15

The sun was warm and bright, falling softly on Gina Sinman's face as she sat in the swaying tram, driven by a gentleman with loud checked trousers and a fine white shirt covered by a good cloth jacket.

The strike that had gripped the town of Sweyn's Eye for the last few days had brought sudden and surprising changes; the rich had taken over the jobs of the working man. The 'plus fours brigade', as they had been laughingly called, had proved adept at keeping essential services running and so had weakened the effectiveness of the strike.

Gina glanced through the window, and saw that groups of men were gathered on the corners of the streets; miners hunkering on haunches, faces grey from lack of sunlight and she felt they were fighting a battle they could not win.

She stepped down from the tram and walked briskly past the slip. The sand was clean and bright, the sea gently rippling into the arms of the bay. It was a fine day for being out of doors and yet Gina's heart was heavy for she was here with one purpose, and that was to spy on Billy Gray. She hated herself for giving even the slightest credence to the word of a woman like Doffy.

And yet she had to know the truth; she was done with being good old Gina, the woman who had waited endless years to be made an honest woman.

As she reached the gate of Victoria Park sunlight was splashing the grass with patterns of light and shade. Children's voices rang out in the stillness, and from across the road the tang of salt from the incoming sea was fresh and heady.

But Gina saw none of it. Billy, her future husband and Cerianne, the girl she loved as her own daughter, were strolling past the green lawns in the company of Delmai Richardson. Gina moved behind the shadow of the trees, her heart beating swiftly. So it was true; Doffy had not lied when she'd said that Billy was up to his old tricks. Gina had wanted to dismiss the words as gossip but something in the confident way the girl had spoken had made her suspicious.

She watched the three figures disappear from sight, then Gina sank onto a wooden bench and put her hands over her face trying to hold back the hot, bitter tears.

Long years she had waited for Billy Gray to take her as his wife and now he was betraying her, yet again – doubly betraying her, for not only had he taken Delmai once more as his mistress but he was allowing her to meet with Cerianne. Gina felt an ache of pain deep within her, she had virtually been the girl's mother; she had brought her up from babyhood and loved her as much as she loved her own son. How could Billy be so disloyal, so treacherous?

After a time, she composed herself and, rising from the bench, made her way back to the house Billy had provided for her. He had bought it in her name, it was her own property and in a mood of hardness, Gina decided that he owed her that much for the years of work she had put in, caring not only for Cerianne but Billy too.

He came seldom to her bed but when he did she had welcomed him with open arms, loving him, always loving him. And what was she to do now? Should she ignore what was happening behind her back or should she make a move right away from Sweyn's Eye and the people like Doffy, who must be aware of her humiliation?

She entered her house and sat in the small kitchen staring at the dying fire. The greying embers were like her love for Billy, she thought, fading away into nothing. She sat still until the afternoon sun waned in the sky and then at last, her decision was made: she would put the house up for sale and move right away from Billy, and all the hurt he had heaped upon her.

Her son was at college now and Cerianne was settled in her job at the office. They were both independent; they no longer needed her – it seemed that no one needed her.

She squared her shoulders. 'There's soft you are, Gina Sinman,' she said aloud, 'self-pity is a poor thing and not worthy of you.'

She moved slowly up the stairs and looked at the many possessions she had gathered together over the years. Here in her little house at the foot of the hill she had been safe and comfortable. But her feeling of security had been built on shifting sand and so she must move on, make a new life for herself.

She packed a small bag with the bare essentials and returned to the kitchen. In the old teapot, high on the shelf, she kept her housekeeping money; it wasn't a fortune but it would have to suffice until she sorted out her long term plans.

As she stood in the doorway, she suddenly felt frightened. All her life she had been able to love and care for those around her; now, suddenly, she was alone with only herself to think of and the prospect was not a pleasing one.

She paused for a moment. Should she leave a note? She didn't want anyone to worry about her and yet, why should she consider Billy? He obviously didn't consider her very much. Tears once again rose to her eyes. She was to have been married soon; she had held everything in the palm of her hand and now it had been wiped away by the few words of a street-walker.

She picked up her bag and looked around her, she had been happy and comfortable in the little house. Her life, though humdrum, had been useful, for she had loved looking after her own son and Billy's daughter.

There was a bitterness within her when she thought of Cerianne, for it seemed that she had agreed to meet her mother without confiding in Gina. She sighed softly. It was pointless brooding, she might just as well get on with it if she was going to make a clean break.

She heard a step on the path outside and froze, bag clutched tightly in her hands. It couldn't be Billy. She closed her eyes. Please God, don't let it be Billy. He came so irregularly to the little house that it would be ironic if he were to call now.

When she opened the door she sighed with relief. '*Duw*, Gerry, man you gave me a fright, mind.'

The man held out a cap with a sheepish look on his face. 'I'm collecting for the miners' fund,' he said apologetically, and Gina bit her lip in sympathy, knowing how much it had cost the man's pride to go from door to door begging.

She dipped willingly into her bag and brought out a few shillings. 'You're welcome to have what I can spare, Gerry,' she said quickly. 'I only wish it could be more. But why are you on strike? I thought you worked for Luke Proud – surely his mine isn't affected?'

'Sided with the boss I did at first, but then there was pressure put on me by my mates; called me a blackleg they did. Anyway, I'm glad you're with us,' Gerry added, 'there's some shutting the door in our faces, mind.'

Gina watched as the miner walked away down the path. It wasn't right that proud men were reduced to begging.

She turned to look into the shadows of the kitchen and sighed. The fire burned low in the grate and the polished brasses gleamed in the flickering light. It seemed that everything was changing; the whole life-blood of the town was threatened by the strike and here was she worrying about her own problems.

A shadow fell over her and she turned quickly, her eyes dazzled by the sun. She put up her hand to shade her eyes and she drew in a quick breath. He stood there, Billy Gray, her husband-to-be, brought to her door, no doubt, by the pricking of his conscience. He was staring at her with a look of bewilderment in his eyes. 'Where are you going, Gina?' he asked, obviously puzzled by the coldness of her manner.

'Away from you,' she said, unable to keep the bitterness from her voice. She had not wished for a confrontation but if there was to be one, Billy would be left in no doubts about her feelings of betrayal.

'You know?' He didn't pretend innocence, for which she was grateful.

'Yes,' she sighed heavily, 'I know. I saw you with Delmai and, worse, you had introduced her to Cerianne. Don't you think I should have been consulted about that, at least?'

Billy shook his head. 'I'm sorry, Gina, I suppose I knew deep within me that it was wrong to keep you in the dark but there seemed no other way.'

'There would have been another way if you hadn't been carrying on your old affair with Delmai,' Gina said harshly. 'You could have talked it over with me. We could have come to some arrangement between us but no, you wanted that dreadful woman in your bed again. You're such a fool, Billy!'

She made a move to pass him but he held her arm firmly. 'Please, Gina, you can't just walk out on us all like this. What are the children to think?'

She looked up at him and the anger in her eyes made him flinch. 'What are the children to think?' she echoed his words. 'They'll think what they like. They are no longer children and can make up their own minds about a man who cheats on his bride-to-be so close to the wedding!' She paused for a moment. 'Oh, Billy, how could you?'

He tried to take her in his arms. 'But, Gina, I can't imagine life without you. You're part of me, I'd cut off my right arm if I could only go back in time and change things.'

She drew away from him and took a deep breath trying to control the trembling that had seized her. She shook her head almost pityingly. 'There's something so familiar about all this, Billy,' she said tonelessly, her anger spent. 'You said much the same thing years ago when I was stupid enough to forgive you for making a laughing stock of me with a little flossie. Well the barrel is dry, Billy, I can find no more forgiveness within me.'

She walked past him then and out into the waning sunlight. 'By the way, I want to put the house up for sale. The proceeds will help me make a new life for myself somewhere far away from you and your treachery.'

Gina stared at him for a long moment. He was a big man with the look of a whipped pup and she forced herself to turn away from him before pity clouded her judgement.

'I'll be in touch,' she said stiffly and walked firmly towards the town as though she had some purpose in mind but in reality she had no idea where she was going to stay.

She made her way towards the Strand where there were boarding houses aplenty. For now and until the house was sold, she would remain in the town and then, who knows, perhaps she would take the journey up to Yorkshire and stay for a time with Billy's sister.

Rhian had always been a good friend and would spare no effort in helping her to make a new start.

But a voice inside her cried that she didn't want a new start; she wanted the safe, comfortable life she'd had before Doffy's spitefully-dropped words had shattered the calm.

Gina carefully scrutinized the boarding houses, though the growing dark did not help matters. She looked at the curtains to see if they were freshly washed and then at the brasses on the door. If they were polished and bright it was a good indication that the rooms within would be clean.

At last, she plucked up courage to knock on one of the doors and deep within the house she heard the barking of a dog. The door was opened by a tall, thin man who stared at her blankly for a long moment without speaking.

'I'm looking for somewhere to lodge,' she said at last, unnerved by the silence. 'Just for a few days until I find myself some other accommodation.'

He rubbed his hand through his already-untidy hair. 'I'm sorry. Please come in, there's just one room left, I'm afraid, but if that suits then you can have it and welcome.'

He led the way into the house and from the kitchen came the sound of a child crying. 'Oh, hell!' He grew red.

'Excuse me, it's the baby; I'll just be a minute.' He seemed harassed and, after a moment, Gina followed him along the passage and into the kitchen. He was holding the child awkwardly in his arms, his face creased with anxiety.

'Can I help?' Gina held out her arms and took the baby. 'Poor thing needs a change of clothing,' she said, smiling, 'he's soaking wet.' She shrugged off her coat while still holding the boy, then she sat on one of the kitchen chairs and unloosed the wet trousers, slipping them to the floor.

'He's my daughter's boy – gone into hospital, she has,' the man said worriedly. 'She runs the place for me since my wife died some years ago but now she's sick herself and I don't know if I can keep the place open.'

Gina felt her strength rise within her. 'Let me help,' she said at once. 'I'm used to keeping house and looking after children.' She smiled ruefully. 'Indeed, that's all I can do but I do it well enough.'

'Well,' he said doubtfully, 'I'd have to pay you, couldn't expect anyone to work for nothing.'

She held out her hand. 'I'm Gina Sinman. What if I help run the boarding house in exchange for my keep? There, how does that sound?'

He smiled and took her hand. '*Duw*, sounds wonderful to me.' He paused. 'I know your face, of course. Seen you in the market many times; don't suppose you've noticed me, though. My name is Geraint Griffiths and this boy here is David – he's my grandson, as you may have gathered.'

'Yes, I'm sure I've seen you about now you come to mention it,' Gina replied. 'My son's name is David, too, but we use the Welsh Dewi. He's grown up now of course, don't need his mam any longer.'

She took the small boy to the sink in the corner of the room and washed him carefully. 'Poor dab, he's getting sore and red. Let's put a bit of egg-white on this shall we? Got an egg, grandad?'

Geraint moved quickly to the larder and, taking up an egg, deftly separated the white from the yolk. '*Duw*, never heard of that before,' he said admiringly,

202

as Gina smoothed the white over the baby's inflamed skin.

'Protects the soreness from any acid in the water,' she explained. 'Good old remedy my mam passed down to me. Now, where can I find some dry clothes for the boy?'

She eventually settled the baby in his pram in the corner of the room and the little boy lay there sleepily, nuzzling his head into the pillow.

'I think he'll sleep now,' Gina said, smiling, 'and it's about time I saw this room of mine, I think.'

Geraint led the way up the narrow staircase to the first landing. 'This should suit you, I hope.' He flung open the door and, as Gina stepped inside she was impressed with the cleanliness of the bedclothes and the freshness of the curtains and covers.

'Your daughter keeps a good home,' she said approvingly, and Geraint smiled warmly.

'Aye, Rachel's a good girl. It's just that she's had this woman's trouble for some time now and the Doctor Soames thought she should go into hospital, have it cleared up once and for all.' He sighed. 'But *duw*, I didn't think it would be so difficult managing without her.' He stared at Gina helplessly. 'When she comes home she'll have someone to help her with the bed-making and such; she'll have to take things easy for a bit.' He smiled. 'Perhaps you could stay on here?'

Gina put down her bag and stared around her. The situation she found here in the boarding house seemed to offer a solution to her problems, at least for the time being.

'Fate, it was,' she said. 'Fate led me here to this house where I'm needed. We'll have to have a talk later,' she added, 'when I've changed my clothes and tidied my hair. I'll come down to the kitchen and you can tell me all about the routine of the place.'

Geraint moved to the door. 'Not much of a routine at the moment,' he said ruefully. 'We've got eight lodgers in all, most of them good men.' He sniffed. 'We did have an Irishman here I wasn't keen on – didn't like his manner at all. To make things worse, Michael Murphy had a very dubious young woman lodging with him. I was glad to see the back of them. When they left, Rachel gave the room a good cleaning and changed all the bedding so it should be spotless in here now.'

Gina had heard of Michael Murphy, Katie's brother – who hadn't? For he made such a noise around the town, rabble-rousing, making speeches against the bosses, causing trouble everywhere he went.

'I'm very glad he's not here now,' she said with a shudder. 'His sort frightens me.'

Geraint nodded. 'Aye, not helping the cause of the workers at all, him – giving us all a bad name, that's what he's doing. No wonder Churchill is writing those pieces in the *Gazette* condemning the workers when there's the like of Murphy roaming the streets.'

He moved out into the passage. 'Enough of my speech-making! I'll give you a bit of time to yourself then, and when you're ready, you come on downstairs and I'll make you a nice hot cup of tea.' He paused. 'And, thank you, Mrs Sinman, thank you very much.'

She watched the door close and then sank down on to the bed. She stared out of the window without seeing the street below. She could not say she was happy, but at least she could feel there was once more a sense of purpose in her life.

She stood up abruptly, telling herself that there was enough of looking back. She would look forward now to building her life in the best way she could without Billy Gray.

The sun shone through the clouds, highlighting for a moment the funeral cortège that wound its way through the paths of Dan y Graig cemetery towards the Richardson vault. Delmai was sitting in the gleaming black car, her face swathed in dark veiling. She lifted a handkerchief to her eyes, blinking rapidly, wondering at the suddenness of the events that had turned her life upside-down.

Beside her, Mali Richardson touched her arm in sympathy. 'Be brave. It will soon be over and then you can mourn in private,' she whispered.

Sterling Richardson smiled down at his wife with such love in his eyes that, for a moment, Delmai felt a real tug of pain. If only she'd shared a quarter of that love with her husband, she would have been happy.

But their marriage had been one of convenience, her father wanting the best match for his only daughter, bribing Rickie into taking Delmai back even after her escapade with Billy Gray. And then when Delmai bore three sons, her father's approbation had known no bound, he had left his entire estate to his son-in-law. Now that fortune as well as Rickie's own estate was Delmai's to do with what she would.

Her eyes gleamed behind the veiling as she thought of her daughter. She could now offer Cerianne everything a girl could want. A season in London, perhaps, to share in the exotic life of parties; smoking and drinking and fun-making that seemed to take place everywhere except this God-forsaken town of Sweyn's Eye.

She sighed softly now that Gina Sinman had taken it into her head to leave Billy. The way would be open for Delmai to manipulate him as she saw fit.

The car drew to a halt and the minister of the church in his black and white robes came into her line of vision – a bird of prey rather than leader of the flock, she thought irreverently.

She had insisted on coming to the graveyard, though it would have been quite in keeping for her to remain at home, shut away from prying eyes. But now she wondered if she'd been wise to attend the ceremony, for it seemed the minister, conscious of the importance of the Richardson family in the town, was bent on making a long sermon out of the burial service.

He talked on endlessly about the virtues of the Richardsons, recalling old Arthur Richardson and his wife Victoria. Delmai could have laughed out loud at the hypocrisy of it all for as everyone knew, Victoria had taken a lover and Arthur was not the father of Sterling, who stood so proudly beside his wife, head erect in the sunshine.

But all that was long past, the sins buried just as surely as the perpetrators and Delmai stifled a yawn, wanting only to have the whole thing over and done with so that she could begin to put her plans into action.

Mali squeezed her arm, obviously taking her restlessness as an expression of grief. And it had all been a shock after all, Delmai conceded to herself. Rickie's sudden death had left her horrified and riddled with guilt because she'd failed to call the doctor in time.

Paul Soames had eased her feeling greatly by telling her that nothing could have been done for her husband, even if his condition had been noticed sooner. A massive heart attack had been the cause of death and Paul told her sympathetically that all his medicines could not have cured a man so far overcome by heart-disease.

At last, the interminable service was over. The vault gates were closed and Rickie Richardson was gone to his last resting place. As Delmai made her way back to the car she glanced over towards the sea, lying like a glittering mirror, and her spirits rose. She was a comparatively young woman, she told herself – she would find another suitor. Not Billy Gray, for now he was too unsophisticated for her tastes.

Perhaps she would accompany her daughter to London and the glorious nightlife that beckoned like an enticing hand.

'Come along.' Sterling was taking her arm. 'Let's get you home, Delmai. There's little point in hanging around here, you'll only distress yourself more.'

She glanced up at him, thankful that he could not see her eyes, dry beneath the dark veiling. 'You're so kind,' she said in an appropriately soft voice. She was not really unfeeling, she told herself defensively, as she settled herself into the car – it was just that she and Rickie were never lovers. He used her as she used him, and they somehow rubbed along. But she had never really forgiven him those early days of their union when, terrified of the intimacies of marriage, she had been forced to do his bidding, however painful and embarrassing she might have found it.

'Why don't you come and stay with us for a little while?' Mali's voice broke into her thoughts and Delmai lifted her veil, allowing Mali to see the tears she had summoned in her eyes. That they were there for herself and not for her husband's passing was her own business.

'That's very kind of you,' she said softly, 'but I must get used to being alone and I might as well start as I mean to go on.'

'Are you sure?' Mali said, her face pale and anxious. She really was quite sweet, Delmai thought, unaware that she was being patronizing.

'Quite sure, dear, but my thanks all the same.' She sank back in the seat and looked through the window of the car unseeingly, busy with her plans for Cerianne's future.

It was a relief to be alone. She thanked Sterling warmly for his kindness and waved to Mali, who had remained in the car. She went indoors and stood looking around her, breathing in the atmosphere of luxury with a feeling of satisfaction. She'd been a fool in the past. She had almost thrown all this away for the delights of being with Billy Gray.

She moved into the sitting-room and pulled at the bell-sash. She would have some tea and then, perhaps, lie down in her own bed in her very own room, where her privacy would never now be violated by any man.

She sighed softly and, unpinning her hat, threw it on the table. She was mistress now of her own fate; if there should be any man in her life, she it would be who dictated the terms.

In the small house at the foot of Constitution Hill, Cerianne Gray sat before the cold, empty grate and stared askance at her father.

'But, daddy, Gina's been gone almost a week now. Haven't you made any attempt to find her?' She brushed back her thick hair with a worried gesture of her slim fingers and Billy, in spite of his mixed feelings, could not help but admire her beauty.

'She doesn't want to be found, love,' he said gently. 'She's had enough of me and I can't say I blame her.'

Cerianne came to him and he felt her slim arms cling around his neck. He closed his eyes. How he loved this daughter of his; she had become the centre of his life and nothing on earth was too good for her.

'Daddy, her pride was hurt, that's all. She didn't like to think of us going behind her back.' She kissed his cheek, grimacing at the two days of stubble on his chin.

'Have a shave, for goodness sake!' She smiled. 'I suppose we were at fault – we should have invited Gina along to meet Mrs Richardson. We both ought to have been entirely open about the arrangements for me to see my mother.'

Billy looked down at his trusting daughter and his heart felt as though it was being torn in two. 'There was more to it than that,' he said. He'd had enough of being underhand; it was honesty that was the best policy from now on.

'I don't know what you mean,' Cerianne said, her eyes wide. 'Come on, what are you trying to tell me, dad?'

'I slept with Delmai.' There, the words were out now. 'Gina could have forgiven me anything but that.' He shrugged his shoulders. 'But now I see that I was simply a means to an end for Delmai – she wanted to get to you through me.'

Cerianne moved away from him. 'You were unfaithful to Gina, now, when you were going to be married?' Her tone was incredulous and Billy realized that his daughter was like any other woman, in that she didn't understand a man's needs. Sleeping with a woman didn't mean that he loved her, simply that he desired her for that moment in time.

'How can I explain?' he asked. 'But it didn't mean anything, love, I still wanted to marry Gina.'

Cerianne stared at him for a long moment. 'If it didn't mean anything, why did you do it when you knew it would hurt Gina so much?' She glanced away and stared out through the window. 'Are all men like you, daddy?'

How could he disillusion his young daughter? 'I don't know.' He rubbed at his eyes. 'No, I suppose not, I've never been a man to conform, you know that, Cerianne.'

She seemed to have moved a million miles from him. He would have spoken, but there was the sound of a car drawing up outside the house and then came a light tapping on the door.

'Delmai, what on earth are you doing here?' Billy was embarrassed and yet impressed with Delmai's appearance. She was wearing widow-black and her large, beautiful eyes appeared filled with sadness.

'I came to ask a favour,' she said softly. 'I'm so alone now up there in that great house. My sons are all away at school and my guilt presses heavily upon me.' She bent her head and to anyone less knowing than Billy, it would have seemed that she was moved to tears.

'What do you want?' he asked, unable to keep the suspicion from his voice. At his side, Cerianne made a movement of protest.

'Come and sit down,' she said gently, taking Delmai by the arm and leading her to a chair. 'What can we do for you?'

It was clear that Cerianne saw her mother as the pitiful victim of men's lust, foolish but more sinned against than sinning. The pulse in his temple began to beat more rapidly. His daughter was being taken in just as he'd been.

Delmai looked up from her chair with dewy eyes. 'I just wondered . . . I know it's impertinent of me to expect anything from you but –' she rushed the words out as though nervous and Billy felt like applauding her performance '– could you possibly come to stay with me just for a few days, Cerianne?'

Billy felt anger explode within him. 'Over my dead body!' he said loudly and as both women looked up at him in surprise, he knew he'd played right into Delmai's hands.

'Of course I'll come and stay,' Cerianne said at once, 'just let me put some things into a bag and then I'll be with you.'

Billy watched helplessly as she hurried up the stairs, her slim body revealing her anger at what she saw as his callous behaviour.

'Don't try to take her away from me,' he said to Delmai and she opened her eyes wide and stared up at him.

'I only want to give my daughter the best in life,' she said sweetly, 'is there anything wrong with that?'

Billy felt beaten and suddenly very old. He slumped into a chair and put his head in his hands. 'This, then, is your revenge,' he said, almost in a whisper. 'You want to punish me for all the discomforts you shared with me so readily, when your blood was as hot as mine.'

He felt her hands touch his hair. 'No, Billy, I don't want to hurt you at all. Why should I? You have given me such a beautiful daughter that I will thank you every day for the rest of my life.'

Cerianne entered the room at that moment and, looking up, Billy saw admiration reflected in her young face. She had heard Delmai's carefully-calculated words and was touched by them.

'Don't worry, dad.' She rested her hand on his shoulder. 'I shan't be away for too long.' She paused for a moment. 'And, dad, try to find Gina, I think you owe her that much.'

The door closed then, shutting Billy in the house alone. He felt suddenly as he'd done all those years ago when he'd been imprisoned within the gloomy walls of Sweyn's Eye's jail. He thumped the table with his fist in sudden anger. This time he wasn't helpless. He would find Gina, tell her what was happening and beg for her help to save his daughter from Delmai's ruthless clutches.

16

The entrance to the Slant Moira gaped like an open mouth in the side of the hill and the sound of wheels upon iron rails rumbled like thunder from within the darkness. Old Cal lumbered forth, steadfastly moving towards the tipping plate, coat dulled with rain and coal dust.

'*Bore da*, boss, you all dressed up today, having a day off, is it?' He didn't wait for a reply. '*Duw*, that's another ton of Red Vein dug from the slant.' Tanny wiped the rain and sweat from his face, leaving smears of white against the dust. 'It's been a busy morning and if the orders keep coming like this I'll be asking for a rise, boss, especially as I'm acting fireman now.'

'You deserve a rise, if it's only for that black eye you're sporting,' Luke said drily. 'You've been having trouble with the strikers, I see.'

Tanny grinned ruefully but ignored the question. 'Hey, Tim,' he called, 'I was just telling the boss here that we should be having a rise, the coal we're pulling out of old Moira, what do you say?'

Tim grinned and moved towards the shed. 'Me, I'm getting in out of the rain – done my job of cutting the coal now. I'll watch the hauliers doing their bit while I sit and eat. Mind,' he continued, 'I wouldn't say no to a bigger pay-packet come weekend.'

Luke's attention was caught by the tall figure striding along the dusty road towards the slant. Jim O'Conner stood for a moment, watching as one of the men guided the dram onto the tipping plate that dropped the coal into the waiting lorry on the lower level.

Jim O'Conner pushed his hat back on his head. He was a strange, silent man, not given to talking unless he had something important to say. It was clear he had come to the mine now to say quite a piece if Luke was any judge.

'What do you want, Jim?' Luke asked easily. The man might be on the other side of the strike but there was a great deal to admire about the way he conducted himself.

'Why are you siding with the government?' Jim said at once. ''Tis blacklegs you are, the lot of you! Can't you see what's behind this strike? Freedom, independence and the right to earn fair wages for our labour.'

Luke eyed him carefully. 'I'm giving my men fair wages. I can't take on the problems of the entire country, man, don't talk nonsense.'

'The bosses of the big pits want fatter profits. They grind the men into the dust, squeeze every ounce of work out of them and then ask them to take a cut in their wages – and you are supporting that sort of action.'

It was quite a mouthful for the usually-quiet Jim and Luke raised his eyebrows. 'A political man, are you?' he asked and Jim took out a pipe and lit it with slow, deliberate movements.

'I like to see justice done.' His eyes met Luke's. 'But already injustice is rife; men will see their children go hungry, see them walk about barefooted before this dispute is settled.'

'I've heard that it will be over in a few more days,' Luke said slowly, 'then where will all the talk of sacrifice get you?'

'The strike may end soon but the lock-out won't, you mark my words,' Jim said forcefully. 'There is much more at stake here than you realize. Why not come to one of our meetings – just listen to the point of view of the strikers?'

Luke thrust his hands into his pockets and stared directly at Jim. 'Not bloody likely!' he said. 'Look at it this way, if you fell down a hole and broke your leg, would it help if I jumped in and was trapped with you?' He kicked at a piece of glittering anthracite. 'I'm not going to see this pit fill up with water, have the headings close up, the timbers snap under the squeeze.

And most important of all, I'm not laying off my men for anyone.'

'That's a selfish attitude,' Jim said, his tone even. 'Don't you believe in sacrifice for the greater good of the working men?'

Luke smiled, revising his earlier opinion of Jim O'Conner, even though he didn't agree with his principles. Luke admired him for his outspoken views, put so succinctly. The man was something of an orator.

'I believe in looking after my own little patch,' Luke said calmly, 'keeping my bills paid and my men employed. If I go on strike is there going to be any benefit in it for me or the Slant Moira? Who is going to give me a higher wage or a shorter working week? I don't want anything for nothing and I don't give anything for nothing, it's as simple as that.'

'Aye, well, every man knows his own poison best,' Jim said, knocking his pipe against the empty side of the wooden dram. He shook the rain from his hat and turned towards the roadway and as Luke watched him go, he wondered what a man of such obvious intelligence was doing in a small mine on the outskirts of Sweyn's Eye.

Tanny appeared at the mouth of the slant clearing the entrance just as a low rumble rose, as though from the bowels of the earth. Luke climbed into the Austin and waved his hand to the men.

'I'll be back in about an hour,' he called above the noise of the engine.

As he negotiated the bend in the road, Luke smiled to himself. On days like this, the Slant Moira almost ran itself. And he had a visit to make, a certain lady he wished to see. He whistled softly under his breath as he drove towards Market Street.

Katie was stacking shelves when he entered the shop. She turned and smiled at him.

'Hello, sure 'tis a surprise to see you in the middle of the day, but a good excuse for making a hot bowl of nourishing soup. Could you do with one?'

'Aye, I could that,' he said, wondering, as he followed her into the kitchen, how it was he felt such affinity with the lovely Irishwoman.

She looked at him and he read the unspoken question in her eyes. He shook his head. 'No, Peta's not come back to me. Her father came over to the house and took her away with him, it was her choice.'

'Have you been to see her?' Katie asked quietly. 'I've heard gossip in the shop and it seems Peta's not well.'

He smiled. 'She told me to go to hell last time I saw her.' He leaned back in his chair. 'It was the first time in months I'd seen her show any emotion.'

'And you admired her for it?' Katie said, her eyes lowered. Without waiting for a reply, she lifted the enamel dish from the stove and began to ladle rich, steaming soup into the dishes standing ready on the table.

'Sit yourself down at the table,' Katie said, 'and tell me to mind my own business about what goes on in your personal life, it's nothing to do with me.'

'That looks delicious; I'll be delighted to have a proper meal.' Luke sat at the table and took the bowl of soup Katie pushed towards him.

Absent-mindedly, he crumbled a piece of bread between his fingers. He could not help but stare at Katie – she was so serene, so natural. 'How's the shop doing?' he asked lightly.

''Twas fine this morning, I did a good bit of trade,' she said brightly, 'I'm beginning to get a good crowd of regulars in the shop now.' She smiled across the white of the table-cloth and he fancied he saw a tinge of colour in her pale cheeks.

'I'm buying my stocks of butter and milk from Alexander Llewelyn and I don't think he'd be afraid of our Michael like poor Sammy was, not with his crowd of brothers and a strong father like Siona behind him.' She paused. 'I might let one of the bedrooms to a lodger though, I'd be happier with someone in the house to keep me company.'

Luke leaned across the snow-white cloth and smiled at her. 'You were walking out with one of the Llewelyn boys,

214

weren't you?' He stopped abruptly. 'There I'm doing it now, poking into affairs that are none of my business.' And yet he felt a pang of something like jealousy to think of Katie with another man. What on earth was wrong with him? They were friends – they could talk together, share an hour or two, that was all. All there could be, a small voice inside him said, for he was a married man.

'I'll ask around, if you like.' He spoke calmly betraying nothing of his thoughts. 'It should be easy enough to get a lodger, I'd have thought.'

She smiled. 'Sure that would be fine and I think I'll just put a notice up in the shop window for good measure. You never know who might see it.'

'Are you working this afternoon?' Luke asked, uneasy that he might be taking up too much of Katie's time.

'No, I'm shutting up the shop; I've got to order some stock and I might as well do it today.'

'Perhaps I can give you a lift somewhere, then?' he said, knowing he was reluctant to leave her. 'It was starting to rain as I drove up to the shop.'

She glanced at him from under her golden eyelashes and smiled, and he felt suddenly light-hearted. He pulled himself up sharply. He was behaving like a beardless youth, a boy courting his first girl.

'No, it's all right,' she said quickly, glancing away from him, 'I'll go on the tram, sure I'm used to it.'

He watched her go with a strange sense of loneliness. Could it be that he was falling in love with Katie?

Later when he returned to his empty, silent house he saw the figure of Hattie toiling up the hill. He pushed open the large door of the house and paused on the step, wondering why Peta was sending her woman to see him.

'What's wrong?' he asked moving to take Hattie's arm. She was breathless, her face puffy from crying, and he caught her hands, feeling them cold with the spiteful rain as he drew her towards the doorway.

'It's Miss Peta,' Hattie gasped. 'She's taken real sick. You'll have to come and see to her, please.'

'What is it?' he asked in concern, and a cold chill seemed to grip him as Hattie clung to him. He led her into the hallway and lit the lamp, the gas mantle popping and hissing as the light grew slowly and filled the room.

'Calm down now and tell me slowly what's wrong. If you cry like that I can't understand a word you're saying.' He spoke gently to the distressed woman.

Hattie took out a handkerchief and dabbed at her eyes; she seemed reluctant to talk and Luke moved to the drawing-room where he poured a glass of brandy.

'Here, drink this, Hattie,' he said, 'and when you're ready, tell me what is wrong with Peta. I have to know sooner or later.'

Hattie sipped the drink and it seemed to give her courage. She glanced up at Luke and gave a shuddering sigh.

'Poor Peta's sick –' she tapped her head '– up there she's sick, can't even remember her name.' The words rushed out. 'Her father sent me for you, says he don't know what to do with her and it's your place to look after her, she being your wife. There's a to-do! Please, Mister Luke, come with me and see her for yourself.'

'Come on.' Luke lead the way outside and opened the car door, gesturing for Hattie to step inside out of the rain.

'I knew you'd want to go to her once you knew how ill she was,' Hattie said anxiously, 'I told her father Peta would be better off in her own home 'cos he's getting on a bit now and don't know how to cope with her.'

Luke smiled reassuringly. 'Don't you worry, we'll have the doctor to treat her. Peta will soon be back to her old self.'

He drove swiftly through the streets and scarcely noticed Hattie clinging nervously to the seat beside him. He jerked the car to a halt outside the house and held the door open for a relieved Hattie to alight.

'It was she who wanted to go home to her father in the first place, mind,' Hattie said. 'So I'd gone off to fetch Mister Cannon to pick her up in his car but when we got

216

back, she was just sitting in her room and not a word did she speak then or since.'

In the hall was a large suitcase and Luke realized that Old Man Cannon must really be at his wits' end. It was clear he intended that Peta should be returned to her own home as quickly as possible.

He mounted the stairs and stood near the bedroom door, appalled at the sight of his wife. She was almost unrecognizable: her eyes sunken, her face so white she appeared near to death's door.

The doctor was at her bedside and hovering near the window was Peta's father, his face grim.

'God,' Luke said in a whisper. 'What is wrong with her?'

Peta was dressed as though for outdoors, with a thick coat and hat, and stout shoes. And there was a wool blanket tucked around her as though she were cold. Her eyes gazed into a distance no one else could see.

'Have you examined her, Doctor Soames?' Luke asked in concern and the doctor shook his head. 'She won't allow me near her. All I could do is give her a sedative; she will sleep soon and perhaps tomorrow I can have a better look at her.'

Frederick Cannon moved from the window. 'There's nothing wrong with her body,' he said positively, 'it's the poor child's mind has been affected by her husband's carryings-on! A week she's been like this, you know, a whole week, and you haven't been near her, Luke Proud.' He puffed heavily as though the speech had left him without breath.

Luke didn't bother to reply. 'Is that your opinion too, Doctor, that my wife is sick in the head?' he asked, and Paul Soames looked at him levelly.

'I can't comment on your wife's mental or physical condition, not until I've examined her thoroughly.' He glanced at his watch. 'All I can tell you is that she is not in any immediate danger – there is no fever and no bones broken. As for heart, lungs and respiration, I can't at this stage form any opinion. As I said, she becomes hysterical the moment I try to open her clothing.' He moved to the door. 'I must go; I'm late for surgery as it is. I'll come round tomorrow and check on your wife's progress.'

Luke watched him descend the stairs and then turned his attention to his wife. He moved to take her in his arms but she pushed herself back against the pillows and put a slim hand over her mouth as though to suppress a scream. Luke sank down beside her and put his head in his hands, a feeling of guilt pressing in on him. He'd known his wife was delicate and he'd treated her badly. He should have reassured her, told her that he loved her; and yet the lie would have stuck in his throat. He sighed and moved to the window where he stared out into the dismal rain. There was nothing else for it, he would have to take Peta home and devote as much of his spare time to her as possible. As for his friendship with Katie, it seemed it must fade away before it was really begun.

Charlotte sat in the kitchen staring at Sheila O'Conner with a sense of panic. Outside, the evening was misty with rain, the lamps in the street glimmering mutedly on wet pavements.

'You don't really mean you're going home to Ireland, do you?' Charlotte asked, her voice taut. 'But that will mean I'll not lose just one lodger, but two – for I won't be able to have Jim in the house, not with me being a woman alone.'

'I have to go.' Sheila's eyes were large. 'I just can't bear to stay away from home any longer. Sure there's going to be a great poverty here in Sweyn's Eye, what with this terrible strike, so I might just as well suffer with those I love as be here in a strange place.'

Charlotte sighed. 'I can see how you feel, but what about Jim? Won't you be sorry to leave him behind?'

Sheila smiled sadly. 'You've seen our Jim at close quarters, you must know that he is a law unto himself. He doesn't need me; he doesn't need anybody, come to that. In any case, you provide such fine hospitality here in your house there should be no problem finding another lodger.'

Charlotte nodded. 'Perhaps you're right, but I'll be sorry to see you go and so will the boys.'

Sheila wiped a tear from her eye surreptitiously. 'Sure an' I'll miss them sorely. Freddy and Denny have been such a comfort to me while I've been here. But for them I'd have been really miserable.'

Sheila rose to her feet. 'I'm going to start packing my things, though I won't leave until the end of the week so long as that suits you, of course.'

Charlotte nodded dumbly and watched in silence as Sheila left the room. She moved quietly as was her manner and closed the door gently behind her.

How drastically life had a way of altering things, she thought sadly. This morning she had woken feeling better than she'd done since Gronow's sudden and tragic death. Her life had settled into an orderly and comfortable pattern, with Sheila and Jim almost like family to her. Now the pattern had altered and Charlotte didn't know how she was going to manage without the presence of the O'Conner's to enrich her life.

The back door opened and Jim entered the room. He swung off his scarf and coat and hung them behind the door. He stood, then, looking down at Charlotte. He was a big, handsome man and until now Charlotte hadn't realized how much she'd come to rely on his good sense and his strength of purpose. Jim was a radical, a man of the people but not in the way her husband had been. Where Gronow had been wild and extreme in his views, Jim was sensible and mature.

'What's wrong?' he asked and she realized she'd been staring at him. She rose quickly and put the kettle on to boil.

'Your sister,' Charlotte said at once. 'She's decided to go home.' The kettle began to sing as Charlotte placed clean cups and saucers on the table. 'I shall miss her,' she added.

'Sure I've been expecting Sheila to return to Ireland, I could see she wasn't going to settle here.' He stood beside Charlotte, close to her but not touching her. 'That won't need to make any difference to our arrangement,' he said in his decisive way.

Charlotte looked up at him and then away again. 'I shall try to find another lodger,' she said, 'because it wouldn't be proper to have an unmarried man alone in the house with me, you must see that.'

Jim took a step closer. 'I don't want to leave here, Charlotte. I don't want to leave you.' He spoke quietly, his eyes looking directly into hers. Charlotte felt the colour coming into her cheeks and suddenly she was breathless.

'I know it's too soon for commitments,' he said, 'but I think in time, we will work out an understanding between us, don't you?'

Charlotte knew what he was trying to say and, like Jim, she was prepared to be patient, to hold at bay any ill-timed feelings. And yet the feelings were there, perhaps had been there since the moment she first set eyes on Jim O'Conner and felt the force of his personality. After a moment she nodded.

He had not touched her and yet she knew that a silent promise had been made, a promise that to them both was as binding as any marriage vows.

'That's all right, then,' Jim said, 'and sure there'll be no more talk of me moving out. I'm not shifting from here so you'd better find another lodger as soon as you like.' He gave her then one of his rare smiles and Charlotte wanted to take his face between her hands and kiss his mouth.

She stepped back a pace as though removing herself from danger. 'I'd better make some tea,' she said a little shakily.

Jim seated himself at the table and began to push tobacco into the bowl of his pipe. Charlotte carried the teapot to the table and thought how right he looked in her kitchen, and she knew that without Jim her life would be empty.

He stared at her through the smoke. 'The lock-out will go on much longer than anyone realizes,' he said. 'I have some savings, fortunately, and I shall be able to pay my rent for some time yet.' He paused. 'Others will not be so fortunate.' He leaned forward, his elbows on the table, his face eager. 'But we must hold firm, otherwise we will never be able to bargain with the bosses again – they will have total power over the working man and power corrupts.'

'I believe you're right,' Charlotte said. 'Gronow was a union man to the marrow, he would have been out on strike with you like a shot.'

Jim nodded slowly. 'Any man you would take as a husband must have been a good 'un,' he said soberly.

Charlotte poured more tea without really noticing what she was doing. She felt able to talk to Jim about anything under the sun, even about her first marriage without feeling awkward and tongue-tied. And now here she was making an unspoken pact to belong to Jim O'Conner once the time was right. She was a lucky woman.

'What about your brother?' Jim asked. 'Do you think he'll stick to his guns and continue to work the slant?'

Charlotte nodded. 'Yes, our Luke is a man of determination, just as you are, Jim.'

'I'm sure he believes in the right of what he's doing,' Jim replied. 'He's a good man and a good boss but he can't see the truth of it – that unless we fight we shall always be at the mercy of the bosses.'

'He's worked hard for what he's got,' Charlotte said slowly. 'I can see why he wouldn't want to lose it all overnight, mind.'

'So can I,' Jim said. 'I respect him for what he's done in the past but I can't agree with what he's doing now.'

'But his mine would be ruined if he neglected it,' Charlotte said quickly. 'All those years of hard work would be wasted.'

'He could just work on safety measures,' Jim suggested. 'Keep the water out and see that the collar and arms are in a good state of repair but stop bringing out coal, that's all I would ask of him.'

'Have you put it to him like that?' Charlotte asked and Jim shook his head. 'It must be his decision. It's not my task to try and browbeat men into making any move they would not make voluntarily. A half-hearted supporter is worse than useless.'

'I suppose you're right.' Charlotte sipped her tea. She felt torn between Jim's arguments, with which she agreed, and loyalty to her brother.

Jim seemed to sense her feelings. 'I'm not against Luke personally, you know that,' he said. 'It's just that the injustice done to the workers sticks in my craw. Sure as it stands, the bosses can impose longer hours on the miner, split up father and son who have worked the same stall for years, insist on a greater measure of coal being brought out for less money – these are injustices that will go on for as long as we let them.'

'I know,' Charlotte said softly. 'I know better than most the grinding dirt in which the miner lives, the dangers of fire damp, of roof falls and, worst of all, the prospect of a miner never seeing the sun throughout the entire winter months.' Charlotte sighed. 'Better conditions and better wages are the right of the miner, I agree with you, and yet when I see the pinched faces of the young children who are going hungry, when I see the queues outside the soup kitchens, I feel afraid and doubtful that the strike was the right action to take.'

'The soup kitchens are what holds the men firm in their resolve,' Jim said. 'They come together for that one good meal a day and they talk to each other, give each other courage.'

'And yet it's such a pitiful sight,' Charlotte replied, 'and then the miners having to go round cap in hand to their more fortunate neighbours; it must be so hard for them to swallow their pride.'

'Sure that's true enough,' Jim said, pressing more tobacco into his pipe, 'and yet it's a big man who can ask for help and get it willingly.'

There was the sound of light footsteps on the stairs and Sheila entered the kitchen. She smiled when she saw her brother.

'I though I heard your voice, Jim. Been talking Charlotte's head off so you have.' She sat down near the fire and clasped her hands in her lap. 'You've heard that I'm going home, have you?' she asked, and it was clear that she was nervous by the way her voice shook.

Jim nodded. 'Sure an' if that's what you want then, Sheila, that's what you must do.'

'Oh, I'm so relieved,' she said breathlessly. 'I thought you'd try to persuade me to stay!'

'Why should I try to alter your mind?' Jim said gently. 'I know how homesick you've been.'

'Well, it's the problem of lodgings,' Sheila said quickly. 'I know it will be difficult for you to remain here with Charlotte when I leave and I didn't want to upset you.'

'That's all right.' Jim smiled but he was looking at Charlotte. 'We understand each other perfectly.'

Suddenly Charlotte felt light-headed, a sense of joy filled her and as she returned Jim's smile, she knew without doubt that a new life was opening up before her.

17

The warmth of the May weather turned suddenly to rain that washed down pavements, clogging drains and causing roads to flood. The sky above Sywen's Eye was heavy with the pall of smoke from the pointing chimney-stacks mingling with the dark rain clouds. The hills of Mount Pleasant seemed to disappear into the mist, the contours blurred overnight.

But within the drawing-room of Mary's house, there was warmth and laughter, a fire crackled in the big grate and the heavy drapes and fluffy carpeting held the dampness at bay.

Mary looked down at the ornate box full of rich chocolate cakes and shook her head. 'Paul Soames, you are spoiling me. I'll be like the side of a house if I keep eating all the goodies you bring me, mind!'

'Rubbish! You're a fine looking woman and you know it.' He took her hand in his and stared down at her. 'You'll always be beautiful to me.'

'Mush!' Stephan, seated near the fire, his long legs spread out towards the blaze, spoke with a tone of indulgent disgust.

'Hush you, my boy!' Mary said with mock sharpness. 'You're still wet behind the ears and anyone the least bit older is ancient to you.'

Stephan rose and holding his stick made his way through the obstacles of the furniture with ease born of practice.

'I'm going to my room,' he said in a tone of good humour, 'leave you love birds to get on with it.'

When the door had closed behind her son, Mary looked at Paul with some humour. 'There's no need to take any notice of Stephan,' she said softly, 'it's only his idea of fun.'

Paul took her hands in his, the sensation was pleasing and Mary found herself leaning closer, her arms creeping around his neck. It was good to be held in a man's arms once again, if only for a moment. She moved away then, abruptly.

'What do you think about this stupid strike?' she said quickly. 'Aren't the workers fools to themselves? They should be shot, the lot of them.'

'I agree,' Paul said smiling, 'but I don't want to talk about the workers, I want to talk about us. I think you may care a little for me and love can grow in the most unexpected way. In any case, I have enough love for the both of us.'

Mary moved away from him. 'Please, Paul,' she said, her eyes searching his face. 'Just give me a little time to think things over, will you?'

He touched her face with his fingers. 'You can have all the time in the world, my love, but please don't condemn yourself to a life spent alone.' He moved towards the fireplace and thrust his hands in his pockets. 'You know I would treat Stephan just as though he was my own son, don't you?'

Mary nodded. 'Yes, I do know that, Paul, and Stephan is very fond of you. So am I,' she added quickly.

Paul smiled a little wryly. 'Fond is such a telling word, isn't it?' He walked towards the door. 'Well, I must get on with my work,' he said briskly. 'There are patients to see and calls to make, and I won't get anything done hanging around here, tempting as the thought might be.'

Mary moved from her chair and, putting her hands on his shoulders, kissed his cheek. 'Come again, soon,' she said warmly.

She watched from the window as he slid into his car and, with a quick glance towards her, drove away, the car skidding a little on the wet surface of the road. He was a fine man – perhaps the only man she could bear to share her life with, so why did she hold back from him?

She returned to her seat near the fire and closed her eyes. Her love for Brandon had been so overwhelming

225

it seemed nothing could replace it. She had quarrelled with her husband, had often disagreed with him and yet underneath everything was a solid love holding them together.

She had slept in Paul's arms for one night only and then she had been crazed with grief believing Brandon had been killed at the battle-front. And yet the union had held a sweetness, a rightness that she could not deny. Paul had taken her with tenderness, he had loved her even then and any betrayal had been on her part, not his.

She shook away the discomfiting thoughts and resolutely got to her feet. Like Paul she had work to do, and sitting near the fire indulging herself in dreams of the past would not achieve anything.

'Stephan!' she called. 'I'm going out for an hour or two. I shan't be long.' She waited for his indistinct response and then hurriedly pulled on a coat and a velvet hat that covered the gloss of her hair. Work. That was the answer. It had always been her own personal antidote to pain. She left the house and closed the door on the warmth and security it contained and turned to breathe in the freshness of the day, for now the rain was easing. She would put the question of marrying Paul completely from her mind, for the moment. But, a warning voice told her, she would not put it off for long. Paul would require an answer and a decision would have to be made.

In the meantime there were matters of business to which she must attend, for her holdings in Sweyn's Eye were blossoming, adding to her not inconsiderable fortune. She was becoming the old Mary, competitive, welcoming a challenge, and suddenly she felt as though new life had been breathed into her, recharging her energies and stretching her horizons. She felt in that moment almost happy.

She slept very little, and in the early morning, Mary, lying in bed staring at the oblong of greyish light from the window, realized her decision had been made. She would gently push Stephan and Paul together, let them learn about each other, see how they got on. Only if her son and her one-time lover found themselves in tune would she consider marriage.

Stephan, always sensitive to her moods, touched her hand lightly. 'Are you going to marry Paul, mam?' he asked in his sweet mixture of American and Welsh. 'I think you should. He's a good man.'

'Oh, my son is ordering my life for me now then?' Mary said with feigned indignation. 'How would you feel about going out with Paul on his rounds, perhaps?' she asked, taking her son's arm and leading him through to the breakfast room.

His face brightened and Mary felt a pang of pain. Had his home become so much of a prison to him that her son should leap at any opportunity to escape from it?

'I'd like that very much,' he said with enthusiasm. 'Can I go with him this morning?'

'I should think so,' Mary said. 'I'll just slip along to his surgery in a moment and ask him. But first, a cup of tea to wake me up is it?'

She sat next to Stephan and watched anxiously as he lifted the cup of scalding tea to his lips. She was always fearful of accidents and yet she knew he must be allowed some measure of independence otherwise he would feel smothered by her. He was such a handsome boy with such a quick intelligence, and her aim in life had been to build up her resources so that when she was no longer with him, Stephan would have the means to care for himself. And yet wasn't there more he needed? The company and the understanding of another man was essential if Stephan were to grow into a well balanced man himself.

Paul was delighted to see her. 'Mary, you look beautiful this morning!' he said, taking her hands in his. 'But why are you out so early – is there any problem?'

'Paul.' Mary was a little breathless from hurrying along the rainswept road. 'Will you take Stephan with you on your calls today? I'd really appreciate it and so would he.'

'Of course I'll take him,' Paul said at once. 'I'd be happy to have his company; he's a very articulate young man, a credit to you, Mary.'

He held her arm as Mary moved to open the door. 'Hang on, I'm ready to go out now. I'll just get my hat and coat and I'll drive you back to the house; I don't like to think of you out in this terrible weather.'

'There's soft you are, Paul,' Mary said. 'I only live a few doors away but you're very, very nice.' She touched his cheek and he took her hand, kissing the palm gently.

'Come on!' He shrugged into his overcoat and set his hat at a jaunty angle on his head. He looked very young and very carefree, and Mary felt infected by his good humour.

The leather seat crackled coldly beneath her as Mary settled herself in the car. She shivered and drew her coat more closely around her.

'There's awful this constant rain!' she said as Paul started the car. She wondered now if she'd been wise to suggest that Stephan accompany Paul on his calls; perhaps she would have been better to leave matters rest until the rain had cleared. She watched Paul negotiate the car past a horse and cart.

The animal whinnied, and reared in fear, hooves flailing, and Paul instinctively put his foot on the brake. The car seemed to pause and then swung sickeningly inwards, crashing against the wooden cart and sending coal flying in all directions over the road. But the car was not halted in its tracks; it continued onwards towards the wall surrounding Mary's house.

She did not feel the impact. She opened her eyes to find blood running down the side of her face. For a moment it seemed to her a nightmare repetition of the accident she'd had when Stephan was a child. She moved cautiously but her legs were trapped and she could not free herself. She lifted her hand to her face and rubbed at her eyes in an effort to clear them. The cart was in splinters on the other side of the road but the driver and his horse appeared unhurt.

Beside her, Paul groaned and she turned to him in alarm. He was slumped over the wheel and the windshield was in sparkling shards around his head. Mary couldn't see his face and she was slumped too far against the door to reach him. She stared at his broad shoulders and the darkness of his hair curling against his collar, and something moved within her. 'Do not die, Paul,' she whispered, 'please do not die.'

The door of her house was opened and Mrs Bush was hurrying down the steps and along the drive. Behind her, Stephan was poised in the doorway, his stick reaching out before him and Mary tried to call out to him to go back indoors. Her voice was so light she could hardly hear it herself and she tried to sit up straighter in the buckled seat.

Mrs Bush was staring at her, eyes wide, and Mary took a deep breath. 'Fetch help,' she said and after a long, agonizing moment, the woman hurried away. Mary sighed and closed her eyes. She was in no pain – did that mean that she was unhurt, she wondered, or had the shock of the accident numbed her senses?

She struggled to see over the edge of the window and a scream rose soundlessly from her throat as she saw her son's efforts to get to her. He was waving his stick before him, moving slowly down the step, his head lifted as he tried to locate her by sound.

'Go back, Stephan!' Mary called but he moved stubbornly forward, stick tapping against the ground. Then what she feared happened. As though in slow motion, Stephan's stick slid away from him. He fell sideways against the wall and the sickening sound of the impact hit Mary as if with a physical blow.

Frantically she tried to release her legs. It was a nightmare from which she could not escape. Stephan lay quite still against the wall, his face resting against the wet ground.

'Help, someone please help!' Mary cried. It seemed an eternity before she heard the sound of running feet. Mrs Bush had called an ambulance and the fire brigade, and the noise of the vehicles rushing to her aid brought fresh hope to Mary.

It took moments only to prise open the damaged door and Mary was lifted out into the coldness of the air. With no thought for herself, she waved the helpers away.

'Please see to the others, I'm all right.' She managed to stand up straight, her hand against the cold stone of the wall and though she was trembling, there was no injury except a cut above her eye.

Paul was being lifted into the ambulance and Mary turned to try to reach her son but strong arms were around Stephan and he too was being carried to the ambulance.

'Come along, missus.' An ambulance man put his arm around her shoulder. 'You'd better come with me and have that wound seen to. Can you walk?'

Mary found that though she was still trembling she could stand unaided. But there was a numb sensation inside her. In the space of a few minutes, tragedy had again struck; her hopes and dreams were in ashes.

She sat in the ambulance in silence, afraid to look at Stephan or Paul and it seemed to Mary in that moment that her world had come to an end.

The fire was burning low in the grate and Charlotte lifted the scuttle reluctantly from its place in the hearth. She sighed heavily. She was tired and lonely; the boys were in bed and it was the night-times that she feared most when with Jim out at a meeting, she would sit alone staring at the four walls around her so aware of her need for Jim's strength.

Since Sheila had left for Ireland, Jim seemed to be out of the house a great deal and Charlotte had been strangely lonely. But that was understandable, she told herself. It was not many months since Gronow had died in the mine and though she still missed him she had picked up the pieces of her life and carried on. The shock of her sudden bereavement was lessening now; she was adjusting to widowhood.

Charlotte knew her two sons still missed their father but she had seen both Freddy and Denny turn more and more to Jim for guidance.

She sighed and hoisted the scuttle higher, she must refill it or she would be cursing in the morning if there was no coal to rekindle the fire.

It was damp and dark in the back yard with a faint moon half-hidden behind the clouds. Charlotte swung open the door to the shed and the creaking of it was loud in the silent air. She shovelled coal from the store and the dust rose up chokingly so that she began to cough. This had always been Gronow's task and she felt tears burn her eyes. He had been a good man and his death was untimely; was she a bad woman to be turning so soon to another man? But they had done nothing wrong and would not. They would wait until just the right time before moving their relationship onto a more intimate footing.

She closed the door of the coal house and pushed the bolt across; she didn't want stray animals sleeping in the coal.

She dragged the heavy scuttle back across the yard and pushed open the door with her foot. The light from the kitchen spilled out in a warm pool against the stones and it was then that the hair on the back of Charlotte's neck began to rise in apprehension.

'Who's there?' she demanded, turning quickly to look over her shoulder. Suddenly, so that she had no time to scream, a hand shot out and caught her arm. The scuttle fell to the floor with a crash and then Charlotte felt a hand clamp over her lips with bruising strength.

She was jerked indoors and the door kicked shut behind her. One arm was twisted painfully behind her back and she found herself thrust into the kitchen.

'Don't scream or shout, for if you rouse your children, it'll be the worse for them.' The voice, coming from behind her, had a trace of Irish in it and as Charlotte began to struggle, it was raised threateningly.

'Keep quiet, you foolish woman and I'll let you go.' She was released abruptly and she fell against the chair, grasping it for support. She rubbed at her arm and turned to face the man in the full light from the gas mantle.

'Michael Murphy, what are you doing here?' she asked in anger. 'I haven't any money or anything worth robbing.'

'You are Luke Proud's sister, that's why I'm here,' he said, glowering at her. He moved closer to her. 'Sure I'm mindful of having my revenge against Luke Proud in any way I can!'

He drew a chair towards him and set it close to her, sitting down on it, his face full of aggression.

'I don't know what I have to do to bring your fine brother out into the open.' Michael's voice was heavy with sarcasm. 'Is he a man or a rat to sit down under the treatment I gave his dear wife?'

'What do you mean?' Charlotte's mouth was dry. 'What have you done to Peta?' She instinctively drew back as he leaned towards her.

'Why, hasn't your brother told you?' He laughed maliciously. 'Keeping his shame to himself, is he? Well I can't blame him.

'Since you don't know, I'll tell you. I went to her house, the house she shares with her dear husband, and I gave Mrs Proud a lesson,' he said slowly. 'I showed her what it's like to have a real man between the sheets.'

Charlotte felt a sudden and burning anger. No wonder Peta had taken so sick that she'd gone out of her mind. She leaned towards Michael Murphy and stared into his face.

'You animal!' she said in a low voice. 'Get out of my house before I take the kitchen knife to you.'

He slapped her hard across the face and she fell back, her head spinning. 'Don't try to be clever!' he said. 'I don't take lip from any woman. Another couple of slaps might teach you to have some respect for me.'

'Respect?' Charlotte said, so angry that she felt no fear. 'Who could respect a man who has to force himself on a poor sick woman?'

'Shut your mouth.' Michael Murphy's face was red. 'And you'd better dig deep into your pockets, find me some money or I might just wreck this little home of yours.'

'You don't frighten me,' Charlotte said quickly. 'I haven't any money and if I did I wouldn't give it to you.' She moved towards the door but Michael caught her arm roughly.

'I can always take payment in kind,' he said meaningfully. Charlotte kicked out at him, catching him fully unprepared.

He released her and fell back, cursing loudly, and Charlotte ran towards the stairs. She would lock herself in with the boys and scream blue-murder through the window until someone came to help her.

Michael Murphy caught her before she even reached the bottom stair and dragged her back into the kitchen. 'Do you keep your savings in the teapot, I wonder? Most women do.' He picked up the china teapot and dropped it purposefully onto the stone floor. Tea spilled like tears across the grey flags. 'No, well, what about in the dresser-drawers, then?' He tugged at a drawer and it fell to the floor with a crash.

'Stop it!' Charlotte said fiercely. 'I've told you, there's no money so you're wasting your time.'

He turned to her then and slowly undid one of her buttons. Charlotte twisted away from him and on an impulse bit the hand trying to open her blouse.

He flung her roughly away from him. 'Whore!' he said furiously. 'I'll give you the finest hiding you've ever had and then I'll go through every stick and stone in this house until I find where you're keeping your money.'

The back door swung open and Charlotte gasped with relief as she saw the broad figure of Jim O'Conner filling the doorway. 'Leave her be,' Jim said quietly, 'and get out of here before I break your neck.'

Michael Murphy moved slowly to the door, his expression guarded. 'What's it to you, Jim O'Conner?' he asked sourly. 'I'm only having my revenge on the man who wronged me.'

'So you vent your spleen on a woman?' Jim's voice was edged with scorn. He caught Michael by the front of his shirt and spoke to him in a low voice. 'You're lucky to leave here in one piece, but if I catch you at this sort of game again, I'll tear your head from your shoulders, understand?'

Michael Murphy moved to the door and turned, a look of apprehension on his face. 'I only had a go at Proud's wife because I expected him to come looking for me. I could have taken it out of his hide then, in a man to man fight.'

'Luke Proud has not come looking for you because I don't think he's got the slightest idea what you've done,' Jim O'Conner said shortly. 'His wife is sick, or haven't you heard?'

Michael Murphy stood in the doorway. 'Well, that's not my fault; and there's still a score to settle, as far as I'm concerned.'

'Sure then settle it with the man himself and not with his womenfolk, do you get me?' Jim emphasized each word. 'Now out!'

Charlotte slumped into a chair, holding her torn bodice together. She was dazed, scarcely able to believe what had happened. She looked round at the kitchen and was filled with renewed anger.

'Oh, Jim, thank God you came back early. I don't know how I'd have held him off for much longer – the man's worse than an animal.'

Jim knelt before her and took her hands in his and Charlotte realized this was the first time they had touched. She felt warm inside as her fingers curled in his.

'There's glad I am you're here with me,' she whispered. She stared at him with wide eyes and for a moment it seemed Jim would take her in his arms but then he rose to his feet, deliberately moving away from her.

'I've been keeping an eye on Michael Murphy for some time,' he said. 'He pretends to be interested in the cause of the workers but he's more interested in himself.' He paused. 'Sure he's been collecting money for the men locked out and putting it in his own pocket. But the word is getting round and I don't think Murphy will be welcome anywhere for much longer.'

Charlotte heard footsteps on the stairs. '*Duw*, the boys are awake,' she said quickly. 'I expect they're wondering what all the noise is about.'

'What's going on, mam?' Freddy entered the kitchen, rubbing at his eyes. 'I heard a bang and then I couldn't get back to sleep.'

'It's all right, boys, back to bed with you. There's nothing to worry about; there's silly you both are standing in the cold with bare feet.' She hurried them out of the room before they could see the disorder Michael Murphy had created.

When she returned to the kitchen Jim was cleaning up the tea that had stained the floor and he glanced up at her, his face grim. 'I could kill that man Murphy,' he said, 'sure I'm ashamed that he's got Irish blood in him.'

Charlotte smiled, 'I thought you were going to spill some of that blood,' she said, 'the way you took him by the throat.'

Jim's face relaxed. 'You're a woman of fine spirit, Charlotte,' he said. 'I'm proud of the way you stood up for yourself.'

Charlotte flushed with pleasure at Jim's praise. He was not a man for paying compliments, which made his words more precious to hear.

'I'll make us a cup of tea,' she said quickly, turning away to hide her hot cheeks. 'I'm sure we could both do with one.'

She rummaged in the pantry and brought out the old brown teapot which – ironically – contained her small savings. 'He wasn't going to get his hands on this,' she said, taking off the lid and emptying the coins onto the table. '*Duw,* it will need a good rinsing before I can use it for its proper purpose, mind.'

Jim picked up the fallen drawer. Charlotte, looking round, could see no sign that Michael Murphy had ever been in her kitchen. He would not dare approach her again. She had seen the fear in his eyes when he'd been confronted with Jim's anger.

They sat then like an old married couple, one each side of the fire. She glanced up and caught Jim's eye, and looked away again quickly. She wanted to express something of her feelings but the words that came into her mind were trite. She rose and moved towards Jim and after hesitating for a moment, rested her hand on his shoulder. He looked up at her and she knew there was no need for words, they understood each other perfectly.

She left him to lock up and went up to her bedroom and stood for a long time looking out over the sleeping town.

'Gronow, my husband, if you can hear me, please send me your blessing, for I have found a good man to care for me and for our sons.'

She saw the lights from the bay twinkling in the darkness. The rain seemed to have stopped and a pale moon was shining, silvering the rooftops of the houses in the town.

Across the sky, against the soft darkness, a shooting star appeared in a sudden blaze of glory, falling away after a moment into the night. Silly and superstitious though it was, Charlotte sighed softly, believing her pleas had been answered. 'Rest peacefully now, Gronow,' she whispered.

18

Charlotte shifted the empty basket into the crook of her arm and paused to take a breath as she walked away from the silent empty shops of Market Street. Once more there had been no groceries for sale.

There was the sudden rumble of heavy vehicles and, turning, Charlotte saw a line of lorries winding slowly along the road. Steel-helmeted soldiers walked at each side of the convoy and Charlotte felt suddenly chilled.

'There's a sight then!' Old Nurse Benson stopped beside Charlotte to watch the procession of vehicles. 'What is it, boys?' she shouted and one of the soldiers glanced towards her good-naturedly.

'Food supplies, missus,' he called. 'We won't let you starve, see.' Nurse Benson shook her head.

'It's all right to bring supplies for them with money but what about the poor miners, then?' The nurse turned to Charlotte. 'And your brother blacklegging, on the side of the bosses – he should be ashamed!'

The cavalcade moved on and Charlotte returned to the silence of her own kitchen. The boys were at school and she was glad of the peace, for it gave her time to sort out her muddled thoughts. She had never been afraid of facing life full-on and yet she was weary of the abuse that was being thrown at her whenever she set foot outside. What Luke chose to do was his business but she was getting blamed.

Jim O'Conner had stood firmly by her, protecting her from spiteful tongues whenever he could and she was grateful to him.

She sighed and rose from her chair. There was work to be done; the washing to put on the line while the sun still shone and a host of small chores that would keep her occupied most of the morning. She opened the back door and stared out over the patchwork quilt of neatly fenced-off gardens nestling close to each other as though for comfort.

She dropped her basket of washing onto the garden, startled by a knocking on the front door. She moved quickly through the long, dim passageway and her pulse was beating swiftly. She did not know what to expect next.

'Luke!' She opened the door widely and ushered her brother into the house with an uncertain smile. 'What are you doing here? I thought you would be working.'

He stood near the fire, his hands thrust into his pockets and Charlotte looked at him with pride. Her brother was a fine, handsome man with success written in every line of his appearance.

The Slant Moira was flourishing against all odds, which was a lesson to the gossips who'd said that a carpenter wouldn't make good as a miner. She could not help being proud of him.

'You look smart,' Charlotte said. 'Getting to be every inch a businessman, aren't you?' He wore an elegantly-cut suit and crisp white collar which emphasized the clean line of his strong jaw. But there was no answering smile and Charlotte put her hand on his arm.

'You're worried sick, aren't you, love?' she said softly. 'Is Peta worse?' She bit her lip knowing she dare not tell her brother what harm Michael Murphy had done to his wife. Luke would be out for revenge and he might get hurt. In any case, the harm was done and nothing she said could change what had happened. It was best, she decided, to let sleeping dogs lie.

'There's no change,' he said, shaking his head, 'she simply sits there staring into the distance. I'm afraid she's going to need special care. Hattie does her best – feeding Peta herbal remedies – but there is no improvement that I can see.'

He seated himself near the chenille covered table. 'It's not only Peta, though. I'm concerned about Katie Murphy, too.' He paused, his eyes meeting Charlotte's. 'I haven't seen anything of her for some weeks.' He rubbed his fingers through his hair. 'I've tried to keep away, if only to be fair to her, and to Peta.' He clenched his hands into fists. 'I keep wondering if that brother of hers is interfering in her life. He's no good, Charlotte, a real bad 'un.'

'I know,' Charlotte said softly, shivering at the memory of the man's hands on her. She leaned forward and touched Luke's arm.

'I went round to the Murphy's shop just now but it was closed like all the shops. I could see Katie, if you like, just to find out how she is. Would that make you feel any better?'

He smiled, his frown clearing. 'It took you long enough to take the hint! Tell her just how sick Peta is and that I just can't see any future for Katie and me together.' He was suddenly serious.

'You should be telling her yourself!' Charlotte said softly. 'Surely there's no harm in you seeing her just for that?'

Luke nodded thoughtfully. 'You're right. Just let her know I'll be calling by this evening to see her.' He put his hand into his pocket. 'By the way, I've something for you.' He placed a packet on the table. 'It's the compensation. It's been long enough coming and I'm sorry.'

Charlotte sighed. 'It's good of you, Luke. I've been living on our savings so far and this money will tide me over for a while again but I must find myself another lodger if I can.'

Luke rose to his feet. 'I'll see what I can do,' he said, 'I have some useful contacts; perhaps I can find you someone.'

She waved to Luke from the window and watched as he disappeared along the winding roadway. He was a good man; a man with a conscience which was keeping him tied to a wife he no longer loved. Life was certainly complicated for him at the moment.

She was happy to be able to help him in however small a way. The sun was warmer now, the air fresher after the recent rain. Charlotte stepped out briskly. She had only an hour or two before the boys returned home from school.

She hurried along Canal Street, hoping that she wouldn't meet anyone who would give voice to the resentment felt against her brother. He was still her kin and she loved him, even though she felt he should be standing by the workers.

She turned the corner of Copperman's Row and Market Street and saw at once the beautifully-arranged window of what had once been Murphys' Fresh Fish Shop. Tins of meat stood in a tall pyramid in the centre of the display and at either side of them were bottles of sauce, packets of flour and an open tin of coffee beans. The convoy must have gone round to the shops supplying foodstuffs for sale and Charlotte sighed with relief – her stock of flour had been dangerously low. She smiled as she saw Katie behind the long wooden counter, weighing cooking apples and tipping them into a brown paper bag.

'Charlotte!' Katie said in obvious delight. 'What are you doing here?' She took the money from the customer and slipped it into a drawer, then gestured to Charlotte.

'Come around the counter and sit down,' she said warmly and Charlotte obeyed, breathing in the aromatic smell of the coffee beans as she walked past the grinder.

'I had to come and see you,' she said softly. She wanted to reassure Katie that Luke was anxious about her but she was almost afraid to speak his name.

Katie, however, had no such compunction. 'How is Luke?' she asked, speaking so calmly that Charlotte felt her tensions ease.

'He's in good health,' Charlotte replied. 'Concerned about you, mind. It's because of him I came here – he'd like to speak to you tonight, it that's all right by you.'

Katie's eyes were suddenly alight. She turned away and stared down at her hands. 'What about Peta, is she still sick?'

'Oh aye, she's sick all right, poor dab.' Charlotte settled herself more comfortably in her chair. 'Doesn't seem to know anyone. According to Luke, she just sits staring at nothing.'

'What on earth could have happened to make her that way?' Katie said softly. 'Surely it wasn't the fault of Luke and me, was it? Jesus, Mary and Joseph, I'd never forgive myself if I'd had a hand in driving her mad.'

Charlotte shook her head. 'I'm sure you and Luke have done nothing wrong,' she said at once. 'Many a man has taken a liking to another woman. *Duw*, half the neighbourhood would be sick if that was the cause.'

'I suppose you're right.' Katie sighed. 'Tell Luke I'm fine sure enough and the business is doing well when we have the supplies.' As if to emphasize her words the doorbell rang and a woman with three young children hanging round her skirts walked timidly into the shop.

'Oh, Miss Murphy, could I trouble you for a loaf and a few spuds, just until the end of the week?'

'Of course you can, Mrs Keys. I've told you before, your credit is good with me.' Katie smiled. 'Ten pound of potatoes enough for now?' She weighed them and placed them into the woman's shopping basket then added a loaf and a quarter of tea. 'Now be sure to come back whenever you need something more.'

The woman's pale lips trembled. 'My man came out on strike, see. One of seven brothers he is and the big boss would only take on three of them again. Trouble-makers he said they were, and my husband as quiet as the day he was born.'

She straightened. 'But I've got a job now – started on Monday, cleaning for the doctor. A good man is Paul Soames, mind.' She clasped the hand of her youngest child and, admonishing the others to keep close to her, swung open the door so that the bell rang loudly.

She left the shop and Katie shook back her red hair. 'Sure an' there's always someone worse off than yourself.'

Charlotte watched as she took a book from under the counter and wrote carefully the amount of money Mrs Keys owed her.

'I doubt if you'll get any of that back,' Charlotte said reprovingly. 'You should think of yourself a bit more, Katie and don't be taken in by hard luck stories.'

Katie smiled. 'Mrs Keys will pay me, if it's only a few pence a week. She's been a customer here since before mammy died.'

'Well, I suppose you know your own business best,' Charlotte said gently but she was studying Katie, noticing the shadows beneath her eyes and the new gauntness in her face.

Katie moved to the door and drew down the blind, pushing the bolt into place. 'There, I've had enough for one day. I'm going to put my feet up and have a rest.'

Charlotte followed Katie along the narrow passage towards the kitchen. A good fire burned in the grate and the room looked cosy and welcoming.

'*Duw*, there's lovely you've got it in by here; it's really warm and nice. I envy you.'

Katie smiled a little sadly. 'Sure it's fine enough but it holds a lot of memories for me, not all of them happy.' She sank into a chair. 'And then there's the threat of Michael always hanging over me. I just don't know when he'll turn up here.'

Charlotte remembered with a glow of happiness the way Jim O'Conner had dealt with Michael. He'd been a man of iron, banishing Michael with a few words, daring him to ever bother her again.

'What your brother needs is a good hiding,' she said. 'I'm sorry, Katie, I know he's your own flesh and blood, but Michael is bad through and through.'

'I know,' Katie sighed. 'He went away from Sweyn's Eye a fine young man, a loving son and brother but sure 'tis a stranger who came back.'

Charlotte pushed back her hair. 'Well, Katie, I've got to get back home. Those rips of mine will be back from school any minute and no tea ready for them.' She smiled. 'And Fredrick is a starver! There's a one for his food – eats like a horse he does, just like his dad.'

Charlotte shivered, experiencing a slip in time, one of those moments when she almost forgot that Gronow was dead. She felt Katie's hand on her shoulder and looked up at her quickly.

'I'm all right,' she said in a low voice, 'it's just that sometimes it's hard to realize I'll never see him again.'

'I know,' Katie said softly and Charlotte remembered that Katie had lost both her brother and her mother during the past year. It was no wonder she was looking pale and thin. On an impulse, she hugged Katie tightly.

'I'm not really self-pitying,' she said in a muffled voice. 'I realize I'm not the only one to lose a loved one, and at least I've got my sons by my side.' As well as a fine, strong man, a small voice inside her said.

'Thanks for coming over, Charlotte.' Katie smiled. 'Sure 'tis good of you to think about me but you can tell Luke he's welcome to call.' She gestured towards the shop. 'Trade is picking up; I'll be rich one day, you'll see.'

Her words were brave but Charlotte had not failed to notice only one customer had entered the shop while she'd been there – a woman who had not even paid cash for the goods she'd taken away.

The bell jangled behind her as she closed the door and for a moment Charlotte felt tears burn her eyes. Poor Katie, what a lonely dismal life she led. She squared her shoulders and moved purposefully down the street. She would make a point of seeing Luke and telling him the truth – that Katie was not doing so well and that she was looking thin and pale. Surely it would not do any harm if he visited her once in a while?

As she hurried towards home, she told herself she must stop trying to sort out other people's problems, she had enough of her own. She smiled; at least now she had flour and could make some bread in time for supper. At the thought of being with Jim, seated opposite him at the table, her spirits rose. She didn't see a small ragged boy pick up a stone and hurl it in her direction. It caught her a glancing blow on her shoulder and she spun round in anger.

'Blackleg!' the boy shouted, but his small pinched face was twisted with misery and suddenly Charlotte felt near to tears. She placed the bag of flour on a nearby window-sill. 'Here, son, take this home to your mam,' she said softly and suddenly her sense of elation had vanished.

Luke wiped his brow. It was warm in the darkness of the heading and sweat made rivulets of lightness in the caked dust of his face. Beside him, Old Cal whinnied softly, wanting release from the dusty tomb and the freshness of daylight outside the Slant Moira.

'All right, boy.' Luke pressed palms against his waist, easing his back as much as he could in the confines of the low heading. 'Only a little while longer and we can haul this lot of coal out of here.'

'There we are then, boss.' Tim pushed the curling box towards Luke, 'that'll make up a good ton, I'd say.'

It never ceased to amaze Luke the way the colliers could assess the amount of coal they had dug from the rock. The dram was full but amongst the good Red Vein anthracite there would be bits of rock and slag, worthless rubbish that would be cast aside before the coal was loaded for delivery.

In the deep pits, up to half a dram of rubbish had to be thrown away for every ton mined and the collier forced to break his back to make up his load before he went off shift. Here in the Slant Moira, things were much easier. Luke Proud did not rely on bullying and force to get the best out of his men, but on loyalty and dedication to make the mine a success. The prosperity of the Slant Moira was their prosperity too, for without it they would most certainly be out of a job.

'Right then, Cal old man.' Luke slapped the horse's rump lightly. 'Let's get out of here.' He sat astride the gun that sloped between the horse and the dram, a dangerous exercise and one that was forbidden in most pits. More than one man had slipped from the narrow shaft to fall beneath the wheels of the dram.

Luke ducked his head as the heading lowered in height and Cal, used to such conditions, hung his big head until his nose almost touched the rails. The horse was willing now, eager to be out in the light and Luke clung tightly as the

244

dram jumped over a piece of loose coal, almost derailed by the obstacle.

'Take it easy there, Cal,' he said softly, 'sure there's no need to rush our fences is there?' He smiled to himself in the darkness recognizing the philosophy that had kept him going even against the hostility and hatred shown him by many of the people in the town. Because he'd stood by his beliefs, kept his pit open in spite of outside pressures, he was being daubed a blackleg and a traitor to his class.

At home there was no relief for he could not talk over his problems with Peta, for she was far too sick. Indeed, she had become little more than a recluse, silent and withdrawn, always sitting in her room beside the fire that burned night and day.

Hattie had managed to cope so far but the woman was looking worn and tired and Luke expected that any day now she would give in and ask to be relieved of her duties. What he would do then he had no idea, but there must be a way out of his worries somehow.

He warmed a little, thinking that tonight he would see Katie, talk to her, look into her sweet face. She was the one stable element in his life and until now he had deprived himself of her company, feeling it wrong to give her false hope about the future. A wife who was well and strong he could leave, but how could he desert poor, helpless Peta?

It was quite late in the evening when he strode along Market Street towards Murphys' shop. He saw the shutters were in place and the heavy front door closed. He made his way around the back and tapped lightly on the door.

'Katie, it's me, Luke,' he said softly. The door was opened at once and Katie drew him into the cosiness of the little kitchen.

'Luke, I've missed you so much,' she said and there were tears in her eyes. He took her in his arms.

'I've missed you, too, Katie but I thought it best to stay away. I have nothing to offer you. I could never leave Peta, not now.'

Katie clung closer to him. 'Luke, I'm not a silly, innocent young girl,' she said gently. 'I'm a woman who has lived and loved and not always wisely. I don't expect the earth but what I do want is your love. I'm lost without it, Luke.'

Slowly his mouth came down on hers. She was soft and pliant in his arms; he held her even closer and she clung to him as though she would never let him go.

'Come with me,' she whispered and drew him towards the stairs. 'I know what I'm doing and I'm not asking you to make any promises, but we deserve a little happiness, Luke; we deserve that surely.'

It was dark in the bedroom and he could hear Katie's soft breathing as she took off her clothes. He slipped into the softness of the bed and she curled close to him. The scent of her was intoxicating.

'Katie, my lovely girl.' He kissed her again and felt the soft thrust of her breast against him. She was beautiful and he wanted nothing more than to be with her, if only for snatched moments such as this one.

There was no more need of words. They moved together as though they were made for each other and Luke felt he had never been so happy as he was at this moment.

Katie's mouth was against his, she moaned softly and he suddenly felt as though he had become ten feet tall. She was giving him passion as well as love, she wanted him as much as he wanted her and it was a wonderful feeling.

At last they lay side by side, quiet and content. Katie's fingers were curled within his and her legs twined around him, as though the two of them had become bound together.

He turned to her in the darkness and touched her cheek. 'Katie, the hardest thing I've ever had to do in my life is get out of this bed and leave you.' he said softly.

'I know, my love, but sure there will be other times; we are one flesh now and nothing will ever be able to come between us.'

'But I'd like to acknowledge you openly,' he said. 'You are too good to be nothing more than a kept woman.'

Katie laughed gently. 'I can't be a kept woman if you're not keeping me, can I?' She wound her arms around his neck. 'We will know that there is true love between us,' she said, 'and that is good enough for me. Go on home now but come back to me soon.'

He dressed swiftly and kissed her mouth gently. As he let himself out of the house he felt he was leaving all he ever wanted in the darkness of the bedroom at the back of Murphys' Shop.

He turned at the end of the road and looked back, and in the silent moonlit night a dog howled miserably. Luke thrust his hands into his pockets, and as he made for home he felt alive for the first time in months.

19

A soft wind was coming in from the sea and poked inquisitive fingers through windows, lifting curtains so that they billowed, ghost-like, in the early morning light. In the drawing-room of her house on Mount Pleasant, Mary sat still before the fire, staring into the flames as they blurred before her tear-filled eyes.

'Oh, Stephan, my little love, please get better,' she whispered.

But she was wasting time sitting nursing her worries, she told herself firmly; she should be getting ready to bring Paul home from the hospital.

Paul had recovered from the crash with remarkable rapidity. He had sustained a badly-sprained arm and cuts and bruising but he was now well enough to come home. Mary had insisted that he stay with her so that she could look after him. She realized dimly that she was at her best when fighting a battle and fight she must, for her son lay silent and unwaking in the hospital ward.

She drew on a light coat and pressed a velvet hat down over her ears. A small piece of hair escaped, falling across her forehead and for a moment, as she stared at her reflection in the hall mirror, she appeared absurdly young.

'Mrs Bush, I'm off now,' she called. 'Please make sure that the fire in the guest room is kept in. I don't want the doctor catching a summer cold on top of everything else.'

Mrs Bush appeared silently from the kitchen and her dark eyes held disapproval of the fact than an unmarried man was to stay beneath the same roof as her mistress.

'I'll make sure everything is all right, Mrs Sutton,' she said, her tone implying that she always did.

Oh, for the warmth and friendship of Old Greenie, Mary thought as she let herself out of the house.

The steps were damp with a sprinkling of rain and the breeze from the sea was fresher. Mary wrapped her coat more tightly around her and moved towards the car. She stood for a moment, staring into the distance, unaware that she cut an imposing figure; tall and upright and with a determined slant to her chin that dared anyone or anything to cross her.

She drove carefully down the steep hill towards the town and turned the car in the direction of the hospital. Her mouth was dry as she wondered what awaited her there. She would see Stephan before picking up Paul, and she could only hope and pray that there had been some improvement in her son's condition.

It had seemed ironic that she and Paul had escaped from the crashed car with very little injury and yet Stephan, who had merely slipped on the muddy pathway, was still unconscious.

The traffic was light and she negotiated St Helens road with ease, finally drawing the car to a halt at the kerb. The gates of the hospital were flanked by trees and the blossoms were beginning to fall. Mary shivered unaccountably before moving briskly towards the entrance.

She lingered for a moment near the door to the ward where Stephan lay. Her mouth felt dry as though she had not tasted liquid for days and the pulse in her head had begun to beat fiercely.

Taking a deep breath, she pushed open the door and moved quickly down the long ward. To outward appearances she was calmness itself.

He lay still beneath the blankets, his eyes closed. He was pale except for where the bruise coloured his cheek blue and purple.

Mary sat beside him and touched his hand. 'Stephan, can you hear me?' she said softly. 'I've come to take Paul home and I want to take you home too, back up on Mount Pleasant where you belong, so please wake up.' She lifted his hand to her cheek and closed her eyes against hot tears, trying through the force of her love to reach him. If only he would show by a flicker of an eyelash that he'd heard her, she would be happy.

She lost track of time as she sat staring into her son's face and it was only when one of the nurses touched her shoulder that she realized she was stiff and uncomfortable in the hard chair.

'Please, Mrs Sutton, don't upset yourself. I've seen youngsters unconscious for weeks and then wake up just as though they'd been having a sleep. They are very resilient, are children.' She straightened and her professional detachment returned. 'Doctor Soames is ready to go, now. He's waiting for you outside.'

Mary touched Stephan's cheek fleetingly and then rose to her feet. 'You'll tell me if there's any change,' she asked, 'any change at all?'

'Of course.' The nurse took her arm as though to guide her towards the door.

'I'm all right.' Mary forced a smile. 'There's silly you must think me crying about the place like a little baby.'

'Not at all,' the nurse said and though her tone was professionally polite there was sympathy in her eyes.

Outside the doors of the ward Paul stood waiting, his arm in a sling and the remains of a bruise in the centre of his forehead. One eye was swollen and puffy but he smiled when he saw her and moved towards her, holding out his uninjured arm.

'Mary.' He held her close and in that moment, she knew that she loved him. Perhaps it wasn't the passion and pain that had marked her relationship with Brandon but it was a feeling of belonging, as though she had come home.

She smiled though her mouth trembled. 'I know this isn't the time or the place, but will you marry me, Paul?'

He closed his eyes and held her even more closely and she could feel his heart thudding against hers. They stood in silence for a long moment and then he led her towards the doors, and down the steps towards her car.

'I'll make the arrangements as soon as possible,' he said softly. 'We'll keep it quiet. I know you wouldn't want any fuss in the circumstances, Mary.'

In the car, she leaned against him for a moment and it was good to know that he loved her. She was an unfulfilled woman if she was not needed by someone. 'Let's go home,' she said softly.

He sat back as she drove through the town and up the hill towards Mount Pleasant. 'We'll have to sell one of the houses,' he said. 'We won't need to keep two establishments going.'

Mary smiled at him indulgently. 'Practical as ever, Paul, but you're right, it would be foolish to maintain two homes.' She glanced towards him. 'I'll sell my house and move into yours, after all your surgery is established there and I wouldn't want to put your patients out.'

She drew up outside her own front door and sighed. 'Another good reason for getting rid of my property is that I can dispense with the services of Mrs Bush. She's so cold and disapproving somehow, though for the life of me I can't think why.'

Paul climbed out of the car. 'It's not like you to be soft, Mary. You should have sent her packing straight away if you didn't take to her.' He took her arm. 'Come on let's go and face the dragon together, I'll give you moral support.'

Mary smiled at him warmly. 'There's soft you are,' she said, reverting to the Welsh. 'I'm not afraid to do my own dirty work and it will be in my own good time, mind.'

Paul held up his uninjured arm. 'All right, you're the boss in this house but it will be different when you move into mine, I assure you.'

The fire burned brightly in the grate and a tray of tea stood ready on the table in the drawing-room. It was almost as though Mrs Bush had got wind of Mary's plans and was making an extra-special effort.

Paul winked slowly. 'Assumptions have been made,' he said drily, 'and the right answer has been found; someone not too far away from here knows your mind better than you do, Mary.'

Mary closed the door. 'But Mrs Bush couldn't have known,' she said, shaking her head. 'I didn't know myself that I wanted to marry you until I saw you standing outside the doors in the hospital waiting for me.'

Paul smiled at her. 'But it's true that the outsider sees most of the game, Mary. Now pour that tea, *cariad*, I'm parched.'

Mary moved towards Paul and placed her arms around his neck. 'You are going to be a bully, I can see that.' She raised her face to his and slowly, Paul touched her mouth with his own.

The kiss was so beautiful Mary wanted to cry. There was love and passion and a great sense of rightness, and when she moved away from him her eyes were shining.

'We're going to make a go of it, aren't we, Paul?' she said softly. 'We'll be good together, you and me.'

They were married a week later by special licence and as Paul had promised, it was a quickly arranged affair. The only guests present were Mali and her husband Sterling. As Paul slipped the ring onto her finger, a shaft of sunlight penetrated the stained-glass windows of the church and Mary felt humbly as though a benediction had been bestowed upon her.

The four of them took tea in a private room in the Mackworth Hotel and Mary felt that if only Stephan was with her, she would be entirely happy. But her son still lay silent and unmoving in the hospital ward, the bruises fading now but leaving him so pale and drawn that it hurt Mary to see him.

She would not speak of him and spoil the party atmosphere that prevailed in the little room looking out onto the bustling Stryd Fawr, but she had made up her mind to bring him home and nurse Stephan herself.

'You're a beautiful bride.' Mali leaned towards her and touched her hand. Mary smiled deprecatingly.

'*Duw*, you have to say that, mind, it's expected of you.' She smiled. 'But there's kind you are anyway.'

'I'm not just saying it.' Mali's tone was soft. 'You really are happy with Paul, aren't you, Mary? You more than anyone deserves happiness.'

'I'm happy with my husband,' Mary said truthfully, 'it's just that Stephan . . . but no, I'm not going to put a damper on today. Today is mine and Paul's and I'm going to put unpleasant thoughts out of my mind just for a little while.'

'Quite right too,' Paul said, catching the end of her conversation. 'Today you are Mrs Paul Soames and you have made me the happiest man in the world.'

Sterling leaned forward in his chair. 'Now, I've got a claim to that title,' he said, smiling.

Mary looked at her friends and then met the eyes of her new husband and a warmth grew inside her. It was good to be loved.

Later, Mary and Paul made their departure and drove through the now-quiet streets towards Mount Pleasant. Paul negotiated the hill and drew the car to a halt outside his house.

Mary moved quickly from the car. 'Now, don't you dare attempt to carry me over the threshold,' she said, laughing, 'I'm far too big a lady for that sort of nonsense.'

Paul took no notice of her. He swept her into his arms and after pushing open the door he carried her into the hallway which, in spite of being polished thoroughly, still smelled of wintergreen oil and Dettol.

'We shall have a little glass of sherry just to warm us through and then we'll go to bed.' He kissed her cheek. 'You're trembling. Come and sit near the fire while I do the honours.'

He moved to the table where the glasses gleamed in the firelight and poured out some of the mature sherry. 'Cheer up, you're not going to the scaffold, mind, but to your marriage bed.'

'I know.' Mary took the glass from him. 'And believe me, I'm happy with you, Paul. We've done the right thing, I feel it deep inside me.'

She held the shimmering glass high. 'To us, Paul, my love – to you and me.' She drank the sherry, swallowing it quickly and it warmed her so that she felt a tingling in her fingers.'

'Hey, take it easy,' Paul said smiling, 'you are supposed to sip not gulp.' He took the glass away from her and drew her to her feet. 'Well, Mrs Soames, shall we retire for the night?'

Holding her hand, he led her up the wide staircase and the silence of the house folded around Mary like a cloak. Paul had given his housekeeper the night off to be sure of being alone.

In the master bedroom, the curtains were drawn against the night. Though the fire had died into mere embers, the thick walls retained the warmth. The double bed was covered in a blue silk spread and the gas lamp spluttered, casting a white glow over everything.

Paul gently undid the buttons at the collar of her velvet dress and it slipped softly to the carpet. Mary stood close to him and slipped her arms around his waist. She felt strangely nervous; it was a long time since she'd been in a man's arms.

Paul tipped her face towards him and kissed her gently at first, then with increasing desire. It was unbelievable that she was still capable of passion after all that had happened to her. Suddenly she felt young again, restored to the girl she once was. She put her hands on Paul's face and her mouth was warm beneath his.

He lifted her and carried her to the bed. She lay there in the dimness, waiting eagerly for him to join her. He was a fine man, broad of shoulder and slim of hip. His skin gleamed with health in the light from the gas lamp and his hair stood crisply from his broad forehead.

He sighed as he drew her towards him and they lay together gently touching, exploring, almost as though they were getting to know each other for the first time. And yet there was that night, long ago in the agony of the war years, when she had gone to him and they had made love; yet it had been desperation that had driven Mary into his arms then while now it was love.

His mouth was warm upon her throat, moving sensuously to her breast. She gasped and clung closer to the silk of his shoulders. She was alive, really alive, for the first time in many a weary year.

He took her gently at first as though afraid of alarming her but as she sighed in his arms he became more passionate, demanding that she move with him in the age old rhythms of love. At last she cried out in fulfilment and together they lay side by side, breathless with delight.

'Have I ever told you, Mary, how very much I love you?' Paul whispered in her ear. She turned to him, her eyes bright.

'And I love you, Paul, with all my heart.'

In the morning Paul arranged for Stephan to come home. He moved about the hospital with such authority – organizing transport in the ambulance, assuring everyone that he was a doctor, quite capable of caring for the sick boy. Mary stood back and marvelled at the strength and purpose in her new husband. She realized suddenly that she admired him as well as loved him.

Stephan lay pale beneath the red blanket in the ambulance and Mary, seated beside him, took his hand in hers.

'We're going home, Stephan,' she told the unconscious boy. 'Paul and I are going to take good care of you. We'll make you better between us, you see if we don't.'

There was no flicker of the eyes, no sign that her son understood her and yet Mary felt that somehow she was reaching him. His face was pale and still as a marble statue, the long lashes curling against the shadows beneath his eyes. He was so beautiful, so like his father that Mary felt tears burn her eyes. She couldn't lose him; hadn't she lost enough when Brandon had died so cruelly?

At last the ambulance drew to a halt and Stephan was carried carefully up the steps towards the doorway. From her own house, Mary saw the curtains flutter and knew that Mrs Bush was there, awaiting her instructions. Mary sighed. She had not yet told the housekeeper her services were no longer required and the house would be put up for sale.

Stephan was carried into the bedroom and as Mary tucked the clothes around his chin, she felt tears burn her eyes. 'Please wake up and look at me, my lovely,' she whispered, but her son was still and silent.

It took a great deal of courage for Mary to cross to her house the next morning and face Mrs Bush with her dismissal.

'You must have realized that I would not need to run two houses,' she said defensively. 'You shall have four weeks' pay of course, and you won't have to work out your notice not unless you wish to.'

'But there's nowhere for me to go,' Mrs Bush said sourly. 'I'll need at least a month to find a new position.'

'That'll be all right, then,' Mary said with a note of false cheerfulness. She felt she should explain that Paul already had an adequate staff but was deterred by the woman's haughty attitude. 'That's all I wanted to say, except that I'll be putting the house up for sale quite soon, but until then, you're welcome to stay.'

Mrs Bush spun on her heel and disappeared into the kitchen and Mary sighed, shaking her head. The woman was impossible to like; she had the most unfortunate of manners.

When Mary told Paul about the little scene, he shrugged his shoulders. 'Don't worry your head about it,' he said, 'she will soon find another place. There's no shortage of work for suitable staff in the big houses around here.' He smiled. 'I managed to get Mrs Reid, the housekeeper, and more recently Mrs Keys to do the rough work with no effort at all. Though I must admit that your Mrs Bush looks more like a grave digger than a housekeeper!'

'Paul!' Mary said reprovingly but she couldn't hide the smile that crept into her eyes. He took her in his arms and kissed her lightly. 'Never mind that old witch, let's go and see Stephan, shall we?'

He took Mary's hand and led her up the stairs, and they entered the bedroom quietly together. Mary sat on the chair beside the bed and took her son's hand.

'It's me, Stephan,' she said softly, 'it's mammy. Can't you let me know if you can hear me?'

She stared into his still, pale face and her heart sank. 'Won't he ever be well again, Paul?' she asked, tears trembling on her lashes.

'Of course he will.' Paul rested his hand on her shoulder. 'If good nursing and loving care can do it, he'll soon be up and about again.'

'It's a good thing you're a doctor and can see that he is nourished properly,' Mary said, grateful to Paul for his support.

Paul took her arm and drew her away from the bed. 'Well I can only feed him liquids, you know, but it's enough to keep him from becoming dehydrated. Come along now, downstairs with you; there is no point in sitting here distressing yourself.'

Mary clung to Paul's arm, glancing back at the still figure in the bed. She had longed for Stephan's sight to be restored but now she would be grateful if he could only speak to her, show any sign that he was still part of her world, not lost to her in some limbo where she could not reach him.

She ate very little of the food set before her on the gleaming damask cloth that bore silver cutlery and ornate candlesticks. Paul was proud of his home and of his achievements as a doctor, and she was proud of him too; but there was just one big shadow on her happiness and that was the sickness that held her son in its iron grip.

'Perhaps we could have a specialist from London to see Stephan.' Paul had read her thoughts correctly and she glanced up at him quickly, eagerly.

'Would that be possible, Paul?' she said breathlessly. 'I know you are doing all that you can but if there is any grain of hope, I must grasp it with both hands.'

He reached across the table and touched her fingertips. 'We'll give it a few more days and if there is no

257

response, we'll have a second opinion, I promise you.'

'Thank you so much for everything,' Mary said and her voice was thick with tears. Paul smiled at her. 'Now let me see you eating something. I don't want two patients on my hands, do I?'

Later, as they lay entwined together in the large double bed, Mary caressed Paul's cheek. He was so dear to her, she had come to love him more and more, and every day they spent together was strengthening their relationship.

He held her close. She burrowed her face into the warmth of his shoulder and softly, as their breathing mingled, she drifted off into sleep.

She didn't know what it was that awakened her. She sat up in the silent darkness and stared ahead of her. At her side, her husband stirred.

'What is it, Mary?' Paul asked lifting himself onto one elbow.

She slipped from the bed and drew on her robe pulling it tightly around her waist. 'I don't know,' she said, moving towards the door. She turned on the light in Stephan's bedroom and moved towards where he lay. He was still and quiet, his breathing light, his face a pale oval in the dimness. She sat beside him and took his hand in hers and there was a tingling sensation in her fingers as though they had communicated with something vital and alive.

'Stephan, it's me, mammy, can you hear me?' she asked. Behind her, Paul put his hand gently on her shoulders. She looked up at him. 'There's a change, I just know there's something different about him,' she said, tears edging her voice.

'All right, take it slowly now,' he said and sat on the bed watching the boy carefully. 'He mustn't be startled, just speak to him normally, keep talking, Mary.'

Excitement flared through her. So Paul believed there was a change in Stephan's condition too. She leaned over her son and brushed the hair from his forehead.

'You had a fall, Stephan,' she said, her voice breaking with emotion. 'You hit your head against the wall, remember? The ground was wet and your stick slipped away from you.' She watched his face but there was no response. Beside her, Paul pressed her arm.

'Just keep talking to him quietly, Mary,' he urged. 'Say anything that comes into your mind, anything at all, just keep trying to stimulate his senses into life.'

'Stephan, Paul and I are married now, I know you'll be pleased.' She paused to gather her strength. 'We went off and did it quietly with just Mali and Sterling as the witnesses and do you know, Stephan, the sun shone on us in spite of the rainy start to the day.'

She ran her tongue over her dry lips. 'All I want now is for you to be well and then I can be happy again. I love you so much Stephan, so very much, my lovely.'

She froze as within her hand the boy's fingers began to move. Softly at first like the stirrings of a butterfly, his hand clasped hers. There was no strength in the boy's grip but he was making a conscious effort to communicate.

'Look, Paul!' Mary mouthed the words at him. 'Stephan's holding my hand.' She felt as though her heart would burst with happiness as Paul leaned forward, and, lifting the lids, stared down into the boy's eyes.

'Keep going, Mary,' he whispered, 'you're doing a wonderful job.' He stood silent now, watching as Mary leaned closer to her son.

'Stephan, listen to mammy, there's a good boy. You'll be all right, I promise you. Paul has been looking after you so well, how could you not get better?' She kissed his cheek and tenderness filled her. 'Come on, my lovely, please come back to mammy, please!'

Slowly, as though he were very tired, Stephan's eyelids fluttered, his eyes opened and he turned his head towards the sound of Mary's voice.

'I'm all right, mammy.' His voice was only a thread but Mary looked up at Paul, her eyes brimming with tears.

'He spoke to me, Paul, what does it mean?' she asked, almost afraid to hope. Paul pressed her shoulder.

'It means that his mind is undamaged, he is going to be all right.' There was more than a hint of gruffness in his voice and Mary knew that he too was moved.

'Stephan, don't try to talk now,' she said as the boy turned his head towards where Paul was standing. 'You must take things very carefully. You have been sick for a long time and we must nurse you back to health.'

'There's something I must tell you, mam,' Stephan said, his voice still little more than a whisper. 'I can see an outline of you, and over there is the lamp. I can see it glowing.'

Mary put her hand over her mouth and stared up at Paul, her eyes wide with hope. 'Is it possible?' she said from behind her fingers.

Paul moved to the other side of the bed and sat down and Stephan turned his head to follow his progress.

'I can only see a hazy picture of you,' he said, 'but I know you are almost as handsome as my father was.'

Mary knew the tears were rolling down her cheeks but she made no effort to stop them. 'Oh, God,' she said, her voice trembling with emotion, 'there's a miracle has happened by here tonight.'

Paul looked across the bed at her. Both of them were holding Stephan's hands and slowly Paul reached out to take Mary's fingers in his own.

'Now we can really start to live as a family,' he said and it might have been a trick of the shimmering, popping gaslight but it appeared there was the glistening of tears in her husband's eyes.

20

The warm May sun brought no joy to Sweyn's Eye, for the general strike was not yet over. Men stood on street-corners, hope dying that the dispute in the coalfields would be quickly settled.

Luke had been listening to the news on his Crystal set and he had been disturbed to hear that members of the public had been recruited to act as policemen. It seemed unjust that the emergency police were being paid two pounds, six shillings and three pence as well as expenses while an average week's pay for a miner was only one pound, eleven shillings and seven pence.

He moved to the stairs and sighing, slowly mounted them. He had enough troubles of his own without worrying about the state of the nation. Peta was still sick; if anything, her condition had deteriorated.

She was sitting up in bed and Hattie was attempting to feed her a thin gruel from a spoon. Peta was as helpless as a new-born baby. She had become painfully thin, her cheekbones gaunt and now, Luke noticed, her usually pallid skin was flushed with bright colour.

He watched for a while in silence before speaking. 'Hattie,' he said at last, 'we'll have to think of putting Peta into a hospital. I think she's worse and it's all becoming too much for you.'

'No, it's not!' Hattie protested strenuously. 'What would I have to do with myself if Miss Peta was taken away from me? Anyway, I couldn't rest thinking of her in one of those awful houses with mad people. You can't do it, mind.'

Luke sighed. 'You're a good woman, Hattie, I don't know what we'd do without you.' He turned towards the door and Hattie followed him quickly, pausing outside the door.

'There's something I've been wanting to tell you for weeks,' she said hesitantly, 'I don't know if it's the right thing to do but I've carried it on my shoulders long enough.'

Luke stared down at her. 'Come on then, Hattie, out with it; it can't be so bad, can it?'

'The reason she took sick in the first place was that she'd been attacked, see!' The words came out in a rush. 'When I was able to persuade her to let me put her in the bath I saw there were bruises on her body, nasty big ones and it was plain that someone had been handling her rough-like.' She glanced away. 'And I found her nightgown. Ripped it was; she'd hidden it away.'

Luke's eyes narrowed. 'Why didn't you tell me this before, Hattie?' he said, his voice harsh.

'I was afraid, see,' Hattie said in a low voice. 'I've been trying to pluck up the courage to tell you for ages.' She bit her lip, obviously trying to curb her tears. 'The bruises they were on her stomach and legs, see, and she had some scratches on her poor little chest.' Tears filled Hattie's eyes. 'I could kill the man that's done this to her, strangle him with my own hands.' Hattie's eyes were large. 'I worked out who did it,' she said slowly.

'Tell me,' Luke said, a pulse of anger beginning to beat in his head. 'Don't be afraid, just tell me.'

'That day, when Miss Peta wanted to go home, well Michael Murphy and his brother met me outside the gate.' Hattie's face was red with embarrassment. 'Kevin offered me a ride in his car over to Peta's father's house. I thought it would be quicker, that's all,' she added defensively. 'And we left Michael Murphy on the roadway outside the house.'

Luke stared at her. 'Peta was raped by Michael Murphy!' he said, anger blinding him.

'*Daro*! It must have been him for when Kevin Murphy drove me to fetch Peta's father, took a long time getting me there, he did, turning on all that Irish charm of his. When we got back, my poor Peta was out of her poor mind.' She paused. 'But keep a cool head on you, Luke, anger will solve nothing.'

Luke touched her shoulder lightly. 'You're right about one thing; I must tackle this with a clear head.' Luke clenched his hands into fists. 'But he will be punished, Hattie, I promise you that.'

Luke ran his hand through his hair. 'We must call in the doctor at once.'

Hattie's eyes were large. 'But the bruising's almost gone; what can the doctor say?'

'He can examine her properly,' Luke said. 'See how much she was hurt and perhaps he can tell us the reason for her constant fevers and her reluctance to eat.'

'I can tell you that,' Hattie said. 'She's hurt inside. Been treating her, I have, mind, with a syrup made of agrimony.'

'I know you've done your best.' Luke rubbed wearily at his eyes. 'But in the light of what you've told me, the doctor must see her.'

Hattie nodded. 'Perhaps you're right. Shall I run and fetch him?' She made a move towards the staircase but Luke stopped her.

'I'll go. I can explain the urgency after what you've just told me.' He turned to look at the sad figure that was his wife and anger rose within him like a tide. Michael Murphy had a great deal to answer for and Luke would see that his day of reckoning came swiftly.

The doctor gave Peta a potion to make her sleep. 'I didn't insist on looking at her before because there was no evidence to suggest she'd been physically harmed, no contusions on her face, for example. And, of course, she was always a highly nervous lady.' He was examining Peta as he talked and his face was grave as he looked up at Luke.

'There's a very bad infection,' he said. 'She was already weakened by the baby – that, or the attack on her caused some tearing that has not healed. I'm afraid that your wife will have to go into hospital.' He washed his hands in the bowl that Hattie placed before him. 'It's a sorry day when a man can't go to his work and leave his wife safely in her own home.'

Luke did not comment. He intended to keep to himself the identity of the man who had raped Peta. He led the way down the stairs and towards the front door.

'You'll see to the arrangements right away, Doctor?' he said slowly and Paul Soames nodded his head.

'I'll call into the hospital on my way home. They'll have a bed prepared within the hour.' He paused. 'I must tell you that she's very weak and it will be difficult for her to fight the infection, but of course everything possible will be done.'

Luke's jaw tightened. 'Thank you for being frank,' he said evenly but in spite of his apparent calmness, anger was running through his blood and he felt the urge to take Michael Murphy and beat him senseless.

It was only when Peta was settled in one of the long hospital ward's narrow beds beneath pristine cotton sheets, with a starched blue and white cover smoothed over her slender figure, that Luke felt able to breathe more freely. He left Hattie sitting by the bedside and strode out into the brightness of the day. He was surprised the sun still shone and the trees were still shedding blossoms like snowflakes onto the ground.

He began to walk towards the Strand, making for the lodging house where Michael Murphy had taken up residence. Luke scarcely saw the tall warehouse buildings rising on either side of him, or felt the softness of the breeze coming in off the water. He had no clear idea of what he was going to do and in spite of his earlier words to Hattie about thinking matters out coldly and logically, his blood was hot for revenge.

The Strand wound upward towards Greenhill and by the time he reached the lodging house he was calmer. He knocked on the door and an icy coldness came over him as he waited to see the face of the man he had come to despise.

But it was Kevin Murphy who opened the door. 'Sure I thought it was the bailiffs,' he said laconically. He stepped back. 'What can I do for you?'

Luke pushed his way inside. The long, dark passageway smelled of clean washing. 'I'm looking for your brother.'

Kevin opened the nearest door. 'This is my room, you're welcome to a jar of ale, but as for Michael I don't know where he is. I haven't seen him for days.'

'I've got business with Michael Murphy.' Luke was not aware that he was speaking through clenched teeth until Kevin replied.

'Looks as if you've got a score to settle with our Michael, and that's none of my business, but I tell you, I don't know where he is.'

'You'd better start thinking about it,' Luke said, grasping Kevin by his shirt front. 'Where is he?'

Kevin drew back in fear. 'Sure he paid up the rent on the room upstairs and left with his fancy piece days ago,' Kevin said. 'He's not here any longer but search the place if you like.'

Luke released Kevin and thrust his hands into his pockets. 'I'll have that drop of ale, now, if it's still on offer,' he said evenly. He took the mug of ale, unwilling to leave without some clue as to Murphy's whereabouts. 'Thanks.' He stared at Kevin over the rim of the glass. 'Are you aware that my wife is in hospital because of your brother?'

Kevin shook his head. 'Look, if you were to knock my teeth down my throat I couldn't tell you any more, I honest to God don't know where Michael has gone.'

It was clear to Luke that he would get nothing more from Kevin Murphy. He was either too afraid to speak or he was telling the truth. Luke put down his glass and moved to the door. 'I shall be watching you,' Luke said coldly, 'don't think I've forgotten your little part in all this.'

As he left, he failed to see the slight figure of Doffy, standing in the shadows of the passageway, a bundle of clothes over her arm. She followed at a safe distance as he left the house and then turning, she hurried along the road towards Market Street, her long tangled hair flying behind her.

'Hell and damnation!' Michael Murphy stared down into the face of the woman standing before him and longed to lash out at her for bringing him news he did not wish to hear.

'You'll have to get out of here!' Doffy cried, throwing down her small armful of clothing. 'It's a good job I went back to get my washing or I wouldn't have heard Luke Proud talking to your Kev, mind.' She sank into a chair. '*Duw*, what have you been up to Michael, that Mr Proud seems to blame you for his wife going in to the hospital?'

'Shut up!' Michael's thoughts were racing. He'd better disappear from the area for a while. It was clear that somehow Luke Proud was only now learning that Michael had given his fancy wife a bit of what-for. Never did any woman harm before, it hadn't, and was it his fault that the silly bitch had ended up in hospital?

'You can get lost for a start.' Michael glared at Doffy. 'Go on, get out of my sight; I don't want to be slowed down by some cheap whore!'

Doffy stared at him, open-mouthed. 'But, Micky, I was the one to warn you, if it wasn't for me, you wouldn't have known . . .'

'Shut up!' Michael raised his hand threateningly. 'Go now or it'll be the worse for you.'

Doffy turned on her heel and walked quickly from the room, closing the door behind her. But she didn't leave the house; instead, she crept up the stairs and into one of the bedrooms and hid behind the curtains.

Michael told himself he had more to worry about than the welfare of a slut. A sudden banging on the door made him jump, he looked out from the curtained window and sighed with relief when he saw his brother moving about uneasily on the step.

He opened the door and Kevin followed him inside. 'By all the saints, it's a good thing you rented this little house,' Kevin said quickly. 'Sure Luke Proud would have taken you apart if he'd found you.'

'I'm not afraid of Proud,' Michael said at once, 'but sure it's as well that I lie low for a bit, just in case he can get the law onto me.' Kevin, who was well used to Michael's sudden disappearances, shrugged.

'Sure an' I'll look after the place, don't you go worrying about that. I want to move out of that scruffy boarding house anyway.'

'Keep your mouth shut about me!' Michael said. 'If anyone comes asking you don't know nothing.'

'Jesus, Joseph and Mary, don't you think I know that much by now?' Kevin protested. Michael stared at him for a long moment.

'I'll be calling in from time to time and I'll be wanting money, so you make sure our sister becomes more generous, got me?'

Michael had collected a bit of money from the fools who thought they were contributing to the miners' fund. It would be enough to get him on a train to London and to set him up for a few weeks.

He scowled as he thought of Luke Proud. He'd expected the man to be after his blood but Michael had not reckoned with Peta Proud being taken to hospital.

He moved easily down the street in the direction of the station in the Stryd Fawr. The sooner the dust of Sweyn's Eye was shaken off his feet the better he'd be pleased.

The station was cold and empty, there was a train steaming and puffing near the far platform and Michael climbed aboard, seating himself comfortably in an empty compartment. He leaned back and closed his eyes. Luke Proud may have won the battle, he mused, but never let him think he'd won the war, for Michael Murphy would be back and then Proud could look out.

Luke left the boarding house and decided he would go to Market Street and see Katie. It was hardly likely Michael Murphy would have gone there – it was the first place anyone would look for him – but then there was no reason with a man like that; it would be just as well to check.

He began to walk along the pavement, striding out quickly, anxious now, wishing he'd thought of going to Market Street first. If Murphy was there God knows what threats he would use to get money from his sister.

'*Duw*, Luke, where are you going in such a hurry?' Charlotte caught his arm then, looking at him in concern. 'What's wrong, love? You look awful.'

'Peta,' Luke said, 'she's worse. I've taken her into hospital.' He paused. 'And, Charlotte, I've only just found out that she was attacked by that bastard, Murphy.'

Charlotte was suddenly pale. She caught his hands in hers. '*Duw*, Luke, there's sorry I am! I could kill that man with my own hands.'

Luke stared down at her. 'Murphy,' he said. 'He's been harassing you too, hasn't he?' He saw her eyelids flicker and the colour rush into her face.

'Yes.' Her voice was so low he could scarcely hear her. 'He tried to rob me but Jim came home in time.' She looked up and her eyes were suddenly glowing. 'You should have seen how he handled Murphy, I was so proud.' She was glancing away from him then. 'You might as well know that Jim and I have come to an understanding.' She was a little on the defensive as though she expected disapproval.'

'I think you've chosen quite a man there,' he said softly. 'There's more to Jim O'Conner than meets the eye.'

'Then you don't mind?' she said breathlessly. 'I thought you'd think me immoral; it's not long since Gronow died. But, mind, we shan't be making any plans, not yet awhile.'

Luke smiled at her and touched her cheek. 'You deserve happiness, Charlotte, and I've a lot of time for Jim. He's not afraid to speak his thoughts, however unpopular they might be.'

Charlotte smiled. 'I'm glad you have taken to him. I know you two are on opposite sides of the fence over this strike business. But forget about that – I feel so sad for Peta; it must have been a horrible experience having that brute attack her. He's dangerous, he should be put away.'

Luke straightened his shoulders. 'Wait until I've finished with him, he'll wish he'd never been born,' he said evenly.

He left Charlotte and made his way towards Market Street; he was anxious to see Katie, assure himself that she was all right.

When he reached the shop, he paused outside the door. To his dismay he saw it was all closed up, the windows dark and blank, the door tightly closed. He knocked loudly and after a time he heard footsteps coming along the passageway.

'Katie, thank God, you're all right.' He moved into the passageway and followed Katie to the kitchen. She turned to look at him and he took her in his arms, holding her close. 'I was afraid Michael would have come here,' he said softly. 'I've got something to tell you about your brother and it's not going to be easy.'

Katie looked up at him from the circle of his arms. 'I don't think I could be surprised at anything he did now. He's not the brother I knew; he's become a stranger to me. Sure mammy would turn in her grave if she knew what he had come to.'

'He attacked Peta, my wife,' Luke said slowly. 'She's very sick in the hospital, some sort of infection. I've been looking for Michael. I can't wait to get my hands on him.'

Katie sighed heavily. 'You go to her; your place is by her side. Sure I'll be all right. If I know Michael, he'll have taken off by now, left Sweyn's Eye far behind him.'

Luke felt uneasy. He didn't want to leave Katie in case her brother showed up and yet she was right, his place was with Peta. He held Katie close for a moment, breathing in the scent of her hair.

'Keep the doors locked, my love. Don't let anyone in, do you understand? Not anyone.'

'Sure, I've told you I'll be just fine,' Katie said emphatically. She smiled up at him as she followed him to the door. 'And try not to worry too much about Peta. The doctors are so good they'll pull her through, you'll see.'

Luke began to walk along Market Street towards the centre of the town, cursing the fact that his car was in the garage for repair. Getting around was so slow on foot, he might have been wiser to borrow a horse from Bertie-No-Legs – at least a horse didn't break down, he thought ruefully.

He paused as a bus chugged past him, the driver enshrouded behind thick wire netting which covered the entire window. Most of the other windows were boarded up, the glass shattered by stones thrown by angry strikers.

And yet the strike had its lighter side. On one of the boards in the window of the bus someone had written a message in red paint!

HOW TO STOP THE STRIKE?

CUT THE HEADS OFF YOUR MATCHES!

Luke smiled. It seemed that a sense of humour still prevailed in spite of the increasing hardships suffered by the strikers, and the miners in particular. He was bringing out very little coal these days, not from choice but from necessity. There was only so much he could do with only old Tim and his two young nephews. But at least the slant was not being neglected. Luke saw that the timbers were replaced when needed so that the heading did not squeeze and close up.

So suddenly that he was taken by surprise, Luke felt a blow to the side of his head. He turned quickly to see a young boy dodging into a doorway.

'Blackleg!' The voice was young and angry and Luke moved quickly before the door could close on him.

He caught the boy by a ragged collar and twisted him round so that he could see his face. The boy glared up at him, his eyes hot with bitterness.

'My mammy is starving because of people like you!' the boy said in a voice thick with tears. 'You should stand by the strikers like my dad. They are only fighting for what is right, mind, but mammy and the baby got to go without, see?'

Luke released the boy. 'What's your name?' he said softly and the boy looked up at him fearfully.

'Are you going to tell the constable about me, is that it?' he asked, his head hanging low.

'I'm not going to tell the constable anything,' Luke said firmly. 'Believe it or not I just want to help you and your mother.'

The door along the dark corridor opened and a woman stared at Luke with large frightened eyes. 'Hugh, what is it, what's wrong, boyo?' she said fearfully.

'It's all right, just a misunderstanding,' Luke said at once. He pushed the boy before him and entered the kitchen. It was clean and neat although not richly furnished, and a small fire burned in the grate. It was clear that the family had little coal; little enough of anything, Luke thought, with a mingling of sympathy and anger.

'I was just telling Hugh to come up to the Slant Moira, I can give him a job if he wants to try his hand at mining.'

'*Duw*, and be a blackleg. Couldn't do that, mister, what would my husband say? Stick together we working folk do, mind. Got our principles we have, whatever you might think of us.'

Luke was at a loss for words. He could not agree with the strike and yet he recognized that others were sincere in their beliefs. He felt for perhaps the first time that they should not be punished for standing firm.

'Can I at least send you a bag of coal?' he asked and just then there was a thin cry from the baby in the crib near the fire.

The woman looked towards the baby and then back at Luke. 'All right; I suppose it wouldn't be wrong to accept some coal just to keep the baby warm. Thank you, sir, but send it in the morning, please, my husband is out then, see.'

Luke moved to the door. 'That's settled, then,' he said quietly, making up his mind that there would be a parcel of food to accompany the coal. 'Well, Hugh, are you going to show me out?'

The boy scampered forward quickly and swung open the front door. Luke put his hand in his pocket and brought out some coins. 'Now look, Hugh, you're a sensible fellow. I want you to take care of this money. Buy your mother some flour and milk and whatever else you think she needs.'

He patted the boy's shoulder and then strode out into the street to come face to face with a large man, who bore the blue scars of the miner on his face and hands.

'What's this, then?' The man looked from Luke to his son and Luke moved forward quickly.

'Your son threw a stone at me, called me a blackleg, which opinion he's entitled to hold. He and I have talked and we have come to an agreement that if he won't break the law, I won't hold any grudges, right, Hugh?'

The boy nodded, his hand in his pocket hiding the coins from his father, and somehow the gesture touched Luke with sadness.

'Well, I apologize for my boy throwing stones.' The man had moved to stand beside Hugh, resting a hand on his shoulder and Luke read pride in the gesture. 'But as you say, he has a right to his opinions.'

As Luke walked away, he glanced back and saw that father and son were entering the house, closing the door on the world.

When Luke reached the hospital, he went immediately to the ward where Peta lay. Hattie was sitting outside on a wooden bench and her face was red and blotchy. Luke's footsteps slowed as Hattie shook her head, the tears welling in her eyes once more.

'She's gone,' she said shakily. 'Slipped away like a little baby, she did, and her not even knowing I was at her side.'

Luke felt frozen, as though he could not understand the words Hattie was saying. He pushed open the door to the ward and Paul Soames was just emerging from behind the screens around Peta's bed.

'I'm sorry,' he said, 'she simply lost the will to live. She was very weak, as I explained. I didn't hold out much hope but then neither did I expect her to go so soon. My sympathies. I can imagine it's difficult for you to accept.'

Luke sat beside Peta, staring down at her face so peaceful in death. He took her hands in his, rubbing her cold fingers as though he could warm them back into life. After a moment, he put his head down on the starched hospital sheet and felt hot tears burn behind his closed lids.

21

Gina drew the curtains against the darkness of the night, her thoughts drifting to when she'd believed in Billy's love and she'd felt secure and warm in her little home at the foot of Constitution Hill. Well, those days were gone. She lived now in the boarding house on the Strand with Geraint Griffiths, caring for the baby left motherless when Geraint's daughter had died in the hospital.

Gina sighed. Geraint claimed he'd fallen in love with her but she knew she could not love again ever. Yet she respected him and even felt a certain fondness for him and together they were making a success of the boarding house.

Geraint, relieved of the strain of caring for little David, had redecorated the house and made improvements; and now the guests were of a different sort – mostly professional men who paid well for the home comforts provided by Gina's experienced hand.

Gina sank down in the chair near the fire. The baby was asleep in the pram in the corner and Geraint had gone down to the Cornish Mount for a pint of ale. For once she was alone and there was time to think. But she didn't like her thoughts. She kept remembering the day Billy had come to beg for her help. It seemed that Delmai Richardson was trying to take over his daughter's life. He'd wanted Gina back not for love of her but so that she could exert her influence on Cerianne. But Gina had firmly refused him her help.

'I've got a new life now, Billy.' She'd spoken softly, aware of Geraint listening in the other room. 'I'm sorry I can't do any more than I've already done; it's up to you now to go it alone or make your peace with Delmai Richardson as you choose.'

'You're still angry with me.' Billy's eyes had been anguished and for a moment her resolve had wavered, but how many years did it take a woman to realize her man had no intention of marrying her?

'I'm not angry,' she said sadly, 'just thoroughly disillusioned, Billy. I'm sorry, there's nothing I can do for you.'

She'd watched him go with a pain deep inside her. But that part of her life was over and done with, the house on Constitution Hill was sold and the proceeds placed in trust for her son. She could not go back, even if she'd wanted to.

As though drawn by her thoughts, Dewi entered the room. He'd come home from College because of the strike. He was taller than ever, still with the thinness of youth about his frame but when mature, he would be just like his father.

'*Duw*,' she said softly, 'you're just like Heinz Sinman come back to earth.' She rose and kissed her son and he pinched her cheek playfully.

'I'm off out, mam,' he said, 'but how about a lend of a few shillings? My pockets seem to be empty.'

'Oh, driving buses for nothing, are you?' Gina said quickly. 'It's a shame they ought to be paying you after the way you get abused and threatened.'

She opened her bag and took out some coins, pressing them willingly into his hand. 'Go on, enjoy yourself, but don't stay out too late, mind, and don't get into a fight about the rights and wrongs of the strike, either.'

She peered through the window, watching Dewi walk jauntily down the street, so like Heinz that tears of pride came to her eyes. How different life would have been if her husband had not been killed in the war camp all those years ago.

The baby stirred in the pram and Gina bent over him, touching his cheek lovingly. All she'd ever wanted to do was love and be loved – was that asking too much of life?

She returned to her chair and was beginning to fall asleep when she heard the sounds of voices raised in anger.

'Sure 'tis turned Commie you have, O'Conner!' The voice was Geraint's and Gina sat up in her chair, her heart beginning to beat swiftly. Would the strike never be finished with and the town returned to normal? Well, whatever the shouting was about, she would not have it, not in her respectable boarding house.

Jim's voice was quieter but the words were plainly spoken. 'We have to stand firm, man, can't you see that?'

The two men entered the kitchen and Gina sank back in her chair, seeing that Geraint was slightly the worse for drink.

'I've brought him home, missis.' Jim O'Conner smiled at her so charmingly that Gina was reassured. 'We've been to a meeting and I'm sorry to say the ale was flowing, though sure I don't know where the bottles came from.'

Geraint sank into a chair. 'Make us a cup o' tea, then, girl, will you?' he said, smiling foolishly. 'I think I've had a drop too much, mind.'

Gina folded her arms across her breasts. 'All right, I'll make you tea but keep your voice down! *Duw*, you're making enough noise to wake the dead, never mind a little baby.'

There was a sudden knocking on the door and Gina looked up in surprise. 'God in Heaven what's going on here? It's like Market Street in by here.' She opened the front door and a dark figure pushed past her.

'I'm looking for a room.' The voice was abrupt and before Gina could reply the man was striding along the passage towards the kitchen.

'*Duw*, come back here, there's no rooms to let, mind.' She hurried along the passageway after the man but he had come to an abrupt halt. Looking over his shoulder, Gina saw that Jim's bulk was filling the doorway.

'Where are your manners, Murphy?' Jim spoke evenly, though there was threat enough in the set of his shoulders.

275

'You've been told that there's no rooms here, so on your way.'

'Why have you got to stick your nose in what doesn't concern you, O'Conner?' Kevin Murphy had been drinking and his words were slurred. He paused for a moment as though uncertain what to do and then he turned away. 'You'll get the beating you deserve one of these days,' he said sourly.

Jim thrust his hands in his pockets. 'Then I'd better remember to look behind me, hadn't I, for you're not enough of a man to attack me face-on.' He caught hold of Kevin's lapel. 'I don't like threats, so bear that in mind, and another thing – that brother of yours, tell him if he shows up around here again, he'll get a very warm reception.'

Kevin turned on his heel and strode away, and after a moment Jim closed the door.

Jim smiled at Gina, 'Perhaps I could have that cup of tea you offered?'

'*Duw*, of course you can. I'll stoke the fire up in there so that you'll be warm, and push the kettle on again. She smiled. 'You put that Kevin Murphy in his place good and proper, mind. I'm glad about that.'

Gina's mood of introspection had vanished along with her weariness. Kevin Murphy had seen to that with his rough words. She stoked the fire, placing coals carefully in the grate, one by one, for it was by being careful that she had made the boarding house into a profitable business.

She moved across the kitchen and peered down into the pram. The baby was still asleep, one finger in his mouth. 'There's a lovely boy, then,' Gina said softly. 'Sleep you and give me a chance to get some supper cooked for your grandad.'

The kettle began to boil and Gina quickly warmed the brown china pot, swirling the liquid round and round. '*Duw*, will you look at that Geraint, fallen asleep he has.' She smiled warmly at Jim. She suddenly felt good and she realized it was because here at Ty Gwyn she was busy and more than that, she was needed.

Her life had been too placid. She'd felt she was growing old before her time and the constant waiting for Billy to make up his mind to marry her had eaten away at her love for him. Perhaps with Geraint she might not hear bells ringing but he was an honest man and steady enough for any woman. She would and could settle for what she had here in the boarding house.

'I'll be bothered! There was me going to cook him a good meal and the ungrateful man has just nodded off. Will you have a bite to eat, Jim?'

'Not for me, thank you, my landlady will be wondering where I've got to, sure an' she will have prepared some supper for me, she always does.'

'Aye, you've fallen on your feet there in Canal Street, just as I have here in Geraint Griffith's boarding house. We've both a lot to be thankful for.' She was slicing a piece of cold ham as she spoke.

With a snort, Geraint awoke. 'What's going on, then, where am I?'

Gina smiled. Geraint did not remember that he'd returned from the public bar of the Cornish Mount under the influence of ale. He was usually a moderate man.

Gina smiled as Jim rose to his feet to leave. '*Duw*, thanks for bringing the blockhead home in one piece,' she said gently. 'I can imagine him putting the world to rights, mind.'

Jim moved to the door, 'He's all right, in spite of the fact he calls me a Commie and no one less a Communist than me, sure enough.' He paused at the door. 'Good night, then. Close the door carefully behind me.'

Gina watched for a moment as he made his way along the road, a tall handsome man and one of principle. It would be a lucky woman who caught that man's fancy.

She returned to the kitchen and stood looking down at Geraint. He had fallen asleep again, his hair tousled around his face. 'Come on,' she said firmly, 'let me get my shoulder under your arm. I'll help you to bed and you can sleep it off or you'll be fit for nothing tomorrow.'

'Sorry, girl,' he mumbled. 'Couldn't be helped, though. Saw some of our lodgers in the public and everybody wanted to buy me a drink, see.'

She pulled off his boots and helped him undress and then, pulling the blankets up around him, she stared down at him for a moment. 'You're a good man, Geraint Griffiths,' she said softly. 'There's a pity that a woman can't fall in love at will.'

She hurried downstairs and picked up the baby. 'Come on little boy, let me change your clothes and then I can tuck you up into bed, too.'

David remained asleep and Gina was thankful, for once the baby was awake, he would want to play and it would be difficult to settle him down once more.

She carried him into the bedroom she shared with him and put him gently into his cot. He was a beautiful child with the bloom of health on his cheeks and she had come to love him as her own. 'Be careful, Gina,' she whispered softly, 'once bitten, twice shy, mind.'

She had given all her love to Billy's daughter, had brought Cerianne to young womanhood and yet in the last months she'd seen nothing of her. It was as though Cerianne had forgotten her existence.

Of course she had her own mother now, which was just as it should be. Still, it wouldn't have hurt the girl to come and see her from time to time.

She heard the front door close quietly and the sound of masculine voices in the hall. Dewi had come home and was talking to the travelling salesman from Yorkshire, whose accent was so broad and distinctive. Gina sighed with relief. The last of the men were home and she could lock the front door now and go to her bed. She hurried downstairs and waved the men towards the kitchen.

'Come on, now, let's have a bit of quiet, is it?' she said. 'I've just put the baby to bed and that's where I'm going too; need all the beauty sleep I can get before the morning.'

Dewi put his arm round her. 'You're lovely as you are, mam,' he said, and she smiled with pleasure. Lately, since he'd been at College he had changed. His accent was flattening out, he was becoming more remote from her and she had feared she was losing him.

The Yorkshireman had disappeared into his room and Gina hugged Dewi close. 'Have a bit of supper now and go on up to bed with you, I'll just lock up and then I'll go to bed too.'

She opened the front door and looked out into the darkness. It was a mild night, but damp, with a hazy moon shining through the clouds. The trees waved fresh young leaves towards the pinprick lights of the stars. What a strange summer it was turning out to be, Gina thought as she turned back towards the light of the hallway.

'Gina, wait!' The voice was low, urgent and she tensed with fear, turning swiftly to see a tall figure emerging from behind the shrubs.

'Billy Gray!' She stared up at him, her mouth suddenly dry. 'What in the name of all the angels are you doing here?'

'I've come to beg you to come back to me,' he said in a low voice. 'I know I've no right to ask you, but I've been so lonely without you.'

She stared at him in disbelief. He couldn't really be standing there before her, expecting forgiveness so easily.

'Come with me now. I'll get a special licence. Marry me, Gina, as we always planned. Change your mind, won't you, please?'

For one blind foolish moment Gina was tempted to go into his arms, to forget everything but the fact that here was Billy Gray, beseeching her to be his bride. Then cold reason asserted itself.

'I can't do that,' she said flatly. 'I'm not one for going back on my word, Billy. I can't throw off my responsibilities as lightly as you seem able to do.'

'I know I've been wrong in the past,' Billy said. 'I've been a fool, I had my happiness there in the palm of my hand and let it slip away from me. But I'm sorry now. Can you forgive me, Gina?'

'I think I can, Billy,' she said slowly and he made a move towards her. She held up her hand. 'But I can't forget, Billy; I can never forget the unhappiness you caused me. I'm sorry, Billy, I couldn't ever trust you again.'

She moved inside and closed the door, then stood leaning against it, shaken and on the verge of tears. But she had done what was right, she told herself, as she forced herself to slip home the bolts.

As she raked the fire in the kitchen and watched the dying embers fall into the shovel, she longed for an instant to run out into the night, to call Billy back to her, to be in his arms once more; arms that were so familiar and safe.

She sighed then and took the ashes out into the back garden where she tipped them onto the pathway and they died into a grey dust. Then she returned indoors and closed the back door with a snap of finality.

The sun was shining, a pale imitation of its summer self, when Gina rose from bed. She stood for a moment on the cold lino, staring out into the morning, knowing that last night she had burned her boats forever. She had said goodbye to Billy and to her past; and now she felt no regret, just a sensation of freedom. She could do what she liked, go where she wanted – she had only herself to think of.

The baby began to cry, reaching out to her with chubby arms and wanting to be lifted from his cot. She knew that she would not go anywhere. She would probably stay with Geraint, grow old beside him as they both gave their time over to rearing David. And, she decided, that wasn't such an awful prospect after all.

Katie Murphy sat in the sun-filled waiting-room looking around her uneasily. She didn't like seeing the doctor and she wouldn't have come at all if she hadn't been feeling so sick and ill lately. Even serving her customers in the shop seemed too much trouble.

It was in Mrs Keys she'd confided her feelings of nausea and the woman who was always so pathetically grateful for the old scraps of bacon and the stale pieces of cheese that Katie put her way, was full of concern.

'I bet I know just what's wrong with you,' she said at once, her huddle of children clinging round her skirts. 'You've got morning sickness, that's what it is. You've fallen for a babba.'

Katie had felt the colour rush to her face. 'But that can't be right,' she'd protested quickly, 'I've only . . . .' as her words trailed away, Mrs Keys had smiled ruefully.

'Look, my lovely, if you only did it once, once is enough. I should know, look at my brood. Now you just take yourself off to the doctor's right away. I clean house for Doctor Soames and he's such a nice kind man, he'll see you all right.'

And so Katie had caught the bus, sitting beside a window covered with planking, feeling hot and ill. She'd been glad to alight and walk along the broad roads of Mount Pleasant to the doctor's house. She hoped she wouldn't see anyone she knew; she wanted to keep this thing a secret at least for as long as she could.

The nurse looked round the door and gestured her forward and Katie felt her knees tremble as she made her way into the doctor's room.

'Morning, Katie.' He smiled at her cheerfully. 'Don't look so frightened; I don't usually bite my patients, you know.'

She looked him straight in the eye, it was pointless beating about the bush. 'I think I'm going to have a baby,' she said quickly before she could lose her courage.

'I see.' Paul Soames took her pulse, his manner reassuringly professional. 'Now when did you last see your courses?' he asked and Katie bit her lip.

'I don't really know. I suppose I haven't taken any notice. I know I must sound stupid, Doctor, but I never imagined anything like this happening to me.'

'No, you're far from stupid, Katie. Many women who are involved emotionally don't think about pregnancy occurring.' He moved away from her. 'Will you take off your clothes? I'd like to examine you.'

281

She waited in an agony of fear and impatience until Paul Soames had completed his examination and then she looked up at him, her mouth dry.

'You're right,' he said. 'You are going to have a baby, but not for some time yet. I'd say you were about a month gone.'

He washed his hands and Katie stared at his back wondering what she was going to do. Her feelings were mixed. She felt joy and then fear, for the thought of confessing her sin to the priest was not a pleasing prospect.

Paul Soames turned to look at her. 'Now you know what to do. You must eat lots of liver and green vegetables and have an orange every day, if possible.' He returned to his seat at the desk. 'Are supplies still getting through to your shop, Katie?'

She nodded. 'Sure, they are a bit haphazard but last week I had a good delivery of tinned goods.'

Paul sighed. 'This strike is gone into the second week now; let's hope it's all over soon and everything can get back to normal.' He smiled at her. 'But remember, take care of yourself. You're carrying something precious, you know – many a woman would envy you.'

Katie made her way out of the large house and walked along Mount Pleasant, staring at the sea sparkling below her. She might be a fallen woman and carrying an illegitimate child but suddenly she was filled with happiness.

Her steps were light as she made her way back towards Market Street; she wondered when she would see Luke and how she might break the news to him. Should it be at once, or should she wait a while? After all, he did have the worry of his wife being ill in hospital.

Mrs Keys was waiting for her return. 'There's sorry I am,' she said at once, 'the children have tipped up the flour bag. I've picked as much up as I could, mind, and sent them into their father for a while. Do him good to have them with him, it will.'

She followed Katie into the kitchen. 'I can see by your face that I was right – you are going to have a babba, aren't you? Never mind, we'll all stick by you.'

Katie was a little irritated by the woman's attitude but sure, Mrs Keys meant to be kind. She put the kettle onto the flames and stared down at the fire, her thoughts far away.

'Oh, there's been bad news going about,' Mrs Keys said quickly. 'That poor Mrs Proud has up and died, sick with childbed-fever she was, or so it's said.'

Katie felt a coldness grow within her. Luke's wife was dead, how awful for him. And then the full import of the woman's words sank in. 'Childbed-fever!' Katie said.

But Luke had told her that he no longer slept with his wife and had not done so for some months. How could Peta have been expecting another child?

'How long does this childbed-fever take to come out in a woman?' Katie asked shakily.

'Right away, either when you've just given birth or just lost a babba. Poor woman, her husband might have given her time to recover after slipping that first little but then look at me; husbands can be so selfish.'

Katie sank into a chair. Had Luke been lying to her, then? Had his relationship with Peta continued? In any case, now that he had just lost his wife, how could she tell him that the result of their lovemaking was to be an illegitimate child?

She became aware that Mrs Keys was leaning over her. 'All right, dear?' she said. 'Is there anyone I can fetch to be with you?'

Katie shook her head. 'There's no one, Mrs Keys, no one at all.'

22

Luke stood at the graveside and stared down at the freshly-dug earth. Beside him Hattie wept unrestrainedly, a large white handkerchief covering her face. He put his arm around her and she turned to him at once, burying her face in his shoulder.

'You did all you could for her,' he said softly. 'No one could have been more devoted to Peta than you.'

Hattie continued to sob and Luke knew that she blamed herself for not telling him sooner about his wife's true condition. He felt anger run through him. If only he had Michael Murphy in his hands now at this minute the man would be in the ground beside Peta.

'Come on home,' he said gently. 'There's little point in standing here any longer.' He looked round. Everyone else had vanished; the vicar in his long robes; Peta's father, whose dour face had been a silent reproof directed at Luke; and the crowd of people – some simply curious onlookers who had watched as Peta was lowered into her last resting-place.

'I'll drive you home,' Luke said more briskly and his tone had the desired effect because Hattie stopped crying and removed the handkerchief from over her eyes.

'*Duw*, there's awful it is to stand by here and know I won't see my lovely Miss Peta again.' Hattie's voice broke and Luke took her arm, hurrying her through the gates of the cemetery. 'But it's God's will, mind, and we must abide by it,' she murmured.

Luke led her to the car and opened the door without replying. If it gave Hattie comfort to believe in divine providence who was he to question her faith? He drove through the streets, not really seeing where he was going. He was thinking of Katie and how long it seemed since he'd

284

been with her, but he felt that the last thing he could do for his wife was to see her decently buried before rearranging his life.

In spite of the gloom of the day and the regrets for the lovely woman Peta had once been, Luke felt a glimmer of warmth when he thought of Katie. She was kind and good and honest and more than any man deserved.

He drew the car to a halt and Hattie, her eyes red, stepped onto the pavement then stood for a long moment staring up at the house.

'It'll be strange without her,' she said, her eyes filling with tears once more.

Luke took her arm. 'Come on inside and make us both a hot, sweet cup of tea,' he said firmly, knowing that it was wise to give Hattie something to do to ease her over the first painful moments in the house now empty of Peta.

'We must remember her as she was before . . .' Hattie's voice trailed away for a moment. 'She was so beautiful and sweet, my Miss Peta.'

'Don't make the mistake of thinking she was a saint,' Luke warned. 'Peta had faults like any other woman and you must remember the bad as well as the good things about her.'

As she made her way to the kitchen Hattie's stiff shoulders told Luke he was wasting his time. To Hattie, her mistress would never be anything but perfect and perhaps after all a bit of self-deception wasn't a bad thing.

She brought him the tea on a tray and then stood before him, her hands clasped together. 'What will happen now?' she asked and her voice trembled.

'I'll still need you, Hattie,' he said at once. 'How would I manage without your help? The place would be in a shambles in no time.'

She relaxed a little but there was still a frown above her eyes. 'Will you be bringing another woman into your house, Mister Luke?' The words were scarcely audible. It had obviously cost Hattie a great deal to speak them.

Luke leaned back in his chair. 'I'm going to be honest with you, Hattie,' he said firmly. 'In time I shall marry again – I'm not a man to live alone.'

Hattie's cheeks were suddenly pink. 'But you won't get married yet; you'll wait for a decent interval, won't you? Out of respect for the dead, mind. If you were to marry straight off, what would people say?'

Luke held up his hand. 'I don't give a damn what people say, Hattie. I gave my wife all the respect I could while she was alive and waiting won't bring her back.' He moved from the chair and into the hallway, pausing to look back at Hattie. 'But don't worry,' he said smiling, 'I doubt I shall get myself a bride not yet a while.'

She nodded her head but Hattie's eyes were still full of tears. Luke shrugged his shoulders into his topcoat.

'You go and rest now, you look all in,' he said softly, 'and don't worry, everything is going to be all right.'

He went outside and stared up into the rain-filled skies, his words of reassurance had sounded fine and it was true he didn't give a damn either way what might be said about him by town gossips. Indeed he was not the most popular of men as it was; what was it they called him? A blackleg and a scab. Well, he would not be dictated to by any man.

He climbed into the car. It was about time he was getting over to the slant; there was work to be done, coal to be brought out of the rich seams. And yet as he put his car into gear, he could not help thinking of Katie Murphy and how much he would like to have been with her today.

As he drove towards the Stryd Fawr Luke heard the sound of voices. He drew to a halt at the kerb for the crowd of men and women were moving excitedly about the roadway, careless of the traffic.

Luke saw a man climb upon a pile of boxes and call out to the crowd.

'The strike is broken, wait, let me speak.' Jim O'Conner was trying to quieten the crowd and watching him Luke could not but admire the man, the force of his personality and the effect he was having on the people.

'Representatives of the General Council of the TUC have been to Downing Street today. They have informed Mr Baldwin that the strike is over,' Jim said in a clear voice that carried to where Luke sat in his car.

He felt a great sense of relief. So the strike was finished. Perhaps now he could get the Slant Moira back into full production. He sank back against the leather seat wanting to join in the cheers of the crowd. But Jim was speaking again.

'Wait,' Jim called, 'things are not so simple. Baldwin has given no assurances that there will be a settling of the miners' problems; he's not even promised an investigation into miners' complaints. And Mr Cook, our representative, has sent telegrams out telling the men not to go back to work.'

A groan went up from the crowd and Luke shook his head in exasperation. Would the workers never see sense? He honked the horn and slowly made his way through the crowded street. Once in the open he drove away swiftly towards the Slant Moira.

Katie sat in the warmth of the kitchen and stared down at the page of writing-paper before her. Suddenly, she snatched it up and crumpled it into a ball, hurling it furiously towards the fire. How could she write a sensible letter of sympathy to Luke when she just longed to be with him?

She rested her hands on her stomach and closed her eyes, his baby was growing within her. If only Luke could be here to share this moment with her she would be happy.

She felt her eyes burn but she wiped them away impatiently – tears solved nothing. She rose from her chair and moved towards the window staring out into the greyness of the rain-soaked garden below. Even the weather seemed dour and angry.

When her baby was born would she still be alone, Katie wondered?

There was a knock on the door and Katie went towards it cautiously. She never knew who to expect these days.

She doubted very much if Michael would show his face in town for some time but with her brother, she could never be sure.

Katie's pulse beat faster. Perhaps Luke had come to see her. She opened the door and tried to conceal her disappointment.

'Ceri Llewelyn,' she said breathlessly, 'come in, it's kind of you to call too. Sure, you're looking well and prosperous, sit down and have a cup of tea with me.' She led the way into the kitchen. 'Come on, sit down, sure you're making the place untidy, standing about there like that.'

'All right, then, just as bossy as ever, aren't you, Katie Murphy? But I'd like a cup of tea for all that.' Ceri took a seat next to the table and rested his elbows on the scrubbed surface. 'I'm not so prosperous, Katie, not these days, with people on strike. Won't buy silver when they need bread, will they?'

'I suppose not. I wasn't thinking, but isn't the strike over now? I thought everything was settled.'

'Well the end of the strike was announced yesterday,' Ceri said, 'but most of the miners are still out of work, more solid than they ever were. It seems they were sold down the river and will have to accept a cut in wages after all.'

'Well, I hoped things were getting back to normal,' Katie said and she wondered how Luke would be taking this further setback. He would work the slant even if he had to work it alone, she knew that, and she was worried for him.

'The railworkers are going back; they've got pensions and such to worry about,' Ceri said, 'so you can't blame them. As I see it only the miners will be left striking, out on a limb they'll be.'

Katie poured the tea and as she looked at Ceri, she couldn't help wondering why he'd come to see her. Their love affair, if it had even been that, was in the past. He was married to Mona now and as far as Katie knew they were very happy.

Ceri caught her look and smiled ruefully. 'You're wondering why I'm here, I can see it in your eyes.' He leaned forward speaking confidentially. 'I've never loved Mona as I loved you, Katie.' He held up his hand. 'I know we can't put back the clock but I've come here to offer help. I know that you're in trouble and I'd like to do all I can to make things easier for you.'

Katie felt a sense of shock run through her. 'But that's impossible!' Katie said quickly. 'How could you possibly know about me?'

'I've been listening to women's gossip, I'll admit it,' Ceri said. 'It seems Mrs Keys who works for the doctor passed the information about you expecting on to Mona.' He glanced at her quickly. 'And to anyone else who would listen, I'm afraid.' He came to her and took her hands in his. 'Let me help, Katie. I've got some money put by and it's yours for the asking.'

Katie tried to draw her hands away. 'No, Ceri, it's not possible, I can't take your money, sure an' can't you see that?'

'You loved me once,' Ceri said softly, 'we almost were married. I still care about you.'

Katie sighed. 'Please, Ceri, I'm grateful to you for your kindness but I'd like to be alone now.' She opened the door and stood there waiting for him to leave. As he walked past her, she reached out and touched his arm. 'I am grateful, it's just come as a shock that everyone knows about the baby. Come and see me again when I'm in a more social mood – and Ceri, bring Mona with you.'

When she was alone, she sank into a chair and put her hands over her hot cheeks. She was so angry with Mrs Keys for spreading the gossip. Hadn't the woman been at all grateful for the help Katie'd given her; the titbits of food, the way she'd been allowed to run up her account?

Katie straightened her shoulders and lifted her head. Well let them talk, all of them, she would not let them upset her. And yet as she moved towards the window and stared out into the rain-filled day, she was suddenly apprehensive about her future.

*

Jim O'Conner let himself into the house on Canal Street with a sense of frustration filling his thoughts. If only he had been able to meet with Baldwin's government, he would have told them a thing or two. Weak men had gone to Baldwin, men who wanted peace at any price. Well, all they had given to the miner was more chaos. Two days after the official ending of the strike the total numbers of men out of work had risen by a hundred thousand.

'*Duw*, Jim, come like yourself.' Charlotte looked up at him; she was in the process of setting the table for supper. 'There's noisy men are, can't shut a door quietly, can you? Well I hope you haven't woken my sons, for they will be down here demanding more food.' She smiled. 'While their eyes are open they will eat, mind.'

Jim moved towards her and stood looking down at her. 'I'm weary of it all,' he said. 'The treachery of the government, the weakness of our leaders – at times I wonder what I'm doing, striving to better the conditions of the working man. When I downed tools and refused to work at the Slant Moira, the men elected me as their local member of the FED as spokesman for them all, and yet they will not listen to me.'

'Jim –' tentatively, Charlotte put her hand on his arm '– it's not like you to talk like that. You are usually so full of optimism and strength; don't let it all get you down, love.'

The endearment had slipped out unintentionally and as Jim looked down at her, he could see that Charlotte's cheeks were warm with colour. He put his arms around her and drew her close and she clung to him, holding him tightly, her slim arms twined around his neck.

They remained together for a long moment and then Charlotte drew away from him. 'Come on, now, let's have this supper.' Her voice was shaking and Jim knew that the moment had moved her as much as it had him. But she had boundaries set around her and these she would not break. Jim loved and respected her enough to wait until the time was right.

'I've got a meeting tomorrow,' he said evenly, as he took his place at the table. 'I must try to make them all see sense.' He took up a piece of bread. 'We must not allow victimization, Charlotte, and victimization is taking place. Already the railwaymen are being asked to do lower-grade jobs. Some are threatened with the loss of their pensions. People must not be intimidated in that way.'

'I know, but leave all that behind you for now and eat your food. What good will you be to anyone if you don't look after yourself?' He watched as she placed a bowl of soup before him and a plate of fresh bread.

'How are you managing so well, Charlotte?' he asked suddenly. 'We never seem to be short of food and yet I'm not bringing you any money in.'

'There are the other lodgers,' Charlotte said meeting his eyes, 'and my brother Luke . . .'

'No!' Jim said quickly. 'Charlotte you must not accept help from Luke, he's a blackleg, a traitor to his class.' He leaned forward urgently. 'Can't you see the position you'd be putting me in if anyone found out I was eating bread provided by a non-striker?'

Charlotte bit her lip. 'I'm sorry, Jim, I hadn't thought of it like that. It was just a case of my brother helping me out, that's all.'

'Think about it, Charlotte, because I can't eat here if I know that Luke is paying for the food.'

Charlotte moved away from the table. 'You're carrying this too far, aren't you, Jim?' Her voice was mild but he could see that her cheeks were flushed.

'I don't think so,' he said. 'I can't take from Luke while the men I'm speaking for are going hungry.'

'Well, then, do you want my boys to go hungry?' Charlotte asked. 'I can't think of just you or myself. I have two growing sons; I'm not willing that they should go without.'

'But their father would have come out on strike, wouldn't he?' Jim rose to his feet. Suddenly he wasn't hungry. Charlotte looked down at her hands.

'Yes, I'm sure Gronow would be with the men, you're right about that, Jim. But I'm frightened; I don't know how long this strike will go on – no one does – and I can't let my sons suffer, I just can't.'

Jim stood for a moment, hands to his sides. He longed to take her in his arms, to beg her to see sense but she had the right to make up her own mind about such an important issue.

'Well, in that case, Charlotte,' he said heavily, 'I can't stay here. I'll find other lodgings. I think that's the best for both of us.'

'Jim!' Charlotte's eyes were full of tears but he turned away before he could weaken.

'I'll be in touch,' he said. 'I'm aware that I must be indebted to you quite heavily by now but I'll repay you, that's a promise.'

'Jim,' Charlotte said, 'please don't go, not like this.' She made a move towards him but then stopped abruptly.

Jim took his coat from the peg on the back of the door and too full for words, let himself quietly out into the night.

Katie smiled at the plump, motherly woman who had entered the shop, her eyes alight with laughter, her double-chins trembling.

'*Duw*,' she said, 'I just saw one of them strikers try to take a poke at my boy, there's a laugh for you.'

Katie leaned on the counter. 'Why, what happened, Mrs Porter – is your Frank working then?'

'Aye, he's just got a job at one of those little slants up the hill there, comes home black as the hobs, he does, but he's earning good money, mind.'

She puffed a little as she sat on one of the chairs Katie provided for her customers. It shook a little beneath her generous proportions.

'Well this man, he come up to Frank, didn't he, called him a scab and what not; threatened to punch him in the nose. Didn't know our Frank is a boxer, he didn't, and there's a surprised look on his face when he found himself sitting on his backside in the middle of Market Street. Teach him to pick on a young boy another time.'

The bell tinkled and Frank entered the shop, his smile as amiable as his mother's. It was difficult to believe he made a hobby of fist-fighting, Katie thought, as he came forward, his fair hair gleaming and his young face freshly shaved.

'Don't want a lodger, do you?' Mrs Porter said. 'I've got my sister and her four coming to stay with me for a bit. From the Rhondda, she is, and they're saying there's people starving up in the valleys.

Katie stared at Frank thoughtfully. He would be a great help with the lifting when the supplies came in and he'd be protection in case Michael chose to turn up again.

'Do you know, Mrs Porter, you might just have found the lodgings you're looking for. I won't charge anything so long as Frank helps me a bit around the place.'

'*Duw*, I was only joking, mind,' Mrs Porter said, 'but as you're offering I won't say no.'

Frank stood watching silently and Katie turned to him. 'What do you think, Frank? Would you be able to put up with an old woman like me for a little while?'

He grinned. 'Do I have any choice?'

His mother cuffed him about the ears. 'Hey, there's manners for you. Katie Murphy is only a snip of a woman, she's not old at all.'

Frank's fair face was flushed. 'Sorry, I didn't mean that. I'd like to stay by here in the shop, it's not too far from the slant or from the boxing club.'

'Don't worry,' Katie said smiling, 'I know when I was about eighteen years of age anyone over twenty was ancient. Go upstairs, then, have a look round, Frank. The bedroom in the front of the house isn't being used.'

As the young boy moved through the shop towards the living quarters Mrs Porter leaned forward and the chair creaked ominously.

'There's pleased I am that I spoke up. He'll be all right here with you and useful he is, mind, strong as a horse. And it'll only be for a little while until this stupid strike is really over and done with.'

293

Katie sighed. 'Sure it seems everyone but the miners are back at work. Let's hope it's settled before much longer.' Then perhaps Luke would able to spend a bit more time with her, she thought ruefully. They'd only seen each other a few times in the past weeks and then she had not found the courage to tell him about the baby.

'That room looks fine and dandy to me.' Frank was smiling. 'I could hold a dance in there it's so big.' He pinched his mother's cheek playfully. 'I'm not going to want to come back home, mind, if I get used to all that space.'

'Well, then, that's settled,' Katie said. 'You fetch your things up here as soon as you like.' She turned to Mrs Porter. 'Now what can I get for you? The supplies are almost back to normal and I've had some nice fresh cheese in.'

As Katie served Mrs Porter, she felt suddenly cheerful. It would be good to have a young boy about the place for company, for sometimes it was very lonely in the night when every creak of the old house could be heard.

'You know something, Mrs Porter,' Katie said smiling, 'I'm very glad you came into my shop today.'

23

The softness and light of the summer morning beautified the coal-strewn mouth of the Slant Moira, the pieces of anthracite gleaming like diamonds against the dusty earth.

Luke shrugged off his coat and stood near the stove in the small shed, staring out at the rise of the hill which gleamed pink in the early light. He had worked hard over the past weeks to keep his mine in production and matters were eased now because he'd found a young man who was not afraid to work the coal against the wishes of the strikers. Frank Porter was amiable and a hard worker. He did not yet know how to handle the coal but he was as keen to learn as Luke was to teach him. They had been kept busy with increased orders and Luke had particularly wanted to take on new customers as well as fulfilling his commitment to Ponty works, one of his best customers. Now that he had only Timmy, his two young nephews and Frank Porter, he was hard pressed to turn out enough coal; but he would do it if it killed him.

He had not been so busy that he had not tried to find out where Michael Murphy had disappeared to. Kevin Murphy had been non-committal when cornered, and even when Luke had grown angry and caught him by his collar he had protested he knew nothing of his brother's whereabouts. Luke had been inclined to believe him, for Kevin was a weak man and an unlikely confidante.

Luke sighed and fixed his lamp to the belt of his moleskin. He must go and talk to Katie and soon, she must be wondering what had become of him. He'd not had much chance to socialize, not with all the work he'd taken on but Katie must know that his plans for the future would include her.

He threw some coal on the stove and replaced the cast-iron top. The shed wasn't much of a place, used both as office and canteen, but he would improve conditions in time. He would build himself a proper office-block and employ a secretary to deal with the paperwork. He meant to succeed and no striker was going to stand in his way.

'*Bore da*, boss.' Tim came into the shed flanked by his nephews who were so much like him they could have been his sons. 'Ponty order today, isn't it? We'd better get young Frank on the loading. He's not much good in the mine.'

'He'll improve,' Luke said, 'and quickly, but you're right, Frank can do the loading while we get out more coal.'

'What's this I'm going to do, then?' Frank said as he entered the shed. 'Got work lined up for me already have you, boss?'

'Aye, you won't be in the mine today, Frank, you'll be out in the sunshine loading the lorries with the Ponty men.'

'That's all right by me, boss,' Frank said amiably, 'I don't mind what I do as long as I get paid.'

He turned to speak to Tim. 'Been put in digs, I have, mind,' he said and Luke listened absent-mindedly. 'My mam's sister is coming from the valleys with a load of kids and so I've been boarded out.' He chuckled. 'I got the best of the bargain, mind – a room of my own and good grub. If my mam's not careful I won't want to go home.'

'All right then, men,' Luke said, 'the sooner we get started the sooner we finish.' He paused for a moment to stare up at the sky for it was going to be a long day and he wouldn't see much of it, not working in the heart of the mine.

By the time the Ponty order was ready, Luke felt his muscles protesting. His back ached and his knees felt as though he would never straighten them again. But he felt a certain satisfaction for the work had been done and there would be a nice fat profit for him at the end of the day.

'Thanks, boys,' he said as the men placed their lamps in the shed. 'There'll be a bit extra in your pay this week.'

He strode out along the rough ground and towards the town, hands thrust into his pockets, cursing the fact that his car was out of action again. It would be good to get home and have a hot bath to wash away the clinging dust.

He had decided to sell the house where he'd lived with Peta; it was not to his taste and it reminded him constantly of his wife.

Peta had loved roses and this was reflected in the drapes and furnishings of the house. The main bedroom was a froth of pink, even down to the silk sheets that Peta had insisted were a necessity. With the thoughts of his wife came the sense of outrage Luke always felt when he remembered her death. The urge to take Michael Murphy by the throat and strangle the life out of him was almost overpowering at such times.

He was walking along the Strand when he saw Jim O'Conner coming out of one of the boarding houses. Luke paused, not knowing what sort of reception he would receive if he stopped to talk.

As Luke approached, Jim nodded in silent greeting.

'Still on strike, then?' Luke said. 'I thought it was all over when the rest of the workers went back.'

Jim nodded slowly. 'Aye, so did a great many people but some of us are made of sterner stuff. Fine body of men are the miners.'

'I'm well aware of that,' Luke said, 'but I'm a miner too remember, and I've my own living to make.' He looked up at the boarding house. 'Are you staying here, then? I thought you were lodging with Charlotte.'

'Aye, well that didn't work out,' Jim said and in that instant Luke saw the truth of the matter – that Jim would not live on the money he knew Luke was giving Charlotte; he would not accept help from a blackleg and Luke did not blame him. Jim was someone to reckon with – not easily duped, a man of unwavering principles.

As Luke hurried towards home, he found himself thinking once more about Katie. She must be wondering why he had not been to visit her lately. He could only hope she understood the urgency of keeping the coal supplies flowing.

Hattie was waiting eagerly for him to come home, for as he stepped into the warmth of the hallway, she came out of the kitchen to greet him. She had a strange look in her eyes and though she was smiling, he sensed that she was all of a flutter about something.

He took off his coat and hung it on the stand, and she hovered round him as he did the same with his scarf.

'Is the water hot enough for a bath?' he asked, moving into the kitchen and kicking off his boots. 'I'm filthy to my skin.' He turned and saw she was rubbing her hands together. 'All right, Hattie, what's wrong?' he asked, smiling down as her. 'Have I forgotten to pay some of my bills or something?'

'Oh, Mr Luke, I don't know how to tell you,' she said, her eyes large. He ran his hands through his hair.

'Come on, you know you're itching to tell me but hurry it up, I'll have a bath and something to eat and then I'm going out again.'

'You're not going to see that Katie Murphy, are you?' Hattie asked with a note of disapproval in her voice.

Luke frowned. 'That is my business. I'm surprised at you for asking, Hattie.' he stared at her for a moment. 'Well, what is it you've been full fuss to tell me? Out with it,' he said at last.

'About Katie Murphy, it is,' she said, her eyes blinking rapidly, a sure sign that she was nervous. 'You know she's made a general store out of the shop in Market Street, don't you?'

'Aye, I do that.' He sighed. 'All right, spit it out. You've heard a bit of gossip about her, have you?'

'Well, Mrs Keys who cleans for the doctor was saying a lot of things about Katie Murphy. There's a man living there for a start, a young man with the name of Frank Porter. A pugilist, he is, a proper ruffian, if you ask me.'

Luke wanted to laugh. 'What rubbish!' he moved away towards the stairs. 'You women believe anything.'

'It's true!' Hattie protested indignantly. 'I went up there but only to get some shopping, mind, and I saw him with my own eyes.'

'So?' Luke was still amused. 'He's lodging with her as well as helping her in the shop, nothing wrong in that.'

'Well he don't go home come nightfall!' Hattie said. 'Can't be right, now, can it – a young man and a woman still unwed living under the same roof. What else can folk think but bad of them?'

'Well I don't want to hear any more about it,' Luke said firmly. 'Folk will believe what they want to believe and to hell with the truth!'

'But there's more to it than that,' Hattie insisted. 'She's above five weeks gone. She's having a baby and Mrs Keys knows that's the truth because she works for the doctor and saw it all written down somewhere, see.'

'Well, I should be careful who you talk to,' Luke said quickly. 'You could end up in court spreading rumours of that sort.'

He stood for a long time staring at himself in the bathroom mirror without seeing anything but Katie in his mind's eye. Katie pregnant, it couldn't be possible, could it? Well there was only one way to find out, he would go up to Market Street and see for himself.

Katie rubbed at her back with her fingertips and grimaced as Frank came into the room.

'I've locked up the shop,' he said and leaned his big frame on the mantelpiece, watching her. 'Aching a bit are you?' he asked sympathetically. 'I know mam used to be bad when she was carrying. What if I was to give you a bit of a rub? Learned a bit about massage, I did, from my trainer, see.'

'Sure an' how did you know anything about me having a baby?' She sighed. 'I suppose it's true that it's all over the neighbourhood now. Well, to the devil with them all, but I don't think I'll risk the massage, thanks all the same,' Katie said smiling.

Frank had become almost like a younger brother. It was true she'd known him only a short time but he was so easy and natural, and even after a day's hard work at the mine he managed to help her. He'd fitted into the routine of the shop as if he'd always been there.

She bit her lip. Frank had told her he was working at the Slant Moira and she longed to question him about Luke. She wished he would come to see her; she would be happy once she knew he was well.

She realized that he needed to show respect for the dead, but surely he could have got word to her somehow? What if he was sorry he'd ever taken up with her?

Doubts tormented her. They had not really talked and she feared he might have heard the gossip about the baby and no longer wanted anything to do with her. But if that was the case, wouldn't he have come to her like a man and told her so to her face?

'Now then, you must settle yourself on the sofa,' Frank was saying. 'Come on, that's right, over on your side.' He grinned. 'I'm determined to show you how good I am at easing away aches and pains.'

Katie sighed in resignation. 'All right, you bully, get on with it, then, if you're that determined.'

She had to admit she felt relief as Frank's hands so big and yet so gentle eased away the ache in her back. 'Sure you should take this up as a job,' she said smiling. 'Should you ever get tired of mining or boxing, Frank, you'd make a fine trainer.'

Frank continued to massage her back until she felt relaxed and she didn't look up when he spoke. 'You stay by there,' he said, 'I'll make us something to eat 'cos I'm starving.'

He left the room quietly and Katie felt so drowsy she allowed him to potter about in the kitchen. She didn't suppose he'd make anything very fancy but she didn't care so long as she could lie so comfortably before the fire.

He returned after a few minutes with a plate of bacon and eggs and Katie smiled encouragingly at him, though the sight of the greasy food made her feel ill. Carrying a child seemed to do all sorts of strange things to her. She felt like an earth-mother, fulfilled and content, although there was scarcely anything yet to show that she was expecting a baby. She no longer felt alone, for as well as her baby she now had Frank's friendship and company. One of the reasons they got on so well was that Frank saw her as he saw his mother and, for her part, she felt for him the same sort of affection she'd shown to her brother Sean.

'You're a very kind person, Frank,' she said, making an attempt to eat some of the egg. She took a piece of bread thickly-spread with margarine and Frank laughed.

'Sorry, I've cut such doorsteps,' he said. 'I never was the dainty sort.' He helped himself to more bacon and she marvelled at the amount of food he could put away and still remain slim and well.

He had proved to be very popular in the shop. The young women stood chattering amongst themselves while giving him coy glances, to which he played up with the utmost charm. Katie sorely missed him on the days when he was at work.

'When is you next fight, Frank?' she asked, giving up on her attempt to cut a burned piece of bacon. 'I've never seen a fight. Are they very frightening?'

'*Duw*, no, I love it all,' he replied. 'The smell of the leather gloves, the roar of the crowds when a good punch lands; it's like magic to me.' He smiled a little self-consciously. 'But then fighting's in the blood. My dad was a boxer before me and his dad before him. Runs in the family, see?'

Katie pushed away her plate. She felt nauseated by the way the fat congealed on the plate. She leaned back in her chair, feeling breathless and sick and suddenly quite faint.

'What's wrong?' Frank's voice came from far away. He sounded frightened and Katie tried to reassure him but the words would not come. The pain in her back had returned and seemed to intensify, spreading in a band that encompassed her body.

301

'Mother Mary, help me,' she whispered. When she opened her eyes, Frank was standing over her, his face pale.

'You passed out,' he said worried. 'I think I'd better go and fetch somebody, you don't look right to me.'

Katie shook her head, trying to clear the mists from before her eyes. 'I'm going to lose the baby,' she gasped. 'Frank, help me, please.'

'Well, you listen to me now, Katie, don't you go moving about, keep your feet up, mind.'

'Frank,' she said breathlessly. 'I'm afraid.' He stood there with a mixture of expressions fleeting over his face. It was clear he didn't know what to do for the best. Suddenly there was a knocking on the door and he gave a sigh of relief.

'Thank God someone's come,' he said, heading quickly for the passageway.

Katie felt a blackness swirl around her once more. What was happening, was she going to lose her child?'

'It's the boss,' Frank said in surprise. Then, miraculously, Luke was there. She held out her arms and he came to her at once.

'Don't worry,' he said softly, 'you'll be all right. Frank, will you go to get the ambulance. Tell them to come right away, it's an emergency.' He turned back to Katie. 'We'll have you safely at the hospital in no time.'

Katie clung to him. 'Oh, Luke, I haven't even had a chance to talk to you about the baby and now it looks as if I'm going to lose it.'

She closed her eyes, feeling sick and faint and Luke held her close. 'Don't try to talk,' he said softly, 'you just stay calm and we'll have you in good hands before very long.'

Somehow, Luke took charge. He calmly brought her a blanket from the bedroom and wrapped her in it. Almost at once, it seemed, the ambulance was outside and Katie was lifted in Luke's arms and carried gently to the door. He smiled down into her eyes. 'Good girl, you're doing just fine.' He climbed into the ambulance beside her and she lay looking up at him, reassured by his calmness.

Katie closed her eyes as another pain caught her. 'Please, Blessed Virgin, don't let me lose my baby,' she whispered under her breath. She couldn't help thinking of how she had miscarried her first baby. It couldn't happen again, could it?

Katie lay still, but sweat beaded her forehead. At her side, Luke took her hand, smoothing back her hair, talking softly, comfortingly to her.

'You're a strong woman, Katie Murphy, you'll keep this baby, you'll see.'

She clung onto his hand, wanting to believe him and yet she was afraid, so afraid of miscarrying their child.

She looked up at Luke. 'You know what the gossips are saying, don't you?' She held his hand more tightly. 'They're saying that Frank is my fancy-man and they are blaming him for the baby.'

Luke leaned forward and touched her forehead with his lips. 'When have either of us cared what people say?' he asked. 'I'm a blackleg and you are a scarlet woman. We go well together!'

When they reached the hospital, Katie was placed on a stretcher and she clung to Luke's hand for just a moment before she was taken away from him. She was tucked into a bed between stiff cotton sheets and after a while a nurse came and sat beside her.

'Will you tell me a bit about yourself, Mrs Murphy,' she said, looking down at the paper in her hand. 'I'd like to know a few details about your pregnancy and about your previous history.'

Katie didn't feel like dealing with the formalities of being admitted to hospital. All she wanted was for a doctor to come and help her to keep her baby. Something of her feelings must have shown because the nurse smiled sympathetically.

'I know this is tedious, Mrs Murphy, but it is necessary so that the doctor has a full picture before he decides on any treatment.'

'I'm sorry,' Katie said, 'but I'm so worried about my baby. I'm not going to lose it, am I?'

'Not if we can help it.' The nurse smiled. 'I'm going to bring you some medicine just to keep you from being over-excited.' She moved to the trolley and came back with a small glass. 'Drink this, Mrs Murphy. It will help, I promise you.' She handed the glass to Katie who swallowed the liquid obediently.

Katie lay back on the hard bed and waited impatiently for the doctor to come to see her. When he did, he simply looked, took her temperature and listened to her breathing. Katie felt that nothing positive was being achieved.

'Aren't you going to examine me?' she asked and her mouth had begun to feel as though there was cotton wool in it.

The doctor shook his head. 'I don't want to disturb things any more than I have to,' he said genially. 'Rest and relaxation are the best things for you right now.'

Katie felt light-headed. She realized that the medicine was responsible for her sense of tiredness. She had to sleep, she couldn't fight it, didn't want to fight it and suddenly everything had dissolved into darkness.

When she woke, bright sunlight was streaming into the ward. She turned her head slowly and saw Luke sitting beside her. She reached out her hand to him.

'Have you been here all night?' she asked and her voice was thick, as though she couldn't quite get her tongue around the words. He nodded and she tried to read his expression.

'Luke, tell me the truth. Have I lost the baby?' she asked and he leaned forward and touched her cheek gently.

'No, you have not lost the baby.' He kissed her mouth. 'And if you'll rest and be a good girl, you will carry our son to full term, at least that's the opinion of every doctor in the hospital and I should know, I've asked them all!'

Suddenly she was laughing and crying at the same time. Luke sat on the bed and took her gently in his arms.

'Don't cry, my love, I'll make sure you're all right because we'll be together, whatever the gossips in Sweyn's Eye might think. You're my woman and that's my child you're carrying, and no one or nothing can change that.'

As they clung together, Katie felt her heart lift with happiness. Her baby was safe and the man she loved was by her side; what more could any woman want?

24

An early sun washed down on the elegant house standing high on the hill overlooking the sea, poking inquisitive fingers into elegant rooms, highlighting the motes of dust that seemed to be everywhere.

Delmai Richardson woke slowly and stretched her arms above her head, staring around the familiar bedroom. For a moment she wondered at the sound of even breathing beside her, for her husband was gone now, buried in the Richardson vault in Dan y Graig cemetery. Turning her head she saw the man beside her still asleep and drew the bedclothes closer around her. God, what a fool she was. She'd taken Billy Gray into her bed, and not in some anonymous hotel room but in her own house.

She tried to remember the party the previous night. How much wine had she drunk? Too much, she told herself, as the room seemed the swirl around her when she tried to lift her head from the pillow.

The party had been in celebration of the the ending of the strike. Her brother-in-law Sterling Richardson had arranged it all. Mary Sutton and her new husband had been present, and she'd been not a little subdued; it seemed she didn't know if she was on the side of the bosses or the workers. But of course she'd come from the lower orders, dragged herself up by her bootstraps, and that sort of thing was difficult to hide.

She sighed and tried to edge from the bed, but beside her Billy stirred and turned to smile at her. She closed her eyes and pretended to be sleepy but then Delmai felt his hand upon her naked breast and her eyes flew open.

'Billy, what's happened, what are you doing in my room?'

He pressed his mouth against hers. 'You invited me, Delmai. Now don't play the innocent.'

'Oh, leave me alone, Billy. I want to get up, I have things to do; I'm a very busy lady, you know.' She tried to push him away but she realized with a feeling of irritation that he was roused by her protests. 'Don't!' She twisted her head away from him. 'This is so silly.'

But he took no notice. He pressed her back against the bed, his mouth hot upon hers. And then he was taking her roughly, without his usual consideration for her feelings. She felt herself warm to his passion as she'd done in the old days when he'd first awoken her to the joys of his lovemaking. She wound her arms around him moaning softly, carried away by the sweetness of the moment.

All too soon, he moved away from her and sighed. 'Well, Delmai, at least I roused some response in you.' He placed his hands beneath his head and she hated the superior way he was smiling.

He leaned out of bed and rang the bell, and Delmai stared at him in amazement. 'What are you doing?' she asked, her voice rising. He laughed and leaned over her and she could see the beading of sweat above his moustache.

'I'm ringing for one of your staff and then I'm going to order a hearty breakfast for us,' he said. He lay back on the pillows. 'We can stay in bed all day, if you like. And, Delmai, make the most of it, for after today we're finished – all communication with me or my daughter is severed, do you understand?'

'You fool!' Delmai, careless of her nakedness slid from the bed. 'You think you're such a fine man, don't you? Well let me tell you that you are a lousy lover.' She punctuated her words by picking up the clothes that were scattered across the room. Her cheeks red, she stared down in astonishment as he laughed derisively.

'You've no idea of how to please a woman,' she continued. 'No wonder you can't get a wife. You're a selfish, conceited man and I don't want anything more to do with you, anyway, so you can just get out of my house before I have you put out.'

'Oh, I'll go, all right,' Billy said calmly. 'When I'm good and ready.'

Delmai walked into the marbled bathroom and ran the water, and to her delight she heard Billy leave the bedroom.

She bathed at her leisure, pouring oils and perfumes liberally into the water. She wondered what on earth had possessed her to drink so much the previous night. Her mouth was dry – a legacy from the wine, no doubt.

She wrapped herself in fluffy towels and returned to the bedroom just as the maid came in carrying a tray.

'Put the breakfast tray down there,' she said, 'and have my clothes washed and pressed as soon as possible. And be careful, Janey, that is an exclusive model you are handling so roughly. God, why am I surrounded by fools?'

'Mr Gray said he's having his breakfast in the dining-room after all, madam.' The maid looked at her curiously and Delmai felt anger burn inside her. Billy was determined to humiliate her. Well, she'd show him that his clumsy manners did not worry her.

'Fetch my clothes from the wardrobe!' she said abruptly. 'I'll wear the red silk with the lace at the neck-line and hurry, girl. Do you have to be so slow?'

Delmai pushed the tray away, suddenly she was not very hungry. 'Did Billy Gray speak to you at all?' she asked and Janey looked away quickly.

'All he said madam was that you and he had got drunk and he'd enjoyed a little fling, but we mustn't make too much about it, keep it to ourselves, like.' Delmai stared at the girl, longing to lash out at her. She was stung at being referred to as a little fling.

Delmai dressed quickly. Who did Billy Gray think he was? He was nothing more than a miner, someone who had actually dug in the ground for coal; he was beneath contempt. Fine clothes and a little money in his pocket didn't make him a gentleman.

Delmai cursed herself for her stupidity in bringing Billy into her house, and yet once there had been so much love and passion between them. Of course she'd soon found that love among the slag-heaps wasn't all that wonderful and had returned to her husband.

Downstairs, Billy was seated in the dining-room as though he owned the place. He ate heartily and Delmai realized he was still a very handsome man. And this morning, he had aroused feelings in her that she'd believed were long dead. She walked past the dining-room and in the hall pulled on a light coat. She would go to town, find some company – a woman to talk to, confide in; but then she had very few friends: she didn't get on at all well with women.

She retraced her steps to the dining-room door and looked in. 'I'm going out now and when I return I do not expect to see you here.' She spoke coldly but that didn't seem to deter Billy. He lifted his hand casually and helped himself to a piece of toast from the silver rack. Taking a deep breath, Delmai turned on her heel and walked away from him.

In town, she decided to go into the Emporium tearooms and see if she could find anyone to talk to. She realized quite suddenly that she was a lonely woman, and yet hadn't she always wanted to be left alone, her life uncluttered by people who would only wish to pry into her affairs?

She sat near the window and stared out into the street. The silly foolish strike that had gone on had changed quite a lot of things in the town. Men in caps and scarves begged at the roadside – out-of-work miners who, if only they had the sense to listen to their betters, would be gainfully employed by now.

'Excuse me, may I share a table with you?' The woman looking down at Delmai was vaguely familiar. Delmai glanced over her shoulder at the empty tables in the room and raised her eyebrows questioningly.

'I'd like to talk to you, if you don't mind. I'm Gina Sinman.' Without waiting for a reply the woman sat opposite Delmai and stared directly at her.

Delmai shifted a little uncomfortably in her seat. Of course, she recognized her now.

'Ah, you're Billy's mistress,' she said icily. 'Well, if you've come to tell me to leave him alone I'm afraid you're wasting your time.' Delmai might not want Billy Gray but she was not going to give this woman the satisfaction of telling her so. Delmai sighed. 'Look, my dear, you're better off without him. He's not really the pipe-and-slippers type of man, is he?'

'It's not about Billy,' Gina Sinman said quickly. 'I don't intend to fight for him; he can have his rich ladies along with his flossies off the streets, for I've finished with him. It's about Cerianne I want to see you. Please leave her be; she's a sweet girl and I don't want to see her spoiled.'

'You must just mind you own business, my dear.' Delmai drew on her gloves. There was little point in staying in the tearooms; it was clear that she was not going to find anyone of sensibility to speak to.

'In any case, Billy's daughter is no concern of mine. I don't know why you think she should be.'

Gina smiled wanly. 'There's soft you must think me, all of Sweyn's Eye knows that Cerianne is your child as well as Billy's.'

Delmai shrugged. 'I don't intend to comment on that either way.' She rose to her feet. 'Now, if you'll excuse me, I have things to do.'

'Wait,' Gina said quickly. 'There's no hope for either of us with Billy, and I, for one, intend to make my life without him, but Cerianne is a different matter. I don't *want* to tell her the truth about you – how when your husband took you back after your fling with Billy it was on condition that you didn't bring your daughter.' Gina rose to her feet and faced Delmai squarely. 'You dumped Cerianne as a baby, literally left her in the house at Spinner's Wharf. She wouldn't think much of her mother if she knew the full truth.'

Delmai was suddenly tired of the whole thing. She hated Billy Gray and she hated this self-righteous woman who stood before her, laying down the law.

'Do your worst,' she said as she moved to the door. She turned and looked back at Gina Sinman. 'Of course yours was the ideal match, you and Billy; both of you from the lower orders. What a pity you couldn't hold on to him.' With this final barb, Delmai strode out into the street. And yet she didn't feel triumphant; she felt low in spirits and very much alone, and suddenly she wanted to cry.

Charlotte sat in the kitchen staring at the fire and listening to the ticking of the clock. The children were in bed and for the moment there were no lodgers in residence. She felt alone and sick with worry about the future.

The general strike might be over but its repercussions went on; everything had been affected by it, even the business of the commercial travellers seemed to be slow, for there had been no lodgers now for over a week.

Money was getting short and in the pantry there was just one bag of flour from which to make bread. After that, Charlotte didn't know what she was going to do.

Luke usually called to see her and always left some money under the clock on the mantelpiece but he was working all the hours he could to keep the supplies of coal flowing. Doubtless he imagined she was all right for money. He wouldn't know there were no paying lodgers to augment her income.

But worst of all was her loneliness and separation from Jim. Since they'd quarrelled about Luke's contribution to her income, she'd seen nothing of Jim, though she waited each day for him to come calling. She couldn't believe that a matter of principle, however strong, could keep Jim away from her.

At last she rose and, sighing, began to rake out the fire. When the embers died she would set the paper and stick in the grate ready for morning, and then she might just as well go to bed.

But even when she lay curled in the large bed in the darkness, she could not sleep. She kept thinking of Jim and how he had left her alone. His love couldn't have been very strong, she told herself bitterly.

Her thoughts turned to the morning and how she was going to bring in some money. Should she swallow her pride and ask Luke for some? He would be only too willing, she knew. But then perhaps he too was having a lean time. There was still the upkeep of the mine to consider and the wages for those men who did go in to work for him: and his profits would have fallen along with his output.

Charlotte twisted and turned, not knowing which was worrying her mind most – the lack of money or the disappearance of Jim from her life. At last she fell into an uneasy sleep and in her dreams Jim sat once more at her fireside.

In the morning, Charlotte gave the boys the last of the oats, cooking them in milk and adding a touch of salt.

'*Duw*, mam, there's thin this porridge is,' Denny said and at his side Freddy elbowed him in the ribs.

'It's lovely, mam. Don't listen to him,' he said and Charlotte felt tears burn her eyes.

'I'll get us some more when I go to the shops,' she said as she sat down at the table.

'Where's yours, mam?' Freddy asked and Charlotte picked up her teacup.

'I'll have mine later when I can eat in peace,' she said. 'I know you boys – you'll have me up and down waiting on you and I won't enjoy my breakfast.'

When the boys had left for school Charlotte began to clear the table, trying to forget her feelings of hunger. She saw that Freddy had left most of his porridge and she knew why: he'd wanted her to have it.

She sat down and putting her head on her hands, began to weep. Later, she took the last few shillings from the teapot and picked up her basket. She would go to Murphys' shop for there she could ask for small portions of cheese, and perhaps some bacon pieces, without feeling embarrassed. Katie was always kindness itself. Indeed, she was sometimes too kind; giving credit to people who had no intention of paying.

Once in the street Charlotte felt a little more cheerful. Perhaps today she might find herself with a lodger again, some good person who would pay her a little money in advance. She lifted her head and walked briskly along the road towards Market Street, determined not to fall into a feeling of despair again.

As she turned the corner past the home that had once belonged to Dai-end-house, Charlotte saw that a crowd had gathered, listening to a man who was talking to them eloquently in a charming Irish brogue. She stopped and her heart was suddenly beating swiftly as she saw the bright hair of Jim O'Conner.

'The government doesn't know what is going on,' Jim was saying, 'Baldwin has said in the House of Commons that he is not out to smash the trade unions but that is exactly what is going to happen.'

He paused and looked beyond the crowd and for a moment, his eyes met Charlotte's. The seconds seemed to tick by and then he looked away and began to speak again.

'It is true that some workers are in the happy position of returning to work on reasonable terms,' Jim said, 'but the miner is not so fortunate. A carrot is being held to the donkey in the form of a three-million-pound subsidy, but that subsidy is only temporary; there will be no lasting benefit from it for the miner. We must continue to resist any motion that means a cut in our pay.'

Charlotte gave Jim a last look before turning away. Jim was so locked into his cause that he didn't even notice her leaving. Charlotte's earlier feeling of optimism had vanished and as she entered Murphys' shop, she felt like bursting into tears.

The shop was quite crowded and, to Charlotte's dismay, it wasn't Katie Murphy behind the counter but a tall, young man who was serving efficiently though without the tendency to generosity that Katie always showed in the good measures she gave.

A woman was speaking to the young man and Charlotte recognized her at once. She was Mona Llewelyn, married to Ceri, the silversmith.

'When are you expecting Katie to be here?' she asked and the young man leaned forward.

'She's not very well at the moment. I dare say she'll be back in a week or two.'

Somebody jostled Charlotte's elbow and she turned to see Mrs Keys looking at her smugly. 'In the hospital is Katie,' she said. 'There's sad that she might be losing her babba, isn't it?' She made no attempt to keep her voice down and the customers turned to look at her curiously.

'*Duw*, Frank Porter, don't look at me like that,' she said to the young man behind the counter. 'Have I spoken out of place, then?' She put her hand to her mouth. 'I thought everybody knew about it by now.'

'Katie Murphy is having a baby?' Mona Llewelyn said loudly. 'Then, who is the father?'

Charlotte felt a sense of outrage at the open gossip about Katie, who was nothing if not kind to all her customers. She moved forward into the shop and spoke quietly but with such a force that the sound of voices died away.

'Don't you think Katie Murphy has a right to her own privacy?' She looked around her. 'There's nasty you all are, talking behind her back. There's more than one of you here have been given that extra twist of yeast or a spoonful more than the correct measure of flour and salt.'

'Good for you missus!' Frank Porter smiled at her encouragingly and beckoned her forward. 'Come on, let me serve you first, from now on you're my favourite customer.'

Charlotte felt her cheeks grow hot. She hadn't meant to make such a speech! She bought a few supplies and left the shop hurriedly. As she walked along Market Street, she heard light footsteps after her.

'Wait!' Mona Llewelyn caught up with her. 'I'd like you to know I wasn't being spiteful and nosey in the shop just now.'

'Oh?' Charlotte said coldly. 'If asking the identity of the father is not wicked, then I don't know what is.'

'I had a special reason for asking,' Mona said, 'it really wasn't just curiosity.'

Charlotte nodded. 'Well, then, you should have been a bit more quiet about the way you asked, shouldn't you?'

She remembered suddenly that Ceri Llewelyn had once been betrothed to Katie. She felt a rush of pity for the woman walking along beside her, it was clear that she suspected her husband of carrying on the affair.

'I shouldn't worry, if I were you,' she said more gently. 'Things are not always what they seem, mind.'

'Why are you being sympathetic all of a sudden?' Mona asked quickly. 'Do you know anything about all of this?'

Charlotte shook her head. 'The first I heard of Katie Murphy expecting was by there in the shop just now.' She moved away. 'I'm sorry, I have to go, I've got to get some bread made before my sons come home from school.'

She hurried back towards Canal Street, wondering why on earth she'd stuck her oar in. What happened to Katie was nothing to do with her. She quickly let herself into the house and closed the door, sighing with relief. She wasn't normally one for speaking up in public and yet she didn't think she'd act any differently if she could go back and relive those few minutes in the shop.

She stoked up the fire and put on more coal. She would have the oven just right by the time she'd made the dough and allowed it to rise.

Soon she was lost in the task of making the bread. Charlotte kneaded the dough with vigour, enjoying her task, feeling that she was releasing some of the tension that had built up inside her.

She was up to her elbows in flour when there was a knock on the door. 'Come in' she called, thinking with relief that Luke had come at last to see her. The door opened and then there was silence. As Charlotte turned her head she took in a deep breath.

'Jim!' She moved forward, careless of the flour on her hands, and put her arms around him. The act had been an impulsive one; she had never been this close to Jim before. They had both respected the fact of her widowhood but now Jim held her close, his cheek against her hair. Neither of them spoke but there was no need of words, Jim had come to her and that was all that mattered.

25

The sunshine shimmered on the wet streets, which was cheering after the way the rain had swept through Sweyn's Eye, and a warm breeze from the sea drove away the last of the grey clouds.

Mona was seated in the window, staring out at the sunshine without seeing it. Ceri's love for another woman haunted her as she saw them together in her mind's eye: Ceri and Katie Murphy, she with her lovely red gold hair and beautiful eyes.

She blushed as she thought of the scene in the shop. She had felt so ashamed when Charlotte had spoken up for Katie. And yet how could she explain that her nosiness was really concern because she felt she was losing her husband?

Now there was a baby on the way, who else's could it be but Ceri's? She rose abruptly to her feet. He'd married her but that didn't stop him from loving Katie.

Mona stood before the mirror and stared at her reflection. She had done a great deal of thinking in the last hour or two. If Ceri was drifting away from her, some of the blame must lie at her own door.

She turned her head slightly. How would she look with her hair cut short around her face? And what if she wore a little rouge or lipstick? Wasn't it time she became a woman in her own right instead of the mousy girl Ceri had married as second-best?

It was about time she stopped apologizing for not being his first choice. He hadn't been forced to marry her; he had done so of his own free will and she had looked after him well. She kept a good house and a plentifully-stocked pantry and she never refused him in bed.

She sighed. Indeed, she could see it now; she had been a doormat. 'Well,' she said to her reflection, 'that is all going to change.'

She moved into the kitchen and lifted the lid of the old china teapot put away high on a shelf. Her fingers encountered the money she'd saved for a rainy day and she laughed at herself ruefully. 'The rainy day has come, Mona Llewelyn,' she said out loud.

She pulled on her good but nondescript coat and picked up her handbag, staring around as she did so at the neat room with the brass well-polished and the carpets swept. She told herself she had been a fool all this time. There was no personality in the place, it was simply a well-kept house that reflected nothing of herself.

It was warm in the street and the sunshine was pleasant and her steps were light as she made her way into town. She would show Ceri and everyone else that Mona was no longer a mousy little doormat; she was about to become a woman in her own right.

She wandered along the Stryd Fawr looking into shop-windows, trying to see which of the latest styles would suit her. When she came to the Emporium, she stood for a moment, looking up at the colourful window displays and her courage almost failed her. What if Ceri was right and silver prices were falling? What if she should keep the money she'd saved? 'Stop it!' she said, and then hurried into the double door, embarrassed by the sound of her own voice.

When the rather elegant shop assistant came towards her, Mona held her head high.

'I'm looking for a complete new wardrobe,' she said firmly. 'I'm tired of dull colours and serviceable cloth. I want something exciting. Will you help me?' she added and the woman seemed to warm to her immediately.

'Yes, of course, come with me.' She led the way across carpeted floors and up the broad stairs to the lingerie department and Mona gasped at the shimmering silks and satins in sweetpea colours, subtle yet exciting. She touched the silk; it felt so soft and so sensuous.

Mona bought six sets of undergarments, all in different colours, and the shop assistant nodded in approval.

'As to dresses,' she said, 'madam is very slim and quite tall, so you can wear whatever style you fancy.' She smiled. 'And with that glossy hair cut just a little more fashionably your high cheekbones would be shown to advantage. Perhaps you would care to visit our hairdressing salon before you leave?'

Mona trembled at the money she was spending. She bought three dresses in fine soft wool, but her favourite was one in cream satin with a low waistline and a gold belt that clasped together over her hips and stomach. She had no idea where she was going to wear it but the mere possession of it made her feel cherished.

She decided she would have most of the clothes delivered to her home but she would wear her bright new coat and the shoes and handbag to match. She smiled as she thanked the shop assistant who glowed in the knowledge that she had helped improve Mona's appearance, as well as in the knowledge that she would have a fine commission on all her sales.

Mona hurried up the stairs to where the scent of shampoo drifted towards her. She would have her hair cut, she decided, and see what the result would be. She sat for such a long time waiting to be attended to that she almost changed her mind; worried that the stark haircut she had opted for might not suit her.

But then she was being swept into a chair, a cloth was spread around her shoulders and the clip of the scissors echoed in her ears. She was almost afraid to look at her reflection when at last a mirror was held up for her to see. She gasped. Her eyes seemed larger and her face a different shape; she appeared almost elfin.

Before she left the Emporium, Mona bought herself some rouge and lipstick in matching colours. She moved towards the ladies' powder-room and experimented with the make-up. At first, she was heavy handed with the rouge and she smiled – she looked like a clown. She rubbed gently

318

until the colour was no more than a trace of a bloom over her cheekbones.

The woman facing her in the mirror was a stranger; tall and elegant in high-heeled shoes, smart and modern in appearance.

Mona sat in the tearooms and as she waited to be served she wondered how many more women were like her, with hidden assets that they were too afraid or too insecure to discover.

She took a long time over her tea and her thoughts were spinning around in her head, exciting, frightening. But she would act now before she lost her courage.

At the till, she enquired pleasantly but firmly about the manager, and the girl taking her money looked at her in concern.

'There's no complaints about the service, I hope,' she said quickly and Mona shook her head.

'Nothing like that, but I do need to know the name of the manager and where I'll find him,' Mona repeated.

'That's Mr Steedman,' the girl said, her eyes round. 'And if you go up the stairs there, his office is on the first floor just before you come to ladies' lingerie.'

Mona thanked her and moved slowly across the carpeted floor. Would she, could she pluck up courage to speak to the man, tell him of her ideas and ask him for a job in the emporium? She forced herself to climb the stairs; then she was standing outside the door of blank, polished wood with a neat brass handle and a plate informing her that this was indeed the office of Mr Steedman, Manager.

She rapped her knuckles against the door and after a moment or two it was opened by a woman dressed in a neat navy suit and a white blouse, hair drawn back severely from a rather bony face.

'Yes?' she said warily, not knowing how to place Mona, who didn't look like the run-of-the-mill customer with a complaint to air.

'I'd like to see Mr Steedman,' Mona said pleasantly but firmly and the woman blinked rapidly.

'Have you an appointment, madam?' she asked, her voice non-committal. Like a blank wall, Mona thought.

'I haven't an appointment but if he has the time, I'd like to see him. I've something of interest to discuss with him,' Mona said quickly.

From within the room she heard a cough and then a gentle-looking, white-haired man appeared in the doorway. 'I'm Mr Steedman. Do come in, I'd be interested in your views,' he said courteously.

Mona was ushered to a seat facing a huge desk. Along the window-sill behind the manager was a range of potted plants and somehow the sight of them made Mona feel that Mr Steedman was a kindly man.

She glanced up at the secretary, hoping the woman wouldn't remain in the room but she sat down at a small table in the corner and bent over some papers.

'Don't allow Miss Foster's presence to bother you.' The manager leaned forward, sensing her reserve. 'Just tell me what you have in mind. If it's some complaint, I'll listen and give what you say every consideration.'

Mona felt suddenly impertinent as she faced the manager of one of the biggest stores in town, yet she had come here to speak of her ideas and speak she would.

'There's no complaint,' she said quickly. 'It's just that I have an idea to put to you. I came here this morning feeling dowdy and dull and in need of an entire new look as regards to my appearance,' she said forcefully. 'I was lucky that I found an assistant who was able and willing to help me but I feel such an important matter shouldn't be left to luck.' She edged forward on her chair forgetting her nervousness.

'I feel that there should be advertising in papers and magazines offering the New You idea to women and there should be a person who is responsible for leading the customer through all the departments of the store, instead of a series of different sales assistants who are not aware of the needs of the customer.'

He smiled and regarded her for a moment in silence. 'Times are not propitious for too much expansion, my dear,' he said at last. 'You must know that many people are still out on strike.'

'But,' Mona said quickly, 'women always need clothes and feel particularly like a new sort of look when times are difficult.' She sighed. 'I do understand that many customers wouldn't be able to afford some of the high prices in the store but what about a cut-price, bargain shop to sell off clothes returned by the wealthier women who have grown tired of them?'

Mr Steedman moved forward on his chair. 'Now there you do have a good idea,' he said at once. He smiled. 'There have been the odd occasions when a customer has brought back a garment – obviously one that has been worn – but with some trumped-up complaint or other in order that they may have a credit-note or even, in some cases, a refund.' He sat back in his chair. 'Let me think about it for a few days and if you leave your address with Miss Foster, we will be in touch.'

Mona walked out of the store as though she was walking on air. She was a new woman and even if nothing came of her suggestions to the manager, she had made an impact with her ideas and had not been turned down flat.

As she walked towards home, she kept turning things over in her mind. If Mr Steedman didn't take up her idea, perhaps she could do something on those lines herself. It would mean renting a shop premises which might be expensive, but on the other hand perhaps she could persuade some one to back her. At any rate, it gave her something to think about other than dwelling on Ceri and his obsession for another woman.

He was home before her and the fire had been stoked so that a blanket of warm air greeted her. The kettle was singing away, steam issuing from the spout and spitting spray onto the hot coal so that it hissed noisily.

Mona went to remove the kettle and then paused, her hand stretched out. No, she would not immediately slip back into her role as housewife. Ceri had put the kettle onto the fire so let him see to it.

She opened the buttons of her new amber-coloured coat, and just then Ceri entered the kitchen. He had been whistling but he stopped in surprise when he saw her.

'*Duw,* what have you done to yourself?' he asked in a mixture of surprise and disapproval. 'You look like one of those fashion models out of a shop-window.'

Mona slipped her arms out of the coat. 'I've bought myself a new wardrobe, most of the things are going to be delivered tomorrow,' she said in the rather cold tone she'd adopted ever since the scene in Murphys' shop. She took off her shoes and rubbed at a small spot of dirt on the heel with her fingertip.

'What have you used for money?' he asked mildly. 'Charged it all, have you, and I'll be footing the bill?'

She looked directly at him. 'So you object to me spending a bit of money on myself, do you? Am I supposed to work in the house, cook, clean, do the washing for nothing just because we're married? Even your father used to pay me, mind, when I worked at the ferry house.'

Ceri looked nonplussed. 'I don't know why you're being so aggressive. You've changed so much lately I hardly know you. Of course I don't mind you buying more clothes and I accept that you're entitled to get something out of our marriage, but you're making it like a sort of business arrangement.'

'What else is it?' Mona asked calmly. 'Let's face facts. You are in love with another woman. I suppose I was blind not to have seen it sooner – you have always loved Katie Murphy and our marriage vows were empty promises on your part.'

'Now, come on, Mona,' he said at once. 'Can you honestly say you were in love with me? When we married, we were both trying to recover from broken romances. We did each other a favour, didn't we?'

'Perhaps,' Mona replied. 'Nevertheless, I've put a great deal into making the marriage work while you have gone behind my back and seen Katie Murphy, and don't deny it, for I've seen you.'

He took the kettle from the fire and set it on the hob. 'It's not true that I've been seeing Katie, not in the way you mean,' he said. 'I've seen very little of her, in fact.'

Mona stared at him. 'From her choice, not yours,' she said softly and there was a pain within her. 'Well, you needn't worry about the money. I've only spent what I've saved over the years, penny-pinching so that we'd have a nest-egg.' She shrugged. 'And then I found out that the nest wasn't very secure.'

'You're wrong, Mona!' She could see that Ceri was growing angry. 'Katie is nothing more than a friend.'

'Well, I didn't know that friendship could make babies. She's pregnant; everyone is gossiping about her, if you must know.' She turned towards the stairs. 'I'm going to put my new clothes away and, Ceri, if you want anything to eat, you'd better make it yourself, I'm not hungry.'

Her small glow of triumph lasted only until she reached the bedroom. She hung the warm coat in the wardrobe and placed her shoes neatly together on the shelf. She sighed as she closed the doors, the brass handles swinging against the dark wood. It was somehow as if she'd put away the new Mona and the old, mousy housewife had re-emerged.

She felt tears blur her vision as she looked around the room at the large double bed. How could she bear Ceri near her when she knew he still loved another woman? And yet he'd argued so convincingly, could she possibly be wrong?

She heard him banging around in the kitchen and moved to the door, then stopped herself, her hands over her face. Of course he was seeing Katie. She must be strong, she must not run to him whenever he cried for help. If she couldn't have his love, then at least she would have his respect. She sat on the bed and the coldness of the room wrapped itself around her, she felt so alone, so unloved.

It was almost a week later when the letter came for her. The envelope was thick and creamy and Ceri handed it to her with open curiosity.

'What's it about?' he asked, elbows on the table. He waited as she unfolded the letter and read it, then he repeated the question impatiently. 'Well, what is it?'

She looked up at him, her feelings warm. She was useful, she did have some worth in her own right, not merely as Ceri's wife.

'I've got a job.' she said briskly. 'I start on Monday.' She rose from the table and hurried upstairs to her room, hugging the letter to her. 'Thank you, Mr Steedman,' she said in a whisper.

She watched from the window as Ceri left the house on his way to work. She would be independent of him now. She'd have her own money to do with what she liked. She would be her own woman and yet the thought did not give her the satisfaction she'd hoped for. She realized now that she loved Ceri and wanted to be with him more than she wanted anything.

Katie had come home from hospital to find that Luke had bought a house for them. It was large and roomy and was situated on the hillside above the sea. Luke was so proud as he led her through the door, watching her face and trying to judge her reaction.

'Do you like it?' he asked anxiously. 'I've even chosen the room for the baby, and I've begun to decorate it, too.'

'Luke,' she said softly, 'it's lovely, but are you sure we should be together so soon after Peta's death?'

'Listen to me.' He took her in his arms. 'Nothing will bring Peta back and what would be achieved if you and I remained apart? You would bring an illegitimate child into the world, and I'm not allowing that to happen.' He smiled down at her. 'Come and see how the nursery looks. Take it steadily now, you're still not strong.'

He led her carefully up the stairs and along the landing, flinging the door wide. Katie walked into the sunlit room, admiring the pictures of small rabbits leaping through green and golden fields.

Luke smiled. 'I take it you're pleased with my handiwork?' he said, putting his arm around her. 'I'm becoming a real expert at papering walls now.'

'It's beautiful, Luke.' She rested her head on his shoulder. 'I don't know what to say. I want us to be together and yet I'm not sure it's the right thing to do.'

He tipped her face up so that she was looking into his eyes. 'We are going to be married, no arguments.'

'But can you afford all this?' Katie asked. 'The house is so grand, it must have cost a fortune, and what with the strike and you not bringing out as much coal as usual – perhaps it's the wrong time.'

'I'm making a good enough living,' Luke said, walking to the door. 'The orders are coming thick and fast these days. I know I haven't got the manpower I'd like but the strike must end soon and then we'll be just fine. In any case I've got a tidy bit of capital coming from the sale of the other house, so don't worry.'

She went with him downstairs, her hand on his arm. She loved Luke and admired what he was doing, yet her doubts remained. He was taking on such a lot of responsibilities and at a time when things were difficult enough for him as it was.

At the bottom of the stairs, Luke turned and took her in his arms. 'I'm a lucky man.' He kissed her gently and then with growing passion and she held him away, laughing a little.

'Sure there's no need getting all loving, there's no bed up there in the room, yet!'

'Well,' Luke said softly, 'we must see to that straight away.' He paused. 'But seriously, I don't like the idea of us living separately, even for a short time, Katie.'

Katie pushed her doubts to the back of her mind. 'Well, it won't be for long, now,' she said. 'When Frank Porter came to the hospital he said his mammy was helping in the shop. I'm going to ask them to do it permanently. They'll run it better than I ever did.' She kissed Luke gently. 'And now, all I want to do is be your wife and mother to your children.'

'Children?' Luke said. 'You're planning to have more, then? In that case we'd better go to town and buy a bed first thing.'

'Luke,' Katie said turning to face him, 'can I ask you a favour?'

'Aye, as long as it's not a diamond ring or a fur coat!' He smiled at her. 'Come on, out with it, what do you want?'

'I want to go down to the church,' she said softly. 'I haven't been to mass since I fell for the baby, it's something I've been putting off.'

He smiled and moved towards her, holding her close to him. 'Of course you can go. I'll take you to St Joseph's in the car. I'm not having you walking about too much, not just yet.'

Katie cupped his face in her hands. 'I know this has been your only day off in weeks and I am grateful to you for humouring me.'

'Say nothing more about it.' Luke kissed her lightly. He locked the large front door and pocketed the key, and Katie slipped her arm in his.

'It's a beautiful day,' Katie said. 'If you've work to do, I can always walk to the church. I'm fine now.'

'Get in the car and no arguments,' Luke said, opening the door for her. She sighed as she sat beside him looking out at the sun-splashed streets. The town had not yet returned to normal; there were soup-kitchens in many of the church halls and groups of men stood on corners with their hands in their pockets, faces lean and worried.

When Luke dropped her off outside the church of St Joseph's, Katie waved him goodbye and Luke smiled at her.

'You can't get rid of me that easily. I'll call up at the slant but I shall be back to pick you up in a little while.'

Inside the church, a choirboy was singing and the sweet pure voice rose to the rafters bringing tears to Katie's eyes.

She touched her forehead with water and genuflected before taking her place in one of the seats. The sweet voice was silent then and the peace of the church eased

Katie's tension. Her worries about Luke's future in the mine added to the strain of knowing she was stepping so quickly into a dead woman's shoes.

But she had her good friends like Mali Richardson, who never changed, and now more recently she had the company and support of Frank Porter. Even his gregarious, good-natured mother seemed to accept her as she was, making no judgements.

Once Katie handed over the shop to them, she would be relieved of the embarrassment of facing customers over the shop counter. Most of them would be polite but Mrs Keys had seen to it that tongues were wagging about the scandalous behaviour of Katie Murphy.

The choirboy was singing again and Katie felt a sense of peace wash over her. She was a lucky woman in every way.

After a time, she rose and moved to the door. The sun was shining outside and it was warmer now. The soft breeze from the sea had died away. Katie looked along the road watching for Luke's car when suddenly she came face to face with Mona Llewelyn. But what a changed Mona. She no longer appeared mousy, her hair was different and she looked vivacious and attractive.

'Good day to you, Katie Murphy,' Mona said and her tone was cold but Katie smiled, thinking she was being over-sensitive.

'Sure 'tis looking fine you are, Mona,' Katie said quickly, 'and me feeling like a frumpy old housewife.'

Mona seemed to relax a little. 'There's nothing frumpy about you, Katie; there never was, especially in Ceri's opinion,' she added wistfully,

Katie suddenly felt unaccountably sorry for her. 'Look,' Katie began, 'please let me explain that there has never been anything wrong between Ceri and me, not since that time when I left Sweyn's Eye to go to Yorkshire.'

Mona stared at her in silence for a moment. 'It still hurts to know that Ceri's still in love with you. He'd have had you into bed without the least thought for me if you were willing.'

'Well that never happened,' Katie said firmly, 'so why don't you put it out of your head?'

'That's easy enough to say.' Mona's voice was low. 'But you're having a baby and I'm wondering if Ceri is the father.'

'What silly nonsense!' Katie said. 'You might as well know, as most people seem to, that Luke Proud is the father. If you don't believe me, sure then stay with me for a while for Luke is picking me up in his car any minute now.'

'There's foolish I feel,' Mona said at once, her cheeks bright. 'Don't know what to say now, I'm so embarrassed.'

'Don't worry about it, I'm only too glad to have cleared your mind about it. Suspicion is a very hurtful thing.'

Mona sighed. 'It's sporting of you to take it like that.' She paused. 'I knew I had to get out of the house, find something interesting to do with my life and I've found myself a job, a very good job down at the Emporium that your friend Mary Sutton used to own.'

'I'm glad,' Katie said at once, relieved that the subject had been changed. 'I'm sure you'll make a great success of it – you were never afraid of hard work.' Katie smiled. 'Sure I remember you years ago when you were nothing but a young girl; how you used to work at the ferry house, helping Nerys Beynon with all the heavy washing. She wouldn't have managed without you.'

Mona nodded. 'Aye, I enjoyed my time spent with Nerys; she's been a good friend to me, always. I'm on my way to see her now, to talk over my new job.'

Katie saw from the corner of her eye a tall figure approaching and took a deep breath as she realized it was Ceri himself. Mona saw her look and turned round, seemingly unperturbed by the appearance of her husband.

'Off down the public, are you?' she said and Ceri nodded to Katie before answering his wife.

'Aye, well, it seems I'm not going to get any dinner today so I might as well have a pint of ale with the boys.'

'Carry on, you,' Mona replied, 'and, Ceri, I'm sorry.'

'Sorry about what, love?' He thrust his hands into his pockets, his tone one of exasperation. Mona smiled.

'I'll have to tell you that later. Go on you and have your drink, I'm just going to the ferry house; I shan't be long.'

Katie smiled at Ceri. 'Isn't your wife looking smart these days and got a job too, I hear.' She tried to edge away but Ceri stopped her.

'I hope everyone is well,' he said politely, obviously trying to make conversation. 'I hear you've been in hospital, is that right?'

'Sure, 'tis right but I'm fine now.' She turned to see Luke's car edging into the kerbside.

'I've got to go. See you both again, some time,' she said in relief. She climbed into the car and, turning to look over her shoulder, saw Ceri and Mona still standing close together. As she watched, Katie saw him take his wife's hand and she smiled. It seemed that Mona's suspicions about her had been laid to rest.

'What's tickling you?' Luke asked, glancing at her curiously. She rested her head on his shoulder for a moment.

'Nothing,' she said. 'It's just that I'm an incurable romantic.' She looked back again and the figures were fading into the distance, blurring into one. Katie smiled and looked up at Luke. 'Yes,' she said again, 'I'm an incurable romantic.'

The silent queue of people spread along the pavement outside the gates of Babell Chapel. Overhead the sun was warm and the new green leaves of the trees rustled softly in the breeze.

'Come on, boys.' Charlotte's heart was beating swiftly. She'd not been to one of the soup-kitchens before and she felt ashamed and embarrassed as she joined the end of the line of people.

She saw several familiar faces; Mrs Keys, with her crowd of children round her skirts first in line, and behind her old

Mrs Benson leaned against the iron railings as though for support.

'Why do we have to come to the chapel, mam?' Denny asked, frowning. 'It's not Sunday, is it?'

Before Charlotte could think of a reply Freddy was nudging his brother in the ribs. 'Be quiet,' he said, 'and don't ask silly questions.'

Charlotte bit her lip, hunger had driven her and her boys to go begging for charity but for days now she had no money to buy food for them. The flour bin was empty and the last of the potatoes eaten.

Charlotte had not told Jim of her true circumstances. He had enough to worry about as it was with the strikers becoming more militant and angry. He had not returned to live beneath her roof partly, she suspected, because he didn't want to be a drain on her slight resources, and partly because with no other lodgers in the house, he would compromise her and expose her to gossip.

She sighed softly but at least they had patched up their differences, and the terrible hurt she'd felt when they'd quarrelled over Luke helping her was lessening. Now, ironically, there was no help from Luke when she so desperately needed it.

The doors of the chapel were being opened and the crowd of people began to move forward. Mrs Keys disappeared into the hall and suddenly Charlotte felt herself being pushed forward, for a crowd had gathered behind her.

As they neared the doors the smell of mutton stew drifted tantalizingly towards them. Charlotte felt her stomach contract for she had not eaten for days. This morning she had given her sons the last of the porridge, pretending that she had already had hers.

'There's a lovely smell, mam,' Denny said, his eyes alight. 'I'm starving hungry, mind.'

'Well today we'll eat with some of our neighbours; that'll be a change, won't it?'

'Aye,' Denny said doubtfully, 'but I'd rather have dinner in our house.'

Charlotte had reached the door and within the hall, she could see a long trestle table laid with a white cloth. Several well-dressed women were serving the stew and Charlotte recognized Mali Richardson, who waved her hand when she saw her.

Charlotte pushed the boys before her but Freddy caught her arm and drew her forward. 'You're hungry, too, mam,' he said in his sober manner, and she smiled down at him.

Mali was about to hand Freddy a dish of stew when Mrs Keys came forward. 'I thought the meals were for the wives of striking miners,' she said spitefully. 'Well Charlotte Davies has got no husband, 'as she?'

Denny looked longingly at the bowl of stew and Charlotte felt a sudden, blinding rage. This woman was trying to deprive her child of food.

Mali intervened quickly. 'Charlotte's husband was killed in the mine and she's as entitled to food as anyone else.' She smiled as she handed the bowl to Denny and then quickly gave Freddy and Charlotte some of the stew along with chunks of crusty bread.

'Take no notice of her,' Mali said, quietly, 'she's known for her spiteful tongue.'

Charlotte moved away to one of the tables, her face crimson with anger and outrage. She stared down at the bowl of stew and her eyes filled with tears.

She forced herself to eat for Freddy was looking at her in concern. '*Duw*, this is lovely stew, mind,' she said. 'I couldn't have made better myself.'

But the food tasted like sawdust in her mouth. She glanced around, wondering if everyone resented her presence, but no one appeared to notice her; they were busy getting on with their meal.

As Charlotte left the hall, Mali called to her. 'Don't you take any notice of that old biddy, mind,' she said firmly. 'You come again tomorrow. You're entitled to the same treatment as anyone else and don't forget it.'

Out in the sunlight, Charlotte took a deep breath. She didn't know if she could face the ordeal of queueing at the soup-kitchens again and yet she couldn't let her sons starve.

'Charlotte, my God, have you been in there?' She looked up into Jim's face and her lips trembled. He caught her in his arms and smoothed back her hair. 'You must never come here again,' he said. 'I could kick myself for not making sure you were all right. I'm a self-centred fool. Come on, I'll walk home with you and on the way we'll call at Murphy's shop and get you some provisions.'

Charlotte leaned weakly against him, grateful to Jim for his concern. 'I have never, in all my life,' she said, 'felt so helpless as when I stood at the table and saw the food almost taken out of my children's mouths by the spite of one woman.'

'Forget all about it, put it out of your mind, for if I have to steal I won't see you going short again, I promise,' Jim said angrily.

'Thank you, Jim,' she said humbly. She clung to him for a moment, feeling faint and ill, and then he was leading her away from the people still milling around outside the chapel hall.

'Come on, Charlotte,' he said firmly, 'I'm taking you home.'

26

Charlotte and Jim sat up talking into the early hours of the morning and she felt warmed and comforted by his presence in the house.

'Sure, the days are spinning past,' Jim said, 'and there's no sign of the strike coming to an end.' He shook his head. 'My men are brave. They've risked everything to make the bosses see sense but I don't know how much longer they can go on.'

'I know, love,' Charlotte said softly. 'I saw it all today at the soup-kitchen. It's shaming to be without food and have to beg for it, mind.'

'Do you know, Charlotte,' Jim said gently, 'that the miners, their wives and their children make up more than ten per cent of the population? What that means is this damn government are allowing five million people to starve.'

'*Duw*, Jim, I didn't realize there was all those people going without. I suppose I'm selfish just thinking of my own family and my own pride.'

Jim shook his head. 'It's only natural that you want to put food in the mouths of your children, love.'

He leaned over and took her hand. 'And I mean to take care of you; so don't worry, you won't go without, I've promised you that much.'

Charlotte was silent. How could Jim earn money for food without breaking the strike? And it would be too much to ask him to go back on his principles.

'I'd better get off to bed, then,' she said, rising to her feet. 'Are you going to stay tonight, Jim?'

He shook his head. 'No, but I'll see you tomorrow.' He moved quickly out of the door then, and as Charlotte closed it and pushed the bolt into place she felt suddenly weary and very near to tears.

In the morning the boys were awake early and Charlotte gave them a small piece of fried bread and an egg. Afterwards they helped her clear away and she was about to do some ironing when Luke appeared in the doorway. He was frowning and she knew he was going to read her the riot act about Jim.

'Go out to play, boys!' she said, her voice trembling. 'Me and Uncle Luke are going to have a talk.'

Denny bit his lip and stared at Luke defiantly. 'I'm hungry,' he said quietly.

Luke put his hand into his pocket at once and took out some coins, but Charlotte spoke quickly.

'No, Luke, I can't accept money from you,' she said huskily. He smiled and shook his head.

'Well, I'm not giving it to you, I'm giving it to my nephews. Go on, Denny, you and your brother get some bread and cheese and a couple of pounds of potatoes from Murphys' shop.' He glanced at Charlotte. 'See, I'm not really giving money away, I'm putting it into Katie's business.'

She hung her head, defeated by his logic. Luke moved towards her and tipped her face up so that she could not avoid his eyes.

'Things are that bad, then? Jim has brought you to this.' He shook his head. 'How can you put up with it, love, seeing your sons go hungry? What would their father have said? Gronow would turn in his grave and you know it.'

'Don't talk like that, please, Luke!' Charlotte said quickly. 'I feel bad enough as it is. But Jim is a good man with high principles and I love him.'

Luke released her and moved to the door. 'Well, principles don't put food in empty bellies,' he said. 'I wanted to speak to Jim but perhaps I'd better do it somewhere else.'

The front door swung open and a tall figure was silhouetted against the sunlight. 'Talk of the devil,' Luke said.

'Please.' Charlotte's hand was on Luke's arm. 'Don't start a row in by here, I just couldn't stand it.'

'All right, love,' Luke said softly. 'Hello there, Jim, I was just on my way out.'

'Well, don't go on my account, man.' Jim moved towards him and Luke had no alternative but to return to the kitchen. 'Come to see Charlotte or was it me you wanted to talk to?'

Luke eyed Jim O'Conner steadily. 'It was you, but I've realized this is neither the time nor the place to say what I want to say.'

Jim moved over to the fireplace and stood before the blaze, hands in his pockets, as though laying claim to his right to be there. 'Spit it out, man, sure there's nothing to be said between us that Charlotte can't hear.'

Luke smiled drily. 'I don't want to involve my sister in the politics of the situation as it stands between you and me. Perhaps it would be better if we took a stroll down to the public bar of the Mexico Fountain.'

'No,' Charlotte said quickly. 'Keep arguments private, if you please, I don't want my name bandied around the bars of Sweyn's Eye.'

Her words were strong but Luke read her well. Charlotte was afraid that he and Jim would come to blows after a pint or two of ale and he couldn't blame her. He thrust his fists into his pockets. 'Well, perhaps some other time then, Jim.' Luke moved towards the door.

'Haven't you got the courage of your convictions, man?' Jim's words were a taunt but Luke smiled evenly.

'What convictions would they be, then – reading my mind for me, are you, Jim?' He opened the door into the passageway but Jim was not ready to give up.

'So you'd see this blasted government rub the faces of the workers into the dust, would you? Sure there's no guts to you; gone over to the side of the bosses to serve your own interests.'

It was clear that Jim was in an aggressive mood and was trying to win Luke over to his side of the fence but Charlotte knew he was wasting his time.

'My mine is so small,' Luke said, 'it can't make a bit of difference to the mighty scheme of things, you must see that.'

'Sure 'tis pointless talking to you, man,' Jim replied, 'got no social conscience at all have you?'

Luke shrugged. 'Maybe not, but I do like to keep food in the bellies of the people who depend on me. I wouldn't see them starve for the sake of a principle.' He paused and stared at Jim pointedly.

'I won't let Charlotte or the boys starve,' Jim said, 'and where were you when they were down at the soup-kitchen, since you're so self-righteous?'

The door was pushed open and the boys came into the room carrying an armful of provisions.

'We've got bread and potatoes, Uncle Luke!' Denny said breathlessly but he stopped abruptly when he saw Jim standing before the fire, sensing the tension in the atmosphere.

'Where did you get the money from?' Jim asked and Denny looked down at the scuffed toes of his shoes, mumbling something inaudible.

Luke's mouth tightened and Charlotte knew what he was thinking: that it was one thing for Jim O'Conner to have his own views, but when it meant Luke's flesh and blood going hungry, it was time he stepped in.

'Put the things down on the table, boys and run outside and play for a minute,' Luke said, forcing a cheerful note into his voice, and Freddy looked up questioningly at his mother.

'It's all right, boy,' she said, 'go on you and play.' Charlotte ushered her son to the door and closed it then leant against it, her face white.

'Now, I don't want any more said about politics in my kitchen.' She spoke firmly. 'I know you both have your own views but this is my house and I want a bit of peace in it.'

'You took money from him, Charlotte?' Jim said. 'After me promising to take care of you.' He'd ignored her words; it was almost as though she hadn't spoken and Charlotte's eyes flashed anger.

'That is my business,' she said. 'Luke is my brother and kin to my boys and as he wanted to help us I couldn't refuse him.'

She turned to Luke. 'I'm sorry, Luke, but I'm asking you please not to come to my house again until this thing is settled. Jim is my man, I believe his views are right but I can't bear all this upset.'

'That's all right, Charlotte,' Luke said slowly. 'I understand that you have to take Jim's side.' He looked directly at Jim. 'But I'll tell you this: if you're any sort of man, you'll keep food in the mouths of those kids whatever it takes to do it.' He moved Charlotte aside and opened the kitchen door. 'And one more thing: keep your subversive ideas to yourself − I don't want you rabble-rousing my men.'

'You still can't see it, can you?' Jim said fiercely. 'If you had come out with us when the strike began, you wouldn't have been helping bosses and faceless men in government to take away the rights of the workers! Sacrifices have to be made if we're to have a say in the way our lives are run.'

'I run my own life my own way,' Luke said at once. 'No man tells me what to do.'

'But you are one of the fortunates,' Jim said. 'What about men who can't speak for themselves, who haven't the ability to make their own way in the world − are they to rot?'

Jim would have said more but Charlotte caught his arm. 'Let him go, Jim, I don't want any more unpleasantness.' She watched Luke go out to his car and she was very close to tears.

Luke scarcely saw the roadways running away beneath the wheels of his car as he drove home. He felt he hated Jim O'Conner and all men like him who bleated on about principles and then let families starve for them. The effects of the strike could be seen in the hollow-eyed children and the lean, worried faces of the men as they stood uselessly on street corners.

He drove up to the house and switched off the engine, staring round him at the folding hills and far below in the distance, between the houses and rooftops of the town, he saw a glimpse of sparkling blue sea.

'Luke, what are you sitting out there for, sure 'tis day-dreaming you are!' Katie hurried out to greet him.

He smiled and slid from the car, taking her in his arms. 'Let's have a quiet cup of tea together, love,' he said, putting his arm around her shoulder. Katie turned into his embrace.

'What's wrong? Sure you're looking like the dog that's had its bone stolen,' she said, trying to hide her concern behind a smile.

'I've quarrelled with Jim O'Conner for a start,' he said ruefully. 'Before that I had a meeting with the men. I had to try to talk them into going back to work but it seems that all of them, even old Tim, think they ought to join the strikers. There's been quite a lot of intimidation going on, love, and I don't blame the men for being frightened.'

Katie hugged him close. 'You look so tired, my love.' She pressed her cheek against his. 'Come on into the house, we'll have an hour or two just sitting quietly by the fire.'

Luke smiled. 'Sounds fine.' He took his watch out of his pocket. 'I'll have to get back up to the mine for an hour later on, supervise the collecting of the coal by the men from Ponty. At least that order is filled.'

He kissed her neck. 'Let's talk about you, shall we?' he said and she pushed him away, her eyes shining.

'Sure an' aren't you a wicked man? One thing only on your mind and that's getting me into bed and in broad daylight, too. Sure you should be ashamed!' Smiling, she led him into the kitchen and pushed him into a chair. 'You sit there, have a rest and tell me what you'll do about working the mine.'

She sat on a stool next to the fire and held his hand. He looked down into her eyes and love for her warmed him,

338

easing the hurt of Charlotte's decision to ban him from her home.

He sighed. 'Being a boss isn't all I thought it would be, but then I never expected life to be easy,' he said. 'But what about you? You look a little pale. That son of ours taking the strength out of you, is he?'

'Sure 'an what makes you think I won't have a lovely little daughter to dress in pretty frocks then, Luke Proud?'

Luke stretched his legs before him. 'So long as the baby is all right I don't mind what we have.' He took a deep breath. 'It's so good to be by my own fireside, having nothing to do but admire my lovely wife-to-be.' He paused. 'You will marry me soon, won't you, Katie? I know times are difficult in more ways than one but I don't see any point in us just living together, the baby must have my name.'

Katie rose to her feet. 'I'm going to make us both a nice cup of tea and then we can talk.' She smiled. 'I know where I stand, sure enough – it's just a skivvy you're wanting round here, someone to wait on you.'

She brought him tea and a plate of Welsh cakes. 'Look at these, will you, I managed to bake them quite well seeing that I'm a full-blooded Irish girl.'

'Aye,' Luke said drily, 'changing the subject you are again. Why is it you shy away when I talk about marriage?'

Katie shook back her hair. 'You've got enough troubles without bothering about a wedding just now.' She sat in the chair opposite him. 'When you go to the mine, I want to slip down to the shop, see how Frank's mammy is managing.'

Luke stared at her anxiously. 'Shall I drive you to town? I don't like to think of you walking about alone not as things are just now.'

She picked up her woollen jacket and slipped it around her shoulders then smiled. 'Let me be, Luke, you're smothering me,' she said gently, putting her hand on his arm.

Luke walked with her to the door. Outside the sun was shining and the roses in the garden lent a flash of brilliance to the day. It was a lovely day and yet for Luke it was overshadowed.

'Don't be long,' he said, 'and don't go wandering round the backstreets.'

'You're thinking about those men who shouted at us the other day, aren't you?' Katie asked, leaning against him, her head on his shoulder. 'Sure it'll be all right – it was just seeing you in the car that got them all riled up. No one will even notice me.'

And yet as he watched her walk away so happily towards the bus stop, Luke for a moment longed to call her back, take her in his arms and beg her not to go. But that was foolishness; it was allowing a few roustabouts to dictate a lifestyle foreign to all he believed.

He returned indoors and resumed his seat. He put his head back and closed his eyes, determined to relax. And yet round and round in his brain he kept hearing the arguments put up by Jim O'Conner, and for the first time he wondered if his own views on the strike could be wrong.

Katie climbed aboard the bus and took a seat near the doorway, glad of the soft breeze that cooled her cheeks. She sensed that Luke had not told her everything. She knew he was worried – why, oh why, wouldn't he talk to her? She supposed it was due to the fact that with Peta he had to take all the strain. He couldn't confide in his first wife and now he had become accustomed to keeping his worries to himself. She paid her fare and smiled as the conductor handed her the change.

'*Duw*, this strike will be the ruin of the town,' he said, hanging onto the upright bar near the open stairs of the bus. 'I wish there'd be a settlement and soon. I know it's wrong the way we get pushed around by the government – they've done what they like with us poor fools and up until now we've been too dull to make a protest – but this time they've pushed the miners too far.'

Katie stared up at him uncertainly, not knowing what to say; Luke's sound common-sense views seemed right and yet the way the bus conductor put it, a fight was apparently a necessity.

She was glad when the bus reached her stop. The conductor held her arm, helping her onto the road. 'You tell your man to hold firm and stick by his fellow workers and we're bound to win in the end,' he said, smiling broadly.

She stood for a moment outside the Emporium staring at the array of clothes in the window and somehow it seemed frivolous to be displaying summer dresses when there were families going short of bread.

She turned away and began to walk along the sunlit pavement, her head full of questions. Was the strike the only way to make the voice of the people heard?

She found herself walking towards Canal Street where Charlotte lived. She would call in and spend a few minutes in gossip; she was becoming too intense, she needed the company of another woman.

Charlotte stared at her warily when she opened the door. 'Katie, what are you doing here?' she said, her voice strangely formal.

'I'm sorry,' Katie said, 'is it a bad time?' She forced a smile though she could not help feeling hurt at Charlotte's manner. 'It's not important. I'm on my way to the shop and I just felt like a natter, but I can call again some other time.'

'Has Luke told you he was here earlier?' Charlotte asked and Katie nodded her head. 'Yes but that doesn't mean you and I have to fall out, does it?' she asked.

'Come in.' Charlotte took her arm. 'The neighbours round here are so nosey.' She led the way along the dark passage and Katie followed her.

'I don't want to seem uncharitable,' Charlotte said, 'but I've asked Luke not to come here again.'

The tone of Charlotte's voice set Katie's teeth on edge. 'Sure, he thinks the world of you and the boys, I can't understand you taking that sort of attitude. Luke is your own flesh and blood.'

Charlotte sank into a chair and clasped her hands together. 'It's all about this stupid strike,' she said. 'Luke doesn't see eye to eye with Jim about the rights and wrongs of it and I don't want them quarrelling with each other in my kitchen. Today I thought they might even come to blows so I told Luke to stay away.'

'Mother of God,' Katie said, sighing, 'Luke is working himself to a standstill to keep his mine from falling down.' She looked at Charlotte. 'What is the right way, do you know?'

Charlotte shook her head. 'I can't understand the logic of men. To me, it seems that negotiations are best – strikes bring out the worst in everybody. The women are frightened; the men frustrated, feeling they've been let down by the unions; and the children starve.' She paused. 'My boys are beginning to go hungry already, mind, for Jim, though he promises to help us, has been out of work for weeks, ever since he left the Slant Moira.'

She rubbed her eyes tiredly. 'I know he's doing it for the good of the working man. He's honest and fair and takes the side of the under-dog and yet I can't help feeling it's so wrong to force people to accept charity, and that's what the soup-kitchens are, believe me.'

Katie hugged Charlotte. 'I didn't realize things were that bad; you must come to the shop in Market Street. I'll leave instructions with Frank and his mammy both that you are to have groceries on tick.' She bit her lip. 'All we can do is to stick by our menfolk in whatever they choose to do,' she said softly. 'But after it's all over, perhaps Jim and Luke will be friends again.'

'I doubt it, love,' Charlotte said sadly. 'This strike will split father from son, mother from daughter. It's all right for all the other workers, they've given in now and gone back to their jobs. It's only the miners who are sticking to their guns.'

She sighed heavily. 'I've listened to the men talk when Jim's held meetings in my parlour; out for blood, some of them and anyone who blacklegs will never be forgiven. The bitterness will go on down the generations, split the whole town of Sweyn's Eye, it will.' She moved to the door and opened it.

'I'd go home if I were you,' Charlotte urged. 'I don't like to think of you out on your own, the mood among the men is getting more violent as the strike drags on.'

Katie felt tears burning her eyes, wondering how she had failed to know the extent of the bitterness the strike was causing. But then since she'd almost lost the baby, she had been cocooned in her own little world.

'Surely Jim doesn't agree with violence, does he?' she asked and Charlotte shook her head.

'He doesn't want anyone to be hurt, he's all for using peaceful means, but I know by the sound of the voices of the men with him that he's not going to be able to control them once they get started.' She put her hand on Katie's shoulder. 'Perhaps both of our men are right and both of them wrong. There should be a middle road on which they could meet. And, Katie, thank you for your kindness, I'd rather accept charity from you than from strangers.'

She stood in the doorway for a moment, a strange expression on her face. Katie looked at her questioningly. 'What is it? Sure you're keeping something from me.'

'I suppose you should know,' Charlotte said. 'Michael Murphy is rumoured to be back in town. I'm sorry, but your brother is here for one reason only and that's to make trouble.'

The words fell into the silence and Katie's heart began to beat swiftly. 'Dear Lord,' she said, breathlessly, 'it never rains but it pours.'

27

The rose-scented air drifted in through the open window of Mona's bedroom. Outside, the birds were singing among the leaves of the elm trees that bordered the garden, and as she opened her eyes the sun was just beginning to rise.

She turned her head slowly. Ceri was beside her, his arm flung across her. He was still asleep. She stared down at his face for a long moment before closing her eyes again. Theirs was a strange marriage, cobbled together for all the wrong reasons. They had both been hurt and rejected, she by Ceri's brother and he by Katie Murphy. And yet, over the past years, Mona had thought some sort of love was growing between them.

She felt tears burn her eyes, she *had* come to love Ceri, she realized it now; her jealousy over Katie Murphy, though quite unfounded, had taught her a lesson. She must work at making her marriage a success.

Last night he had made love to her with more passion than he'd shown for a long time and hope had begun to flicker within her. And yet she would not give up her new found independence, not now that she had created a niche for herself in Mr Steedman's shop.

She slid carefully out of bed, not wishing to disturb Ceri. He'd been having a tough time of things lately, the strike playing havoc with the silver trade.

She washed in the kitchen and dressed quickly in one of the good fine dresses she'd bought for herself. When she looked at her reflection in the mirror, her spirits rose. She had become a woman of some elegance with her short hair, and the carefully-applied rouge and lipstick highlighting her good features.

She left the house quietly and as she walked along the street, she turned her face away from the ragged groups of children, some of them barefooted, making their way to school. The strike was dragging on through the summer, bringing hardship to the town, but it was not her fault and there was nothing she could do about it, she told herself. Yet she could not help but be disturbed; the divide between the rich and poor, it seemed, had never been greater.

She caught the bus on the corner of the road and sat near the door. The sun was rising higher now, it was promising to be a fine day. She saw the glance of a man sitting opposite and read admiration in his eyes. After a moment, she looked away, but she felt uplifted – happy that she'd put away the mousy image and become a woman who was attractive enough to catch a man's eye.

She alighted from the bus in the Stryd Fawr and walked the short distance to the Emporium with a jaunty step, feeling more confident as each moment passed. She paused to look with a critical eye at the window she had helped dress the previous day and smiled. No one would believe the clothes displayed so invitingly were second-hand, except for the poster that stood boldly before the models.

HIGH-CLASS GARMENTS SKILFULLY RENO-VATED AT PRICES TO SUIT MOST POCKETS.

The diplomatic wording pleased Mona as did the clothes themselves. She would be buying one or two of the more expensive articles herself once she had earned enough to pay for them.

The range covered most kinds of clothes from ordinary daywear to the more elegant and lavish evening-gown and Mona had found her customers among women who were fairly comfortable but who could not afford the exclusive designs at the full price.

Mona had been surprised by the number of very rich women who took advantage of the service and brought in garments scarcely worn. Most of the ladies were induced to buy something new with a discount for the returned goods. This meant that the Emporium could scarcely lose.

345

She was met by a smiling Mr Steedman as she walked into the carpeted store and Mona returned his smile, still a little in awe of the man who had the power to change her future. So far, he'd been more than satisfied by the venture but it had scarcely had time to be tried and tested, and might well fizzle out.

She straightened her shoulders. She would not allow it to fizzle out; not if she had to go out onto the street and drag customers inside.

'There is a lady waiting to see you, my dear,' Mr Steedman said in that gentle voice which hid an iron determination, as Mona had learned. 'Mrs Sterling Richardson, no less.'

'Ah.' Mona looked up at the large clock on the wall. 'I should have been here to see her. I'm sorry, I'm a few minutes late – the bus, you know.'

'No matter.' Mr Steedman turned back towards his office. 'If business continues this way you should soon be able to afford your own car.' His eyebrows rose a little. 'Though perhaps a good watch might do for a start.'

Mona hurried through to the dress department and smiled politely as she saw Mali Richardson seated on one of the plush chairs admiring an oyster satin gown decorated in finest coffee lace held up for inspection by one of the young assistants.

'Hello, Mona,' Mali said, looking up and smiling. 'Isn't this gorgeous? Is it an exclusive dress?'

Mona felt her hairroots tingle. If Mali would only buy one of the second-hand garments and wear it in the company of her friends, it would put the seal of approval on the business.

'Yes, it's come from Paris originally, and brought to us by a lady who lives in London.'

Mali smiled. 'So I'm not likely to be embarrassed by meeting the previous owner.' She fingered the satin.

'It has been thoroughly cleaned and pressed, of course,' Mona said easily, 'though I don't believe it could have been worn more than once, if at all.'

Mali looked up. 'Good sales talk, Mona, but I must admit it looks beautiful and if I hadn't known better, I'd have thought it completely new.' She allowed the shimmering material to slip through her fingers. 'Except, of course, the price gives it away.'

Mona took the garment from the young girl who had been holding it and held it against herself. 'See how the skirt swings. The material has been cut on the cross to give it more flare; it's beautiful.'

'I'll take it,' Mali said, 'though I don't think it will look half as good on me as it would on you.' She rose to her feet. 'I think you should have a fashion show and you would do very nicely as the model. I think I'll suggest that very thing to Mr Steedman.'

Mona felt herself blush with pleasure. She knew Mali was being kind because of their mutual connection with the Llewelyn family. Ceri's father was Mali's uncle and to be fair to her, however rich she'd become, Mali had never forgotten her origins.

As she became involved with the business of the day, Mona forgot Mali's words and so it came as a surprise when Mr Steedman called her into his office.

Miss Foster's frosty look had melted a little and Mona didn't know whether to consider that a good or a bad sign. She walked towards the chair in front of the desk and at a gesture from Mr Steedman, sat down.

'One of our customers made a very good suggestion today.' The old man pressed his fingertips together. 'And one that I intend to implement.' He leaned back in his seat and smiled. 'We, this old-fashioned establishment, are going to ape Paris and London, and hold a fashion show.'

Mona stared at him, wondering what to say. She licked her lips and waited, and after a moment Mr Steeman continued.

'You will organize the whole thing.' He smiled his bland smile and his watery baby-blue eyes regarded her steadily. 'I'm sure a young lady with your forcefulness will manage it all very nicely.'

Mona's mind went blank. How on earth did she even begin to go about such a venture? She lifted her head and stared the old man in the eye.

'I shall be happy to organize such an exciting event,' she found herself saying smoothly with no outward sign of panic. 'I think you've made a very wise move, Mr Steedman.'

'We shall see,' he said in equally smooth tones. 'If, as I'm sure it will be, the event is a success then there will be an immediate rise in salary for you and, of course, there will be promotion to fashion-buyer for the entire Emporium.'

He smiled. 'Since I took over here, the trade has not been all I would have wished. I think the place has now become too old-fashioned; we need young, enterprising people to put us old fogeys on the right road, eh, Miss Foster?'

He paused for a moment and now he was quite serious. The twinkle was gone from his eyes and the steel beneath was clear to see. 'Anyone who can increase my profits is an employee to be valued.' He rose to his feet, indicating that the interview was at an end. 'I'm sure you are not going to disappoint me, my dear.'

Mona felt as though she were in a dream. She took her coat from the cloakroom and without as much as a by-your-leave, left the Emporium. There was work to do and she would not be doing it by standing in the store selling dresses, however expensive.

Her mind was a morass of thoughts and ideas; they spun round in her head like a kaleidoscope of moving colours. She would consult fashion magazines for the latest information from London and Paris. She would need to organize a stage for the models to show off the garments to their best advantage; she would need the models themselves – where was she going to start?

Suddenly, she was laughing out loud. She ran through familiar streets not even seeing them until, breathless, she fell onto the sandy beach of the bay and lay on her stomach, staring out at the ships clearing the harbour, leaving on the afternoon tide.

She felt alive and almost delirious with pleasure. She did not know how she was going to do it but she was going to put on the best show Sweyn's Eye had ever seen. There would be gilt-edged invitations going to every important household, she would have posters painted and hung in the windows of the Emporium, there would not be one woman of means left in the town who would not give her eye-teeth to buy a rare model.

She put her head on her hands then and felt the gritty sand beneath her cheek. She had Ceri's love, now she could be happy.

Slowly, as the days passed, Mona put her plans into action. The house was cluttered with books about fashion and every evening Mona spent hours trying her hand at copying sketches from the magazines. She knew nothing about the rights of a big store to copy the great designers but, just as a precaution, on each drawing she altered a garment just enough to make it different.

She was working late one night when Ceri came into the kitchen where she sat at the table.

'Don't I even rate a meal these days?' he asked wryly and she looked up at him in astonishment.

'I'm sorry.' She rubbed her eyes. 'I'd forgotten all about supper.' She pushed away the papers and rose to her feet. 'There's some cold beef and pickles or a bit of cheese,' she said, making for the pantry.

'Damn it all!' Ceri's tone of anger startled her. 'I wanted something hot, not a make-do meal. I've been working all day, don't you realize that?'

'I've been working all day too, mind,' Mona began placatingly. 'I've said I'm sorry, I can't say more.'

Ceri moved towards the fire and threw some coal on the dying flames. '*Duw*, it comes to something, can't even watch the fire and you're sitting on top of it!' He slumped suddenly into his chair and put his head in his hands.

Alarmed, Mona went towards him. 'Ceri, what is it? Are you sick?' she asked anxiously. He looked up at her, his face drawn.

'I'm ruined, Mona. There's not even a scrap of coal left in my shop and so I can't smelt the little silver I have left. In any case, look at the world out there – really look at it. People are starving, Mona. I saw one woman faint in the street she was so weak, like a walking skeleton, she was.' He sighed heavily. 'It's just as well you've got this job because I'm not capable of supporting my own wife any longer.'

'Support? Is that all you think my needs are?' Mona asked softly. 'I'm a woman – I need loyalty and love and only you can give me those things, Ceri.'

'But I'm a failure, Mona, even my father brings in a good living, ferrying people across the river. His wife and children won't starve.'

'Siona's in a different position to you,' Mona said at once, 'his work has to go on so that folk can get about.'

'And what shall I do?' Ceri said bitterly. 'Queue up for the food-vouchers that are being handed out, go to the soup-kitchen in the chapel, perhaps?'

Mona put her arm around his shoulder. 'We are a team, Ceri, and until this damn strike is ended we'll live on what I earn. It's all right, I promise you.'

Ceri rose suddenly and left the room, and Mona heard him take the stairs two at a time. She bit her lip and returned to her chair. Ceri was a proud man and he would not take kindly to being kept by his wife, but there was no alternative. He should be thanking God that someone was bringing in the money.

Mona had organized the show with great speed but even so, it would take place in the last dying days of summer. Invitations were sent out, models found and carpenters employed to erect temporary staging. Dressmakers were ten a penny and all eager to work but Mona went painstakingly through the list of applicants choosing only those with exceptional flair and ability.

It was the talk of Sweyn's Eye, taking women's minds away from the ever-present threat of strikes and setbacks, all of which seemed to have no real bearing on the lives of the ladies of the town.

Mr Steedman was genial about the entire matter but Mona was wise enough to know that if the venture failed heads would roll and hers would be the first. But it would not fail. She was determined that the show would be only the first of many such events to take place at the Emporium.

But when the moment actually came for her to step upon the stage before some of the wealthiest women in the town, her courage almost failed her. She looked down at her dress made entirely from amber lace with seams sewn in such a way as to shape the dress to her slender figure, and tried to draw strength from the fact that she looked as affluent as any lady in the audience and much more fashionable than any of them.

She must remember Mr Steedman's words, that she was youth, setting future trends. Taking a deep breath, she stepped out from behind the velvet curtains and then she was facing the sea of expectant faces turned up towards her.

She began the speech she'd prepared and her voice rang out clearly in the large room. She talked with authority about the new designs and the latest exclusive models, and after a few moments her nervousness left her. She found she was actually enjoying herself, talking about what had become an all-consuming interest – the fashion world.

'So, ladies,' she concluded, 'please look at our gowns, new gowns made at a fraction of the prices charged in the big cities of the world, and yours to choose from tonight. Not forgetting, of course, our range of exclusive garments made in the Paris fashion houses and thoroughly and expertly renovated by us.'

She stepped back in a flurry of applause, allowing the models to walk out onto the stage to display the satin evening-gowns which were slickly cut and shown to perfection on young, slender bodies. Each button and belt-buckle was covered in satin and every stitch was faultless.

After a time, tea was handed around and the ladies took up the cards provided then proceeded to make their choice, vying with each other, eager to snatch at not only the new models but the exclusive second-hand gowns.

'I think you can say it has been a success, my dear Mona.' Mr Steedman's voice cut into her thoughts. She turned to him with a smile.

'Yes, I think I can say that, Mr Steedman, and so it's a salary increase and promotion for me, then?'

'I like that: straight to the point, that's young people for you today.' He chuckled. 'Come and see me in the office in the morning, I think we'd better draw up a contract. I don't want some big city store tempting you away from me.'

It was almost dark when Mona returned home. She was more weary than she'd believed possible. She opened the door and was surprised to find the house in darkness.

'Ceri,' she called, 'are you home?' Somehow the silence was eerie and with a prickling of her scalp, Mona lit the gas mantle. As the light lifted the shadows filling the room with a whiteness, Mona turned towards the stairs.

Her scream echoed around her head, going on and on until she thought she was going mad. At last the tears came.

'Oh, Ceri why did you do it!' She forced herself to look up at the bare feet swinging to and fro in accompaniment to the creaking beam. On the very night of her great triumph, Ceri had taken his own life.

28

Charlotte moved up the hill towards the Murphys' shop, her basket over her arm. Her purse was empty, her food-vouchers used up and her sons were going hungry again. Subdued, Charlotte had braced herself to ask for the 'tick' that Katie Murphy had offered her.

Outside the shop was a crowd of women. Mrs Keys was at the forefront, brandishing a brush covered in whitewash.

'Let's go up to the Slant Moira and get the blacklegs!' she shouted. 'Go back to work, would they? Break the strike? Well, we'll show those blacklegs a thing or two. That Rory calls himself a fireman, does he? Well, he'll know how hot hell is before we finish with him.'

Charlotte turned away before she was seen, her heart beating swiftly with apprehension. Luke must have persuaded some of the men to go back to work; not too difficult with their families near starvation, which meant Luke would be in danger too. She turned and hurried up the hill towards the slant. She knew what the women had in mind. They would use the whitewash on the men to humiliate them and then the brushes would become weapons with which to beat the strikers.

Charlotte quickened her pace. Although she was breathing heavily, her basket bumping against her side as she ran, she hardly noticed the pain, so anxious was she to get to her brother's mine before the crowd of angry women.

She saw Rory at once. He was standing outside the mine and from the cloud of dust in the air, it was clear he had just completed blasting.

'Rory, where's Luke?' Charlotte called. 'You must both get away from here – the women are on their way with buckets of whitewash.'

Rory turned pale. '*Duw*, the boss is in town.' He looked around nervously. 'I'd better get out of here, then. You get old Tim from the shed and tell him he must hide in the mine with his two nephews; never run away in time, they won't, see.'

Rory turned and hurried across the sloping ground, uphill away from the slant and in the opposite direction to the town. Charlotte crossed to the shed where Tim and the two young boys were eating their snap.

'What's the shouting about?' Tim asked, chewing laconically at his bread and cheese.

'Some of the women are coming from the town. They want to get at the blacklegs, so you'd best hide in the mine; they won't look for you there.'

Tim shrugged and continued to eat and Charlotte wanted to shake him into action. 'I don't think you'll get far enough away if you try to run!' she said desperately.

'Not going nowhere, me,' Tim said, his gnarled hands curved around his pick-handle. 'Not afraid of a gang of women, mind.'

Charlotte stiffened as she heard the sound of excited voices and turned to see the group of women coming over the rise of the hill.

'It's too late,' she said. 'I suppose the only thing to do is try to reason with them.'

'Don't waste your breath, girl,' Tim said, 'I've seen it all before, mind. The only thing they'll understand is a bit of their own violence turned back on them.'

Mrs Keys panted to a stop, staring into the shed, her face flushed from her exertions. 'Charlotte Davies, so you've turned blackleg as well, have you?' she said venomously. 'Came up here to warn your brother, I expect. Well, it won't make one jot of difference, we'll get you as well.'

Tim moved forward, the pick in his hand. 'I'd think again if I were you, my girl,' he said but Mrs Keys rushed at him catching the old man off balance and he fell to the floor winded.

Mrs Keys dipped the brush into the bucket and slapped whitewash along the old man's back. 'We'll teach you to go against the rest of the men,' she said hotly, 'we're starving for the strike and you are putting food in your old belly that should be in the mouths of our children.'

Charlotte stood in horrified silence as one of the other women grasped one of the young boys and whitewashed his coal blackened face. The whimpering of the frightened boy galvanized Charlotte into action. She moved forward to push the woman away from the boy.

'Take it out on the defenceless, would you?' she said. 'And do you think that's a good principle, then, humiliating old men and children? Is that what this strike is all about?'

For a moment, the women looked at her in silence and then Mrs Keys stepped across the old man and slapped Charlotte across the face with the brush. The lime stung Charlotte's eyes. She gave a scream and launched herself at the woman, catching her by the throat and bearing her to the ground.

'My sons are as hungry as yours!' She shouted the words into the startled woman's face. 'My own belly is empty and I am all for the strike, but I can't see the sense in hurting those too weak to fight back.'

Mrs Keys dragged herself away and struck out again at Charlotte with the brush. She was past reasoning and lashed out again and again, encouraged by the shouts of the other women.

Charlotte's groping fingers encountered the pick dropped by Tim. She caught it and swung it in a circle around her so that the women fell back in fear.

'Get away from here before there's murder done!' Charlotte cried, tears running down her cheeks. The women fell silent, staring at her as though she'd taken leave of her senses and perhaps she had, but there'd been enough violence.

'Keep your distance, mind,' she said as she lowered the pick to the ground.

'What have we become?' she asked more quietly. 'We're like packs of wolves ready to tear and rend anyone who stands in our way.' She watched as Tim staggered to his feet, white and shaken. One of the young boys was cowering in the corner, hands over his head.

Charlotte faced the women defiantly. 'We are all lucky that no real harm has been done here today. Someone might easily have been injured,' she said. 'And now I think we'd better all get off home.'

The women mumbled to each other uncertainly and were about to turn away when a band of policemen came over the hill.

'*Duw*,' Mrs Keys said, 'we're for it now!' None of the women attempted to run – it was pointless, they were far outnumbered.

Charlotte felt herself being grasped roughly by the arm and she looked up in surprise. 'But I'm not part of all this,' she protested. The man ignored her, dragging her towards the roadway.

'She's telling the truth,' old Tim called out but the constables were busy grouping the women together and herding them towards the town.

Charlotte tried to pull away. 'I'm not one of them,' she said again and the constable looked down at her whitewash-spattered clothes with indifference.

'We'll let the magistrates sort you lot out,' he said, pushing her forward.

The women found themselves being unceremoniously chained together. Charlotte tried once more to protest but she was being dragged down the hill towards the town. At her side, Mrs Keys was sullen, her head bent, her hair hanging in untidy tufts over her face. Charlotte could only guess that she was looking just as bedraggled as the other women in the silent group.

As they were being marched through the streets, faces appeared in windows and doors were flung open, and a cheer rose from the spectators.

'Good for you, girls!' a voice called. 'You showed those blacklegs from the Slant Moira what you can do.'

Charlotte looked up and saw Michael Murphy and his brother standing at the side of the roadway, cheering the women on. She shuddered and felt herself being pulled forward. What was she doing here among a crowd of violence – crazed people who only wanted to strike out and hurt?

The women were being herded towards the police station and at the step Charlotte tripped and fell to her knees. Two pairs of young arms encircled her and she looked into the faces of her sons.

'We're with you all the way, mam,' Freddy said, 'we're proud of you.' At his side, Denny was white-faced and frightened, trying hard to control the trembling of his lips. Charlotte looked at him for a long moment before she was being dragged forward into the doorway of the station. She looked back over her shoulder and Freddy was comforting his younger brother, arm around the thin shoulders.

'Who will feed my boys?' she asked of the nearest constable. He shrugged and turned away, his reply indistinct.

'You should have thought of that before you broke the law,' he said but there was no conviction in his tone.

'Please,' she said to him, 'let Jim O'Conner know that my boys are alone, please, I'm begging you.'

'All right,' the constable said, 'I'll see what I can do.'

The women were being separated and placed in bare rooms, and Charlotte shuddered as the door was slammed upon her. She turned her back against the door and felt the tears run hotly down her cheeks. And then there was only a deep, frightening silence.

29

Katie had been uneasy for days. The spirit of unrest that had gripped the country was reflected in the mood of the people of Sweyn's Eye. She had stood behind the counter of her shop in Market Street and heard the stories of her customers with horror; there were tales of whitewashing of blacklegs and, worse, the stoning of some of the unfortunate culprits. Times were bad indeed.

Frank Porter was continuing to work sometimes at the mine but more often in the shop, along with his cheerful and talkative mother. Mrs Porter was a good worker and got on well with their customers, and Katie would have no hesitation when the time was right to leave the shop entirely in her hands.

These days, Luke was not willing for Katie to be alone, especially not now with Michael back in the town and he, no doubt, having a hand in the way the violence had escalated in the last few weeks.

This morning he had insisted on Katie remaining at home. He felt she was looking pale and strained and indeed, she was feeling under the weather but mainly through worry about Luke. The incident up at the mine where a band of women were arrested for attacking old Tim and his two young nephews, had frightened her.

She moved to the door where Luke's car stood outside, leaning drunkenly on one side, for during the night someone had removed two of the wheels. Luke had been angry but determined to work at the slant, undeterred by what he thought of as an act of sheer spite.

'No man shall dictate whether I work at my own business or not,' had been his final word on the matter. He had warned Katie that she must remain indoors for her own safety and she had obeyed him, knowing that to be cautious made sense, especially in her condition.

She put her hand to her mouth as Luke's tall figure came into sight. 'Thank God,' she said in relief, but by the time Luke reached the door, she was standing at the table calmly carving a piece of cold ham. She looked up and smiled, though she searched his face anxiously – he seemed pale and drawn.

He sank into a chair and rubbed his hand wearily over his eyes. Katie went to him at once. 'What's happening, love?' she asked and he looked up at her, shaking his head a little.

'I can't believe it. Our Charlotte was one of the women taken into custody for attacking Tim and his nephews. It doesn't seem possible that my own sister would turn against me. None of the men turned up for work today and I can't say I blame them.'

'Are you sure Charlotte was involved?' Katie asked. 'I can't see your sister running with a crowd of mad women.'

'Well her name is on the list of the women arrested, all right; I saw it myself.'

'Are you still going to keep the slant working?' Katie asked and Luke's jaw tightened.

'So long as there's any strength in my muscles, I'll work my own coal,' he said. 'Even if I have to go it alone.'

'Luke, must you be so hard-headed?' Katie said gently. 'Couldn't you at least take a few days off until all this violence is settled? There are police on every street corner and the strikers are getting more desperate. There's bound to be more trouble to come.'

'I can't sit on the fence.' He smiled. 'Don't fret, I'll be all right.' He sat back in his chair. 'In any case, I've got to work, there are the horses to be fed and the collar and arms to be checked, otherwise the timber will split and the roof will fall in on the new heading Rory has recently opened.'

'But you can't do it all on your own,' Katie said desperately. 'Sure the horses can fend for themselves for a day or two.'

'I'm going to be all right,' Luke said firmly. 'This madness is not of my doing so let the workers stew in their own juice. All I mean to do is go to my own mine and look after my own interests.'

'Why are you so sure, Luke?' Katie said. 'Can't you not feel even a bit of sympathy with those men who are fighting for what they believe is right?'

'Aye, I've sympathy, but I'm not going to ruin myself out of pity.' Luke rose to his feet.

'Where are you going?' she asked anxiously. 'Sure you've only been in the house a few minutes.'

He smiled at her reassuringly. 'I've got to get the car sorted out,' he said. 'I'm going to Johnson's garage, see if someone can come and put new wheels on it for me.' He put his arm on her shoulder.

'Now don't go worrying, I am quite capable of looking after myself.' He kissed her cheek. 'I won't be long.'

She went with him to the door. 'Luke,' she said, 'I'm frightened.'

'I'll be back before you know it.' He paused for a moment and took her in his arms. 'Now you just look after yourself and that baby you're carrying and soon, once this damn strike is settled, we'll be wed, I promise.'

She watched him walk away into the darkness and there were tears in her eyes. It was so easy for him to tell her not to be frightened but he didn't seem to realize there was danger everywhere.

She drew the curtains across the windows, shutting out the darkness. She bolted the doors and then sat near the fire, staring into the flames.

'Bring him home safely, Mother Mary,' she said in a whisper.

Luke moved through the quiet streets of the town feeling weary and low in spirits. He could not believe that even Charlotte had turned against him, but strangely the opposition made him more determined to hold out against the strike.

The lights spilled forth from public bars, but within the smoke filled rooms there was no cheerful conversation and no singing. Men could be seen huddled in small groups, either morosely silent or speaking in whispers: it was as though the town had died. And everywhere, as Katie had said, were the shadows of the constables moving about silently, as though biding their time.

The doors of Johnson's garage were firmly closed and Luke made his way around to the back of the building. All was in darkness except for a small light in the upstairs window. He knocked loudly and after a time footsteps could be heard on the stairs, then the door was opened a crack.

'Luke Proud. *Daro*! What are you doing here, man? This is no place for bosses, mind.'

Luke stepped forward a pace. 'Aye, I'm a boss but I'm as much a working man as you are.' He gestured with his hand. 'You own the garage but that does not stop you from being a worker, does it?'

Johnson glanced at the constable standing on the opposite pavement and moved back a pace. 'All right, then, get inside. We can't stand here arguing on the doorstep.' He led the way up the stairs and into the backroom that smelled of oil and smoke, and Luke realized that a meeting was in progress. He moved into a seat, unnoticed by Jim O'Conner who was addressing the men.

'We were caught unprepared,' he was saying. 'Councils of Action were set up long ago to control the strike at local levels. And –' Jim emphasized '– the government now demand that we give in totally. They want us to go back to the eight-hour day and take a wage-cut into the bargain. Our answer to that is that we withdraw safety men from the big pits, let the water run in and the pit-props rot and see what the bosses have to say then.'

Luke stood up and he saw Jim's eyes turn to him questioningly. 'Something to say, Luke Proud?' he asked evenly.

'Why don't you call off the strike?' Luke spoke forcefully. 'Can't you men see you are playing into the government's hands? Your actions will only serve to increase the size of the police-force in the town which will lead to more disorder, perhaps even to bloodshed.'

Jim thumped the table. 'We know even too well about the police,' he said, 'and the military are against us, too. From the onset of this strike tanks were stationed at Wellington Barracks in London. Hundreds of thousands of special constables were enrolled and arrests have been made, unfairly and without warrants. We haven't let ourselves be intimidated yet and we won't start now.'

'*Duw*,' a voice spoke from the body of the room, 'even the women are attacking us now, what can we do against that lot, then, man?'

Luke peered across the crowd of men and realized it was his fireman speaking.

'We can continue to fight, whatever happens, Rory!' Jim replied. 'We won't let the bosses push our faces into the dirt.' His fist was raised. 'We can show them that we won't be intimidated by their might; we mustn't give in now, not after coming so far. If we stick together we've got a chance.'

Rory raised a cheer and the men began talking amongst themselves. It was clear that the meeting was at an end. Luke stood at the back of the room unnoticed.

'Right, men.' Jim called the meeting to order. 'Go home now, I don't want violence. Sure we've got enough problems as it is without giving the constabulary the gift of a charge against us. Go to your homes quietly and I'll let you know when I'm going to call the next meeting.'

Luke stood near the door as the men filed out until only he and Jim were left in the room. After a moment, Luke held out his hand.

'I admire you, Jim,' he said. 'I'm not saying you are right and I'm wrong but at least I've heard a little of your side of the argument and very impressed I am.' With a smile, Jim took his hand and shook it.

'Sure it takes a big man to admit that,' he said. 'How about a pint of ale together in the Mexico? I want to talk to you about Charlotte.'

'Aye, right,' Luke agreed, 'explanations are in order on the subject of my sister. You go on, I'll just see Johnson about my car and I'll be with you.'

It took him only a few minutes to explain to the owner of the garage what was wanted, and the man pushed back his cap and scratched his head.

'*Duw,* there's a strange thing to do,' Johnson said, 'pinching your wheels. I can't see any of our men having the time to do such a daft thing.' He replaced his cap. 'Anyway, I'll see to it tomorrow, first thing.'

It was so dark when Luke stepped out into the yard that he didn't see the man standing in the shadows. Luke's keys slipped from his hand and he leaned forward to pick them up, which probably saved his life for he felt a crashing blow across his shoulders and the splintering sound of wood.

He spun round, senses alert and his eyes, becoming accustomed to the gloom, saw the man crouched, ready to spring. Luke moved aside quickly and so only caught a glancing blow from the man's fist. Luke brought up his knee and with an agonized groan, his assailant fell to the ground.

Luke was upon him then, his fist connecting with the man's jaw. It must have been a good punch for he fell limply onto the pavement. Luke dragged him towards the streetlamp and saw the gleam of red hair in the light.

'Michael Murphy!' Luke said in disgust. 'I might have known it was you.' He dragged him to his feet and thrust him roughly against the wall, rage burning in his head. He wasn't aware that he was throttling the life out of Murphy until he felt a hand on his arm.

'Don't, Luke.' It was Jim O'Conner. 'Killing's not the answer to anything.'

Luke dropped Murphy to the ground. 'Don't get up or I might have to start on you again,' he said.

Michael leaned on one elbow. 'I'm not finished with you yet, Proud,' he snarled but Luke ignored him.

'Thanks, Jim. Now let's have that drink and you can tell me how come my sister was involved in this attack on my men.'

It was only later when he made for home that Luke felt the ache across his shoulders and the smarting of his knuckles, but he was smiling as he walked uphill for Jim had assured him that Charlotte had gone to the mine to warn his men and to prevent trouble. He sighed. First thing in the morning he would go to the police station and make a statement to that effect. Rory could back it up, as well as Tim and his young nephews. But for now, all he needed was a sound night's sleep.

Katie was waiting for him, her face anxious. He put his arm around her shoulder and stood with her before the dying glow of the fire.

'You know what's happening?' he said. 'These new crystal-set radios are a weapon against the workers. Baldwin is able to speak to the nation saying that the strike is a threat to constitutional liberty.'

'Well, how do you know that? And sure, Luke, you're not changing your tune and siding with the workers, are you?'

'No, I'm not, but my blood began to boil when I listened to Jim telling me of the dirty tricks that have been played against the strikers.'

There was a sudden rapping on the door and Luke put Katie to one side. 'I'll go,' he said.

Rory was red from running. He leaned against the doorjamb for a moment, trying to catch his breath. 'It's Jim,' he said. 'There's trouble in town and he's gone alone to try and sort it out. As Jim's supposed to be looking after Charlotte's boys I though I'd better fetch you.'

Luke picked up his coat and Katie caught his arm. 'Don't go,' she said but Luke shook his head.

'You know I must go; I can't see Freddy and Denny left on their own, can I?'

He held her for a moment in his arms. 'I love you,' he said softly. 'Don't look like that. I'll be home before you know it.'

As the door closed, Katie rubbed at her eyes. It was pointless to cry, she told herself; crying helped no one. She began to clear away the dishes. She would try not to think of what might be happening outside in the streets of Sweyn's Eye.

Michael Murphy looked round at the scene before him and his eyes gleamed in triumph. He'd seen to it that the news was spread quickly round the town that the women caught at the Slant Moira were to be taken to Port Talbot Court the next day and charged with intimidation and unlawful assembly. The women would almost certainly be liable for fines of anything up to forty shillings and as none of them were capable of paying, prison sentences might be imposed.

The strikers were beginning to congregate in the Strand; on the corner a band was playing a rousing hymn and Jim O'Conner was at the centre of a group of men trying to talk reason to them. But, Michael thought, the man was a fool if he thought he could keep the protest march peaceful.

Michael was jubilant. It seemed that two of his enemies were about to be paid back in full this night: Jim O'Conner and Luke Proud.

He moved back into the dimness. He had business to attend to – even if Proud should escape the anger of the mob who saw him as a blackleg, there would be nothing left of his precious mine.

He looked around him, cursing his brother Kevin. He was never there when he was needed. He moved away from the crowded street, listening in satisfaction to the shouts of the men; they were fools, all of them, dogs baying at the moon.

He left the Strand and made his way along the silent backroads and at last came to the hill leading towards the Slant Moira. He would teach Luke Proud a sharp lesson. No one pushed Michael Murphy around and got away with it.

From out of a doorway came a slim, shadowy figure and Michael paused in his tracks. 'Micky, it's me, Doffy!'

He slowed his step, but only for a moment. 'Don't stop me now, woman, I told you to get out of my life once and I meant it.' His voice was harsh and Doffy, knowing better than to argue with him, disappeared like a shadow.

Michael was breathless by the time he reached the slant and his legs ached with weariness. His face was still sore from the beating Proud had given him and he paused a moment to gather his strength.

Nappa, the small pit-pony, came ambling towards him, looking for something to eat. Michael was about to thrust him away when he realized it would be easier to hitch up the animal to the dram and ride deep into the mine, planting the charge where it would do the most damage. His escape too would be so much quicker.

In the shed, Michael found a lamp and enough black powder to blow up the valley. Proud was an arrogant fool.

He called softly to the horse who seemed nervous and ill at ease as Michael hitched the gun to the harness and clambered into the dram.

'Get on, stupid animal, right into the heart of the mine. There will be nothing but dust left here for Luke Proud.'

The animal was reluctant to move and Michael slapped the horse's rear savagely. 'Get with on you, I said!'

The silent darkness was unnerving. Michael was used to deep pits – had worked them for years – but they had always rung with the sounds of men's voices. Here there wasn't so much as the squeak of a mouse, only the grinding of the wheels of the dram upon the rails and the snorting of the frightened horse.

Michael stopped the animal and lifted the lamp, staring at the junction where several headings met before deciding that it would be the ideal place to plant the powder.

He carefully gouged holes into the rock and in several places, so that there would be no mistake, and filled them with shot. He coughed a little in the dust-laden air. He turned the horse before lighting the fuse and then began his retreat.

'Back, you stupid creature!' he shouted and the sudden noises set the horse off at a gallop. Michael had time only to leap onto the gun and cling tightly to the edge of the dram. It was not a comfortable way to ride but at least the animal was moving faster and every second brought the entrance of the mine nearer.

The frightened animal stumbled in panic and Michael cursed its stupidity. And then the world seemed to slip sideways; the gun that held the dram to the harness appeared to bend. Michael felt himself falling and he screamed out before, suddenly, he was plunged into darkness.

The breath was knocked out of him but thankfully the horse had stopped its frightened run and was standing shivering in the darkness. Michael could hear the snorts of fear and he tried to push himself upright, cursing as the weight of the dram seemed to be pinning his legs into the mud.

He leaned back and over his shoulder he could just see the entrance to the mine. 'Help!' he shouted, as he realized he could not free himself. He struggled, trying to force the dram away from him, fear pounding in his brain.

He heard a scraping behind him and, leaning over backwards, he could see a bulky figure outlined in the entrance to the mine.

'Help! Get me out of here!' he called. The figure moved forward and stood staring down at him in unnerving silence.

'For God's sake, don't just stand there!' he cried. 'This place is going to blow at any minute.'

'At your old tricks, then, are you, Murphy? Playing with explosives like the time you killed my horse. Daisy was a good friend to me and I've never forgiven you for what you did that day.'

'In God's name, who is that?' Michael tried to drag his leg free, panic filling him.

'It's Big Eddie Llewelyn. Your little girlfriend Doffy told me which direction you'd run in and I followed you. I guessed you were up to no good.'

'Get me out of here!' Michael said. 'Don't you realize we could be killed?' His voice rose on a note of hysteria but Eddie calmly walked towards the horse.

'Come on then, Nappa, silly old animal; nothing to be frightened of. Big Eddie will get you out of here, now.'

'Don't bother about the horse!' Michael shouted. 'My leg is caught under the dram, I can't move.'

'I'll just take Nappa out first,' Eddie said smoothly. 'I don't see why another poor dumb creature should die because of your madness.' He looked down at Michael contemptuously. 'Don't care about man nor beast, do you, strikers nor starving little children? All you care about is you, Michael Murphy.'

Michael watched in disbelief as Eddie unhitched the bent gun and began to lead the horse to the entrance of the mine.

'Come back you fool!' Michael screamed. 'You can't leave me here to die!'

But it was too late, the rumbling like the cracking open of the earth was all around him. There was a blinding flash of light that encompassed him, searing and choking, and in its wake, a deep crushing blackness.

30

Katie stood beside Luke on the hillside, staring in dismay at the heap of rock and coal that had once been the Slant Moira. The explosion had ripped the headings apart so that in the main roadway was a gap, as though a giant tooth had been pulled.

It had been the early hours of the morning when Big Eddie had knocked on the door, bearing the news that there had been an explosion at the mine.

'I was there, see,' he gasped, 'managed to save Nappa but there's sorry I am, Katie, your brother . . .' He had shrugged his big shoulders expressively.

'Laying a charge, he was, didn't know enough about it; must have gone off early, I reckon.' Katie had felt a stab of pain; she couldn't believe that Michael was dead.

Men were working now among the ruins trying to find him. A coffin waited, the pale pine wood ghostly in the morning light. It was to Katie as if the world had turned a complete circle and she was back at the moment when she had stood in the same place and waited for her young brother Sean to be brought out of the mine, his young spark of life extinguished forever.

And now, she could not help but grieve for the small boy Michael had once been, lying in a pram with no wheels, or playing on one of mammy's rag-mats before the fire. But the man he'd become was shameful to her and he had died ignominiously, taking his revenge by trying to ruin Luke.

'This is no place for you.' Luke turned to her. 'I want you to go back home, please, Katie.'

But she leaned closer to him and clung to his arm, staring up at his white, angry face, afraid for him. 'What are you going to do, Luke?' she asked softly

369

and he stared out across the ruined mine, his eyes clouded.

'I'm going to hire me a lorryload of men from the Ponty works,' he said, his words clipped. 'I shall get new headings dug as soon as I can and carry on working, that's what I'm going to do.'

'But Luke,' Katie said quickly, 'to bring in outsiders will surely cause more trouble – you know what's happening to blacklegs.'

'I'm not going to be intimidated by anyone,' Luke said. 'Now go home, Katie, before you become even more upset. I don't want you falling ill.'

She turned away, tears in her eyes as she made her way obediently towards her home. The pale October morning was chill and damp and the mountainside seemed an unfriendly place to be. She quickened her step, pushing from her mind the horror of Michael's act of revenge backfiring on him so that he lay buried somewhere beneath the coal. It seemed the Slant Moira had taken a revenge of its own.

In the kitchen she knelt before the fire and lit the paper beneath the network of sticks. Carefully she added coal, fanning the flames, sitting back on her heels with a sheet of newspaper held out as a blower across the fire.

Soon the room began to warm and Katie sat in her chair, coal-blackened fingers resting in her lap. She felt weary and ill from emotion and lack of sleep and she wished Luke would come home.

She hoped he was not serious in his intentions of bringing in the men from Ponty works to set up new headings, for his act would be seen as one of rebellion and would be met with more violence.

As daylight filtered into the room, Katie forced herself to rise from her chair and make herself some hot tea. She felt stiff and uncomfortable, her heavy skirt too tight around her waist. She pushed the kettle onto the fire and listened to the water begin to sing, wondering why all the strife and trouble of the strike should happen now when she should simply be happy as Luke's wife-to-be and the mother of his child.

The sun came up as she sipped her tea and the lightening of the day seemed to lift her spirits. When Luke returned she would talk to him, beg him not to do anything provocative; at least to hold his hands for a few days until things had calmed down.

She stood in the window for some time and watched as the sun climbed higher in the sky warming the land and touching the grass with tips of gold. Soon the troubles must end for what had begun as a nine days' strike for everyone else had become for the miners seven months of hardship and depression.

When Luke did not return home for a meal, Katie decided to walk to Market Street and look in on Frank Porter and his mother, see how they were getting along in the shop. She felt she could no longer bear the silence of the house, empty without Luke.

It was a cool day in spite of the sunshine but Katie decided that a walk would do her good. The sun was pleasantly bright, washing the roadway with dappled patterns as it shone between the trees. She felt her spirits lighten. Soon, she was sure, the town would return to normal and she could marry Luke and live a quiet life as his wife.

Frank greeted her with an uneasy smile. 'Katie, there's good it is to see you looking so well.'

He was cutting a small piece of cheese for one of the customers and as Katie moved behind the counter, Frank glanced at her anxiously. Mrs Porter came out of the kitchen and, opening her plump arms, hugged Katie welcomingly.

'*Duw*, there's an improvement in you; looking well you are now, girl, but perhaps just a bit worried?'

'Mam!' Frank said quickly. 'Don't be so soft. It's no wonder Katie is worried, you know what I told you this morning.'

Katie brushed back her hair. 'You've heard about the explosion at the slant, have you?'

371

'*Duw*, 'course we have and your brother killed in the accident; there's *twp* I am opening my big mouth and putting my foot in it.'

Katie didn't bother to explain that the explosion was no accident, there would be enough speculation as it was. 'What worries me,' she confided, 'is that Luke is talking about getting a lorry full of men over from Ponty to try and clean up the mine.'

She heard a sound behind her and turned to see Mrs Keys holding the piece of cheese in her hands.

'For shame!' the woman said. 'There's us starving and you and your kind making money out of our misery. And that sister-in-law's just as bad trying to tell the magistrate she had no part in the riot up at the mine, ringleader she was, and I told them so.' She smiled in triumph. 'Let the rest of us go, they did, give us time to pay an' all, but kept her they have.'

'But I thought that Rory and Tim would tell the police the truth that Charlotte was trying to prevent trouble,' Katie said in dismay.

'Aye, well, who is going to let them blacklegs get to the police and tell more lies? Stopped them, the men have, and they won't go to work no more, not until the strike is ended, see.'

Mrs Keys turned and left the shop and Katie bit her lip. Frank put his hand on her arm.

'Don't worry about her. I'll just go and have a word – owes this shop some money does Mrs Keys.'

'No,' Katie said, 'sure I don't want to see her children suffering because of her evil ways; let it be.' And yet even as Katie moved towards the kitchen urged by Mrs Porter to have some tea, she wondered if Mrs Keys might use what she'd just heard to make more trouble.

Charlotte stared at the wall of the cell. She'd stared at it for three days now, her mood swinging from optimism to despair and there was still no sign of her release. She had told her version of events time and time again to the constables. Even though different men were sent to question her, her unwavering replies were beginning to make an impression.

Charlotte hated the silence of the bare room, the locked door and the dimness but, even more, she hated the way the whitewash had dried on her hair and clothes.

One bright spot in it all was that one of the women who cleaned the cells had smuggled in a note. It was from Jim telling Charlotte that the boys were well and cared for and he would have her out of there as soon as he could.

The heavy door swung open and a constable came into the bare room, carrying a tray of food. He put it down on her knee and lifted the cloth for her to see.

'Bit of *cawl* today; better than dry bread and water, isn't it, girl?' He smiled kindly but Charlotte looked up at him with suspicion.

'Why am I having special treatment?' she asked. 'Or are the other women having the same?'

'*Duw*, the other women have all been released, girl,' he said, 'you're the only one left.'

'Well, when will I be released?' Charlotte asked indignantly. 'I did nothing wrong, so why am I kept here after the others?'

'Well, girl, the magistrate must decide if you're telling the truth or not. Don't want to fine a woman whose done no wrong now, does he?' The constable moved to the door.

'Well, when shall I see the magistrate, then?' Charlotte asked. 'You know I've got two young sons to think about.'

'Perhaps in the morning,' the constable said, 'we'll see.' He left the room and Charlotte felt tears of frustration burn her eyes. But she must keep calm and not let them get her down. She had done nothing wrong so why should she be punished?

She had just begun to eat her soup when another constable entered the cell. He stared down at her and she looked at him questioningly.

'You want to go back to your sons?' he said. 'Well, that's easily fixed. All you need to do is confess your guilt and pay your fine and off home to go.'

Charlotte rose to her feet and put the tray of food down on the bunk. Her hands were trembling and some of the *cawl* spilled from the bowl, a fact that did not escape the constable's attention.

'Nervous are you, Mrs Davies? No need to be, we don't knock people around, not unless we have to, mind.'

'I have done nothing wrong.' Charlotte repeated the words she'd already spoken many times. 'I went up to my brother's mine to warn him that the women were coming.

'But Luke Proud wasn't there, was he?' The voice was reasonable as though the man was talking to a child.

'But how could I know that?' Charlotte asked. 'I thought he'd be working as usual.'

'As usual,' the constable repeated. 'So you know nothing about any explosion then? Surely one of your illicit notes would have told you about the trouble up at the mine?'

He didn't wait for a reply. 'Isn't it true that you are living with a man by the name of Jim O'Conner?'

Charlotte was bewildered at the turn the conversation had taken, she looked at the policeman with anger.

'I'm not living with him, not in the way you mean,' she said quickly. 'He was my lodger but that's all.'

'A lodger.' The constable walked to and fro across the small space. 'So that's why this same lodger is taking care of your sons; just a business arrangement, nothing more. You don't feel anything of a personal nature for this man, then?'

'I didn't say that,' Charlotte replied. 'I do feel something personal for him but I haven't been to his bed if that's what you are insinuating.'

'Insinuate, me?' he said. 'I should watch your tongue, my lady, if I were you. Such talk might get you into trouble.' He moved to the door. 'I knew your husband – same type as this Irishman. Troublemakers. Communists, the both of them.'

Charlotte drew herself up and took a deep breath. 'You're right, officer. You do not insinuate – you blacken a man's character right out in the open, but when one is dead and the other not present to speak in his own defence.'

The constable gave her an angry look and then without another word took up the tray of food and left her alone in the bare room.

Charlotte sat down on the hard bunk, clenching her hands into fists. She'd not had a proper meal since she'd been taken into custody but her anger and her sense of injustice was so great that she didn't feel hungry any more.

She closed her eyes and leaned back against the coldness of the bare wall. Patience, that's what she told herself she needed, and the knowledge that her sons were safe. Yet tears, hot and angry, ran like salt into her mouth.

It had grown dark in the little room with the coldness that came with night, when the door of the cell was swung open abruptly.

'Well, Mrs Davies, you can go now.' The words, spoken by the constable who had questioned her earlier, buzzed around Charlotte's mind. 'Go on,' he said, 'we've bigger fish than you to fry tonight.'

She rose to her feet and made a tentative move towards the door, expecting yet another trick. It was only when she was outside in the moonlit roadway that she felt relief sweep over her. She was free!

The town was strangely quiet but there were bands of constables everywhere. Charlotte began to walk towards home, conscious of her bedraggled appearance with whitewash dried onto her clothes and hair. She wondered what was happening to have the police-force at the ready, truncheons in hand, the sense of calm was eerie, like the prelude to a storm and suddenly Charlotte was frightened.

She began to hurry uphill towards her home, the silence stretching around her. She was breathless and as she paused to rest, she heard the sound of a lorry chugging along the street behind her. She stood in a doorway, watching it pass and saw that it was going in the direction of the Slant Moira.

She realized then what was happening. Luke must have had an accident up at the mine, the explosion the constable had talked about. Perhaps it wasn't an accident but a deliberate act of violence. In that case what was Luke liable to do? The answer was clear, he would bring in men from outside.

She felt her breath catch in her throat – that was it, the police were expecting trouble and they would be ready to deal with the strikers should they protest about blackleggers being brought in.

Jim would certainly be involved, Charlotte thought. She began to run towards Canal Street, pushing herself onwards, hoping desperately that she would be in time to prevent Jim leaving the house.

As she burst into the kitchen, she saw Freddy and Denny seated at the table. Before them was a loaf and a large piece of cheese.

'Mammy!' Denny ran to her and flung his arms around her waist, hugging her in delight. She touched his hair, trying not to cry.

'Hello, mam.' Freddy moved towards her sheepishly feeling himself too old to cling to her and yet longing to be in her arms. She hugged him and the three of them clung together.

'Jim has been looking after you, then?' she said, pointing to the food on the table. Freddy remained silent but Denny smiled wickedly.

'Pinched 'em we did, mam. Got the loaf from old man Parish's shop, took it when he wasn't looking, and the cheese came from the co-operative.'

Freddy's words of warning came too late. 'You weren't supposed to tell,' he said, pushing his brother's arm.

Charlotte bit her lip. 'Freddy,' she said, 'did it have to come to stealing?'

Her son looked up at her. 'Mam, if I hadn't done it, Jim would and I knew how much he would have hated it. In any case, mam, all the kids are doing it, it's expected now.'

'*Duw*, I didn't think things could get any worse.' She looked round. 'Where Jim?'

'Gone to a meeting, mam,' Freddy said quickly, squeezing Denny's arm to silence him. 'Just a meeting, that's all.'

'Freddy, it's important; I've *got* to find Jim,' she said. 'The constables are out in force because a gang of men are coming in from out of town; there'll be rioting for sure and I don't want Jim involved.'

Freddy sighed heavily. 'All right, mam, they're going to meet in Johnson's Garage but you can't go there by yourself, mind.'

Charlotte touched his cheek briefly. 'I want you boys to stay here. I can run down to the garage and warn the men, then I'll come straight back home, I promise.'

She pulled a coat over her bedraggled clothes and looked outside. Everything appeared calm and still, and she wondered for a moment if she was wrong. Perhaps there would be no trouble; but then the constable had told her quite clearly that he had bigger fish to fry – that must mean something was expected to happen.

She hurried along the lamplit streets with not a soul in sight. Somewhere a dog howled, a lonesome, eerie sound. Charlotte's heart was pounding. She felt so frightened she could hardly breathe.

At the back of Johnson's Garage, she knocked lightly on the door. It was opened almost immediately by the owner and he looked down at her in surprise.

'Charlotte, they've let you out of prison, then, and not before time too. Cheeky beggars, holding a woman in custody.'

'Mr Johnson, can I speak to Jim, please? It's urgent,' she said, catching his arm. He moved back a pace.

'Aye, come on in, girl and welcome. Is it one of the boys – no sickness, is there?'

'It's not that. Will you just send him out to me, please?' she asked more quietly. Mr Johnson disappeared up the stairs and a few minutes later, Jim's broad-shouldered figure came into sight.

'Charlotte!' He took her in his arms. 'How I longed to break into that police station and get you out!' he said, his voice thick with anger.

'Jim, listen,' she said urgently. 'I suspect that Luke is bringing in blacklegs to work at his mine. Am I right?'

'Sure,' Jim said softly, 'and we can't allow them to reach the mine. We're going to stop them before they get to the slant, so don't worry about Luke, he won't be involved in any fights.'

'Someone has fooled you,' Charlotte said. 'The lorry is already on its way, it went up past Canal Street about half an hour ago.'

'Damn!' Jim caught her shoulder. 'Go on home and stay there. I don't want you hurt; stay right away from the slant and I'll do my best to see that the demonstrators don't lose their heads.'

Charlotte watched as the men filed silently out of Johnson's Garage and made their way like swift dark shadows up the hill towards the slant. She bit her lip, knowing in her heart that there would be violence. The clashes between the strikers and the blacklegs had become more fearsome as the months went by and the interference of the police was likely to escalate the trouble.

She walked slowly back to the house, clutching her coat around her. She must go to her sons, make sure they remained indoors where they were safe. As she slipped through the silent streets, Charlotte felt a sense of doom as she knew in her bones that this night would bring tears.

Katie awoke to a loud, persistent banging on the door. It was dark and she reached out her hand towards Luke but he was not in bed with her. There was the sound of booted feet running up the stairs; the door of the bedroom was flung open and men's faces stared down at her, eerie in the light of the torches they carried.

'Where is Luke Proud?' One of the men moved closer and Katie recognized him. 'Mr Keys,' she said calmly, 'do you make a practice of bursting into a woman's bedroom?'

He fell back a pace. 'He's not here, men,' he said. 'Let's get up to the slant.'

He turned and then the men were following him, running loudly down the stairs and out into the roadway, calling to each other. Katie rose and began to dress with shaking hands. She must get up to the mine and warn Luke. She would take the short-cut across the stream. As she pulled on her coat, she saw again the angry looks on the faces of the men and she could taste fear in her mouth.

She hurried out of the house and up the sloping roadway towards the slant. The street seemed alive with bands of men, running together like packs of wolves, she thought fearfully.

She caught sight of Jim O'Conner and she pulled at his arm. 'Jim! I know you're a fair-minded man; please don't let anything happen to Luke.'

'Go on back home,' he said softly. 'Sure I'll do my best but there's not only my men to deal with here, there's outsiders come in to punish the blacklegs. Go back; sure there's nothing you can do but get out your rosary.'

He hurried away and after a moment's indecision, Katie turned across the fields and, holding up her skirt, waded across the shallow stream. The rest was a steep incline up to the slant and she was just coming over the rise when she saw flames leaping skywards, yellow and red, dancing higher even as she drew closer.

She stopped running and leaned against a tree, looking at the roadway leading to the mine. A lorry had been tipped over and set on fire and smoke and flames gushed upwards into the night, highlighting the bands of men who danced like demons in the glow.

'Blessed Virgin, help me,' she said clinging to the tree for support. Through a haze, she felt someone touch her hand. She looked round quickly to see Charlotte staring at her, hair tangled, eyes wide.

'My boys!' she said. 'Have you see Denny and Freddy? They're not at home and God, I don't know where they are.'

'Sure I'm sorry,' Katie said, 'I'm sorry.' But all she could think of was Luke. She pushed herself upright and even as she began to move forward she heard a blood-curdling cry. Then, as if from nowhere, a crowd of police constables with truncheons at the ready were streaming towards the men gathered around the burning lorry.

Suddenly the night was alive with cries and screams from the wounded who lay on the roadway unable to escape. Slowly Katie moved forward. She gazed around her and saw that one man was being beaten about the head and shoulders by a policeman's truncheon. Everywhere men were fighting each other. A stone was hurled and it grazed past Katie's face.

'Luke,' she called desperately, 'Luke, where are you?' She began to search among the still figures on the ground and as she moved nearer to the overturned lorry, she saw something move.

'Luke!' She was on her knees, lifting his head, holding him close to her. He opened his eyes and blood was streaming from the cuts that covered his head and face.

'Oh, love, what have they done to you?' she whispered, but it was clear that Luke had been stoned, the punishment meted out to any blacklegs. She tried to raise him but he stopped her.

'It's no use, Katie,' he said and his voice was thin and thread-like. 'It's no use.' He paused, struggling for breath. 'I'll never live to see my son,' he gasped, 'but the house, everything, is in your name. You'll be all right, my lovely.' His hand was raised to touch her cheek but it fell back to rest against the cold ground. Slowly, his eyes fluttered and closed.

Katie looked down at him. 'You can't die, Luke,' she whispered. 'You can't leave me alone!'

Strong arms were lifting her to her feet and she looked into the face of Big Eddie. 'Come on home, missus,' he said, softly.

'I can't,' she said, 'not without Luke.' Eddie nodded in understanding.

'*Duw,* we won't leave him here. I'll bring him home, don't worry.'

He picked Luke up in his huge arms and carried him towards the roadway while Katie walked beside him with her head high.

'I won't let you down, Luke,' she whispered softly. 'I'll bring your son up to know you fought to the death for your beliefs.' And then, silently, she began to weep.

Charlotte pushed her way between men who were cursing and shouting and lashing out at anyone near. She looked frantically for her sons. She was convinced they had come to the slant; to them it would have appeared to be a great adventure.

'Freddy!' Charlotte heard an answering cry and in an instant, she was running over coal-strewn ground, for the voice was that of her son.

'Denny!' she called. 'Where are you?' She stumbled over the uneven ground, almost falling in her haste. 'Freddy, answer me.'

She saw her sons, then; both of them were kneeling on the ground, warding off blows from a constable. A tall figure loomed out of the darkness and a fist caught the man right on the point of the jaw, and he fell to the ground without a sound.

'Jim!' Charlotte said. 'Jim, boys, thank God you're all safe.' She stumbled towards them and fell into Jim's arms. He held her close for a moment, his lips against her hair.

When she looked up, she saw that the battle was over and the police were rounding up the subdued men. Two burly constables approached Jim and his arms were caught and held.

'You'll do eighteen months' hard-labour for what's happened here tonight,' one of the constables said heavily. Jim's head was high, his mouth curved into one of his rare smiles as he looked into Charlotte's eyes.

'Wait for me?' he said and Charlotte went to him putting both her arms around his neck and pressed her mouth to his.

'Our first kiss,' she said softly. 'Of course I'll wait for you, Jim, if I have to wait the rest of my life.'

The sun was beginning to streak the sky with red, painting pale shades of purple over the higher hills. Charlotte took her sons' hands and led them towards home, and the small pieces of coal on the roadway sparkled in the dust like a thousand tears.

THE END

SPINNERS WHARF
by Iris Gower

Rhian Gray left her home in Sweyn's Eye to make a life for herself in Yorkshire, where she learnt the skills of spinning and weaving. She also learnt to love Mansel Jack, a charismatic and ambitious mill-owner, who wanted to make her his mistress.

When Rhian returned to Sweyn's Eye, it was to a town torn apart by anxiety and uncertainty, by the vicissitudes of the Great War – a town whose workers' lives were governed by fear and uncertainty.

Amidst the anguish and dedication of the women who were left behind, Rhian must decide where her own future lay – in respectable marriage to Heath Jenkins, her former sweetheart – or in the arms of Mansel Jack.

0 552 12638 1

A SELECTED LIST OF FINE NOVELS
AVAILABLE FROM CORGI BOOKS

☐	12387 0	**COPPER KINGDOM**	*Iris Gower*	£2.99
☐	12637 3	**PROUD MARY**	*Iris Gower*	£2.99
☐	12638 1	**SPINNERS WHARF**	*Iris Gower*	£3.50
☐	13138 5	**MORGAN'S WOMAN**	*Iris Gower*	£2.95
☐	13315 9	**FIDDLER'S FERRY**	*Iris Gower*	£3.50
☐	10249 0	**BRIDE OF TANCRED**	*Diane Pearson*	£1.95
☐	10375 6	**CSARDAS**	*Diane Pearson*	£3.95
☐	10271 7	**THE MARIGOLD FIELD**	*Diane Pearson*	£2.99
☐	09140 5	**SARAH WHITMAN**	*Diane Pearson*	£2.95
☐	12641 1	**THE SUMMER OF THE BARSHINSKEYS**	*Diane Pearson*	£3.99
☐	12607 1	**DOCTOR ROSE**	*Elvi Rhodes*	£2.99
☐	13185 7	**THE GOLDEN GIRLS**	*Elvi Rhodes*	£3.95
☐	12367 6	**OPAL**	*Elvi Rhodes*	£2.50
☐	12803 1	**RUTH APPLEBY**	*Elvi Rhodes*	£3.99
☐	12375 7	**A SCATTERING OF DAISIES**	*Susan Sallis*	£2.99
☐	12579 2	**THE DAFFODILS OF NEWENT**	*Susan Sallis*	£2.50
☐	12880 5	**BLUEBELL WINDOWS**	*Susan Sallis*	£2.99
☐	13136 9	**ROSEMARY FOR REMEMBRANCE**	*Susan Sallis*	£2.99
☐	13346 9	**SUMMER VISITORS**	*Susan Sallis*	£2.95